DANGEROUS BEAUTY

Cuatro Cienegas. She was there.

The lilies weren't the only nice thing in the water. Or, Ninon amended while standing in the tree's small shadow, not the only *beautiful* thing. The other creature—while splendid—might not be nice at all.

The man was tall, with dark hair and pale skin that glistened with either sweat or water. Perhaps it was a reflection of the golden grass that partially screened him, but it almost looked like he was covered head to toe in gold paint. He was lean, carrying no extra baggage on his frame. He was also not an *indio*—at least, not full-blooded. Spain's tentacles had reached far into Mexico while searching for gold, but Ninon doubted it was the conquistadors this man had to thank for his pale skin and height. Perhaps the stork had gotten lost while making his delivery and left this baby under a cactus instead of the correct cabbage patch in Iowa.

Cherie, the voice in her head warned. *This is no time to get distracted. There is danger.*

Oui! Oui!

But she had always liked dark men....

Other books by Melanie Jackson:

THE SAINT
THE MASTER
DIVINE FIRE
STILL LIFE
THE COURIER
OUTSIDERS
TRAVELER
THE SELKIE
DOMINION
BELLE
AMARANTHA
NIGHT VISITOR
MANON
IONA

MELANIE JACKSON

DIVINE MADNESS

LOVE SPELL   NEW YORK CITY

For Jennifer Reese,
the genuine resurrectionist
who brought light when it was dark.

LOVE SPELL®

September 2006

Published by

Dorchester Publishing Co., Inc.
200 Madison Avenue
New York, NY 10016

ISBN 0-505-52690-5

The name "Love Spell" and its logo are trademarks of Dorchester Publishing Co., Inc.

Printed in the United States of America.

Visit us on the web at www.dorchesterpub.com.

DIVINE MADNESS

Man is put into the world for a limited time; if yours were the choice, to what age would you extend life?
—*Letter from Ninon de Lenclos to Saint Evremond*

The other day they seized an odd man who told us his name was St. Germain. He will not tell us who he is or from whence, but professes he does not use his right name. He plays the violin wonderfully, is mad, and not very sensible.
—*Letter from Sir Horace Walpole to Horace Mann upon the arrest of Saint Germain in London, Dec. 1745*

First—That pleasure which produces no pain is to be embraced.

Second—That pain which produces no pleasure is to be avoided.

Third—That pleasure is to be avoided which prevents a greater pleasure, or produces a greater pain.

Fourth—That pain is to be endured which averts a greater pain, or secures a greater pleasure.
—*The Epicurean philosophy of Monsieur de Lenclos (Ninon's father)*

PROLOGUE

Scotland, Summer 2002

Miguel Stuart sank his turf spade into the sodden ground, grunting with the effort. The morning was cool and clean, the mist no more than a memory to the sunny moorlands.

This was wonderful—sun, sweat. He should have taken a vacation months ago. Work had kept him away too long. He loved what he did, but this place . . . The Highlands were magical. Here he was a different person. He thought different thoughts. He stopped looking for patterns and explanations and could even feel hope. And his oddities were nothing. No one except his father knew he was damned.

He tossed another square of black peat aside, enjoying the birds' chatter as he finished his father's chores, taking pleasure in using his body and not just his mind. He'd enjoy it even more if he stopped thinking altogether, but that would be hard. His brain had been nagging him of late, reminding him that his father was old and sick—far sicker than Cormac would admit—and that his oft-broken bones could no longer do the work required at the croft. Cutting peat should have been done weeks ago so that there would be time for drying, but the old man hadn't had the energy and had been too proud to call his son in America and ask him to come home. Miguel had been working full time since he'd arrived to catch up on the chores, but they'd still have to have coal brought in for the winter.

As if to remind him that winter was coming soon, a sly bit of autumnal wind slipped beneath his woolen shirt and ran a cold finger down Miguel's spine. The birds fell suddenly silent and then sped away, all except a solitary crow who perched on the stone wall and eyed him coldly. Miguel shivered and tried not think of the *hoodie craw* as being an ill omen, the harbinger of death. Autumn was coming and on her heels bitter winter, the time of darkness, and that was what he was sensing. Nothing more. And the best thing to keep cold at bay was a good peat fire and a mug of dark tea. Remembrance of his early years in Scotland had him suddenly craving hearth and mug with a hunger that was almost as strong as the other hunger. The dangerous one. The one he kept hidden from his father, though the old man had to know, or at least suspect, that the beast rode him hard these days.

The crow opened its beak and hissed at him and then stared over his shoulder. With a great flap of wings, it launched itself into the air.

"Miguel!" an urgent voice called. He turned and saw Mistress MacGuinn lumbering toward him. A part of him was glad to know what had frightened the birds away. "Miguel!"

"I'm here!"

A different kind of cold ran down his spine as he saw the splashes of crimson on the front of Catriona's apron. He didn't need to hear her next words to know what was happening, but she yelled them anyway.

"Make haste—it's yer da. His lungs are bleedin'. Miguel, Cormac's dying!"

Miguel dropped his turf spade and ran for the cottage.

*   *   *

"Promise me you'll gae on with your life in the States when I'm deid and in ma grave. Promise me ye'll stay away frae *her*." Her. Miguel's mother, who was also dead but not in her grave. "I ken ye thirst, but ye canna drink frae that cup o' misery. Promise me." Cormac Stuart's voice was hushed but urgent as he forced the words past his blue lips. Catriona had gone to fetch the doctor though they all knew there was nothing he could do. Miguel's father finally admitted that he had cancer in his lungs and stomach.

Miguel wanted more than anything to comfort his father, but the thing Cormac Stuart hated most in the world was lies. He compromised with a half-truth.

"I've no plans to go to see my mother," he assured the man who had sired him and whom he loved, but whose blood no longer flowed in his veins. And he didn't want to go back—that was truth. Because if he went back to his mother, it would be because the demon inside him was winning.

Satisfied, Cormac nodded and closed his eyes. Miguel stayed by the cot and held his hand until his father's sprit slipped away.

Miguel had his dark tea then, and a fire in the grate, but without Cormac to share stories and puff away on his old briarwood pipe, the ritual had no meaning. And Miguel knew that he'd never do it again.

The time had come to face his demons, the real ones living in Mexico.

NINON:

HER STORY

. . . Till the monster stirred, that demon, that fiend,
Grendel, who haunted the moors, the wild
Marshes, and made his home in a hell
Not hell but earth. He was spawned in that slime,
Conceived by a pair of those monsters born
Of Cain, murderous creatures banished
By God, punished forever for the crime
Of Abel's death. The Almighty drove
Those demons out, and their exile was bitter,
Shut away from men; they split
Into a thousand forms of evil—spirits
And fiends, goblins, monsters, giants,
A brood forever opposing the Lord's
Will, and again and again defeated.
—*Beowulf*

What hast thou done? The voice of thy brother's blood
crith unto me from the ground. And now art thou cursed
from the earth, which hath opened her mouth to receive
thy brother's blood from thy hand; when thou tillest the
ground, it shall not henceforth yield unto thee her
strength; a fugitive and a vagabond shalt thou be in the
earth. And the Lord said unto him, Therefore whosoever
slayeth Cain, vengeance shall be taken on him seven fold.
And the Lord set a mark on Cain, lest any finding him
shall kill him.
—*Genesis 4:10–15*

CHAPTER ONE

Christmas, 2005

The woman with red-gold hair and coal-dark eyes pushed the late-arriving Christmas cards aside and read the cable again. Her lips twitched at the *"C'est un vrai cinglé, ce type,"* that concluded the brief report. Her informant was wrong, of course, though she understood his mistake. The great poet, Byron, wasn't a nutcase. He was just involved in some unusual projects that produced somewhat suspicious behavior.

Which was fortunate for her, because it seemed that he had taken care of the Dippel problem with commendable thoroughness. There remained just one other difficulty for Dippel's few remaining afflicted, and she didn't know if this was the proper time to openly challenge le Comte de Saint Germain about his intentions.

"Will there ever be a time?" she asked Aleister, who politely cracked an eye at her meditative enquiry. The cat yawned, showing his dainty but very sharp teeth, which was his way of shrugging.

Je ne le crois pas, his pea-green eyes said as he stared down from the mantel. She sighed heavily, suggesting to the cat that she agreed. "But what then do I do? What course is best for me to follow?"

Aleister sniffed once at the frangipani-scented air. He had no suggestions to make. That was regrettable, but then, really, it was not his problem. He had just eaten a large plate of fresh steamed shrimp, and it was time for him to drop back into a deep, contemplative state that closely resembled a nap but was actually where he thought about important cat things and listened to the splashes in the koi pond where his fantasy meal swam.

Being a perceptive creature—she was almost a feline, Aleister felt—the woman took the subtle hint and politely left him to his work.

She walked silently across the room, not disturbing the grass mats on the floor. Carefully, she struck a match and lit one of the many candles on her old-fashioned writing table. The small flame was barely enough for a normal person to see by, but she didn't bother to light any of the others. There was no need; she saw everything required. There wasn't a great deal to see. There was no computer on the desk, and no phone.

To write or not to write?

Several times in the nineteenth century she had come close to contacting Byron. Then the poet had disappeared from Greece, not to be found again until the late twentieth century. It was tempting to look him up because she could use an ally. She was quite aware of his continuing interest in her. But now?

No, she would wait. It wasn't likely that anyone was following her yet—she had done a good job of faking her disappearance in the Devil's Triangle—but it was within the realm of the possible that her position had again been discovered and she would have to move. She wouldn't risk leading the Dark Man's son to Byron and his new consort. It was possible that Saint Germain didn't yet know that the poet lived. Tabloid rumor had it that Byron—or at any rate, the current alias under which he was known—had been killed or kidnapped by aliens last Christmas Eve. If Saint Germain thought him dead, she would not be responsible for bringing more evil into Byron's life.

Sighing again, the woman who had once been Ninon de Lenclos folded the cable into fourths and then fed it to the candle's greedy flame. When the last bit of ash was crushed and then swept into the waste basket, she turned back to the cat and smiled fondly at his delicate snores. She loved to watch him slumber. It was one thing she missed most from her old life, being able to sleep untroubled by dreams and ghosts. Still, there were other compensations.

She coughed softly. It wasn't painful. Yet. But she would have to do something and soon. This was a sign that it was nearing time to renew.

"Très bien," she said softly to the floral scented air that wafted in the window. She leaned over and blew out the candle. As her silk blouse fell forward, any passing person might have observed the small golden scars over her heart. But there was no one passing by on this side of the island. That was why she liked it.

On the night of her eighteenth birthday a stranger was announced and, being much alone and tired of her sickbed, Ninon received him though he gave the servants no name. The man who appeared before her was very strange—old and yet ageless with eyes as black as midnight that matched his long black cloak. She had the strangest conviction that she had seen his face before, perhaps in a dream.

"My visit surprises, perhaps terrifies you," he said. "But be not afraid. I have come on this night to offer you one of three things; either highest rank, or immeasurable wealth, or eternal beauty. But you must choose without delay. At the count of seven the opportunity will be gone forever." He reached out a hand to push back his hood and she saw his skin was covered in a fine net of gold scars.

"Then I choose eternal beauty. But tell me—what must I do for such a great boon?" she asked flippantly, not truly believing this man was any more a great magician than the disappointing creature she had seen earlier in the day at the caves in Gentilly, the one she had sought because he might have a cure for stagnant lungs.

"You must sign your name in my tablet and never tell a soul of our secret compact." A thick stack of parchment appeared in his hand.

"Do I sign in blood?" She coughed again.

The dark man smiled cruelly. "That will not be necessary. Ink will suffice for this part of our contract." Then, when Ninon had done as he said he told her, "This is the greatest power that a person may have. In my six thousand years roaming the earth I have only ever bestowed it on four mortals; Semiramis, Helen, Cleopatra, and Diane de Poitiers. You are the fifth and last to receive this gift.

We go now into the night so I may finish my work. Look for me before fifty years have passed on the night of a great storm. When you see me again, tremble, for you shall have but three days to live unless you pay the toll I ask at that time." He pulled his hood back over his head. "And remember that my name is Noctambule."
—*Saint Evremond's supposed account of the meeting between the Devil and Ninon de Lenclos*

[Saint Germain] is supposed to have intercourse with ghosts and supernatural beings who appear at his call.
—*Landgraf von Hessen-Barchfeld*

CHAPTER TWO

Mexico, 2006

The woman who was Ninon but who was now calling herself Seraphina Sandoval drove deep into the desert, doing her best to get completely lost before trying to find herself again. Her mind was like the scenery around her: red, empty of other life, monotonous. The only other living thing braving the brutal heat of midday was her cat, who had been Aleister but was also now someone else, though he was mostly unaware of it.

It was late spring in the desert and the earth followed its natural cycle. Hawks took to the thermals, prairie dogs scampered, the agave bloomed. Everything was getting on with the job of living. Even she was, though there was greater urgency to her movement because unlike these animals, the woman knew she was dying. Again. And someone was trying to speed her on her way.

"Poor kitty," she murmured in French as she stroked him, finally rousing herself from her deliberately blank-minded reverie. Then, hearing herself, she frowned. She had to remember to speak Spanish now—even in her head. Even when she didn't feel watched. *"Pobrecito. But you still have eight lives left."*

The cat glared at her from his place in the passenger seat. His singed fur, dyed as black as his mistress's hair and which now matched her obsidian eyes, was slowly growing back. But he was still far from his beautiful and dignified self, and the taste of the chemically altered hair infuriated him when he bathed. Ninon didn't care for her hair color either, but the Devil—or at least the Devil's son—was on their heels and there was nothing for it but to hide who and what they were.

The changed appearance and identity might work for a while, though there was no guarantee. After years of dividing her time between her island and New Orleans, burying herself in what she had thought was complete obscurity, she had awoken one dawn to find herself in a wet hole in the ground about the size of a grave with the world on fire around her. An explosion. Had she not been who and what she was, and had the fish pond not been filled with water, that would have been the end of her. And of her cat.

"Reeoow."

"We must work on your accent. Anyone would know that you are a foreigner. You must learn to hide your disdain," she said absently, trying for a note of gaiety but falling far short. Her smoke-damaged larynx hadn't fully recovered. She was also coughing again. But that had nothing to do with the explosion.

The cat was not buying her false cheeriness.

Things had come apart on New Year's Day at about one in the morning on what should have been the start of a new and better year, had her old enemy not caught up with her in the form of a fire bomb delivered by some unknown means. It had had no note with it, at least none that survived, but she knew who the sender was anyway. He'd been after her for a long time—two centuries at least.

At first his attacks had been subtle, oblique, things that inspired anxiety more than presenting actual danger. But after his father the Dark Man's descent into insanity and then death at the hands of Lord Byron, Saint Germain had turned to a more overt form of war. He must be getting desperate, fearing he would go the way of his sire and looking for a cure for the insanity that came when too many brain cells died in the needed electrocutions. Just as she sought help from outsiders, so too would Saint Germain. It was a race to see who would find help first.

Her hands tightened on the steering wheel. She didn't usually dwell on her many brushes with death, but this had come so close. If she hadn't been outside, rescuing Aleister's midnight fishy snack, she and the cat would have both died. Vaporization and fire were two sure ways to kill her. As it was, her poor koi had been boiled.

Ninon pulled her mind back to the present and worked on keeping it calm and blank. Strong emotion was bad. It seemed to work like a sort of beacon, calling her enemy to her if he were anywhere nearby. Once she could have controlled her feelings, but her mind was every day less and less her own. She couldn't risk leaving any sort of a mental pathway that he could use to track her now that she knew—more or less—where she was going. She had been careful not to leave any electronic or paper trails for Saint Germain or others to follow, used no credit cards, debit cards, or cell phones. But that wasn't the only way they tracked her.

"I'm sorry. That is banal. So, I shall choose a new name for you, yes? How about Corazon?" she asked, and then realized that in her mind she had already named him this. "It's pretty, and it would be an excellent disguise for you. You must not be a gender bigot."

The cat closed his eyes. He was not a sweetheart, and it was a matter of indifference to him what his mistress called him so long as she produced proper sustenance at regular intervals and scratched him under the chin.

Ninon understood this and didn't judge him harshly. Though her closest friend, he was an animal and had an animal's experience of the world. He needed food and shelter and an occasional physical display of affection. She was not so simple. Not any more. For a long while—since a form of immortality had been visited upon her—she had been plagued by a complex question: Was she just a thinking animal who occasionally had glimpses of a spiritual realm; or was she in fact a creature of spirit, trapped on earth so that she could learn from earthly experience before moving on to another life? If it was the latter, then she had certainly miscalculated when she allowed her enemy's father to extend her life with his Promethean fire. How could one move on to the next world if one could not die at the appointed hour?

It was not like her to dwell on unhappy things, to second-guess herself. She agreed with Charlotte Brontë that regret was the poison of life, and did her best to never sip from that cup. But having someone's hate endure unto the second generation and then a good deal longer—hate grand enough to prompt a man to multiple murders and to hurt a cat—that was just cause for momentary reflection, and perhaps even to review one's life choices.

But not right now.

Ninon sighed and shifted in the Jeep's less-than-luxurious seat. How she missed her Cobra! But that much-loved car and her other house were both in New Orleans where she could not go without risking Saint Germain's spies finding her. Had he not sent his minions to open the already weakened levees after the terrible hurricane? He had drowned her beloved New Orleans in another attempt to kill her, and also to hide the evidence of his own systematic looting of the old graveyards.

Her nose wrinkled. The smell of exhaust was strong. It was expected. The tailpipes had smoke like that from a fire-breathing dragon. Her current vehicle was a probably reject from a demolition derby, but that was proving to be handy in a place where nice cars were like friendly dogs, tending to wander off with any passing stranger who knew how to hot-wire an engine. It was also faster, more stubborn on hills, and more loyal than any other desert vehicle she might have asked to face this Hell at high noon.

And it seemed to always be high noon—all day, every day—in this land suspended somewhere between what had been once and what was yet to be. Man was an unwanted intruder here. Sometimes gray clouds appeared on the horizon and hinted at cooling rain, but Mother Nature never followed through with her promise. Ninon had come to suspect that She was on the enemy's payroll, trying to degrade his victim's will by frying Ninon in the sun while denying her the renewing fire of the storm. That would be one way for Saint Germain to kill her. Not as quick as decapitation, but just as sure.

Of course, the nine-millimeter pistol Ninon had tucked under her leg didn't help her comfort either.

Corazon chuffed. He didn't care for the smell of gun oil or exhaust.

"We must endure," Ninon muttered.

The Americas were a strange place. She had been in the New World off and on for nigh on three hundred years, but her eyes had still not adapted to all the varied landscapes. The scenery was simply too bright, too bold, too big. And this land was too dry. *Por Dios!* Would it never rain?

The people were different too—brash, uncivilized, disinclined to play by any rules. Even rules they themselves made.

Like you've ever played by anyone's rules? a voice that might have been her conscience asked.

I had rules. They were just my own.

The cat lifted an eyelid and glared. He seemed to know whenever she started talking to herself, though the dialogue was strictly internal. The voice had always been there, but it was only in recent weeks that it had taken to visiting daily, forcing her into a slightly insane Socratic dialogue. Maybe it would go away when her concussion healed—when all of her healed in the heavenly fire.

Hoping to stop the voice in her head, Ninon pushed a tape into the player and the sounds of Sourdough Slim filled the Jeep. The cat glared some more. He did not care for yodeling.

Ninon glanced down at the gas gauge. She was still fine for fuel and she was in sight of a major highway—the 111, if the map was correct—and there was a town located at the outskirts of a nature preserve that would be at the junction of this highway and the 30. There was at least a quarter of a tank and she had begun seeing signs for a place called *Cuatro Cienegas*. Four Lakes—that was good. Of course, after the *Sierra del Muertos*—Dead Man's Mountains—anything sounded good.

Oui, but you still do not know why you are running or even where.

Nonsense. She was running to . . . She looked down and read the words she had scribbled on the map: Hotel Ybarra.

That's not what I mean, cherie.

I know. But you also know that we have to . . . to do something. There is no one left in Europe who can help—Saint Germain has killed them all. The lead in Greece was faulty, and the only other place we have heard any reference to people being resurrected by fire is here in Mexico.

They were being resurrected by other things as well, if legend were to be believed. Tezcatlipoca, the Smoking Mirror, God of the Night, was apparently big on vampiric priestesses culled from women who died in childbirth. These creatures were scary, not like the usual neck-sucking Euro-trash so popular in movies. They liked brains as much as blood. This was a bit of a drawback, but Ninon needed help badly enough to brave brain-sucking fiends. She just wished the ancient stone tablet she'd sought hadn't been stolen from the museum before she could see it. She would have had a clearer understanding of what she was up against.

So now you seek out the blasphemous Aztec gods to aid you?

Look, I'd seek out the Dev—she started to say and then paused.

Not *the Devil?* the voice asked. *But why, if he can help?*

You know why. I think it may have been the Devil who got me here. Or at least one of his henchmen.

Perhaps. Regardless, we are now touring the hellholes of the New World looking for a way out of troubles. Is that wise? Have we exhausted all other options?

Yes, they are exhausted, most dead and buried. I wish the answers were in heaven—do you really think I wouldn't rather be in Cancun sunning myself on a beach? But I tried paradise for a savior, and all I found was a serpent. And no rain—no storms even where there should be. It has to be Saint Germain's doing.

The voice didn't answer. Perhaps because the cat had stuck his claws in her leg. Corazon looked worried. He seemed to know that his mistress's mind was going somewhere bad.

Actually, when she thought about it, Ninon's paradise had been free of serpents for a long while, and there had been plenty of rain if no lightning. But as always happened, the modern world had started intruding on her Eden, and paradise had been slowly losing its allure. Before, where there were lush crops of tropical flowers, the land had sprouted expensive homes—which would have been lovely architectural sculptures if people hadn't come to live in them.

Her end of that island had been inhabited mainly by American expatriates with money and relaxed personalities—trust fund babies mostly, who had no urge to follow in Mummy and Daddy's well-shod footsteps, or to provide them with kids who would have an III or IV tacked onto their names. Some were unfortunate first wives bought off when their former hubbies went accessory shopping for their midlife crises and came home with new girlfriends—invariably younger and dumber—instead of hot cars or Rolexes. A few were retirees from Silicon Valley who were tired of fending off corporate raiders who treated acquisitions as a kind of blood sport now that the dot-coms were a bust and the dying companies were chum in the water that attracted sharks. Though, now that she thought about it, one of the men on the island had been a retired Silicon Valley dot-com hit man himself.

There were some accountants, also victims of the tech bust, who had official people looking at the books they'd cooked and deciding things were neither rare enough nor well-done enough for their tastes, and who were issuing warrants in complaint. There was even one guy who made a living as a urine donor for professionals who couldn't quite pass company drug tests on their own. They'd been fun neighbors, easygoing, having many of the same appetites as the rest of the modern world but possessing slower metabolisms. They reminded her a bit of the society in which she had been raised, people who came from families where "summer" and "winter" were used as verbs—as in "We'll summer in the Hamptons and winter in Vail"—but they had left much of that behind in favor of smaller, more private lives. They understood that geographical proximity did not mean friendship.

However they'd come, most were now Jimmy Buffett's spiritual children, laid back and fond of margaritas. And they'd also been incurious about her. That had been a huge plus. True, there wasn't a great depth of intellect in those neighborhoods and that had left her feeling a bit lonely, but she had been mostly content with her situation. Certainly she had liked it better than the way she was living now. Being homeless sucked. Ninon sighed and the cat did too.

It was unfair, actually, to say that every place they had visited since was a hellhole—though she had begun her most recent stay in rural Mexico at a small hotel in Guanajuato near the *Museo de Momias,* and that had to be listed somewhere in Hell's zip code.

What had prompted her gruesome impulse to visit that museum she could not say, since there was no particular resurrection myth associated with the mummies, and as a rule she avoided places like it, cemeteries and churches that served up feasts of corpses for the morbid. She'd had more than enough of that on her eighteenth birthday. Still, something had guided her into the dreadful glass house raised for the dead.

The back story of the museum was partly appalling and partly, if you had a dark sense of humor, amusing. The poor corpses in the cemetery of San Sebastian had actually been dug up in 1853 because of back taxes due the local government—though how the dead were expected to pay taxes . . .

You managed it, the voice in her head spoke up. *And you've been dead for centuries.*

The words prompted from her a horrified giggle.

The franchise tax boards should try this, the voice went on. *A yearly cemetery tax levied on every family in America. It could be added to the property tax bill. And if you fail to pay, the penalty would be to have Grandma dug up and put on display in a museum.*

Ninon clapped a hand over her mouth to still her horrible laughter, which transformed into a cough. Death and taxes weren't something she usually found amusing, singularly or in conjunction. It was one more sign of her weakening mental state.

There had been one hundred and ninety-nine souls disinterred that first year, their bodies buried in carbon and lime, pulled from their crypts and moved to a new building at the edge of town, the guide gleefully informed the museum's visitor. Once they began looking, other cemeteries were found where natural mummification had taken place, and they, too, were dug up. One thousand, two hundred and eighteen in all. They had continued to be dug up until the law was amended in 1958 and put an end to this practice of charging a cemetery tax.

If Ninon had properly understood the guide, whose Spanish was as far removed from formal Castilian as it was possible to be, there was evidence that several of the corpses had been interred prematurely and the poor souls woke in grim boxes in the suffocating darkness of those severe vaults where they were stored. One poor woman had her arms raised overhead and there were long claw marks on her face. Living inhumation—that's what it was called. It didn't happen much in these days of modern medicine. Unless it was on purpose, of course. Sometimes during revolutions the soldiers got a little hasty with shoveling the bodies of their enemies into mass graves. And there were always psychopaths with certain kinds of tastes.

Ninon shuddered at the thought. She knew about waking up from death alone in the dark.

All the exhibits in the museum were depressing, many corpses wearing nothing but shoes and socks, but she'd found the dried body of a pregnant woman to be the most disturbing of all. The guide had talked on about natural salinity and nitrates that caused mummification, oblivious or inured to his visitors' horror at the sight. Then, as Ninon leaned over the display case containing the world's youngest mummy, she had felt the now familiar weight of someone's hostile gaze, and since the only person in the room was a man long dead and eyeless to boot, she had known familiar dread. Sickness crawled up through her body, making her as cold and weak as vampire's prey. It never occurred to her that her fear was irrational, a bit of imagination run amok. Instinctual awareness had come calling too many times for her to be mistaken about the danger that shoved this cold alarm before it like a sickly shadow. She had always known when Saint Germain stalked her dreams. Sleep became a twilight of fearful shadows, an endless corridor lit by the sinister light of stolen Glory Hands harvested by his father. But this was the first time he had found her during the day since she had fled New Orleans. That was not good news. It meant that his search was narrowing in on the same areas she was traveling.

She had left Guanajuato immediately after contact, heading for the Chihuahua Desert because there had been reports of strange ceremonies being conducted during the summer lightning storms—resurrections of the dead, shape-shifting, levitations—and because it was away from where she had told the hotel clerk that she planned to be. Nothing concrete prompted her precipitous departure from town, skipping a long-anticipated shower at her hotel, except this well-developed sense of danger that said her pursuer was close, and that she again needed to run as fast and as far as she could.

Aleister—no, Corazon—wasn't enthused about further travel that day in their Jeep, which was one of the early, primordial models that didn't have much use for things like shock absorbers. But for a while he seemed entertained by the birds in the spiky agaves and the odd appearance of an alarmed Mexican prairie dog. When they passed a long pipe-organ cactus, sentinel of the true desert, he ceased watching the wearying landscape and returned to his nap. He was wise this way, knowing he needed a solid eighteen hours of sleep to be at his very best.

Ninon had groaned in understanding and reached into her purse for a piece of black licorice to soothe her cough. It reminded her of the aniseed dragées she used to take at bedtime to sweeten her breath for her lovers. The taste of licorice exploded on her tongue and flooded her mouth with sweetness. It was a strange counterpoint to the rest of the world around them. This place was certainly more bitter than sweet. In fact, it actually hurt the eyes and furred her tongue as it dried her tissues. Some soft lands appeared almost edible, every plant a possible culinary delight. Her childhood home had been like that—fields of sweet strawberries filled with sunlight, orange groves living in glass houses, dairy farms of tender grass where farmers made vast wheels of goat cheese and baked rustic brown bread that they would offer to travelers and runaway school girls. And then there had been the vast flower fields of Grasse . . .

Corazon twitched and gave a soft growl.

But this was not such a place and even the cat knew it. Everything here was hard and came with thorns. A person lost in this wasteland would starve or be poisoned, if not killed by the sun first. Best to simply sleep through this hell if a siesta was an option, even if sometimes you rolled over and smelled Fate on the pillow next to you, and you knew that Death had come and lain beside you while you dreamed of demons and ghosts.

She needed to rest. Still, respite from worry proved elusive. That night, though exhausted in mind and spirit, she and Corazon lay unsleeping in a shabby, sweltering hotel in a town too small to have any name—though hotel was an elevated word for the two-bedroom, rotten adobe sweatbox built against a crumbling cantina erected with short-lived hopefulness in 1929. Neither the hotel nor the cantina where she risked having dinner—and risk was the word—seemed to have seen a dust rag or a mop since. The yellowed sheets in her room were also suspiciously fuzzy and she had stripped them off the bed, preferring to sleep on her sleeping bag on the bare mattress. The bed was probably more bug-ridden than the floor, but there was clear evidence in the corners of the room that the floorboards were a highway for rodents of various types and sizes. A few scorpion tails suggested what the preferred meal was.

Yes, sleep eluded her, but safe behind her thick walls and heavy door, locked by the expediency of a chair shoved beneath the door knob, Ninon finally took the time to stop panicking about what had happened in the museum and to think sensibly about what she should do. Living the rest of her life in places like this was not acceptable—if this could even be called living. What had become of the woman she had been? All she now did was run, never confronting her enemy. Worse still, she hadn't allowed herself a friend—a human one anyway—for the last two decades. And there had been no close friends or lovers since Saint Evremond died. She was alone except for the mice and flies—and her cat.

As though summoned by her thought, a small cockroach crawled through the door's keyhole and then along the back of the room's only chair. La cucaracha paused midway along the chair's back and then reared up on his hind legs. He seemed to sneer at her—*Buenas noches, Senorita Gringa. Welcome to the first of many perreras where the unwanted dogs of the earth go. I am sure you will be with us* para siempre—*forever—now. My million cousins and I shall enjoy getting to know you, sleeping with you, sharing your food, swimming in the same cesspools. I shall return* inmediatamente *and tell them of your arrival. We shall have a party tonight,* si? Then he sang: *Porque necessito marijuana que fumar.*

La cucaracha might have said more, but Corazon chose that moment to eat him, and since the cockroach had been mocking her, Ninon let her cat enjoy his snack. She wasn't crazy about his new eating habits, but she didn't think the bug would hurt him. After all, he had taken to eating rock scorpions last year, even though they had enough poison in them to euthanize all nine of his lives, and the island's indestructible wild goats too. He was also missing his favorite treat of frozen green peas and inclined to be cranky about changes in his diet.

Ninon watched while he ate, welcoming even that disgusting distraction. The bug dinner didn't lasted long, though, and she and Corazon soon returned to brooding in the quiet that was as deep as the hush of a cathedral, but one where perhaps murder was to be done.

She had known all along that she had to eventually stop running from Saint Germain and formulate some definite plan for dealing with her nemesis. The man now called himself Ramon Latigazo, a supposed real estate tycoon, but she knew he was really the son of the Dark Man. Yes, Ramon or Saint Germain, he was the son of the serpent who had offered her the fruit from the tree of unhappiness. It was he who chased her, not the Dark Man himself. She had to remember that. The son was not the father. The Dark Man had died on Christmas Day last year in New York at the hands of Lord Byron—and many blessings upon the poet for ridding the world of that insane beast. Her present nemesis had other strengths and weaknesses.

The next step of their deadly dance could be up to her—if she chose to take it. That was a dreadful thought, but her chances of survival would improve if she went on the offensive, if she took a stand.

The one good thing about Saint Germain's many attempts on her life was that Ninon no longer felt guilty for planning on ridding the world of him. There was no time for guilt about his murder. It was self-defense. Her brain, the storehouse of several lifetimes of knowledge, applied logic, and bruising memories, was failing. And she was beginning to feel blurred around the edges. Her ability to project a confident image, to control her expression and hide her superior reflexes, was bleeding away in a painful trickle. Every day she appeared less human. Her lungs, too, were beginning to relapse into their diseased state. But that was no longer what drove her to fight Saint Germain and seek this darker gift of Mexico, this gift that would surely damn her if she were not already condemned. No, she sought to renew her strength not to save her life or end her pain, but because she had to stop Saint Germain before he unleashed whatever new evil he planned to loose on the world. That he meant the world harm she did not doubt.

And she would do it as soon as she was strong enough.

Or before, if she never were truly strong enough.

In the next room the bedsprings began to creak and the filtered sound of at least one party's lust seeped through the cracked plaster. The other party remained silent, so silent that Ninon wondered if she might be of the rubber blow-up variety. She listened with slight interest as the man began exhorting his manhood in original if graphic terms, some of which she had not previously heard—at least not in Spanish. Two long minutes later the moaner climaxed with a self-congratulatory yodel that would have impressed Slim Whitman, though it made Corazon sneer. Ninon sympathized. She had nothing but contempt for a job done hastily and sloppily.

Why did you do it? the voice asked suddenly. *Why did you take the dark gift from Dippel?*

Ninon turned from the wall and shrugged. At the time, it had seemed the right choice to make, to accept that astonishing offer of everlasting beauty. So many of her friends had died young of terrible diseases. Many more were disfigured by pox, their personalities as marred as their flesh while their chances of marriage were destroyed and the bitterness and loneliness infected their souls. The year she had succumbed to Dippel's plan, the hand of death had been suspended over her neighborhood in Paris, striking out at almost every household with plague. Her own health had been failing when the Dark Man appeared at her door on the eve of her eighteenth birthday. His offer of long, healthy, beautiful life had seemed the answer to a prayer. He hadn't told her that it was life everlasting, though. Or about the lightning, the Saint Elmo's fire—that heart-stopping fire she would have to bathe in every half century in order to sustain herself but whose power to heal would slowly fade. He hadn't told her that she would live forever, her brain slowly slipping away unless she would commit the sin of suicide.

Sin? Do you really believe in that anymore?

Yes, a part of her still did. You could take the girl out of the Church, but you couldn't take the Church out of the girl. That was sadly all too true. As a child she had lived in a world of religious constraints that had threatened to repress her soul. Mass three times a day and hours of prayer in between. She had finally sought to escape the constant boredom by living with her hedonistic father, and then through a traditional male education that exercised her active mind. Neither act of societal defiance had set her truly free, because though one unchained her body and the other her mind, neither could unchain her soul. One parent or other had to win the tug-of-war for their child's philosophy, and she had decided on music, mathematics, learning—and, yes, hedonism—over life in the convent. But in spite of her decision, her mother's early teachings had deep barbs that she felt in her heart, an anchor to her past. She worked diligently to rid herself of her mother's indoctrination, but some clung like burrs in shoelaces. Memories of childhood could be the cruelest of taskmasters, tyrants of the mind that refused to be dethroned. She might love God, but she also feared Him.

Her decision to visit the magician at Gentilly had been her last naive effort at external escape from that parental tug-of-war. Shortly after her encounter with him, she had learned one of life's most valuable lessons: The things that constrained her were within, and no one on the outside could ever set her free as long as she chose to limit to herself with others' expectations.

Mea culpa. But Christ-on-a-crutch! Who'd have ever guessed it would come to this?

Cherie, I wish you would not use American English to swear. It's vulgar.

Ninon looked at her cat, who had two tiny wiggling legs

still sticking out of his mouth, and she thought: *Now that is vulgar.*

"You need a napkin, my pet."

Corazon just licked his lips and then belched delicately. He returned his eyes to the oil lamp he watched with fascination. He always had enjoyed candle-gazing, especially at night when there was no moon. He was the perfect familiar. She shared his need of light that evening. Night was vast in the desert, far larger than it was in the city. But even this darkness did not provide adequate hiding places for them. They were in a dark part of the world now where dark things with dark sight dwelled, and she also liked to keep a night-light on.

Not that she needed external light that night. Ninon looked at the shutters where slices of moonlight cut the darkness. Unwillingly, she thought again of Saint Germain. He had a smile like the moon, only it went through no dimming phases, so it shone almost endlessly on everyone around him. Like the moon, it was beautiful and cold. People did not notice the cold, so dazzled were they by his physical presence. And what his beauty could not seduce, his drugging voice could. He was charming, he was handsome. And he was soulless. In so many ways, he was worse than his father, who had at least been drawn to the dark arts out of scientific curiosity.

He scares you badly, the voice said. *More than the father.*

She had seen the Dark Man only once in the last century, but that had been enough to repulse her. The first thing she had noted about Saint Germain's father was that he called to mind rotten cheese. He had certainly been malodorous to her heightened sense of smell, a faint stench leaking out through the pores in his waxy skin. His flesh itself has been yellow like rancid tallow, falling into the small craters that pocked his face and hands. It was as though he were rotting from the inside out.

Still, as bad as that was, the father wasn't half so scary

as his beautiful son. That beautiful, crazy son. And he was evil.

As was she. Well, she was slightly insane and very beautiful. She couldn't say if she was evil. It was the burden of the condition; most evil things were not self-aware. They did not know that they were wicked.

Of course he frightens me. Seeing him is like looking into a dark reflection of myself, a warning of what I might have become. This wasn't thought with vanity. Ninon had long since abandoned any pride at the famous beauty and charm that had made her the toast of Paris for more than three-quarters of a century. Like Saint Germain, she too had been a gifted artist and musician, lauded—even lionized—by society. They had both been courted for their opinions and their ability to sway others.

That explanation was also not the entire truth, though. She feared Saint Germain mostly because once he had nearly seduced her. And it wasn't until she had looked into his eyes, unveiled by a premature moment of triumph over breaking through her reserve, that she had understood that he wanted more than her body, wealth, and secrets. He wanted her soul. To do what with it, she could only guess.

What a fool she'd been! How blind!

Her inner voice sighed.

Well, there is some use in crying over milk that is spilt. You should sleep now. Aleister is standing guard.

Corazon, she corrected. *Aleister died in the fire, and so did I.*

Ninon awoke resolved. The time had come to make a stand.

She and her cat left the hotel early, declining breakfast but filling up the Jeep and its two spare gas cans. Smelling the gasoline made her think of the fire that had nearly killed her and how wretched she'd looked with singed hair.

You're not entirely sane today, are you?

Ninon laughed grimly and then started to cough. Laughter was not the appropriate response to such a question, but it was one she seemed to be making more and more often as her control slipped away.

Is this plan wise? The paper said that the local police were holding practice drills in the area. Supposedly looking for drug dealers, but who knows? There are rumors that the United States military knows about you too. All of you, Dippel's experiments.

Ninon shrugged. That could be true, since the U.S. government had raided Byron's high-rise. But anything they gleaned would hardly be knowledge that the U.S. would share with the Mexican *Federales*. No one sensible would risk talking openly about Frankenstein-like experiments to corrupt officials in a foreign land. And even in the U.S. there were very few loonies with the kind of security clearances that could be had only by generals and tin gods who would hear and believe such a story. At least this was how Ninon comforted herself. Her protection was the utter ridiculousness of the truth.

She laughed again, the sound without humor.

It was good that there was no traffic around on these back roads, because she wasn't in any mood to slow down or practice caution. Anymore. Yes, she had awoken clearer than ever about the where if not the why of her next destination. She and Corazon were going to the land of eternal white, *Cuatro Cienegas*, to find a murderous god who lived in a cave and traveled on an underground river where he collected souls. That sounded insane, of course. And dangerous. But she was running out of options. People said it was better to deal with the Devil you knew—but they were wrong. Sometimes the Devil you hadn't had dealings with was the better choice. Especially if you needed special powers, the kind that would help you take on a enemy who could practice magic and summon demons. At the very least this god could call her a storm.

Demons? But were such things real? Could she trust her perceptions? Might they be just monsters of the mind?

They're real enough, she assured herself. And she needed help against them and the man who sent them.

They say, cherie, that there is no free lunch. Best think of this. Why should the god Smoking Mirror help you?

Ninon sighed. *I know there will be a price. Believe me, I know. But whatever it costs, I'll pay.*

She had no choice.

Ninon took up the quill and then wrote quickly:

Let no vain hope come now and try,
My courage strong to overthrow;
My age demands that I should die,
What more can I do here below?

This would serve as a farewell. She wished that it was possible to spare her friends grief at her supposed death, but it was time to leave. She could no longer disguise the fact that she was not aging.

And this might be her death in truth, should the lightning fail to revive her. It was her third time to submit herself to its fiery embrace, and each healing had been slower than the last, her heart and brain ever less eager to recover. There could be no long delay of this process either, for she knew how swiftly age could come upon her. In less than a month, her hair would fall out, her joints knot with arthritis, her vision would fail, and her lungs would fill with water. Lifetimes of delayed disease would gnaw on her innards. But she probably would not die.

A part of her wanted to give in and end it all. But was that suicide? If God had not intended for her to live, would he have sent the Dark Man her way? Surely she was intended for some important purpose.

She had lived ninety years, surrounded by the finest philosophical and religious minds, but still had no answer to this question. So, she would put it all in God's hands. If he willed it, she would live. If not, she would die in the fire.

Ninon laid down her pen and sighed.

Where the carcass is, there shall the eagles be gathered together.
—*Matthew 24:28*

The greatest potential for control tends to exist at the point where action takes place.
—*Ninon de Lenclos*

No initiate was welcome if he could not heal—aye, recall to life from apparent death those who, too long neglected, would have died of lethargy.
—*H. P. Blavatsky on the cult of St. Germain, from* The Secret Doctrine

· Chapter Three

The dirt road she traveled might have been a relic from the days of Cortez, or at least Pancho Villa, and the longer Ninon traveled it, the more she felt that she was driving into the past instead of the future—and she wasn't at all certain it was where she wanted to go. She also wished that her *Buns of Steel* DVD had actually given her a solid-metal butt. Along with a cast-iron bladder.

This land was closer to the Bronze Age than any New Age, and the old gods felt closer, too, probably because people still needed them and their call was answered by an artesian upwelling of power that seethed out of soil watered with their sweat and blood. The idea of wanting to be with these gods was alien, but she supposed that there was some comfort to be had in seeing aspects of your gods in their animal totems wandering your backyard. Her own bodiless deity, who only visited churches and cathedrals, felt uncomfortably far away out here in the desert.

In the blinking of a tired eye, the dirt track filled with birds, became a bowling alley of poultry with a death wish, which was Corazon's favorite kind of meal and had him meowing excitedly. Not sharing her pet's desire for a bloody strike, Ninon applied the brakes, forcing the cat to put twenty more holes in both the upholstery and the dashboard where he was leaning. Disgusted at her cowardice, he spat once and then leapt from the car's open window to fetch his now-fleeing lunch.

"Corazon—*merde!* The dry crunchies aren't that bad!" Ninon killed the engine and jumped out after him. She shoved her pistol into the back of her jeans. Possibly there was some law about abandoning a vehicle in the middle of the road, but she was willing to risk it. "Come back here, you black-hearted cat," she called, but softly. The sudden and utter quiet demanded a lowered voice.

Her eyes itched, tired of the dust and from the soft brown contacts she always wore these days. The dust aggravated her lungs as well, causing her to cough more frequently.

She trudged after the cat. Over the crest of a white gypsum dune capped with stunted conifers, she came across a small pond—a *poza*—colored the deep brown of coffee and rimmed with dead golden grass that curved away like eyelashes on a coquette. A nice selection of water lilies bloomed in the tar-colored water.

Cuatro Cienegas. She was there.

The lilies weren't the only nice thing in the water. Or, she amended while standing in the tree's small shadow, not the only *beautiful* thing. The other creature—while splendid—might not be nice at all.

The man was tall, with dark hair and pale skin that glistened with either sweat or water. Perhaps it was a reflection of the golden grass that partially screened him, but it almost looked as if he were covered head to toe in gold paint. He was lean, carrying no extra baggage on his frame. He was also not an *indio*—at least, not full-blooded. Spain's tentacles had reached far into Mexico while searching for gold, but Ninon doubted it was the conquistadors this man had to thank for his pale skin and height. Perhaps the stork had gotten lost while making his delivery and left this baby under a cactus instead of the correct cabbage patch in Iowa.

Cherie, the voice in her head warned. *This is no time to get distracted.*

Oui! Oui!

She had always liked dark men, though. She found them more enthusiastic than the blond ones—like that anemic poet, Rombouillet. It was different in the north, of course. The Norse were quite strong and vigorous. But among the civilized southern peoples, she preferred dark men.

Feeling her gaze, the man stuffed something in his sock and spun about quickly. He stalked toward her, a shotgun ready, though it was unlikely he could see her clearly with the sun in his eyes and her in dappled shadow.

Ninon was not tall anywhere except in intellect. There she towered—or had until her brain had started to die off. But brains, even great ones, were not much help in certain situations, and there were many men who saw a woman alone and tended to think petite meant easy pickings. That was where they went wrong with her. She didn't have a lot of weight, but every ounce of it could fight when it had to. As much as she didn't care for it, there were some situations that benefited from the constructive use of applied violence. That was why she kept the nine-millimeter pistol in the holster in the small of her back. That made for a great equalizer when reason failed and one got stuck in deadly pissing contests with morons.

Innocents found the idea of preemptive violence shocking, but aggression was like a drug—the more you used it, the less it affected your sensibilities. Ninon was no longer a virgin and didn't flinch from it. She wondered if this man was himself a habitual user, a violence addict. It was impossible to tell. The gun didn't mean anything either way. Only an insane person would go out alone into the desert and not carry a weapon for protection.

Apparently the man agreed with her, because he carried a twelve-gauge shotgun. It went nicely with the dark sack of rocks he had dropped before starting toward her.

The shotgun would be bad news if he used it. Ninon could probably recover from a single blast, if it wasn't to the head or heart, but it would hurt like a son-of-a-bitch and delay her for days, and would also waste precious time and energy in healing the wound.

Decision time. Hide or take the ride Fate offered?

She looked about at the available cover. Though she was small, it was smaller. Hiding in the sparse brush wasn't an option. *Merde!* She was going to have to take the ride, wherever that led her.

"Hello!" she called, stepping into the sun and waving with an ineffectual finger flutter. She gave the stranger a smile she used only rarely because it caused men's IQs to lower to dangerous levels. Stupid men and guns were a bad mix. She added quickly in American English: "Have you seen my cat?"

There was a moment of utter shock when the man's steps faltered and his expression transformed. The widening of his eyes almost made her laugh. He couldn't have looked more stunned if a clown had reached out and played honk-honk with his penis.

His eyes—a brown that was nearly black, she could see now—traveled the length of her body and then returned to her face. She knew what he saw: pale flesh, skintight jeans, a sheer white blouse that barely contained her breasts, and lots of loose windblown black hair. A rear view might have alarmed him, since it would have shown off more than her jean-clad butt if he looked under the ruffle of her blouse, but from the front she looked like a walking, unarmed wet dream.

His gun lowered and he started laughing. The sound

was low, though, as though he were aware at some level that there could still be danger nearby and didn't want to risk sound carrying beyond the white dunes of the Sunken Region.

"Hullo. I thought you were a hallucination." He had a slight accent, probably part Highland Scots. The rest was black magic. Language as well as skin tone said he was not one of the proletariat who toiled in the fields—but was he a gentleman?

"Did you say you were looking for your cat?"

"Yes, he ran off after some road runners—thinks he's a coyote or something."

A slow blink veiled the man's beautiful dark eyes and he started to climb toward her. He said, "I've seen no kitties out here." His head tilted down for a moment and he added to himself in a voice she was not meant to hear: "But why not a cat? We've everything else."

Ninon heard him loud and clear, in spite of the whispering wind, but she didn't say anything, just kept smiling, looking harmless. She wanted to give him complete peace of mind. That was important when the other person carried a shotgun.

"Well now, I don't suppose that you are a thief or a spy who just happens to be traveling with a cat," he suggested when she made no more effort to engage in conversation or come any closer. Apparently understanding that a lone female might be alarmed by the gun in his hands, he slung the weapon over his shoulder and climbed the last five feet of slope slowly. He tried to look harmless but didn't succeed. The small hairs of Ninon's neck were standing on end.

"Not today," she said truthfully, making sure not a bit of her French accent came through. She didn't feel Saint Germain's unfriendly gaze upon her, but she agreed with this stranger that there was some odd tension in the air. They were in a place haunted by something that liked to watch and listen, and maybe to act. "Were you expecting one?" She gestured at the gun, putting her back to a tree and thrusting her breasts slightly forward. She reached out a hand as though supporting herself against the rough trunk, keeping it near her pistol, though she wondered how effective the weapon would be if she had to use it.

"Expecting?" He laughed. "Not exactly. Let's just say that I am always alive to the possibility out here. Lots of wild animals, you know."

Many of them human. Many of them not. She understood.

"And what did you think I had come to steal? Your rocks?" she asked, pointing with her other hand at the rucksack he'd dropped by the pond. It appeared to be filled with wet stone shards.

"Well now, perhaps I was worried that you were after my heart," he answered easily. "Men have been known to lose them out here."

Flirtation. She had invented this game and was good at it. He seemed genuinely taken with her, too, but that meant less than nothing. Even a stone-cold killer could enjoy looking at a woman's breasts and exchanging a few witticisms or sexual innuendos in between cutting people's throats. Even her throat.

Before Ninon could decide how to respond to his opening gambit, Corazon appeared, stalking toward her with a confident swagger. There were light brown feathers around his mouth. She wanted to kiss him, feathers and all, for providing her with confirmation of her story. Nothing else would have been half as disarming.

"You really were looking for your cat." He sounded slightly surprised. Actually, he sounded wonderful. His voice carried a sudden caress as he decided she was safe. It raised the tiny hairs on her arms and she prayed he didn't notice, or if he did, that he thought it was simple attraction, arousal. "It looks like he caught his lunch too. He must be fast."

"Of course." She knelt carefully, pretending not to be

alarmed when the stranger drew even closer. "Corazon, you bad kitty. Where were you?"

"Corazon?" He sounded amused. His voice was flexible, capable of expressing any and all emotions. She sensed he could be anything she liked. "You do know that he's a male cat?"

"Oh yes," she said airily, suppressing an urge to cough. Coughing didn't help shift the weight from her lungs and it was unattractive. It made men think about tuberculosis instead of kissing. She smiled again, confident now that her cat was there. She had learned to play an American ditz really well. "I just call him that sometimes."

Tall, Dark, and Handsome appeared fascinated, willing to fall for her conversational sleight of hand. She wanted him distracted so he wouldn't look closely enough to doubt her contacts, makeup, and hair dye, or any of the other tools she used to dim her unnatural radiance. She was careful with her voice too. Stunning with a quick smile was one thing, seducing with a voice was another. She had been good at both before—able to use her words to assure whole groups of people that they were singularly and collectively the most witty, beautiful, and insightful beings that she had ever known, and that there was nothing in the world she wanted so much as to hear their next insight, poem, song—whatever they offered at her shrine. She was even better at it now. Practice did indeed make perfect, and she'd had centuries to hone the art.

Yet, even with her amazing gifts, she sensed she wasn't in this man's league. His voice was inhumanly beautiful. She'd only heard one that even came close, and that man had sold his soul to the Devil to get it.

The voice in her head *tsk*ed at her irreligious paranoia, but Ninon didn't let down her guard. Lucifer, the angel of light, had been beautiful too. That didn't mean he wasn't dangerous. No, she'd relax around this man when pigs fielded an Olympic swim team.

Shadows passed overhead and they both glanced up.

Buzzards. Ninon didn't like them and had to force herself not to frown. It was hard though. If she died out here, the vultures would rush in to pick over her bones. That's what they did—stole from the dead. That they would see her as potential food made them seem even less attractive than they were.

"Why? I mean, why do you call your cat that?" the man asked, again moving a little closer.

"Because he annoys me." She flicked another look up at his face and noted twin scars on either cheek right below the bone, the kind that came from a cut with a very sharp knife or a perhaps large needle. A moment later, they were gone.

"Why?" he asked again. His body took on a relaxed pose, an arm resting propped up on a knee that rested on a low boulder, but she could see that his muscles were still coiled. That was probably just the way he came; naturally wary, but she did her best to look like the kind of girl who didn't know physical from metaphysical. "I mean, how? Chasing birds? Chasing other pussycats?"

She shook her head, both in response and also to clear it.

"He looms. When I'm sleeping. He gets on the pillow and towers over me while he breathes in my face."

"*He looms.* I suppose I should step back," the man suggested. "I seem to be looming too—though hopefully not breathing in your face."

"Oh no." She peeped up at him again. "You could tell me your name though."

Her eyes lowered back to his feet, as though she were modest. The man wore dusty hiking boots and thick socks. But that wasn't all. The additional item was not standard with most hikers, and wouldn't have been visible to someone standing, but Ninon, still kneeling could see a blade tucked carelessly into a sheath in his right sock. It was black but not a traditional Scottish *sgian dubh*. It was carved out of obsidian, and had a short buttonlike handle that fit between the fingers and nestled into the palm. She had seen knives like this hidden in belt buckles, though never made of obsidian. She actually had something similar in her own sock. Her interested was piqued. Thinking back, she'd seen one almost like it in a museum in Mexico City years ago. It had been used in sacrificial rituals.

She looked at his hands. Calloused and dexterous, but covered in tiny nicks. She was betting that in a tight spot he would use the blade effectively. There were benefits to using a knife in certain situations—like a lack of ballistic evidence. They were quiet, too, in the hands of an expert. This insight didn't make her any happier.

"I'm Miguel Stuart—Doctor Miguel Stuart. Mum was a local girl," he explained, also doing his best to look harmless and charming. His eyes never dipped to her breasts, though she had left one too many buttons open. She returned the favor, though his bare chest was impressive.

"But Dad wasn't?" she asked.

"No, he was a geologist from Scotland, and we weren't around here much when I was young. I spent more than a few years with him on the other side of the ocean. It gave me an accent."

One that clearly came and went as needed or wanted.

"Cross-pollination produces some unusual things," she suggested, and then regretted it when his eyebrow rose. That had been a slip. A real ditz wouldn't know a word like pollination, let alone that it could be crossed. She had to be more careful!

She came to her feet swiftly, but not too swiftly. She had learned long ago to hide how quick her altered reflexes were.

"I'm Seraphina Sandoval—of Spain and California. Mostly California." She didn't offer her hand. Touching might be dangerous.

"The pleasure is mine," he said formally.

She dimpled. "Probably, but we'll have to see."

He gave another slow blink. The flirtation was back

on. She could feel his sexual energy reach for her through the air.

"What do you call him the rest of the time?" Miguel asked, looking down at the cat, who bathed nonchalantly. He seemed intrigued by the animal's complete unconcern with his presence. Usually predators were uneasy around one another. Put two dominant males together and they would fight.

"Oh . . . Soul-sucking Bastard," she said untruthfully, but earned another surprised laugh. She liked keeping this man off balance in this dance of flirtation.

"Perhaps that is what he is doing when he sits on your pillow at night," Miguel suggested.

Ninon shuddered. The idea of Corazon as an incubus was unappealing. He'd be entirely too good at the job.

"And why is Doctor Miguel Stuart out here?" she asked after a moment, taking a chance on the question because an innocent person would be curious, especially if she were attracted.

"I'm a researcher for the United States National Aeronautics and Space Administration."

It was her turn to blink. That sounded entirely too respectable an occupation for Miguel Stuart of the ready shotgun and obsidian knife. Also, his hair was far too long for NASA—unless they'd taken up with drug dealers to finance their shuttle program. His words sounded like a lie, or at least only a half-truth.

Still, she couldn't condemn him for being hesitant about explaining himself completely. She herself had a biographical detail or two that she never mentioned.

"I'm collecting stromatolites," he continued easily. "Algae gets caught in layers of silt and then compressed into rock. These rocks were around two billion years before the dinosaurs. It's about as close as we can come to knowing what a planet's early formation is like."

She nodded, doing her best to look both interested and

yet not quite bright enough to understand and therefore be any threat to his research—if research was truly what he was doing here. She didn't think it was. She had seen a science show about stromatolites and these stones looked nothing like them.

"I didn't know anyone was working down here," she said. "The place looks deserted."

"There's no team this time. I'm here unofficially," Miguel said. "I still have family in the region and I come back periodically to . . . renew old ties. It's a sort of busman's holiday."

This, she believed. He had old ties like she had old ties, and from his expression he didn't relish them either.

The wind kicked up suddenly. It had teeth, and was inconsiderate enough to bite at her bare skin. Usually the cold didn't bother her, but she was getting weaker and every day grew more vulnerable. A raven flew overhead, jeering loudly as it passed. Corazon looked up consideringly, though the creature could easily be half again his size, and he had to be full from lunch.

"Damn birds," Miguel muttered. "I hate them. In Scotland they are sometimes seen as harbingers of bad luck or even death."

Ninon laughed and scooped up her cat, holding him in front of her, enjoying the warmth of his muscled body. Ditzes didn't know about harbingers, and it was high time she left. She nodded.

"We should go before Corazon decides to do something really rash. I don't think he is aware that he isn't a puma."

Miguel nodded. "Perhaps he was in another life. Are you staying nearby?" He asked casually.

Hide or take the ride? Ninon had only a second to make a decision. "I'm at the Hotel Ybarra."

Miguel nodded again. "I know it. They have a fairly nice bar—if not a nice manager. Perhaps I will see you some evening."

"I'd like that," she said, and almost meant it. She

backed away carefully, letting him think that she was reluctant to break eye contact. Really, she just didn't want to risk him seeing her gun before she was back in the shield of agave and cactus along the road.

Miguel Stuart—if that was his real name—might work for the National Aeronautic and Space Administration in some obscure capacity, but she had real doubts that rocks were what had drawn him to Mexico. Nor was he your average man.

He wasn't like her—not exactly. But he was something that was no longer completely human. Assuming anything that beautiful had ever been human. This was either a very good sign of supernatural activity in the area, or else a very bad one.

Corazon growled and looked up at the sky. Ninon hoped Miguel was wrong about the raven being an omen, but knew he probably wasn't. After all, Death was never that far away.

It is strange that modesty is the rule for women when what they most value in men is boldness.
—*Ninon de Lenclos*

Sometimes he disappears for considerable time, then suddenly reappears and lets it be understood that he has been in another world communicating with the dead. Moreover, he prides himself on being able to tame bees and to make snakes listen to music.
—*J. van Spesteyn on Comte Saint Germain*, Historische Herinneringen

She rode in her carriage by moonlight, the city as peaceful and empty as it ever got near the Place d'Armes. Her driver was black but not a slave. She loved the freedom and spirit of Nouvelle Orleans, but not slavery of the dark people, so her cook and maid and driver were all free. She had even taught her maid to read since the girl had an aptitude, though this was kept secret. Actually, if anyone were to be pitied, it was the Irish who had come to dig the city's canals and who died by the thousands of yellow fever.

The air was damp, drowsy with heat, and the night was full of smells both pleasant and terrible. Plants blossomed madly, but they decayed too. The city had been wrested from the nearby waters and she sometimes wondered if the water resented it. Certainly it was vigilant, always looking for a way back in. It was a fecund city—perhaps doomed. What wasn't taken by water was slowly being pulled back into the earth by beautiful but destructive vines.

She also wondered how much longer she could remain there before people began to notice that she wasn't aging. It wasn't that she would mind being thought a voodoo priestess, but her fame would spread. And that would attract the two men she never wanted to see again.

Invisible hands seemed to reach out and touch her face. She turned her head aside, knowing it was only phantoms of her mind but still dreading their touch. There had been an attempted seduction and then an attempted rape. From that day forward, though she had left the Continent, a ghost had always been with her, conjured to life by her anger and hate and—yes—fear. Someday she would find a way to exorcise it. Someday.

CHAPTER FOUR

She had been expecting another down-in-the-heels hotel, but the Ybarra was fairly nice. Not too friendly though, and not fond of cats, she thought, putting down Corazon's carrier. Of course, the feeling was mutual. The cat didn't like places that had the nerve to insist that he be kept in a cage.

The clerk was a woman with streaky foundation that looked like it had been applied with a wide-toothed comb and allowed to harden into textured plaster like the wall behind her. She didn't bother to smile back at Ninon. Perhaps she couldn't without cracks. Still, Ninon sensed a certain hostility and disapproval caused part of the facial immobility—and it was undeserved because the woman didn't know her and she had actually buttoned her blouse almost all the way to the neck. Nor was Ninon traveling alone. She had a cat with her. Women bent on licentious behavior didn't usually bring pets.

Then Ninon saw the woman's husband and understood the hostility. She hoped she wouldn't have to break his fingers because he tried sneaking into her room late some night.

The man came forward from the dark alcove behind the desk, sucking on a cigarette, a man with a big chest and too little brain, one always looking for something easy to fill the void in his mind and heart. He smelled of beer and sweat. The odor leaked from his pores, telling her he was a habitual drunk. Ninon wondered if he suffered from beer impotence yet. If not yet, he would soon. Beer droop went with beer belly.

He swaggered as he walked, moving as if his *cojones* were too big to fit in his pants. A quick glance told her that the problem was strictly psychological. If anything, he seemed more likely to have tiny equipment. Odd, that he wasn't aware of his shortcomings. But then many men weren't. It just went to prove the power of the self-delusion.

Ninon smiled again at the clerk, this time recognizing that the heavy makeup was a cover for bruises, and she decided that perhaps she wouldn't be sorry if she had to break the man's fingers after all. Men who beat women disgusted her.

Checking in did not take long, and Ninon was pleased to discover that she had an actual shower in her room. Soap and toothpaste were not essential to her survival, but her brain preformed better when her body was comfortable. Corazon, freed from durance vile, joined her in the bathroom, as happy as she to wash the dust off his paws in the sink, though he declined the use of her shampoo or the tub.

Ninon got out of the shower and found herself being scrutinized. There was a small statuette of a feathered serpent god on the window sill, looking fearsome even in its diminutive state. She smiled. The old religions were here still, just obscured by the hardening sediment of four hundred years of enforced Catholicism. This was a good thing, at least for her purposes.

Still wet, she stood in front of the spotted mirror over the sink and examined her body. It was outwardly healed from the explosion. The burns were gone. Her only marks were the fine mesh of golden scars that covered her torso like lace. It looked like a clever tattoo, but wasn't. These powers of recuperation still amazed her. She should have been incapacitated by the fire bomb, her skin burned black and peeling, but even with her powers waning, she had managed to stagger away from her grave with only minor burns on her chest and legs.

Still, that had been a close call. She and Corazon had left on a boat that very night, borrowed clandestinely from a neighbor, a gut-shot cocaine-trafficker who had given up smuggling but kept the yacht for auld lang syne. Or whatever. She felt that he would have approved of her actions had she taken the time to contact him.

The crossing to the main island had been rough, but she couldn't complain about the price of passage or the slutty clothes she had found lying on one of the bunks. And once there, it was easy to join the other tourists from the cruise ship making a surf-n-turf port of call and get lost among them. She'd made a few calls from a pay phone to friends who had friends who did useful and illegal things for large sums of money, and Seraphina of California was born two days later.

She had debated sending Byron a telegram or e-mail to warn him of what had happened, but was certain that he and his lover Brice had left her home and that they were already on the run. And if they weren't, her action might actually put them in harm's way, alerting the authorities or even Saint Germain to the fact that the poet was alive and probably involved somehow in that incident with Dippel at Ruthven Towers. Instead, she had simply crossed into the U.S. at one of the illegal border crossings and headed for Byron's wife's last known address, hoping to pick up their trail on the way.

The next morning she'd heard about an "incident"

where some illegals had been gunned down. It was hard not to wonder if the killers had been looking for her.

She'd known that she was too attractive to fool the other illegals in her group that she was traveling to the U.S. to pursue a career in agriculture, but no one had doubted that she would be taken care of in the land of opportunity. She looked the sort of girl who relied upon the kindness—and bedside tips—of strangers. Of course, that image only held together until someone looked into her eyes. If a person were even moderately perceptive, the role of high-priced mistress began to delaminate. A few hours in her company and the whole role came apart. Some women would never be whores. The men had wisely left her alone, and she'd left that group and joined another as soon as she could, both for her own protection and for theirs.

She'd thought about abandoning her plan. Whore wasn't a role she needed to play often or for long, and it was unlikely that the government would be looking for her among the illegals further north, so this was safest.

So you will be going back to the States when this is done? the voice in her head had asked.

Of course. As soon as I have help with my problem.

Ninon ran a hand down her belly. Smooth—not one hint of scar tissue. Amazing. The only evidence of the fire was Corazon's hair. Not one bit of her own body showed any damage.

She had once asked a former island friend who was a retired sports doctor—retired early for prescribing too many steroids for what were deemed trivial reasons—to check her out on the pretext that she was thinking of running a marathon. The results of the examination had astonished him and made him want to recheck the results. Her maximal heart rate was around four hundred beats per minute—nearly twice that of the cyclist Lance Armstrong. Her muscles refused to build up lactic acid so she almost never fatigued—at least not physically. Mentally she was vulnerable to exhaustion, especially near the time when her body needed to renew, but there was no way to measure that fatigue unless she gave herself over to a neurologist or headshrinker, and she didn't want either near her.

Ninon leaned into the mirror, peering down at her legs. She smiled a little at the patch of red-gold pubic hair she had neglected to color. She would take care of it as soon as she found a drug store that carried hair dye. There had been just enough color for her head and the cat; her nether regions had had to remain unaltered. She didn't anticipate getting naked with anyone in the next few weeks, but she knew the importance of details. Perhaps she should just shave.

Turning, she reached for the bottle of skin tanner and began smoothing it over her body. She had to reapply it almost daily. Corazon wrinkled his nose at the scent of soggy cornflakes and hurried away. He was an hour late for his early midafternoon nap anyway.

Ninon waited for the lotion to dry and then dressed with care. She had found a lovely turquoise and sea-green blue sundress by Alfred Shaheen in an antique store in Texas and been unable to resist. She carefully adjusted the angel wings over the bust. She made a perfect vamp—seductive but the tiniest bit innocent. She hoped Miguel would approve.

She touched her dress a last time, marveling in its texture and construction. She loved the feel of the bark cloth, the color, the exquisite architecture of the dress's form. She was an outlaw in vintage designer sheep's clothing, she thought, grinning briefly. But so was Miguel Stuart. And that meant there were no rules of engagement that she felt compelled to honor. Anyway, she liked pretty clothing for its own sake and wore it whenever she could. To have done otherwise would be to buy a racehorse and then cut its hamstrings. Of course, in this backwater town, she'd stand out like a whore at a church social in this dress.

The thought made her grin again.

On the run for your life, and still you have time to appreciate clothes. The voice in her head was amused.

Of course. And Miguel Stuart would be coming to see her tonight. Ninon was dead certain of it. He was not the kind of man who waited politely for what he wanted.

As if to underline this fact, a short note and a bundle of flowers—bird-of-paradise obtained who knew where— were waiting for her on the bedside table when she emerged from the bathroom. She didn't think the maid had brought them in.

You'll have to see about securing that door tonight.

Indeed. Though legend had it that no lock could keep out a vampire, if he'd been invited.

A vampire?

Perhaps.

Ninon frowned as she looked at the tidy, straight script—likely a result of expensive schooling in Britain that even a long stay in America had not broken. It was her experience that some of the most ruthless men had the most controlled handwriting. It was about power and not being careless, ever.

Of course, it was also possible that Miguel Stuart had had his hands beaten with a tawse until the training took. Children learned what they lived. The thought of childhood made her a little sad. But only until she thought about the fact that this supposed offering was Miguel's way of checking up on her story, and that whatever he had lived as a child, he had less than honorable intentions toward her now. Sentimental compassion was not an emotion that she could afford to indulge.

I do not know if you have cause to fear her. But, my son, if you feel you must kill her then know you do so with my blessing. However, you must act at once, before she discovers your intent and pulls on the strings of your heart with her wily hands. I have long observed her and can say with conviction that hers is not a citadel that will fall to romantic siege. Especially beware her voice, which can enslave, and also her eyes that are like an invading horde sacking one's brain and demolishing one's will. For where her voice and gaze fall, there even wise men are made captive, and their hearts and minds are made to burn until they are but ash which her smiling lips may blow away. She is slow to rouse, but where she finally attacks, she gives no quarter.

—*Letter from the Dark Man to his son, Comte Saint Germain*

So his father had also attempted a seduction and failed. This was not surprising because she was lovely as well as a vessel of power. But if she could not be had one way, then he would find another. This was dangerous, perhaps even stupid, but faint hearts did not kill fair ladies.

The beautiful magician stepped into the moonlight and raised his right arm on high. In his left hand he held a silver blade.

"I call thee, Evil Spirit, Cruel Spirit, Merciless Spirit: I call thee who sittest in the cemetery and takest away the healing of man and eatest his soul. Go and place a mark on the one called Ninon de Lenclos. Put a knot in her brain, in her eyes, in her mouth, in her tongue, in her windpipe, and put poisoned water in her belly. I call thee and those six knots that you go quickly to her and kill and bring me her soul, because I wish it. Here is payment of my blood. Amen, Amen, Amen."

The one called Saint Germain smiled as he slashed his wrist and watched his black blood spill onto the frozen ground.

Ninon, now called Ana St. Cyr, boarded the train at Gare du Nord in an uneasy frame of mind. Standing under the metal-vaulted canopy in the cathedral of modern transportation, she had her first small frisson of disquiet. Foolishly, she did not obey the intuitive tug on her skirt that told her to return home. There was no sensible reason for her to abandon her luggage or forestall her visit to London where she had heard Lord Byron was presently staying.

She paused at the top of the steps. There were others on the train, all swaddled in scarves and buried in winter coats, but not so many as normal because the unseason-

ably harsh weather and illness had kept them at home. There were also few porters about, and few vendors trying to hawk their wares. An eerie quiet surrounded them.

Ninon walked along the dim corridor, the back of her neck and palms tingling in an increasingly unpleasant manner. She drew near her assigned compartment, feeling steadily more alarmed though she could perceive no peril in the deserted car.

The car shifted as though buffeted by a strong wind. The hair on her nape began to rise and something tickled at the back of her throat, a bit of poisoned air perhaps. Ozone was gathering, a lightning storm.

But that was impossible. Not inside the train station.

Danger. She couldn't ignore it any more. Something bad was close by. Perhaps a ghost. Perhaps something worse.

Ninon stopped. She took a deep breath, allowing her eyes to focus on the curtained glass of the door across from her. Glass, mirrors, still pools all induced in her a hypnagogic state where she could access other senses. She stared into the glass, looking past her reflection.

Something moved inside. Something man-sized, but not man-shaped. And dark. A vague scent of rot and sulfur floated toward her.

Dippel? Could it be him? Or one of his sick creations? But why? And why here?

The train began to move, pulling her off balance in her tiny heeled slippers. She put a hand to the wall and turned her head slowly in the dark shape's direction. There! At the end of the corridor, someone waited behind an opened door. Someone very large with black shoes and dark woolen pants.

The feet moved, rocking forward slyly, and she saw that it wasn't shoes at all. She was looking at hooves. And the thing wasn't wearing trousers, it had knotted legs covered in fur. As she watched in frozen horror, a long snout eased around the corner of the door, drool running down the long tusks that burst out of the mask of bristling quills.

*Horns glittered on its bull-sized head. A long black tongue
unrolled, flicking in her direction. She thought to herself
that this impossible thing had to be a hallucination.*

Then it looked into her eyes and smiled.

*Revulsion rolled through her body, freeing her limbs.
She turned and fled back toward the door where she had
boarded, intent on nothing except escape. She had seen
ghosts, and felt the final trembling shivers of malevolent
magic worked in a desecrated graveyard that had been
looted by Dippel, but never experienced anything like this.*

*Demon. The word popped into her head. Then: Saint
Germain. Was this a rejected suitor's revenge? He was
certainly egotistical enough to want her dead.*

*The stench warned her first. She stopped so suddenly
that her legs nearly slid out from under her a second time.
As it was, she still nearly ran into the thing—or another
thing that looked just like the first one—that stepped into
the corridor from the opposite end of the car, its ape-like
arms spread wide. Taloned hands with too many fingers
reached for her. Its head slashed from side to side as
though demonstrating how it would gut her with its horns
when it had her pinned to the floor.*

*With a scream that died before it escaped, strangled in
her throat by terror, Ninon thrust open the first door she
backed into and tumbled into the empty compartment,
slamming the door with all her fear-induced strength.
The small window cracked and glass tinkled behind the
curtain.*

*No lock. Not that any man-made device would stop the
infernal thing, especially not if it was a thing of the mind.*

*Hail Mary, full of grace—blessed is she among
women—*

*The train was running fast now, but Ninon didn't care.
All that mattered was escape and finishing her frantic
prayer.*

*She rolled to her feet and lunged at the window, tearing
off her thick coat. Using all her strength she wrenched*

open the frozen sash. Behind her, the door was flung wide and something cold and loathsome began to pour into the room.

Not wasting another instant, even to look back at what stalked her, Ninon threw herself off of the train, legs kicking violently as she propelled her weight over the fulcrum of the windowsill. She prayed that there was not another train approaching on the opposite tracks where her body landed, and began to tumble with a distressing cracking sound that meant bones were breaking as well as corset stays.

The somersault finally ended. Snow swirled around her as she fought for a first painful breath.

No train. Merci, bon Dieu! Though, even if there had been, terror would have still forced her from the window. An iron horse did not scare her as badly as that creature did.

She rolled onto her back, unable to breathe smoothly through the pain in her ribs, and watched as the locomotive disappeared. She couldn't be sure, but it seemed to her that there was something impossibly huge and dark bulging out of the window she had just exited. Was it flesh, or was it phantom? Probably it didn't matter. If luck favored her, the demons would return to their summoner and demand he provide them with his own life as payment for their loss. She'd never been that lucky, though. He'd buy his way out somehow. The best she could reasonably hope for was that Saint Germain would be so inconvenienced by the monsters' demands that he would not call for these evil things again.

Damn! They'd found her once more, the Dark Man and his son. She had to prepare.

She exhaled painfully and rolled to her knees, gathering her torn skirts with her left arm because her right was broken.

Men! Even the brightest of them were still terrified by

women who could think, and these two—cowardly bastards! Eventually something would have to be done about them. If only she knew what. How did one kill what would not die?

CHAPTER FIVE

Ninon felt the weight of every assessing male stare as she strolled into the cantina. The jukebox in the corner was old but still giving valiant if ever-fading service. "Forever Nightshade Mary" came to an end and a long silence followed until the pool players recalled that they were there to have a game and not stare at the petite *gringa* who somehow managed to stroll with the long-legged walk of an Amazon.

Ninon sauntered to the old juke without giving the slightest sign that she was aware of the attention, though she felt it as surely as the sweat on her skin and the heaviness in her lungs. She understood that if they thought her a Latina then she should be insulted by their scrutiny. If she were an American tourist then she should feel flattered. As a Frenchwoman she was merely amused, but that wasn't a response they would understand, so she kept it simple and gave them what they expected.

It amused her also to see mixed in with the juke's salsa music some old American pop tunes, including "St. Elmo's Fire." Her fingers hovered over D9, but then, not feeling like tempting fate, she moved on to E2. Again she hesitated. She liked some of Nine Inch Nails because of the genuine emotion in the songs, but didn't think that this was the kind of place where a lone woman should have Trent Reznor singing to the world that he wanted to "fuck her like an animal." Instead, she chose Patsy Cline's "Crazy." She kept her back to the room as the song engaged, allowing herself to sway to the music, and also allowing the men to look their fill at her body. A sexual fantasy was a lovely gift to give a stranger. And anyway, she never knew when she might need one of these men to help her. This was her way of putting them on retainer.

In the tarnished mirror above the record player she watched the hotel manager. He was behind the bar counting the take in the cash box—still staring at her, still smirking, still begging to have his fingers broken. Her gaze was not inviting but his conviction of his great sex appeal was inviolate. Ninon truly pitied his wife. She also gave Miguel credit for seeing this creature for what he was.

Ninon inhaled slowly. The bar seemed to be serving beer, tequila, and *vin ordinaire* that smelled a bit too *ordinaire* for her tastes. There were only so many compromises a woman could make.

She knew by the frisson that passed over her skin when Miguel arrived, and she turned slowly to face him. He was dressed all in black, a shadow. Dark on dark, he moved smoothly through the dim, smoke-choked room on silent feet. The other men didn't exactly scatter in front of him, but whenever he arrived at a space, it was empty and waiting.

He seemed at ease with the gift of beauty that Mother Nature—or the Father of Lies—had bequeathed him. It was Ninon's experience that scientific types didn't dress up well. If they managed a suit or tie they chose the one their mothers had dressed them in for high school graduation circa 1968. Miguel didn't have that problem. The delicate lawn of his shirt and the crisp linen of his slacks both begged to be touched so that their superiority could be known. And he wore no gun—though she was willing to bet there was still a knife in his sock. She evaluated the cost of his clothing right down to the handmade shoes on his narrow feet. Science was paying well these days. Or perhaps he had other sources of income, like an annual tribute of gold from superstitious villagers.

His eyes moved over her, every bit as appraising. She was willing to wager that he recognized who had designed her dress, and that it was a vintage piece belonging in some design museum and not in a cheap cantina. His eyes were hot. Maybe he wanted to touch her clothes too. Certainly he wasn't seeing her for what she was and thinking she had a fine analytical mind and athletic body. Later he might find that her ability to think clearly, to resist being be-spelled—and able to take a bullet too—belonged on her list of attributes, but not right now. She was willing to bet that nowhere was there an internet ad placed by Miguel Stuart that said: Single smart male seeks same in female. Must live forever, be able to fight sorcerers, and jump from speeding trains without hesitation.

She knew a moment of melancholy. Which was stupid—how could any woman have a man stare at her with such fierce attention and be disappointed? It was just . . . What? That she wanted to be appreciated for what she was? And what was that—a monster far stronger than any normal man?

"Crazy," Patsy sang, "I'm crazy for feeling so lonely."

As had been pointed out lately by the voice in her head, Ninon was crazy too.

He's a handsome devil, she thought.

He's not a devil, cherie.

No. But he is probably a blood relative. He has to be. Look *at him.*

"You're staring," she said when he stopped a pace from her. It wasn't an accusation, and it was said softly so that it didn't disturb the soft hum of male voices around them.

"Around here, you don't see too many women who dress like they love their bodies," he answered. That surprised her a little. It was a clever thing to say—if he suspected she had a brain. Perhaps they were going to play a game with more than one level of meaning. She had always loved subtlety.

Remain focused, the voice warned. *This is not a game.*

But it is *a game—survival.*

"My body does many things for me. I like to give it pretty clothes as a reward." Unspoken was the suggestion that her body could do many things for him too. She sat down on the edge of a bar stool and crossed her legs.

"Will you have dinner with me?" Miguel asked. He too sat. His voice was liquid, a rolling tide of seduction that could not be deterred.

Thus spake the spider to the fly.

Is this wise, cherie? He is very good. . . .

It's what I came for. She didn't know if it wise, though. Wisdom was another luxury she could not afford.

Ninon answered, "Sure," sounding very Californian and laid-back, though it remained to be seen who would be eating whom at this meal.

A brief image of her naked body pressed up against his flashed through her mind, pointing out that her thoughts at least had more than one meaning. The subconscious double entendre startled and annoyed her. She also wondered if the image was her own or if she was picking up something from his mind. Perhaps he was sending out subliminal lures. Could that be part of his power?

"You've made my night," he answered. His body, expression, and voice all said that he found her fascinating and couldn't wait to hear what she had to say. She knew it was his natural—or unnatural—charisma and nothing personal, a lure he used on everyone. But it was still hard to resist.

He held out his hand, but she did not take it. She was prepared, in control—and yet there had been that small erotic image of the two of them in her brain. She couldn't chance touching him. Not here. Not now. His clever fingers might drink in both her nervousness and attraction, and she didn't want him certain about either feeling, though he had to suspect both.

"Would you like to bring your chaperone? I am sure that for a suitable tip, Corazon would be permitted to join us." He was amused by her hesitation and showed it with his suggestion. He didn't touch her though, seeming to realize that it would mean risking losing his fingers to her bite. Not that he was the type to fear pain, but he was probably clever and knew it was too soon in their relationship to let one's prey know things could get bloody.

Still, it wasn't a bad idea to fetch the cat. A witch should always stay close to her familiar. . . . But, no. She could not risk putting Corazon in danger. He was just a cat, not a demonic imp.

"No thanks, he does not care for the local cuisine. He is on the Atkins diet and avoiding carbs. Beans and tortillas would never do." Ninon made herself smile.

"I don't suppose there are many carbs in feathers," Miguel agreed.

"None, I shouldn't think. Anyway, he has a bad habit of licking the salt off my margaritas."

Miguel smiled again, and this time she felt it was genuine and personal, a smile just for her. It made the muscles of her abdomen clench and she had to look away. She had not counted on this intense physical attraction.

A quick glance out the deep sill of the window revealed something unusual. An impressive palisade of black clouds was building on the horizon. They would finally have rain. And lightning. Had Saint Germain left Mexico and allowed Mother Nature to resume her natural course? Or did this mean just the opposite?

"It will be here soon," Miguel said softly, looking in the same direction. "I've always loved the rain. It's such a miracle in these dry lands. Sometimes I go out in the storm and let it bathe me."

Naked. He went naked. As did she, though it wasn't water she bathed in, but fire. Her breath caught on the image of the two of them naked, stuttered, and then stopped altogether.

"Let me buy you a drink—with extra salt if you like. The firewater is safe here too, though I wouldn't touch the wine," he said. He moved a little closer and the hair on Ninon's arms raised slightly as though pulled erect by static. "Then we can go on to dinner."

"A margarita please," she agreed, looking away from him, away from the storm. She stared at her gold-gilt toes peeping out of her sandals and tried to regain her lost breath.

A moment later a drink appeared in his hand. Either more time had slipped by than she was aware of, or he had somehow managed to both anticipate and communicate his wishes to the bartender before she voiced her order.

"Here you go," he said. Sensing her hesitation, he had dialed back the raw desire. It was uncanny how he read her. This was a master manipulator.

"Thanks. And extra salt too."

She took the glass reluctantly—she should have been watching to be sure that nothing besides lime and tequila had gone into it. Ninon sipped cautiously. Some tequila was corrosive enough to cause second-degree burns on the lips and throat, but that wasn't what she feared.

Her worries were foundless, the drink was smooth, and her keen tongue and nose said that there was nothing dangerous in her glass except his intention to relax her enough to bed her. Miguel sipped his own drink and then curled his tongue over the rim. Again came the flash of an image, his tongue traveling up her body, after the salt of her sweat. Hers or his? She didn't know. Ninon stared, reluctantly intrigued.

Then, something else. She had seen only the quickest of glimpses when he licked the salt from his glass, but she was certain that he had black racing stripes on either side of his tongue. Natural coloration in tongues was not unheard of. Some breeds of dogs had blue and black tongues, but this looked deliberate, symmetrical—like the fine scars on his cheeks. But who the hell tattooed his tongue? It had to hurt like hell.

At least it isn't forked.

She transferred her gaze back to the window. It seemed the safer place to look.

"Shall we step outside?" he asked. "There is a gazebo where we could sit and watch the storm."

The idea of being outside where there was lots of room to run appealed to her. Ninon also enjoyed the contact high she got from nearby lightning. Of course, if it came too close she would have to leave him. Under her fake tan were the gold lines, evidence of her previous encounters with St. Elmo's fire, and they would begin to glow if the lightning came near.

"That sounds perfect," she said, lying, but not too much.

They walked side by side on the paved path lined with whispering palm trees that were also a white man's import. The gazebo was raised, slightly Moorish in its architecture, and had a view of a church, Iglesia de San Jose, which was little more than a pair of perpendicular white towers topped with bright red cupolas. It was not a thing of architectural beauty, but she made note of it because it was the tallest structure in town. She might need to make use of it if her time came and she had not found any help.

Miguel was being cautious, still respecting her obvious desire not to be touched, but she could feel his gaze on her face as they climbed the gazebo's stairs. She knew that both his curiosity and hunger were growing. Who was she? What was she? Why did she not instantly fall into his arms? This was probably a new experience for him.

Take the ride or hide? Stop playing games? Should she

tell him what she was and what she wanted? Assuming he didn't already suspect.

No. Not yet. She might be genuinely attracted to him, but that meant nothing. Passion was not honest. He could be another Saint Germain. Only a fool would assume him to be a knight-errant because of his beauty. Other women in the first throes of desire might be trusting, but she had always thought intense attraction was like watching a two-year-old play with fire. She had been badly burned and was more cautious.

"Tell me a little bit about what you do," Miguel urged.

Ninon smiled.

"I used to be a sort of Mary Poppins for those with relationship problems." He blinked at her so she explained: "You know, Mary Poppins, the magical nanny who'd arrive with the North wind—or maybe it was the East, I never can remember. Anyhow, she'd work with a child until things got better, and then when the wind shifted, she'd fly off again."

"I know who Mary Poppins is," he said. "The image was just so . . . incompatible that it threw me for a moment."

"Well, I work with adults, not children, but the idea holds." She mounted the steps, letting her hips sway. Let him look at something besides her face, which she was having trouble controlling.

"So, you're a sort of sex therapist?" He seemed to mull this idea over, perhaps feeling that it would explain her differences, why she could be sexy but not be ruled by sexuality.

"A sex therapist. I like that. I was thinking of myself as more of a counselor but—"

"I like counselor better," he said.

So, he had a few old-fashioned prejudices. That was good to know. It also amused her, and that made her feel more in control. Men! It was so simple for them: Women were either Madonnas or whores.

"You're sure? I think sex therapists would wear better

underwear," she said, resuming their flirtation. "Assuming they wore any, of course."

Ninon set her drink on the flat railing of the gazebo and leaned against the ancient wood as well, forcing herself to finally meet his gaze and smile with an appearance of calm. She had left her gun in her room inside Corazon's carrier, but she could feel the trench spike inside the satin sheath that rested on her thigh. It was made of pure steel and had a deadly sharp blade. It wasn't being shown as a summer accessory in any of the fashion magazines, but like a good Scout, she believed in being prepared—and you just couldn't count on someone else having a trench spike lying about when you needed one.

"You're even more beautiful at night," he said, changing the subject. A cliché, but his voice made the phrase seem like it was being spoken for the first time. That voice! Either he was pulling out all the stops for her, or else the reason he spent so much time in deserted pozas was because he was tired of beating off the females.

"Oddly enough, so are you." Her voice wasn't as even as she would like. "So, tell me something about yourself. A favorite color—or do you have a nickname? A pet?"

His head tipped to one side.

"Yes, I have another name. It is a difficult name. Many have trouble uttering it. Would you like to hear it anyway? Or perhaps you would like to choose a name for me."

Ciuateto, the ozone-rich breeze seemed to whisper.

His eyes! Damn! It took only a moment of contact and she was again lost in their dark reflection, caught in a hall of mirrors where each glance showed her own desire, multiplied to infinity as the longing bounced from her gaze to his gaze and back again down the dark tunnel of long-denied need. Meeting him at night was a mistake. That was when certain dark powers held greater sway and when she was weakest.

And she could read what was in his mind now. He had looked inside, sensed her want and he had a message just for her: *Come close. I know what you need and do not judge. Just ask—pleasure, pain, amnesia, even death. I can give it all. Just say my name. Ciuateto. Say it, and I will give you everything.*

She forced her eyes not to answer, grateful for the plastic film of the contacts that helped veil what was there. No longer innocent, she felt fear and longing in equal measure.

Was this his standard seduction? Or did he realize his particular appeal to her? She'd come from an age of sexual and moral repression, so his offer of freedom and acceptance, lust without limits or moral judgments, was the ultimate seduction. And the thought of punishment— well, that was seductive in its own way. The desire to accept his offer was stronger in her than it would be in any modern counterpart who had never known what it was to be forbidden sexual expression on pain of death.

Ninon tried to think, tried to pull back, but it was useless. The stronger part of her wanted to see this contest through. She was stronger than he! She had to be.

But looking at him, she knew he would transgress even her firmest sensual boundaries, that he would take her deep into the world of lust—as deep as she wished to go.

And perhaps even deeper. Was she ready to be sacrificed, even tortured? The voice in her head asked, *did she really think that pain would bring absolution?*

No, but she needed to know—how strong was he? Could she resist if she needed to? If seduction was her only recourse, the only means of persuasion, could she encounter him and survive? More importantly, was he stronger than Saint Germain?

Who is in control here?

I am, but I think I will let him assume that he has power for a while longer. Ninon hoped this wasn't a lie.

You play with fire, cherie.

For the last four hundred years. It's what keeps me alive.

Resolved, she exhaled and then turned her face upward, letting her eyelids fall, inviting a kiss. She leaned closer. In legend, vampires had to be invited into someone's home; maybe Miguel—whatever he was—had to be invited before he could make a move.

His eyes widened slightly at her invitation. This was apparently not what he had expected given her earlier resistance. Perhaps he was thinking of Venus flytraps. Slightly wary now, he nevertheless moved a step closer. Slowly, though without hesitation, he lowered his head, holding her half-veiled gaze as he set his mouth to hers.

Take what you will, his eyes seemed to say. *And I shall too.*

Mouth pressed to mouth. She had no warning, and obviously no previous conception of what desire truly could be, which might have given her armor against him. It was joy. It was terror. It was a mad tingling in every nerve as electricity ran over her skin and made her muscles spasm.

She gasped and stumbled away, landing on one knee, barely holding herself upright with the aid of the railing. Horrified, she could see the golden lace of scars on her arms glowing in the darkness, burning as they did when true lightning ran through her body.

He did it! He had called them out! Nothing but lightning could do that.

So now you know. He isn't human.

And he knows that I'm not either.

Her only consolation was that Miguel looked equally startled, and seemed to be staring at his own arms rather than at hers. She couldn't blame him for this, because he glowed, lit from within by a luminescence that rivaled the moon, and it showed that he also had some strange scars. In anyone else, she would have called them the marks of the stigmata.

"What are you?" he whispered, finally lifting his gaze to hers. There was no seduction there now. His eyes were the shade of the coldest deepest lake. He had reeled his power back in. Perhaps that was what made him burn like phosphorous.

"I . . ."

She sensed it then, the terrible overshadowing of her mind. Saint Germain had felt the moment when she lost control and was questing for her, following the path of the emotional flare she had inadvertently sent up. Her stomach clenched and all her heat drained away.

Frowning, Miguel looked up at the sky. Ah—he sensed it too!

A part of her still wanted Miguel, regardless of the danger, wanted to mingle their light and reunite the parts of the emotional storm that had been pulled apart. But her mind was no longer her own to control, and her past did not want to be known just then. Her terror was strong of Saint Germain. She suspected that if she got too close, her subconscious mind would try to maim or kill Miguel—anything to prevent revealing herself to her enemy. Survival instinct superceded lust. Barely.

So instead, she pulled herself to her feet and vaulted over the railing. She landed lightly on the paving stones, unhurt by the fall.

"I'm sorry," she called as she ran for her hotel. "We aren't safe now."

Miguel did not follow, but she heard his sharp answer in her mind.

Later then.

Everyone tells me that I have less to complain of in my time than many another. However that may be, if anyone had proposed such a life to me I would have hanged myself.
—*Ninon de Lenclos in a letter to Saint Evremond*

Actors ought to be larger than life. You come across quite enough ordinary, nondescript people in daily life, and I don't see why you should be subjected to them on the stage too.
—*Ninon de Lenclos*

At all events, it is palpable that his knowledge has laid the seeds for him of sound good health; a little of which will—which has—overstepped the ordinary time allotted to man; and it has also endowed him with the means of preventing the ravages of time being visited upon his body.
—*From a letter of Count V Gregg, upon on seeing Saint Germain after a span of fifty years*

Whenever she thought of the First World War, she thought of the terrible smell—perforated bowels, gangrene, death. And noise. To this day, she hated the sound of thunder because it sounded like distant artillery fire.

In Belgium at the time of the invasion, she had volunteered at one of the hospitals, hoping to do something to relieve the terrible suffering she saw all around her. She knew it was what her mother would want; that she use her dark gift, her immunity to disease, to help others. Was that not what Christ taught they should do?

At first, spirits were high at the hospital, in spite of the steady trickle of casualties that came weekly. It was said again and again that Antwerp was unassailable, impregnable, and she would never fall to the German war machine. But Ninon knew better. History had taught her that eventually any place could be defeated.

Still, it was safer than many other cities. Preparation had made Antwerp an immense complex of ugly but strong defenses. All around the city were seas of deep trenches for the soldiers to retreat to, miles of barbed-wire snares just waiting to be powered with generators that would electrocute the enemy. There were primitive defenses too, pitfalls hidden by downed tree limbs containing stakes to trap the unwary cavalry. Other fields were peppered with sharpened stakes hidden in tall grass, designed to skewer the cavalry's horses—a sight that she had seen before and which made her ill and haunted her to the present day.

Just outside the walls of the city were wide moats no vehicle could cross, alternated by tall, grass-covered fortresses, bristling with armaments. All roads into Antwerp passed over at least one bridge, and each had *been mined. With the touch of a button the whole thing would blow. And, lastly, great gates of iron pierced the city walls, where nervous soldiers stood guard night and day. They were safe, everyone assured her and themselves. The city was unassailable.*

But, just as she had feared, none of these clever preparations was of any use when Death came calling, because no one had reckoned upon the siege guns and long-distance howitzers the enemy had. And they used them effectively, because the city had spies.

The small towns fell first after days of ferocious battle that smashed their lesser fortifications like a sand castle on the beach at high tide. The towns' destruction was a bloody harbinger of what was to come, though everyone continued to deny that it could happen to Antwerp. The human carnage poured into the city in ambulances, bodies hopelessly broken and mangled when parts were not missing altogether. The operating theater ran around the clock for as long as the battles lasted but many died anyway. And every day the Germans drew closer. Fear invaded the city. And ghouls. There was at least one. She had seen it late one night, dining on the dead in a makeshift morgue. That was when she had taken a trench spike from a dead soldier. If she had the chance, she would kill the thing.

Shells began to fall on the city itself. Eventually enough damage was done that the water supply failed, and disease quickly spread through the embattled metropolis. Nurses and doctors fell ill and had to be bedded beside their bleeding patients. Animals starved in the streets and there was no one to haul the bodies away. Everyone was on the edge of panic. Except Ninon. She hated the shelling but she had no fear of illness. As the bombardment continued, she worked without sleep, doing what she could for the wounded while they awaited evacuation.

It was on the final night before deliverance that she herself was wounded, shrapnel tearing a hole in her leg.

Knowing she could not let any medical person examine her, she crawled into the basement of a nearby ruin that she shared with a half-starved cat and the slowly rotting bodies of the former owners while she waited for her wound to heal. It might have been delirium, but she thought one night that she saw Saint Germain and a small pack of ghouls walking among the wounded and dead left in the street. He never stopped smiling as he examined the corpses and tossed the living to his pets.

CHAPTER SIX

Corazon's human changed her clothes immediately when she reached her room, throwing her dress into the sink to soak. He was glad, because the smell of fear and helplessness had to be washed away. He couldn't stand the scent of either. Knowing she felt bad at losing her fight, Corazon tried to interest Ninon in a game of chase-the-dental-floss—reclaimed from the wastebasket for just this purpose. That was, after all, what he liked best when he was feeling down.

Unless of course he was feeling down because of hairballs.

Staring at her consideringly when she failed to respond to his offer of play, he decided that perhaps she needed some private time to cough up whatever was bothering her.

Ninon patted her distracted thanks for his perspicacity and went into the bathroom where she began running water into the ancient tub. Corazon debated on joining her since he liked this faucet. Water was often sly and played dirty tricks, but it came out here at only a trickle, and it had some color and a rusty odor so he could tell where it was at all times. Also it was fun to chase cockroaches around the tub until they ran into the water and tried to swim. He'd left one in there earlier for just this purpose. It was to be his bedtime snack.

And yet, he was a French cat and had manners. One did not intrude when someone was coughing up hairballs. He would allow his human to play with his toy by herself. She never ate his things, so it would be all right. He could snack later.

He paused by the door until Ninon gave a small gasp and made a sound of disgust, and then he knew that she had found the cockroach in the tub. Satisfied with his work, he curled up on the bed and waited for her.

Leaving the shower, Ninon decided her cat had the right idea. Curling up in bed with Corazon, she buried a hand in his fur. She had her ears cocked at the door, a part of her waiting for the sound of Miguel's footsteps in the hall. Corazon was not interested and clearly thought she was worrying over nothing—if worrying was the word she wanted.

She did not sleep until the moon was set and the smell of morning rode the air. Instead she stared at the window and thought about her past, an activity that she had never really relished but seemed to be doing with distressing regularity these days.

Men! They were always there, the markers in her life— father, lover, son, deadly enemy. They had brought her the greatest joys and her greatest sorrows. Her greatest danger too.

Her second lover had approached her when she was fifteen. Refusing him after her first had not been easy, but she knew that in spite of his oft-stated admiration for her, she had to stay away from him. He was a dangerous man. After all, he was the power behind the throne, answerable to no one and therefore often capricious and cruel. Cardinal Richelieu also had an ambition so large that there was no space around him for affection to grow. This might have troubled another man, but his personality was likewise so vast and overshadowing that few people—himself included—realized this flaw, especially not the king, who was even more dazzled than she. And by the time awareness had dawned it was too late. Poor Louis was not so much seduced into losing his power as he was overwhelmed by the stronger personality.

Saint Germain was much the same as Richelieu, but he did not work in the same way. He was also a societal seducer, but a dandy who distracted with his jewels and accomplishments; he was a charmer who seduced without sex. That made him colder than the Cardinal. And because he was not obviously sexual in his conquests, people did not realize that they were actually being led astray by the deadliest of sirens. He was a magician using sleight of hand to distract his audience from his real agenda. He appeared to give away for free what others would hoard and charge dearly for—information, jewels, contacts with others in places of power. But once the supposed gift was cast into the world, Saint Germain reeled his bait back in, carefully concealing his delight when his victims followed the lure. And in the end, they always paid for their free gift.

Isn't there a saying: It takes one to know one?

Oui. I am also a seducer.

In her era, Ninon had been something of an emotional and mental transvestite, an ambiguity of feminine logic that intrigued most males; the judgment and education of a man housed in a beautiful woman's body. And she had been—was still—a capable seducer. Of course she was! All wise women of her era were, for how else were they to have any power or protection when the means of brute force employed by men had been denied them by nature? It wasn't as though they could appeal to the law for aid either. At least not until that nasty little general, Napoleon, changed the law so that women could finally buy and sell property in their own right

The voice in her head didn't answer. It wasn't condemning in the silence, simply waiting for her to finish her thought. Ninon stroked the cat, who was likewise alert and pensive.

Yes, she seduced. Seduction was a delicate act of war practiced both on individuals and on society, as politicians, priests, actors, and kings have always known. Such a method was usually thought to be a woman's tool because of the simpleminded belief that it was beauty and sex that drew men in. Saint Germain knew this. But he also knew that true seduction was a matter of psychology and could be used on either gender by either gender. Like a gun, the power didn't care who wielded it. Given the tools and the will, anyone could entice.

Some people—then and now—considered seduction a bad thing. But that was only because they had not chosen their pleasures wisely. They hadn't hungered after the right things. Whether being seduced by a person or an idea, one always had to be cautious—as Ninon knew from painful experience. Had she kept her hungers to a longing for education or respect of her peers, she would not have been so grievously injured. But the desire to preserve her beauty and above all her health . . .

You were young, her voice consoled. *Your chest hurt more each day and the pox was everywhere.*

Do you think God will see that as cause for mitigation? If I thwarted His will by accepting the dark gift? And does He care that I turned from the Church not because what it asked was hard and I was lazy, but because they were venal and cruel and I longed for equality for my sex?

The voice didn't answer. Perhaps it didn't know.

Would God understand? And forgive? Even if she didn't repent? For she did not regret most of her actions. That was the truth of it. She did not repent either her life of sexual adventure, nor that she had turned from religion at an early age because of the utter corruption of the clergy—many of whom tried to seduce her after her father had fled France and she was alone. And she certainly did not feel shame in being one of the *précieuses galantes* who had insisted on rights for women—she believed then and now that all women should be able to reject marriage, and not be forced into convents and have their money and property taken if they refused. She did not regret taking on the Faculty of Theology when they tried to ban Descartes and his works because they threatened Church authority and the frightened clergy deemed them blasphemous. Nor did she regret upholding Molière's right to produce satirical plays about the corrupt Court and Church, though it had earned her the hatred of the local priests he lampooned. The Church had decried her impiety again and again and said she was damned, but she had still fought for what she knew was right in the Court of the King, in the Court of Law, and the Court of Public Opinion. And she was not sorry for any of it!

The main difference between her seductions and Saint Germain's was that, other than her one transgression with the Dark Man, she used her power only to secure her safety and that of those close to her. She had not sought political rule or great fortune—though opportunities for both had presented themselves many times. Nor had she ever purchased her happiness by stealing it from another. She did not kill to sustain her life or political position.

Still, the voice was right. She may have done wrong for the right reasons, but it took only one false step to fall from grace. And the two of them were too close to kin for comfort; she and Saint Germain were opposite sides of a very thin coin that could be used to buy both good and evil.

And now there was Miguel Stuart. What was he? He might be the greatest seducer of all.

They say set a thief to catch a thief.

They did. But the real question was, could one set a seducer to catch a seducer? And without getting caught oneself. It might be possible, if Miguel cooperated. He'd need to turn down his charm when he was with her. Perhaps he would be inclined to, now that he knew there was more to her and the situation than he imagined. She had spotted his unhuman nature; surely he had seen hers as well.

Or maybe he would just head for the hills and save himself from the complications of involvement with her. It all depended on how curious he was. How badly did he want to know who and what she was? Had he religious training? Most humans drew a line—this was life; that was death. Life was short, death was long. But Ninon's line wasn't so straight and she didn't draw it in the same place most people did. In fact, hers kept shifting as she again and again delayed natural death. It was the curse of the inquiring mind. Maybe Miguel was the same.

It was a pity that time was running out for her, but it was. A decision had to be made. The Dark Man had ended insane, his mind burned up by repeated trips into the celestial fire. It could happen to her as well if Fate ruled against her in this eleventh hour. Her next renewal could be her last, if it destroyed her mind.

That couldn't happen. She had to stop this deterioration, even if it went against all natural and moral law. And Saint Germain could not be allowed to go on with his plans.

Even if there were eventually dire consequences for you or Miguel?

I'll take the chance.

Oui, *but should anyone else have to pay for your salvation? Does the end justify the means?*

That was the question. Would anyone else be hurt and have to pay if she continued her fall from grace? And who would decide what the penalties would be? And when they would be assessed? Some laws were immediately enforced without divine help. Like gravity—there was no avoiding that one. Drop a glass, it falls and breaks. But other laws had delays built in. Like sin, which you paid for at death—or so most world religions believed. Could one avoid that by not dying? And then there were those man-made laws. Those tended to be enforced only to the degree of strength of will of the men making them. Those were the easiest to get around, as she well knew. She had no doubt that Miguel could evade any man-made laws that he had to confront. Even murder.

This isn't a man's law you face. Clever argument will not save you. Or him. You cannot win a fight with God.

I know—but it is not God I go to battle.

Are you certain of this? Could this not all be God's will?

No! Ninon answered at once. But could it? Could God actually want this horrible thing to happen, to let evil loose on the world? How could she know, when God was mute? She stood at a crossroad again and had to choose. Just as she had had to choose before. But the way was narrower now, her options diminished to three—unnatural life, death, or the unknown. And even this triad of choices might be an illusion, because Miguel, the unknown option, could be anything.

She bowed her head and tried to pray. Words would not come, though, and finally she just said—*If this is wrong, please, show me a sign. I will do Your will.*

But, as ever, God remained silent. She would have to find her own way.

Miguel . . . If only she didn't like him. If only he were truly evil! But she did like him, and he didn't seem wicked. He wasn't human, but that didn't make him a soulless thing of evil. She had no right to seduce him and involve him in her battle.

I agree.

If she could find some other option, she'd take it. But she'd have to find it quickly. Time was running out.

Indeed, this infernal temple, from its great height, commanded a view of the whole surrounding neighbourhood. From this place we could likewise see the three causeways which led into Mexico ... And this Tezcatepulca was the god of hell and in charge of the souls of Mexicans, and his body was girt with figures like little devils with snake tails.
—*Bernal Diaz,* Verdadera Historia de la Conquista de Nueva España

The true Mexican vampires were the Ciuateteo, women who had died in their first labour. They were also known as the Ciuapipiltin, or princesses, in order to placate them by some honourable designation. Of these Sahagun says: "The Ciuapipiltin, the noble women, were those who had died in childbed. They were supposed to wander through the air, descending when they wished to the earth to afflict children with paralysis and other maladies. They haunted crossroads to practise their maleficent deeds, and they had temples built at these places where bread offerings were made to them, also the thunder stones which fall from the sky. Their faces were white, and their arms and hands were coloured with a white powder."
—*Montague Summers,* The Vampire's Kith and Kin

CHAPTER SEVEN

Lilly pads sailed calmly on the still poza, crewed only by small frogs and small winger insects that were surely kin to the damselfly. They were not at all disturbed by the human who waded among them.

Ninon took a seat on a flat rock and watched Miguel work. He certainly seemed to be collecting stones, fitting broken pieces together, but she was having a hard time imaging that NASA really cared about these ancient rocks. He had to be up to something.

Hide or take the ride?

Damn! It was too soon to decide. She turned away, annoyed at her indecisiveness. Maybe it was just an excuse, but before she spoke to Miguel she wanted to see the *lago*—the lake—where the carved stone tablet stolen from the museum had been found. That stone . . . it would have told her so much. If there was some way for her to accomplish her goal without involving him, she would take it.

You're rationalizing your delay. This is a fool's errand.

We should go to the next village and see the shaman for a cure.

We've tried. There is no cure.

She always had been—and still was—a cheerleader for rational cognitive thought. The difference was that she no longer looked for consensus about reality from the rest of the world. She relied on intuition and followed her instincts. That said, there was comfort in her belief that Miguel—whatever he was—saw what she saw, knew what she knew, and therefore wouldn't think she had sat down for tea with the Mad Hatter if and when she told him her story.

But he could be dangerous. Understanding could make him extremely dangerous. That was the fly in the ointment.

Cherie, he is dangerous. All that remains to be seen is if he is dangerous to you. Why tempt Fate?

Ninon stood and walked away.

She had thought her life—her lives—broken into segments: childhood, her teens, her first lover, her last lover. As each era, each identity passed, they were broken off and set adrift so that she would not become weighed down with regrets or remorse or grief. But it seemed that not all of her past had floated away in the stream of time. Perhaps Ana and Coco and Angelique were gone, but her memories of her life as Ninon were now always close by. Not just in the voice in her head, but in her dreams. She was haunted and worried about repeating past mistakes.

The past never leaves us.

One island neighbor had called her otherworldly— which of course she was. Her first life was as *other* as it could get. There were few places in the modern world that had survived as long as she had. Buildings and statues, yes—some of them. But philosophies? Perceptions? Beliefs? No. Her world was long gone and the modern mind could never understand the part of her that still lived there and thought old thoughts and believed old teachings.

Do you think Paganini was one of the Dark Man's get? the voice asked suddenly. *How I loved his music.*

Maybe. They say he sold his soul to the Devil. How many Devils can there be?

I don't know, but even one is too many.

She nodded and then pushed the thought away. Paganini's was one ghost she did not need looking over her shoulder. She had found some of the Dark Man's creations, but not until many were already murdered by him.

"What a horrible place this is," she muttered to herself. "Hard to face the idea that I might die here."

There was a violent beauty to this sun-assaulted land, but it was frozen in time—not alive, not evolving. She'd driven through a lot of small towns down here that were dead but would be slow to get a decent burial because the inhabitants were stubborn about clinging to the corpses of their old lives. The way to Hell wasn't paved solely by good intentions; there were also a lot of lost dreams and broken hearts of people who couldn't let go. She'd learned to avoid this trap long ago—adapt or die—but she still pitied those who lingered as human ghosts, unable to move on.

Her eyes were growing tired of this place. This landscape was the same for as far as the eye could see. The world had ghostly colors not found in any crayon box, and it was a place that had no shadows, no secrets from the sun.

There had been rain—hard rain—sometime in the past few weeks, and it had gnawed with voracious hunger at the stream's banks as they overflowed their edges. Larger plants had been ripped away, but tiny opportunists had moved in to replace them. In a few more weeks there would be no evidence of the upheaval. This place did not like change.

World without end . . .

Amen.

Ninon found the *lago* mentioned on the stone and then

walked north. She stopped outside the cave where the hieroglyphs had indicated that the god of the Smoking Mirror was supposed to appear on the final days of the year. She sniffed the air cautiously, but smelled nothing obviously sulfurous. She looked for signs of ornamentation that befitted a god, but from the outside at least there was nothing to mark this cave as special, a place of worship, just some large stones that had been defaced by manmade tools so long ago that they had again grown smooth. She reached out with other senses, but felt no ghosts, no shades of old violence. Yet legend insisted this was where the god, Smoking Mirror, lived and was worshipped.

Ninon took in another lungful of air and opened her senses. Nothing. There was nothing strange about this place. No nerve-tingling power, no aura of supernatural dread. It was, if anything, less alive than the desert around it. Annoyed, she stared at the spreading ring of mushrooms that had stopped only when they reached the edge of the turgid creek that disappeared into the cave. She knelt down, not sure why they should grab at her thoughts and insist she study them, but willing to be led by intuition.

Mushrooms. There was nothing special about them. Small, brown, they looked a great deal like Haymaker's mushrooms, the fairy rings that were quite common all over the United States. The only thing interesting about the species was that the Haymaker mushrooms were not individual plants that marched outward in a magical expanding ring, but were actually only the fruiting part of a larger underground fungus that crept through the soil like a disease. The roots were part of the interconnected fibers of something that looked a bit like the synapses of a giant human brain.

Ninon blinked and focused on that thought.

They were each part of a larger entity. Like groves of aspen trees that spread from rhizomes and were in fact interconnected—a single plant that looked like many trees. Actually, she recalled that many plants did this. And there were scientists who insisted that it made them aware at some level. Damage or stimulus to one was recognized by all. Certain plants knew when insects were attacking and would emit chemicals to repel them, but didn't react when the damage was caused by fire or crushing. Because they were part of a collective awareness?

She stepped closer to the river and looked down into its coffee-colored water that sparkled like broken obsidian. The long stringy grasses within waved sluggishly. Could it be true of the strange dark grass snaking through the underground rivers of this area—were they tapping out a watery Morse code? Might that be how Smoking Mirror kept track of where people were and when sacrifices were brought?

Too bad there wasn't a botanist nearby to answer her questions. The other way of testing her theory was so much more dangerous.

Don't step in the water. The voice in Ninon's head was alarmed. *Go back to Miguel if you must.*

But this could be another way—something that would not involve Miguel. If I can call the god himself . . .

She listened intently. Frogs ground out their painful songs at the creek's murky edge. If she didn't know better, she would swear that nothing urgent ever happened here, that she was imagining things. Except . . . sunlight seemed to stop at the mouth of the cave as though turned away by a solid darkness.

"Hello—anybody home?" she called softly, dipping a finger into the water.

Cherie, don't!

Something stirred the air and it eddied slyly. A long tentacle of grass curled around her index finger. A foreign awareness touched her.

Oh yes, *something* was there, even if was just lackey fungoids and grasses passing on the message of her arrival. She pulled her hand back, wiping it on her jeans. It felt . . . unclean.

"I've come to ask for passage to the god Smoking Mirror." She kept her voice calm and rational as she turned toward the source of silent power, though she knew that what she was saying and thinking would sound patently irrational to anyone who shunned information acquired through sources other than the standard five senses, the classroom, or CNN.

She rose and walked forward, stood at the mouth of the cave, half in the dark, half in the light. She saw nothing unusual that was common to places of natural worship—nothing beautiful, amazing, or even sinister. Looking closely, she could see that the cavern may have been natural but clearly man had been at work inside it, smoothing the floor and such. And after the heat of the desert it seemed pleasantly cool, offering thousands of years of thick insulation against the sun. It tempted her.

There was a current in the air, though—an eddy of power that only a fool would ignore. The darkness felt tangible. It rubbed on her skin and she tasted it on her tongue. It was faintly metallic. Actually, it tasted of blood. If she went any farther, she would be wading into the torrents of the supernatural. Was that really what she wanted?

Hide or take the ride. Did she go back to Miguel and ask for his help, or stay and face the unknown?

She peered at the water that moved so sluggishly, a black worm burrowing through the cave. This was the local river Styx? It seemed rather dark and narrow, and generally uninspiring for a place of epic death and rebirth. But perhaps Hollywood had given her unrealistic expectations of the underworld. Would a smart god want any obvious markers guiding people to his lair?

Especially if he weren't a god at all, but merely a very long-lived monster.

She slid a foot a few inches further into the cave and had a moment of disorientation. There was north and south, east and west, up and down—and then there was this place, this time. It felt terrible—dead. Evil. Her courage failed her.

Cherie, run!

Okay, I'm outta here.

Suddenly a body welled up out of the dark river, an upright form but not of a man. Fast as she was, there was no chance for Ninon to get away. It dragged her into the dark and she found herself at the edge of the water, laid out flat on a small altar she hadn't noticed before, her mind knocked clean of all logical thought as something powerful and terrible rolled through.

He was a giant, twice her size, with a face of stone and jaws wide enough to bite off her head. But that wasn't what terrified her most. It was the feeling of power that surrounded him, an invisible aura that nevertheless burned her eyes. If he wanted, he could stop her heart, sear her flesh, cremate her mind. She was helpless, her body a prison that held her heightened senses at his mercy.

And it was slightly cliché, but the god smelled of sulfur, just as she had expected.

His obsidian eyes watched her as she tried to recall how to breathe. Something moved against her leg, inching upward. It paused at the gun she had shoved in her pants and patted the weapon curiously. She wished she thought the moving thing was a penis, but knew it was not. An image of a giant leech popped into her head, something thick like an elephant's trunk, looking for a place to latch on to her bare flesh and suck her dry. Also, behind the gaps in his giant, grinding teeth she saw something move. It gleamed like a silver needle but was as long as an ice pick. It reminded her of a scorpion's tail.

It didn't seem likely, but Ninon prayed that somehow the telegraph plants outside had also carried a message to

Miguel that she was here and needed help. Her desire to keep him from her affairs had fled in the face of this monster.

Cherie? This would be a good time to panic, but if you feel that you cannot do that, perhaps you could think of something to say to distract him.

Say? To this?

But the voice had restarted her brain. Ninon stared at her captor and tried a tentative probe on the god's mind.

When she looked with her senses, she could see into his brain, but it was through a veil of smoke where most detail was hidden. Even what she could see made little sense. Tezcatlipoca, he thought himself, god of the Smoking Mirror . . . He had thoughts that she couldn't follow because there was no human context for them, no words for what he was in any human language. He dreamed about things for which humans had no conceptualization, had been things that humans had no name for, and trying to understand him made her hurt.

He probed back. His will was unsubtle but he didn't look deep, seemingly happy to feed on her surface fear. She tried to relax, to allow her reason for coming here to present itself to him. She willed him to stay at the surface of her brain, to look no more deeply into her mind where he might find the things she truly feared. He would not be gentle and wouldn't care how much damage he did he as he rummaged through her mind, and there were thoughts there she did not wish to share.

"This is the frontier of the dead," the god said, speaking with a physical voice but also in her mind. "Sometimes people grow confused and the living find themselves among the dead souls, and the dead among the living. That a body moves does not mean that it has a soul. That it is still and dust doesn't mean the soul is gone. In this land, all is mine."

Ninon nodded at this prepared speech. She was afraid to ask if he meant she was soulless. She was more afraid to ask if he was claiming her. Her plans for the day hadn't included immediate sacrifice to a blood-drinking god. If that was what he was.

"I see there is a man following you, one you fear."

Rather than try to hide this thought, Ninon concentrated hard on Saint Germain. Better to think about him than having her blood sucked out of her body by that vicious straw attached to Smoking Mirror's tongue.

"This man who chases me—there is no confusion about what he does," she said softly, ritualistically, hoping Smoking Mirror could understand. "It's no accident that he is here in your land. Like his father before him, he has called the dead. He still calls the dead—even your dead. And if no one stops him, he will do it again and again until he has raised an army."

"He would call the dead in the land of Itlachiayaque?" The god used his other name. "Has he no respect of the gods?" Smoking Mirror's face shifted, for a moment appearing almost feline. Legend said that he could shape-shift into a jaguar, and she wondered if that would be a bad thing. A cat would probably be somewhat smaller and would put less weight on her already heavy chest.

It would still be large enough to rip out a liver.

"He has no respect for my God either," she said. "He respects nothing. He is a thief."

"But what are *you,* almost daughter?" Smoking Mirror asked, the black reflection of his eyes showing no reaction to her words. *Almost daughter*—that was either very good or very bad.

Ninon shook her head, not denying but not knowing how to answer. She realized with a sinking heart that this creature was insane. She recognized the signs, and wondered if all long-lived beings were eventually driven mad. How could she get away from him?

"Pale woman, what are you?" The black, bottomless eyes stared into hers, daring her to lie. His gaze pierced her brain. "Why have you really come?"

"I don't know what I am. I'm not normal—not one with my people. Not anymore." She told that much truth because she had to. The god appeared to be considering this and she lay very still, trying not to think about the fact that she was stretched out on an obsidian altar, the kind where victims had their living hearts ripped from their bodies. She added, "I came because I need help, strength to fight my enemy. Now your enemy." She added, "I come as penance for an old sin."

She couldn't tell if he believed her. Or even if he understood.

"Why does this magician follow you?" the god's voice asked, a rumble in her head. The words and feeling were foreign, and the forced emotional and verbal translation actually made her ache.

"Because he covets," she answered in a whisper, unable to blink. Her eyes began to tear.

"You?" Probing tines slid deeper into her mind. She had to stop him.

"My power. All power." She told the truth; to have lied would have been to rip her brain in two. It might be torn apart anyway. She added desperately: "He is not content with immortality. He wants to be a god. To do that, he believes he must gather up all the power his father bestowed on others. And he needs something more—just as I need more to fight him."

She added the last plea, but knew it would do no good. This god did not care to help her.

"So you are a priestess. One who has sinned." But he wasn't thinking about her. The god's mind and face shifted again, and He Who Would Not Be Named By Man paused, perhaps pondering the idea of a rival, someone actually arrogant enough to challenge him. That obviously hadn't happened for a long time. Perhaps he was thinking it would be most expedient to cut her throat so that Saint Germain would have no chance at transforming himself if he found her. Maybe the god thought he could take her power for his own use. All Ninon could do was wait for his verdict. She didn't try to correct his assumption about what she was. One didn't argue with an insane god.

A shadow fell over the cavern's small mouth, and she sensed when Miguel joined them in the cave. Her first reaction was relief, but it was followed swiftly by caution. She sensed that the balance of power could be tipped either way, and though she did not want to die, she didn't want Miguel hurt either.

"Seraphina, I see you've met my . . . father, S.M.—The Source of Discord, Patron of Sorcerers, God of the Smoking Mirror," Miguel said. She saw that he was breathing hard but trying to control it. "Or perhaps I mean my grandfather, since he at once gave birth to my mother and yet also fathered me into a new life."

His father?

She felt the god's attention shift away from her, and some of her mental pain eased. *Patron of sorcerers?* She didn't like the sound of that. Saint Germain didn't need a patron. It would be bloody annoying if she'd accidentally led her foe to what he needed to consolidate his powers.

"Relationships are often complicated," she answered, and felt the moment when He Who Would Not Be Named By Man was finally moved to something other than anger and suspicion. She thought he might actually be amused, though by her words or Miguel's, she didn't know. The god shifted back on his knees—if that's what they were—and the golden bells at his ankles tinkled musically. She finally dared to turn her head and look at Miguel, still unsure if she should be relieved that he was there.

The sight of him caused her a small pang. In the dim light he looked a lot like Louis de Mornay, the man who had so long ago fathered her son. The memory of her last meeting with her lover passed through her mind, leaving sadness in its wake. The god probably felt this. She hoped he would think her feelings were for Miguel.

Miguel's eyes stayed on the god. He was clearly wary,

son or no son. He went on, speaking to her: "The thing about us—my people—is that we feed on emotion. Any emotion, good or bad. As long as you feel anything, it's enough to interest us. And our capacity to absorb is endless, our appetite unquenchable." Miguel's eyes were somber, a warning. All trace of his Scottish accent was gone. Ninon realized then that her original role of ditz was also on a long bathroom break, perhaps trying on lip gloss, maybe swallowing some tranquilizers while her logical mind dealt with this monster.

She forced herself to nod again.

"I'm trying hard to be unfeeling—really I am."

Miguel smiled a little, but she sensed his fear for her. And maybe of her. Well, fair enough. She was afraid of him and for him too. She was in this horrible place only because she had wanted to spare him from involvement in her troubles.

"You want her, my only son?" the god asked. His jaws cracked open and Ninon could finally see clearly the long scorpion tail at the end of his tongue. "Shall you be the one to bring her to us? If I let her live this morning, will you take her offering yourself?"

"Yes," Miguel said. His eyes flicked over her. He swallowed something bitter and added, "I will."

Somehow, she knew this wasn't good. Miguel seemed a better choice, at least on the surface, but there was some power struggle going on between him and Smoking Mirror.

And Ninon really didn't like the word "offering." She had always suspected that she would probably have to die someday. Especially in order to become a vampire. But she hadn't planned on it being today, right now. In a cave, on an altar, at the hands of a death god's reluctant son while his sadistic father looked on?

"Then do it," the god commanded. He looked pleased— way too pleased. "Take her as your first, and I shall have the sorcerer for myself."

Neither Miguel nor Ninon reacted openly, but Ninon

was appalled at this command—though Miguel was clearly the lesser of two evils. Whatever he might have in his mouth and pants, it had to be better than a stinger the size of an ice pick and a leech-like penis that could function as a third arm. And if she survived, there might still be time for her to get to Saint Germain before the god did—because she *had* to now. In spite of his arrogant words, she could sense that the Patron of Sorcerers couldn't be trusted to kill Saint Germain. Smoking Mirror would be too intrigued. He would try talking to Saint Germain, and the Dark Man's son was the Scheherazade of magicians. The world could not afford having that monster gifted with any more life or power from some godly but psychotic patron.

Merde! There were times when she wished desperately that she could trade superior wits for superior strength. She'd break the god's neck right then and there if she could, even if it meant she went insane the next time she renewed.

"N-now?" she asked the god. Then, thinking urgently of ways to delay: "But I haven't been cleansed or anointed. And there is no storm. We need lightning. That is how I am reborn. That is my way to new life when I cross over. I would not wish to be a less than perfect offering."

Would he believe this drivel? He thought her a priestess, so maybe . . .

Miguel looked at her like she was insane. She knew what he was thinking—that those whom gods wished to destroy they first made mad—but his father considered her words.

Ninon kept her face meek and her thoughts corralled. In this way, if no other, the god was at a disadvantage. Smoking Mirror had not kept abreast of the times. In his world, women were for sex, having babies, and were—in a pinch—a second-rate sacrifice only marginally brighter than a chicken or sheep, even if they were priestesses. It was inconceivable to him that she could be anything more that that.

He wasn't the first to make that mistake.

"You wish to be reborn in the sky-fire?" he asked. "That is how you would make your offering?"

"Yes."

"And you believe that you can be born again that way?" That sounded like skepticism, but she wasn't sure.

"Yes." She was very sincere.

"Very well. Go and prepare. Tonight there shall be a storm. You will have your chance at rebirth in the sky-fire."

She had a sudden instinct that he was lying. Perfidious bastard. He didn't want her to be reborn—he planned that she would die at Miguel's hands and, failing that, in the lightning storm. This angered and frustrated her but she kept her defiant thoughts locked up. She used stolen fire from the gods, took life from heaven itself—she would steal his power too if she got the chance.

Miguel said nothing.

The god backed away and Ninon sat up slowly, getting a good look at the god's body. Panicked thoughts filled with revulsion skittered through her brain as he changed form into that of a cat, but she kept them suppressed so the god wouldn't sense them. As far as he was concerned, she was an awed worshipper.

"You have until moonset," he said to Miguel. "I've waited long enough."

As she and Miguel watched, the god backed into the river and disappeared in its murky depths, becoming one with the dark water. The last of the pressure eased from her brain. Ninon sagged with relief at the lifting oppression, but still felt overloaded by rage, and a bit drugged. These days she got high only on meditation; a yoga buzz wasn't adequate preparation for having her brain invaded by a god of death.

"What sky-fire? Or was that just bullshit to keep from

getting killed this instant? Not that I blame you, if you lied." Miguel helped her from the altar. They backed toward the mouth of the cave, keeping a watch on the underground river. Apparently Miguel had trust issues with his father too.

"It's a long story."

"I think you had better start telling me. I don't like the sound of this man chasing you. S.M. seems unhealthily excited by him. And trust me—anything that gets him excited is bad for you and me. In fact, we are in what is commonly referred to as deep shit." Miguel usually looked vibrant. Right now he was just vibrating. The aftermath of terror took some people that way.

Ninon exhaled slowly, trying not to cough. It took some effort to keep her surface thoughts calm while she spoke of other things. Having both the god and Saint Germain trying to eavesdrop on her was annoying. The god would hear some of her conversation with Miguel—she was almost certain of this—which was why she couldn't tell him anything of her real plans. She needed the god's power now more than ever. Saint Germain could not—absolutely could not—be allowed to join forces with Smoking Mirror.

"You're right—and I'm sorry about this. I had hoped to keep you out of this . . . this affair."

"I doubt that is or ever was possible."

"I'm beginning to doubt it too. But maybe this is for the best." She shook her head. "The first thing you should know is that I am not Seraphina Sandoval from California. I was—am—Ninon de Lenclos of Paris."

Miguel stopped moving. This news would likely mean nothing to the god, but it did to Miguel.

"*The* Ninon de Lenclos? The woman who taught Frenchmen of the seventeenth century how to make love? Who edited Molière's plays, advised Cardinal Richelieu, educated Voltaire, and fought for women's rights—and was the love of the philosopher Saint Evremond's life?"

"Yes. *C'est moi.*"

"Holy shit." And then he started laughing. He took her arm again and urged her out of the cavern. Electricity danced over her skin where he touched her, but it did nothing to warm her.

"Want to hear the really funny part?" she asked, not sharing his laughter.

"Hell, yes. I can always use a good laugh. Especially when we're about to die."

She ignored that.

"The man chasing me—the one your father wants to meet—that's the Comte Saint Germain. And *his* father was the man you know as Dr. Frankenstein." She paused. When a stunned Miguel said nothing, she added: "His real name was Johann Dippel. He *made* me. I am one of his . . . creations. He fed me drugs and then electrocuted me during a lightning storm. And I have lived for centuries because of it."

They backed into the purifying sunlight. Miguel was no longer laughing.

"That makes what I have to say rather anticlimactic," he complained. "And I suspect you already know the truth, and that's why you're here."

"Yes, but say it anyway. I think we'd best have all our cards on the table." They turned and faced each other, letting the sun bathe them in purifying rays. They were both about three shades paler than they should be.

Miguel said slowly: "I'm the son of a death god who made my mother a vampire along with the corpses of many other women who died in childbirth. I've resisted making the change so far, because he hasn't completed the ritual—I think because of how powerful I might become when he does. But unless we can think of a way out of it— like a high-speed jet to the north pole or a mutual suicide pact—you're going to be my first. S.M. wasn't kidding about tonight being the night. Believe me, death would be better than letting me near you."

First kill? First victim? First meal? Ninon didn't ask.

"My initiation," he explained softly, guessing her thoughts. "But here's the punch line. If you're thinking of some movie vampire's smooth seduction, forget it. We don't have nifty little teeth for biting necks. That's not how we . . . drink. You're a smart woman, and I know you have to be in dire trouble to come here, but trust me—you don't want to be one of Smoking Mirror's priestess sacrifices. Mine, either."

She stared at the twin cuts that had reappeared on his face, and guessed how he had received them. It was all she could do not to shudder at the thought of the god's tongue piercing his flesh, cutting it open. Miguel was right. She didn't want to be Smoking Mirror's sacrifice. However, she was out of options. Every other lead had gone cold. There was no one else.

"Not his, but I want to be *yours*," she said. *As long as you don't suck out my brains*, she added to herself. *Do you have that much control?*

His eyes widened and he licked his lips. His expression was part fear and part desire. He might resist the monster growing within, but it was there, alive, and it hungered.

"I *am* good, but the sex won't be worth the cost," he managed to say.

"I'm sure it would be," she argued. "But I do want to avoid the dying horribly part. Look, you can't have a . . . a stinger like your father, and I think that gives me better odds, don't you?" There was nowhere to hide a stinger, except maybe in his pants.

"Yes. His is impressive, being right there on the tip of his tongue. Mine is to scale. It cuts, though, deep enough to reach arterial blood. And other things. Not that you have to worry," he assured her. "I would never do that to you."

But she did worry. "Other things" meant brains. His faith in his restraint was touching, but he had never been tested.

"Does it hurt?" she asked with a show of reluctance, in

case the god was listening. It would be natural for her to be nervous.

"I imagine so. His hurt me," Miguel said. "But I think my initiation was meant to be painful. It was revenge. He thought I was dead when he called my mother over to the dark. He wanted no male children from his women because there's some legend that basically says there will be some father-son rivalry that can't be worked out peacefully. One of us has to die. I haven't figured it all out from the stone tablets I've salvaged, but it boils down to this: Conflicting amino acids on our genome preclude a quiet ending."

"But you're still alive. There must be a reason he hasn't killed you." That also suggested Miguel was strong— which was good. He would need to be very strong.

"Alive? Sort of," he agreed. "I've never known why he let me live. Maybe he thought I would suffer more, having my humanity drained gradually. He's into suffering—as long as it isn't his own, of course."

"Of course. Perversity. It's a god's privilege." She forced herself to breathe slowly. Panting only made her chest pain worse. Damn. She hoped the god was sincere at least about bringing a storm. She had to renew herself. The weakness and pain grew stronger with every passing hour. And her self-control diminished accordingly. Now when she coughed, evil red flowers bloomed on her handkerchief.

Miguel glanced at her, perhaps wondering why she was being flip. She laid a finger to her lips, cupped her ear, and then shook her head. She mouthed *"Later."*

"You're very calm," Miguel said, giving a small nod of acknowledgment that he understood her warning that they would be overheard.

"If I thought hysterics would help, I'd have them," she assured him.

"I'm still considering them. I really wish we'd had a chance to talk before now. Maybe we could have avoided Smoking Mirror."

Could this have been avoided? she wondered. Maybe, though she doubted that anyone except Smoking Mirror could have forced Miguel's cooperation, given his obvious resistance to giving in to his vampire side. So in the end she would have still needed to confront the god.

Poor Miguel. There was so much she needed to tell him. And she was certain that there was a lot that he could tell her about his power that would help her fight Saint Germain.

"We need to plan," she said finally. "We'll keep our options open from here on. Remember, the nice part is that it's never too late to panic."

Miguel shook his head at her at what he thought was her levity.

"You just don't understand," he said.

But Ninon looked into his fevered eyes and was sure she did. Her heart ached for him.

"Look," he said. "You have to know that I . . . I want you more than I've ever wanted anyone. But I don't know if I can do this to you." She just stared at him, and eventually he went on, saying what she knew he must. "Of course, if I don't, S.M. will. . . ."

She nodded, connecting with the hunger lurking in his eyes, in his heart. He couldn't hold out much longer. Poor, innocent Miguel. It might cost him his soul, but he could do this. He *wanted* to do it.

"Neither of us has much choice, Miguel," she said.

He looked away, part in shame and part in excitement. Her words, though kind, clearly didn't console him. Why should they? A part of him had to know that sating lust—even this one—would never compensate for one's fall from grace.

"Better you than the alternative, *non?*" She turned away, not wanting him to see the sudden sheen of tears in her eyes.

Please, bon Dieu, *this is not his sin. It's mine. Do not punish Miguel for this.*

Upon entering the tiny village of Gentilly we inquired after the dwelling of the celebrated necromancer known to us in Paris as Perditor. A guide soon presented himself and conducted us thither under a watchful eye. Presently we arrived in front of a yawning cavern surrounded by deep ditches. Our guide made a signal and immediately a man dressed all in red livery appeared on the opposite side of the ditches and asked us what we wanted.

"I wish for the philter," I replied, "which will make my beauty last the full length of my life." I did not wish to admit in front of the count that I felt unwell and needed a cure for my lungs which grew heavier every month.

"And I," said the count, "wish to see the Devil."

"You shall both be satisfied," the man said calmly, as if we had asked for the most natural things. Then he lowered a sort of drawbridge over the ditch, and once he had crossed, he admitted us to the cavern, where we found ourselves in almost complete darkness. In spite of this, I felt not a bit nervous. We had yet to come into the presence of evil.

"Do not be afraid," the count said to me, "I have my sword with me, a dagger, and two pistols. With them I can defy all the sorcerers in the world."

I nodded, but wondered if a sword and pistols would scare the Devil should he actually appear.

After proceeding for several minutes along underground galleries and passages we found ourselves in a sort of circular chamber hewn from solid rock. Some resin torches cast a gloomy glare up at the vaulted roof. At one end of this hall, upon a platform draped in black, was seated a personage in the garb of a magician who appeared to be waiting for us.

"That is the Master!" said solemnly the man in red. And he left us alone in the other's presence.

"Approach!" cried Perditor, addressing us in a terrible voice that made the hall vibrate. "What do you wish?"

"I wish," murmured I, in a trembling voice that was quite unlike my own, "a philter to preserve to me my youth and beauty all of my life."

"Forty crowns—pay me first."

Taking out my purse, I laid down five louis, appalled at his tone and also reconsidering the wisdom of this act. No normal man of business would be so bold.

The count did not wait for man's question.

"For my part, Sir Necromancer," he said, "I am only interested in seeing the Devil. How much do you want to show him to me?"

"One hundred livres."

The count was sly. "At that price, what gifts you must be able to bestow."

But the lord of the cavern made no reply. He took the money from the count with a large and dirty hand, and he put it in a big purse hanging at his side, along with my louis. Then he laid his fingers upon a bell, which sounded as loud as the strokes of the Notre Dame tower. At this signal, which nearly deafened us, two nymphlike young women, fairly pretty though not too thin, dressed in white and crowned with flowers, rose from the ground nearby. Perditor pointed me out to them with a dirty finger, then handed them an empty crystal phial. Again he struck the fearful bell that vibrated in my skull. I gathered that they had gone to mix my potion.

"And now," continued the necromancer, turning. "You are both decided that you will see the Devil?"

"Very decided," said the count.

I did not answer, for I was not certain that I wanted to witness Satan firsthand.

"Your name?"

"Is it necessary to give it to you, sir?" I stammered.

"It is indispensable."

"It is Anne de Lenclos—called Ninon," I admitted reluctantly.

"And," added my companion, "I am called Georges de Sandrelles, Comte de Lude."

"You swear never to reveal that which is about to take place before your eyes?"

"We swear it." The count answered for us. Again, I did not speak.

"You promise not to be afraid, and not to invoke Heaven or the saints?"

"We promise." Georges smiled insolently. The notion that he would be frightened of anything amused him.

The magician rose. He took a long wand of ebony, approached us, and traced a large circle in the dust, inscribing it with a number of cabalistic figures. Then he said to us—

"You can still go away—are you not at all afraid?"

I wanted to answer in the affirmative, but the count mocked. "Afraid of the Devil? For shame! What do you take us for? Get on with it."

And at that same instant we heard a thunderous peal— the voice of the magician barely heard above the uproar. He gesticulated, shouted, and spoke in some unknown tongue in a violent flow of diabolic invocations as he raised his arms toward the heavens. It made my hair stand up all over my body and revulsion seized me. I clung to the count's arm, and implored him to leave that fearsome place.

"The time is past for it!" cried the sorcerer. "Do not cross the circle of protection or you are dead."

Suddenly, to the noise of thunder, there was added a sound like the rattling of chains being dragged along the depths of the cavern. Then we heard a miserable howling. The necromancer's contortions continued, and his cries redoubled. He uttered barbaric words and appeared to enter into a frenzy. In the blink of an eye, we were enveloped in a circle of flames.

"Look!" cried Perditor.

A cry of terror broke from me as I saw in the midst of the wild tempest of fire a black goat, bound with glowing red chain. The howling grew more fearful, the flames burning with appalling intensity, and a troop of repulsive imps began to dance around the animal, waving torches and making angry noises in a tongue I did not know. The goat reared on its hind legs.

"Ah, for God's sake!" cried de Lude, "The comedy is well-played, I own; but I am curious to see the stage and to examine the costumes of the actors closer. Come with me, Anne!"

He grasped his pistols and made as if he were going to step over the circle, but at a shout from the magician, the blaze was extinguished, and the chained goat and demons disappeared. We were plunged once more into deep gloom. Before my eyes could comprehend the change, strong arms seized us, and we were dragged hurriedly along the passages and flung outside the caverns.

I was only too glad for the end to our adventure, and did not ask to go back for my philter, willing to leave the magician my five louis.

The count was not at all happy. He insisted on piercing to the enigma and unmasking the pretend Devil. We had been the victims of a hateful charlatan, he insisted. But I did not feel as convinced of this as he, and the grotesque display we had witnessed would not leave my imagination. For the rest of that day and the following night, I saw nothing but imps dancing among flames and howling at thunder.

—*An account of seeing the Devil the day before her eighteenth birthday, from the diary of Ninon de Lenclos*

It is not the essence of things that causes indecency. It is not the words, or even the ideas; it is the intent of him who utters them, and the depravity of him who listens.

—*Letter from Ninon de Lenclos*

Our worst fear is not that we are inadequate. Our deepest fear is that we are powerful beyond measure. It is our light and not our darkness that frightens us.

    —Nelson Mandela's inauguration speech

CHAPTER EIGHT

Many women prepared for a date with a hot guy by putting condoms in their purse. Ninon was practical and carried epinephrine. Just in case she saw more than metaphorical fireworks and her heart actually stopped during the proceedings. She also dressed for the shotgun wedding, or perhaps funeral, like it was a real ceremony—which it would be. Though she was the only one who knew there would probably be a second part to this wedding where the bride liberated her bridegroom.

Corazon growled.

"I know," Ninon replied. "I feel stupid primping."

On the one hand, what was happening was impossible—at least it would appear so to anyone whose definition of reality was handed down to them by twenty-first century science-trained westerners stuck in a very limited definition of reality. But she had already seen and participated in the impossible, and didn't doubt the situation was real and dangerous. It wasn't a hallucination, a bad dream, or a drug trip, and she could die tonight. She could also end up killing Miguel, either in self defense if he attacked her, or possibly if she talked him into her newly formed and dangerous plan.

At least the god had kept his word. There would be a lightning storm to backdrop their ceremony. It had come on like a psycho's rage, which wasn't surprising given who was causing it. The sudden heat and humidity lay on her skin as mercilessly as a hair shirt, but she didn't mind as long as the static kept Saint Germain from reading her mind. Wiser men than she had advised against trying to fight a war on more than one front. Smoking Mirror was challenge enough for one day.

She took a last look at the gathering clouds and then closed her shutter. The wind driving the storm was warm and fetid like a coyote's breath, and it loped steadily in her direction. Ninon was willing to bet that if they changed locations, the storm would too. Miguel was presently the focus of his mad father's tempest. That would change.

She also suspected that, in spite of the local gale providing white noise, Saint Germain's antennae would twitch at the moment she gave herself over to Miguel. Certainly he would know if she were struck by lightning and resurrected. And that was fine as long as he didn't know her exact location. She wanted him to come to her in a rush, unorganized and maybe blinded with anger. Her best chance of catching him out would be if he made a mistake.

A short while later, Ninon stepped into the clearing where she and Miguel had agreed to meet. It was a safe distance from the town and also any body of water that might harbor Smoking Mirror or any of his priestesses. Supposedly the female vampires and their god needed water to travel, but Ninon kept a wary eye out just the same. Smoking Mirror had already surprised her more than once that day.

"Hello," she said softly when Miguel appeared. He looked wonderful, with wind whipping around him, making his hair fly. Ninon realized she was relearning the lost art of the genuine smile. She smelled the storm on his body and knew he'd been outside for a while.

Miguel's gaze probed as he walked toward her, and this time she let it draw through her. She let him *see*. Not everything, but she wanted him to know what she was feeling—because she did need and want him, and she knew that he would need this encouragement to do what must be done.

There were surprises waiting for her too. Though she had feared the sensual part of her might have died in the years of loneliness and solitude, she had not after all forgotten what desire was, and even under these circumstances she was glad to have rediscovered it. Passion made everything more bearable—a little sugar to help the medicine go down—and so she shared it with Miguel, for the first time ever, willingly opening her mind to another.

"Your mouth," he said at last.

She nodded. She knew what he meant. She had worn no makeup and her unglossed lips were smooth, unlined, pink like peach or melon, the mouth of a girl too young to have been kissed or to have worn anything except an innocent smile. Her face was also very young when she forgot her makeup. This was normal for her. She had been changed, frozen in time, when she was little more than a child.

Except for her eyes. Those were ancient and knowing.

Miguel didn't try to speak again. His hand's first tentative touch on her cheek asked if she was certain. Her body answered affirmatively. The removal of clothing was a quick negotiation. Ladies first, but she had on less so near nakedness was accomplished before she ever reached for his shirt.

Around them, the wind cycloned, drawing ever closer, and Ninon wondered if Smoking Mirror was actually going to allow the condemned a last chance for the happiness of sex. From her reading, she knew that it wasn't part of the original sacrifice ritual, but Smoking Mirror might let it happen because it would make what he foresaw as the inevitable betrayal all the more awful.

She knew that she shouldn't get drawn too deep into the emotional waters, but didn't want to close her mind to Miguel. Unfortunately, the lifeline ran both ways and she felt his desire as if it was her own. When she touched Miguel's bare chest with hands and lips she was as awed as if she were touching the moon. The muscles were hard but the skin was velvet—only better, because it was vibrant, warm, alive. She could feel the muscles shift, spring-loaded like a gymnast about to take to the mat. And he wanted her to the point of insanity; it was in his eyes. There might be reluctance behind the wildness— fears, doubts, and questions about what they were doing—but carnal desire was there too. His attraction fueled her need. It was a poor time to get distracted from her goal, to let down her guard but . . . men could be beautiful in their own hard way and she had always loved the male body—their greater size, the hard muscle under soft skin, the tease of crisp hair on their broad chests so different from her own. Miguel was especially beautiful, the most beautiful man she'd ever seen, because though not entirely human he was still humane. Unlike Saint Germain, he had not forsaken his soul. And she frankly physically adored the muscles that roped his body and made his belly hard and firm. He appealed to her mind, yes; but even more, he appealed to her senses.

And she loved his penis. She was not shy about letting him know this. She let him read all of it as she ran a hand down him in a slow stroke and then reached around to cup, to lift him up. Ah! She loved the way he gasped when she pleased him. It would be so easy to lose herself in his pleasure, to forget everything else and be in the moment with him.

But that would be foolish, because they were not alone. She could feel eyes upon her. They were hot and greedy and gloating.

Perhaps unaware of the witness, Miguel in turn ran a finger down the midline of her body, his touch subtly electric—especially on the pendant that covered her chest. It was an old-fashioned piece, too heavy for today's tastes, and only women who worked out five days a week at the gym could wear it without neck strain. Most people would be distracted by the enormous jewels in the necklace and never notice the steel prongs on the back of what was actually a chest-plate, prongs that could be driven into the flesh right above the heart. But not Miguel. He saw and his touch moved around it, calling her golden scars to life. His hand was gentle on her, though she suspected now that this went against his basic nature. Miguel was lustful and preferred things rough and wild. It was in his blood—unwanted perhaps because he had been raised a civilized man, but there all the same. And the wildness was rising. The beast had been called to feast, and long denied, it hungered. She would have to somehow persuade him to set it free, because she did not doubt that if Miguel balked at the last moment and refused to make her a sacrifice, that Smoking Mirror would do it instead.

The electric, skimming touch was a strange pleasure, one that crossed the fuzzy border of pain and made her breathe hard and fast. Was this introduction of pain deliberate on Miguel's part? Did he know what he was doing to her? Or was it just the gathering thunderstorm? The air was highly charged—dangerously so. Soon sheet lightning would appear. Then the much needed St. Elmo's fire.

Did the god plan to kill his son, too? She suddenly wondered. Everything she had read about this species of vampire said that they were terribly strong but not immortal. Only Smoking Mirror had that gift. Lightning could kill Miguel. Or it might simply force him to bloodlust and madness, so that he killed her before the blood exchange was completed. Ninon looked into his eyes and saw a predator hiding there. It would not take much to push him over the edge.

Careful.

Oui. The plan was to be made only a little dead, not completely so. She forced herself to retreat a little and to think. She had learned long ago at the hands of Cardinal Richelieu that there was an art to feigning surrender during sex with a dangerous partner, a way to avoid courting extreme risk by directly challenging the predator within by acting as prey. Of course there were always dangers both emotional and physical in making love; in spite of his civilized facade, Man was a killer, a marauder at heart, and sex was very often a substitute for pillage and plunder. After the first time when she had so foolishly given up her deepest feelings to a lover—love certainly, but also pride—Ninon had never again completely surrendered. But this time she would have to let go. Miguel would know if she did not. She had to accept and ride whatever pain—emotional or physical—the animal Miguel inflicted when he changed her. He would probably need access to her soul as well. Everything she had read about the vampiric transformation said that it was the vampire who held his lover's identity and soul while she crossed over into death and then was born again. Assuming Ninon still had a soul for him to hold.

And it would be far better for Miguel that she enjoy the experience if that were possible. Their minds would bond at the moment of transformation. If she suffered too much he would be tortured as well, and she did not want to make his first time a nightmare. It was the bloody god who demanded this sacrifice and who would revel in it, not Miguel. Before satisfaction, before reward, there had to be pain—some inflicted, some received. That was the minimum price demanded. And Ninon doubted it would be as simple as feeling desperate longing or having physical pleasure denied. The god would likely demand much more from both of them because old gods rarely learned new tricks, and this one was a monster who enjoyed bloodshed.

Yes, she would give him what he wanted—a pound of flesh even—if he gave fair trade. Thanks to the Dark Man's legacy, she could withstand practically any physical damage short of having her heart ripped from her chest or being decapitated. She would not offer love or worship though—nothing beyond basic human caring for the god's so-called son, the man made a vampire in what had amounted to rape. This resolution was not made solely in anger at the god, but also for Miguel's well-being. This would be a life-altering event, but it had nothing to do with love and it would be wrong for either of them to fool themselves. Miguel was vulnerable—she felt it—and he hadn't her experience in these matters. Romantic delusion most often happened when one person was certain that the lack of something inside could only be filled by someone else. Out of desperation, people went out and sought mates, usually some equally damaged person whose psyche's ruins matched up nicely with their own. But this was wrong—so wrong! And though she was lonely now and desperately in need of help, Ninon knew it was unwise to mistake this unholy attraction for anything more than what it was. She and Miguel were helping each other out of a tight spot. She knew this and he needed to understand it too.

Miguel took her in his arms and slowly lowered her to the stony ground, which seemed to know why they were there and welcomed them.

"Beautiful. So perfect. I had never imagined. . . ." The beast had been pushed back, at least for a moment. His delight was sincere. Some words were like kisses, sweet and arousing. Ninon sighed in answer, and they paused a moment to savor the feeling of closeness, the last bit of calm before the storm.

People were touchingly naive, she reminded herself. They thought sex brought understanding, while it so seldom did. This was different, though, and they both knew it. This would be more than a meeting of bodies. Once taken, they could never retrace their steps. There would be no time-outs or do-overs. It made them both hesitate, though they knew there was no turning back.

Something hot and dark blew by them. They felt the instant when he entered his son, and both froze with shock at the intrusion. Smoking Mirror shouldn't have been able to reach into them physically—unless there was an underground stream . . . ?

Ninon looked down and, sure enough, water was welling up around them, a dark artesian broth that was thick like heart blood. It wasn't enough for the impatient god to appear, but enough to carry his vengeful spirit.

Miguel's body temperature spiked upward and his skin flushed dark. His eyes went flat black. It was Miguel's mouth that finally spoke, but the thoughts that issued forth belonged to Smoking Mirror.

"The dry earth was my womb and blood of war the seed that quickened me. Violence of flood and fire marked my mother's labor, and death came with my birth. I woke hungry and, as a god, it was my right to feed." These words were not sweet and arousing, and Ninon closed off her mind before he poisoned her.

A tear fell from Miguel's eye, a golden drop that painted his face with a visible trail. It was not shed in sorrow, though, and it burned when it rolled from his chin and struck her lips. She did not look away. To show fear, to attempt to flee was to provoke the predator to strike. Miguel wouldn't hurt her—wouldn't want to, but he might not have any choice about his actions. He was being violated, invaded—mentally if not physically—as surely as she was. She would do nothing to provoke the god while he was in his son's body, nothing that could hurt Miguel.

Try to touch him, cherie. Find the man inside.

Looking into those dark eyes that were so beautiful, though now so far from human, she felt behind the god's gaze Miguel's soul-searing pain, a despair so complete that she knew he would not survive whatever the god had planned. It was a long shot, but she hoped against all logic that the god would not actually kill his son or drive him into an act so horrible that he could not live with it after. She had to make the god understand this and back away.

"It's all right," Ninon said to the power behind Miguel's eyes that seemed slightly more understandable, if more despicable, now. Contempt had stifled awe—a monster was a monster was a monster. Anyone who would do this to their son was filth. Her lips still burned and were going numb; in fact, the numbness was spreading over her cheeks and down her throat. The tear was some powerful anesthetic. She used every trick she knew to seduce men and lied: "I know you wish to spare your son my anger at what he must do. You think to take my hatred and aim it at yourself so he won't suffer. But it isn't necessary." It was hard to say *necessary*—too many ess sounds. Her words were slurring. In another moment she would be unable to speak. "I do not hate Miguel. And I will not hate him. I have known pain and I have sinned. I am not afraid to make this sacrifice. He wants to take me."

The god blinked. Miguel blinked too. So good to know that she could surprise them. Of course, the god might not believe her. It was a bit far-fetched, the whole kill-me-because-I-deserve-it speech. But the idea of having Miguel betray his own morals would appeal to the son-of-a-bitch god. She was nothing to him, just a tool, a means to an end. Miguel's suffering was what would please him more.

She went on gently and truthfully, forcing these manufactured thoughts out where the god could easily read them: "I sought this out. I came to you for this. For what happens now—and after—I take full responsibility." That was good. The drug wanted her to be submissive—a victim—but her nature was not inclined to give in completely. The compromise was perfect, passive but not an out-of-control thrashing that would cause him to strike instinctively.

She waited a moment, and then with tremendous effort, she forced her mouth to move, her vocal chords to function a last time.

"Please let Miguel do this on his own. He'll be fine, and it's only right that a god's son have his own sacrifice." And he might have to learn how to do this if her plan failed, in which case there was no time like the present. The other thing all the legends agreed on was that once a vampire took his first victim, he had to go on taking them to feed the hunger inside.

Ninon looked hard, searching for Miguel until she found him. She wasn't sorry to be his first, but she did regret that there had to be any first at all, and wanted to make it a positive experience. At least, as positive as it could be. Committing the act that destroyed one's soul and damned one in God's eyes could never be an easy thing. Being forced to do so would take away any possible pleasure, and might actually drive him to suicide.

The god in Miguel's eyes stared at her for a long moment, and then started to laugh. The sound hurt her ears and inside her skull.

Cherie, he is a god that demands human sacrifice, and frankly he doesn't seem the type to spare anyone for any reason, her voice whispered.

Ninon knew the voice was right. The god was a heartless bastard—and an arrogant one. She counted on that. They would deal with it. If she could live with what happened, Miguel could too. She just needed to get him to cooperate for a few more minutes—just until she could catch the storm—then she would break the god's power.

"How I would love having you as my own!" the god lied. Miguel's eyes shone with his unholy amusement. "Still, my son has refused his destiny for so long, it *would* be amusing to watch him have to make this first kill on his own. Perhaps I should ask his dead mother to come as well. She has been prideful of his resistance to me. I would love to see both of them humbled."

Yeah, that will be fucking hilarious, making your son

into a murderer while his mother's spirit watches. Ninon thought it, but didn't say it aloud. Inside, though she tried to stifle it, she thought: *You better hope that I die today, Smoking Mirror, because if I live, I'll come back for you. I don't know when or how, but I* will *destroy you. My soul is already in peril. I have nothing to lose.*

This is still better than Saint Germain? Or do you have a new greatest enemy? her inner voice asked, forcing her to back away from her rage.

No, Saint Germain still tops the hit parade.

Then focus, the voice chided. *Let your anger go before he sees it.*

Easier said than done. Her fear was controlled, but a divine madness brought on by rage had seized her, and instead of dividing her thoughts, it focused them like the beam from a laser that was ready to burn down her enemies. Saint Germain first—he was the greatest threat. The god was just a petty monster ruling his little kingdom. And he would probably stay that unless Saint Germain helped him become something larger.

The god didn't know that she had no intention of being his victim or letting Miguel be either, and it was a pleasure to thwart him. Smoking Mirror was not getting her blood or emotions, not her loyalty and certainly not her free will or soul. Not even her life. Nor would he get Miguel's, if she could prevent it. Miguel would become a full vampire tonight, but he would not truly kill because his victim would not die.

And then *she* would change *him.* Give him the power to make his mind safe from this monster who tormented him.

The god was wavering. Which was more fun, the forcible rape of his son's mind, or watching Miguel betray everything he held dear by committing murder on his own?

Betrayal won. The god began to back away, his control to ebb. Ninon lay still and thought that she would place flowers on his grave on the day she used his tainted blood to rid the world of Saint Germain. Because she *would* kill them both. There was no hesitation now. The stakes had been raised. This allegiance could never be allowed. She would do murder because Saint Germain was planning some great evil for the world, and because Smoking Mirror would help him. She would kill for Miguel because Saint Germain would hunt him as well, and because it was wrong to help him escape one monster for it just to be replaced with another. And mostly she would kill because she was tired of hating and fearing the Dark Man's son.

Hate and fear. Next to love there were no more intimate emotions, and she was weary of feeling them. Day and night, they haunted her. She would never be able to move on with her life as long as she was so troubled. The time had come to finish old business.

I think he hears you. Ninon's inner voice was suddenly terrified. *He knows what you're planning!*

But the voice had to be wrong, because suddenly the god pulled back. He wasn't gone, but Miguel again looked out of his own eyes and had control of his body.

"You are either the bravest person I have ever met, or the craziest." He rested on his forearms above her. His dark hair fell around them like a curtain, giving the illusion of privacy. His face was anguished, filled with hate and shame, but he was trying to hide it and also that there was a monster inside him that wanted to hurt her.

"You too. Frankly, I don't think the two are mutually exclusive," she answered. The words were mush. Her entire face was paralyzed. That should have frightened her but it didn't. It wouldn't last long. Already her body was throwing off the effects of the drugs. Anger was helping.

"Thank you for the kind thought," he said. "I appreciate it, even if he doesn't."

"Make love to me. Lose yourself in my body. Now," she slurred. "We'll fit the blood-letting thing in at the end." Though it was doubtful he could understand her, she added, "Have faith. All will be well."

Or perhaps he did comprehend, felt her optimism, and believed, although he had to think the situation hopeless.

His head dropped and he began kissing his way down her body where she could still feel. The drug paralyzed but did not block sensation. Her face and head were almost frozen in place but the rest of her could experience and savor. At the moment, that was an excellent thing. The caress at her navel made every muscle in her abdomen contract. Sensing this, he used his lips mercilessly, trying to lose himself in the act.

She moaned. He could probably do push-ups with that tongue. Under any other circumstances, she'd be ecstatic.

Miguel smiled against her skin.

The god's listening. Miguel's probably still in your head and passing your thoughts on to him, the voice warned.

Maybe. But he's just on the surface. Now hush. I'm busy. She wasn't thrilled with having an audience—especially one that could intrude at any moment—but if the god thought to add to her discomfort by hanging around, he would be disappointed. She did not have performance anxiety.

"Make love to you? Perhaps I can. I feel . . . energetic," Miguel said at last with a slight smile. His voice was heavy, drugged, and his eyes glittered. He was giving himself to the animal, letting it do what he could not. The beast was scary, but it was still partly Miguel. "I have to be careful with my sibilants now or I'll end up stabbing myself."

He moved back up her body until he was above her. He lifted his tongue and unfolded the stinger on its end. It was no more than three-quarters of an inch long.

I like it better than teeth, she thought at him, willing him to hear. Then, in amazement: *Miguel, are you stoned?*

"Oh yeah. I took a bit of *datura inoxia*—jimsonweed. For some reason, I thought maybe I wouldn't enjoy this." He chuckled, and Ninon found herself wanting to laugh with him. It was half hysteria and half relief. It was probably the drug that was keeping the beast in check. "I am having the time of my life—isn't that weird? This isn't true love though. I just want you to know."

I know, she thought. And she did know, and was glad he knew. She didn't believe in true love. It was an illusion that could lead to broken hearts and, worse, marriage when both parties were taken unaware by the rush of first uncontrolled emotion. Even in this day and age, a woman could find herself imprisoned by a wedding ring before the hormone high wore off, and that little finger band could be harder to break away from than any slave's shackles. And falling back out of love was messy in court.

"I'm not the marrying kind," Miguel assured her, reading some of her thoughts but seemingly unaware that he did. The drugs had provided his psyche with a strong cushion, which was all to the good. He didn't need anything else to disturb him. "I might kill you in a blood frenzy, but I'd never force you into marriage."

Thanks, she thought. And they were both laughing. His high was giving her some kind of contact buzz. This probably puzzled Smoking Mirror.

"So, what do you like? Push-ups? Sit-ups?"

Sex was something more than isometric exercise, though if done right, it could be an excellent workout. She was fit—more than fit—but it was getting harder to participate because it felt as though gravity had doubled around her, making her limbs heavy. Her lungs also began to labor.

She looked down at her body and saw it as Miguel did; pale except for the gold lace of lightning scars. Her breasts were soft, her belly slightly rounded, everything small, delicate, defenseless. It was great camouflage. Less discerning people mistook delicacy for weakness. Delicacy might bring out Miguel's protective instincts. It might not. In any event, her body would keep him from focusing on her thoughts and feelings. She really didn't want him in her head right now. She would open up at the very end, but for now needed to gather herself.

O quam misericors est Deus. Her inner voice was wry, but it spoke true. God was miraculous. Her body was a testimony that miracles existed. It hurt and it was hard to breathe, but she needed to have some faith that all would be well. Surely God would grant her strength in the face of this great evil.

She smiled a little at the thought. Neither Miguel nor his father knew of her delicate-looking body's relentless urge to heal itself—*and thank you,* bon Dieu, *for that.* The god merely thought of her a poker chip that could be used to up the ante in the nasty game he played with his son. And as for Miguel . . . his motivation was harder to understand. Certainly he wanted her, but this wasn't about sex. At least, not entirely. He could have fled, avoided this confrontation. Maybe it was guilt and an un-willingness to play the coward's role, but she thought that he also had to want something else very badly if he were finally giving in to his vampiric nature. In time she would discover what that was.

She ran her hands down his back, feeling a series of scars along his spine, unnoticed until she touched them, calling them to life along with the rest of his erectile tis-sues. The scars were round, too large for a normal needle. These were not from a medical procedure; they were more like bullet holes.

Or stab wounds. And she suddenly knew who had made them. Did Smoking Mirror like spinal fluid? she wondered, repulsed.

Miguel shuddered under her touch. Like her, his plea-sure was proving to be very close to pain.

He reached again for her necklace, but she batted his hand away.

"Leave it," she said. Only it came out more like "Ee-i." She tried to think her message at him but feared it was too complex. She had to make him understand that if she were struck by St Elmo's fire, she needed to direct the cur-rent to where it would do the most good.

"This is it then," Miguel whispered. His hair danced about him, lifted by the rising static. His eyes were wild and beautiful, and her soul yearned for him to be part of her at least for a while.

For a moment, they both held their breath and waited. The instant of anticipation surrounded by fear of the unknown on one side and possible death on the other made the moment of hesitation as sweet as the last breath of air for a man condemned to walk the plank.

A last look into Miguel's eyes, and then she gave in to her desire and let it blind her, and through the conduit of the god, Miguel. Rationally, she knew that attraction of the magnitude she felt was a form of slavery, at least temporarily, but he wasn't seducing her into its bonds this time. She had placed herself here—just as she had said to the god—and she took responsibility. It might be stupid, allowing herself to touch him empathetically, to be intimate with his mind. She was allowing herself to be seduced first by his pain, and then by soft hums of pleasure, which were not deliberately enticing—and this was probably because they were not intentional and therefore pure and beautiful and, most rare of all, honest. She simply craved his touch. And to touch him, his black hair as it lay fanned on his strong shoulders, his powerful scarred back and his long muscled legs and, yes, his delightful male parts that reacted so wonderfully to her touch. But above all, she needed to not be alone. Not right now. And not for always. Her soul was cold with fear at the step she took and needed to be warmed at these passionate fires, however brief they might be.

The sex was rough but she found it sweet, and there was a certain wicked pleasure in giving in to the paralysis of Smoking Mirror's drug and letting Miguel have his way with her, to pound into her with all his strength and not resist. But then came the part where he had to drink from her. He waited until she was lost in ecstasy, but even so she felt the pain of his spike driven into her flesh, piercing muscle and vein. His saliva burned like acid. Agony was a clear signal to her body to heal, and to her mind to clear. Her brain began pouring out endorphins, helping her manage the pain, perhaps even to enjoy it because it meant that she was close to her goal.

Miguel's eyes changed as he drank. The black of his pupils expanded to cover the iris and then continued to bleed over into the whites until he had the eyes of an obsidian statue.

Pleasure, or something else, convulsed him a second time. She forced her arms to move, to hold him. To offer comfort, but also to remind him that she was there, alive and suffering and that he must remain aware enough to rein his monster in before it truly killed her.

It was a near thing, the struggle between Miguel and his beast, and if she had been unaltered she would have died of blood loss while the battle raged. Miguel finally mastered the killer, though. He released her abruptly and rolled onto his side. Ninon could feel a trickle of blood on her throat and smelled copper in the air. But that was all she could feel and smell. He hadn't offered her blood. He hadn't given her any power.

"You didn't finish," she said, her words barely audible above the moaning wind and still a bit slurred. As she had hoped, the electrical interference of the storm made it easier to hide her thoughts from both the god and Saint Germain.

· "He didn't want me to—and I wanted to spare you. You have no idea of the pain involved, the eternal craving." He opened his eyes. They looked almost normal again. Only his pupils remained dilated, and that was probably from the jimsonweed.

"I don't want to be spared. I need to be changed, Miguel, if I'm to live. But we'll have to exchange blood later. There is something else I must do right now."

"It isn't blood," he said, frowning. "I told you—forget

all that Dracula crap. You don't drink my blood. That isn't how it's done."

"Then what . . . ?" She suddenly understood the scars on his back. "You inject something into me."

"Yes. Into your spine. I crack open your bones and shoot poison into you—and it will eat at you like acid, like decay. You can't want that."

She looked at Miguel, so concerned for her—and, emotional slavery or not, she cared back. The thought was mildly dismaying.

Smoking Mirror, you had better not try doing anything else to your son, because he is mine now and I will protect him.

"But I do want it, Miguel. However, we have to get out of this storm before you get fried," she said, finding that she could talk clearly again. Bless her body's superior metabolism! Fear and anger left her by degrees, allowing her lungs to expand as they needed so that she could draw deep breaths and prepare her muscles to move. The returning calm was welcome.

You are still very annoyed, though. I've never felt you so angry.

The lightning did not affect her own inner voice. Why had she thought it would?

That's because I am you, cherie. As long as you can think, so can I.

I am annoyed—enraged even. The god tried to kill me with his damn drug, and he stopped Miguel from finishing the ceremony and giving me his power. That's hostile and breaking our bargain. I didn't die, true, but as far as I'm concerned, it's the nasty thought that counts, not whether or not Smoking Mirror succeeded. And I don't trust him to kill Saint Germain when he should. He'll try and suck out his power, or maybe make him a protégé. I can see him thinking that Saint Germain would be a swell son. After all, Saint German would kill without qualm.

And you think Saint Germain might win that encounter and steal the god's power?

I think it's possible. The god is stupidly arrogant. And it would be too much to hope they'd get into a pissing contest and kill each other.

I suppose . . . well, we'd best make haste. The storm draws near. The voice paused a moment. *Cherie, are you actually thinking of trying to kill him. A god?*

He isn't a god in anything except name. He's just a monster. And I admit that the thought has crossed my mind a few times in the last few hours. I don't know how yet, but I have learned one thing from Saint Germain and the Dark Man—the only thing to do with an enemy is bury them as soon as you get the chance. You don't leave pissed-off people behind, and looking for revenge.

The voice sighed but didn't argue. *You've grown hard.*

I've had to.

"I thought you wanted lightning!" Miguel shouted over the storm as she sat up. He couldn't talk in her head anymore either.

"I do, but not just now. We need tools. Help me up," she commanded. Smoking Mirror was trying to pull the storm away, but it was too late. She had hold of it now.

Miguel reached for her and hauled her to her feet. He didn't seem surprised by her recovery. She wondered what he knew about their encounter, about how much blood he had taken, and that it was supposed to be fatal. He hadn't guessed that the storm was just window dressing to keep her pliant until she was paralyzed. He didn't know that his father was going to have him kill her and then let him live with the shock and guilt. The son of a bitch, Smoking Mirror, deserved to die.

They dressed quickly. There was no basking in post-coital glow, or napping as they cuddled and talked.

"Wouldn't it kill you to be hit by lightning?" he asked as they began to run toward town. As she suspected, he had no trouble keeping up. Perhaps because she was still somewhat under the influence of Smoking Mirror's paralytic drug.

"I don't know. In my current state . . . maybe. If it were the wrong kind. What about you?"

"I don't know." Lightning crashed behind them, followed by almost immediate thunder. So, the god was feeling pissy. Too bad. He was going to follow through with their bargain now whether he wanted to or not.

"Why did you lie before about the storm and your reasons for coming here? And why tell the truth now?" he asked, sounding curious rather than judgmental.

"Because neither the god nor Saint Germain can hear me right now with all this electricity in the air. They could before—and they can't know what we're doing until it's too late to stop us. This storm isn't window dressing. It's a tool—a weapon."

He digested this, perhaps recalling that he had been able to read her mind.

"What *are* we doing?"

"For one thing, you're going to finish that ritual and give me your blood or whatever."

"But—"

"It won't affect me the way he thinks," she yelled above the wind, trying to sound completely confident. "Also, if you want, I can make you like me."

"And I would want that why? So I can be what I am forever?" he asked. She saw his point—he already had one rather large handicap.

"Well, if it goes according to plan, you'd be able to slow or even halt your vampirism and still go out in the daylight—something that might be impossible for you now that you have completed the cycle and taken blood. Look, I'm not sure how it all works with vampires or even with humans. I should need to eat constantly with the way my metabolism changed, but I actually need very little food to survive. I don't age or get sick. I think it will be the same with you and blood. Also, I had a fatal, degenerative lung disorder and it was halted by the . . ." She didn't want to say electrocution. "By the treatment."

For the first time he looked genuinely startled. She knew he was thinking that there had to be a downside to what she offered, but almost any consequence seemed better than the one he was facing now.

Cherie, what if it has the opposite effect? What if it turns the vampire in him loose and makes him strong and ravenous?

Then we have a problem, she admitted.

Are you prepared to kill him? If something goes wrong.

Yes. But I won't have to. He'll kill himself.

Perhaps, but it will be immeasurably harder once you have transformed him. You know how hard it is to die.

I know. And it would be harder for her to commit suicide as well when she had changed into a vampire, but she already knew that she would end it all if the vampirism couldn't be controlled. Sin or no sin, that was the only option for her. She would not become a parasite preying on the innocent. That was a line she would not cross, not if she had to send her soul to everlasting hellfire to avoid it.

"Sounds good to me. I'll chance it," Miguel decided, interrupting her grim internal moral lecture. "What do we need to do?"

"We're going to the church roof. I left some things there."

"What things?"

"Things we need to safely electrocute ourselves with St. Elmo's fire. Don't worry, the roof is the perfect spot for it. Those bronze angel statues and the bell are like a massive conductor."

"Splendid. How do you know there'll be St. Elmo's fire there?" he asked. To his credit, he hadn't flinched at the word "electrocution."

"It'll be there. I attract it whenever there's a storm. I'd have done this sooner, but Saint Germain has managed to keep the clouds away."

"That's why you asked Smoking Mirror for a storm?"

"Yes." It wasn't the whole truth, but she didn't think he was ready to hear the rest.

He digested it.

"Not to be a wet blanket, but what happens if something goes wrong?"

"Then we die." Either in the transformation, or by their own hands after.

He thought about that. But not for long.

"I can think of worse things," he finally said. "You know that S.M. will probably kill us for disobeying him?"

"He'll probably try." *Again.* The high from the electricity in the air made her manic enough to sound cheerful. "If we're lucky, he won't succeed. Now tell me, do you have any strong feelings about patricide?"

"Very strong. I'm completely for it—at least in this case. I really think he actually meant for me to kill you tonight. He thought I'd lose control and drain you dry. It could have happened."

"So, you knew his plan. I wasn't sure." She wanted to say that she was sorry he'd had to face this, to offer comfort. But there was none to put forward. His father was a murderous bastard who would torture and even kill his own son if it seemed expedient. Sorry didn't begin to cover that.

"I suspected." Miguel thought some more.

"What? There's something else bothering you." She picked up speed. Again, he kept pace. "Ask now, or forever hold your peace. Once we do this, there's no taking it back."

"Is your life always like this?" he demanded.

"Pretty much. It's go, go, go, when you have a homicidal magician on your trail." Fully recovered, she put on a final burst of speed. As she had hoped, Miguel did too. He was physically strong. He should be able to withstand electrocution.

Please, bon Dieu, *I am not worthy. But make him able to survive the fire and for it to chain the beast. Don't let me be the one to kill him. Saint Germain, yes—and Smoking Mirror. But not Miguel.*

She found the stone in a small catalogue from the National Museum in Mexico City, published in 1929. It was believed to depict the standard female sacrifice ritual to the god of death, Mictlantecutli, in a ceremony of fire. What interested Ninon was that it was shown with lightning in the sky, bolts of which were hitting the altar. Some of the victims had lightning bolts hitting medallions on their chests as well. The presiding god had his tongue extended—as all gods do, because they are immortal and like sticking their tongues out at the world—but he seemed to have some kind of dagger or needle attached to the end of it. He also had something that resembled a serpent attached to his body in the general region of his penis. In no other stone was the god shown this way and some scholars, the pamphlet said, questioned whether this was even Mictlantecutli. Might he be some representation of the vampire cult that had flourished before the Conquistadors wiped it out?

Strangest of all was the calendar on the back of the cylinder. The Aztecs had a two-hundred-sixty standard day calendar broken down into eighteen equal months. At the end of that, they had a time called Nemontemi—five "lost days" that were to appease the gods. These were frightening days when the gods had to be propitiated or evil would come into the world. That was when the fire sacrifice took place.

Scholars were puzzled. Ninon was intrigued.

She visited the museum as soon as she could but was told upon arrival that the stone had disappeared more than seventy years ago, right after the catalogue was published. Would she like to see the stone of the sun instead?

Unhappy, she had nonetheless seen the stone of the

sun—and every other stone in the museum—but nothing offered her any clue as to what the first engraving had meant. Her only hint was where the stone was found. It was discovered at the bottom of one of the pozas in an area called Cuatro Cienegas.

For too much love of living,
From hope and fear set free,
We thank with brief thanksgiving
Whatever gods may be
That no life lives forever;
That dead men rise up never;
That even the weariest river
Winds somewhere safe to sea.
— *"Garden of Proserpine" by Algernon Charles Swinburne*

I was on the road to Tournai and was informed of the presence of M. le Comte de St. Germain at an inn and desired to be presented to him. An interview was granted with the restriction that he would appear incognito and that I not press him to partake of food or drink.
—*Casanova*, Memoires

CHAPTER NINE

"Undress and lay down," Ninon urged Miguel, unzipping the backpack she had left on the roof. She quickly began unrolling chains that she wrapped around the church's bell and secured with an S-hook. They were heavy, made of iron instead of aluminum. As soon as he was naked, she began draping them around his wrists and ankles and waist where she hooked them in place. She ordered her hands not to tremble. It was difficult because the increasing electrical charge in the air made her muscles jumpy. Also, she was a little bit afraid—which was only right when preparing to steal fire from the gods.

"This is a bit kinky," he said, lifting his wrists. She gave him a quick smile. The wind was whipping about them, lifting her hair into the sky. Now that she had stopped moving from place to place the storm was closing in quickly.

She knelt beside him, plucked the medallion off her own chest, opened it, and laid it over his heart. She pressed down hard so that small spikes pierced his skin.

"Ow. I guess you owed me one."

"Sorry—we need iron over the heart," she said, but the wind tore most of her words away. She didn't really want to explain what was happening anyway. Most people would balk at the idea of constructing a lightning rod over their heart.

"Didn't you want me to—well, *change* you first?" he asked.

She looked toward the storm front, then shook her head regretfully.

"No time. We'll have to do it after." Assuming there was an after.

She got out a second medallion—this one not decorative—and drove the prongs into her own body with a hard slap. The gesture was practiced and was probably reassuring to the watchful Miguel, though he had to notice the small trickle of blood running down her belly.

"I'm sorry. I didn't have time to find topical anesthetic," she yelled. She didn't add that there was also no time to apply a barrier between the metal and their skin. The whole thing was makeshift and they would probably be burned. The wounds would heal quickly, but would hurt until they did.

Miguel nodded. The lightning was close now. He counted aloud the seconds between the flash and the thunder. "One-one-thousand. Two-one-thousand."

"It's not too late to change your mind." She had to say this. There had been no time to explain what this transformation would mean—having to put oneself through the fire every few decades, the slight but ever mounting brain damage that occurred with each electrocution that would some day lead to insanity. And that whatever ailments you had when you transformed might come back—always stronger—each time the effects began to wear off. In his case, vampiric bloodlust.

If there had been time, she would have waited until she contacted Byron and asked him for help. The poet didn't seem to have to renew himself as often as she did. Perhaps

Dippel had improved his process by the time he had "cured" the poet's epilepsy.

"Yes, it is. Years too late." He looked into her eyes. "If there is any chance that this will help control the vampirism, I must take it. I have been on the borderline for a long time and I know I'm getting worse. It's only a matter of time before I kill someone."

She understood. Sometimes the Devil really was worse than the deep blue sea.

"Anyway, you can be my training wheels while I learn to ride this bike."

"Okay." Ninon loaded a dose of adrenaline and amphetamine into a second syringe. The first was retrieved from her bag. The last thing she did was remove her contact lenses—it would be bad to have them melt in her eyes. She looked up and he saw her unveiled gaze for the first time and sucked in his breath. She knew that her irises were black—completely black. Her skin was also beginning to glow. She hoped no one was looking at the top of the church or there would be wild rumors about angel visitations at the *iglesia*.

"I wish I could spare you this next part," she said, between wind gusts.

"I don't ask to be spared."

"Nevertheless . . ."

"I know. I'm not crazy about hurting you either."

Ninon stripped off her own remaining clothes. Carefully, she laid herself down over his body, belly pressed to belly as she grasped in tight fists the chains that bound him. His heart thudded beneath her. The pose might have been erotic under other circumstances, but neither of them could feel much but anticipation and dread.

"One-one-thousand . . . The lightning is following me, isn't it?"

"No, it's after me now. Hang on," she murmured. "This part isn't great."

Miguel turned his head eastward where she looked, as

the storm boil toward them over the crenellations of the church's wall. He glanced again at her face. She wasn't watching the clouds. He looked down a few degrees, following her line of sight. The two syringes she had prepared were close by, cushioned on top of the backpack. Her dose, the smaller one, was closest at hand.

"I have to get to it immediately because my heart will be stopped and my eyesight gone," she explained. "We'll be blind and have only a minute, perhaps two, to work before brain damage begins to occur. If anything happens to me you must—"

The thunder came before she was done speaking. The air around them froze, crackling like ice cubes in water.

One-one—His lips counted, then they were hit with the strange blue lightning, a strike that they could feel but not hear.

Ninon would have screamed if her lungs had not been paralyzed. It felt like a nest of maddened wasps attacking her skin and then chewing into her muscles. There was thunder on the inside of her skull, like a grenade set off in a small room, exploding in her brain, scrambling the cells that it touched. Light and heat entered every fiber of her body, spreading cruel fire. It was the fire of annihilation but also creation. But it didn't burn like normal flames; rather it melted and reshaped everything inside. It filled the head with merciless sound, noise not understood by the ears, but rather a pulsation that altered the tissues, disturbed the very molecules of the body and drove them into violent rearrangement.

Her brain sizzled and confused synapses at once smelled and tasted every odor and flavor she had even known. There was also pain as every nerve in her body overloaded. This had to be what Hell felt like.

Then the flock of black birds—a murder of imagined crows—swooped in and buffeted her brain, confusing her and making it so she could no longer tell what was happening to either her own body or Miguel's, though Ninon knew that death was closing in quickly for both of them. She knew she was being electrocuted. So was Miguel. His inhumanly strong body had bowed up, lifting both of them off the church's roof. It lasted forever, pain and light and the vicious birds trying to pull her soul from her body.

Noooooo! she screamed at the birds in her head as her agony reached its pinnacle.

And then it was over. The last thing her failing eyes saw was lightning dancing over the clamoring church bell. The St. Elmo's fire died out slowly, a last climax of eerie, incandescent light. Her world went dark. She was blind. She was dead. Again.

But she had expected this. It happened every time. She was not afraid. Not for herself. Miguel was another matter. She had to move quickly. The first time was terrifying, being lost in the blackness of death but still partly alive and all aware. There was no knowing how the vampire would react. That part of him might become violent, and the chains would not restrain him for long.

Her muscles were dead weight, but she gave her hand a command and it groped until it found the syringe, though every movement was dull agony.

Pick it up! she ordered her hand. And again it obeyed, though not as quickly as she would like.

Miguel first? No, she needed to see what she was doing. Anyway, she might not be able to reach his syringe. Her hands were losing all feeling now as they realized she was dead.

Ninon made a huge effort and rolled onto her back. She pulled the medallion aside and turned the needle on herself, plunging it into her chest, angling it in below the breastbone and thrusting upward. She did it before she had time to consider the pain it would bring.

At first there was nothing. Then her heart stuttered back to life. Her vision slowly returned. She didn't wait for full sight, but immediately pushed the medallion away from Miguel's chest and retrieved the second syringe. Her hands were still clumsy, but she managed not to drop the hypodermic. She rolled onto her knees, straddling him. Finding the proper spot below his sternum, she plunged it into the bull's-eye of burned flesh that lay around Miguel's heart.

For one long second nothing happened. Then his eyes popped open and he gasped, drawing in his first breath of air. His face was a mask of agony, his tongue with its stinger distended popped out as he exhaled with pain; but she was reassured. You had to be alive to feel hurt.

Church bells began to peal, shaken by the last gust of wind that had reversed its direction, pulling the storm away. *Ask not for whom the bell tolls. . . .* Fireworks and bells—that made for a grandiose first time. It should have been more fun. Instead it was all fire and pain.

"Welcome to my world," she said softly when Miguel's breathing quieted and his muscles relaxed. She put a hand to her own chest. The assaulted skin glowed gold over the scarring that sealed her renewed heart inside. *"Laissez les bons temps rouler."*

Miguel managed to lift his left hand and lay it on her thigh. His gaze was clear but very strange. His eyes were black and it was a bit like looking into a mirror.

"I saw stars," he whispered finally. "Did you?"

She smiled at his small joke and didn't say anything about the murderous crows that always swooped down on her at the moment of death, as if they were trying to tear apart her soul. If he saw stars, that was far better.

"Just do it," she said, lying on her stomach in a puddle. The storm was gone but the roof was still wet.

Miguel stared at her slim back, so nearly childlike. Her skin was milky pale. She looked impossibly fragile and he felt ashamed that this should arouse him.

"Haven't we done enough for one night? Surely it can wait—"

"No, the storm is clearing." She turned her head in his direction. "That means Saint Germain and maybe your father will be able to get back into our heads if they are anywhere in the area. They'll try to stop you. We have to have this finished before they can interfere."

Miguel hated her answer but knew she was right. Smoking Mirror would do anything to stop him from creating another truly like himself. The god reserved that right unto himself.

"Okay. But neither of us is going to enjoy it."

"I never expected to. Anyway, it can't be worse than electrocution," she said softly.

Feeling reluctant and more than a little unsure of what he was doing, Miguel stuck out his tongue and let the small stinger underneath unfold over his lower lip. He wasn't sure where to inject her. The lower back looked strongest, but his stinger wasn't that long and . . .

"The neck," she whispered. "That would be easiest."

He nodded, uncertain if he could speak without lisping.

Miguel worried that his small stinger might not be strong enough to crack the bone of her spine, but it turned out he didn't need to. By feel alone, he managed to slip it between the vertebrae, through the cushion of the disc and into the spinal cord. His lips sealed tight on her skin. Injecting the venom happened with no effort on his part. It felt something like a climax.

Ninon gasped once as the stinger went in, but she didn't react otherwise, though he knew she had to be in pain. Vampire venom burned like nothing else. He withdrew as quickly as he could, feeling ill but also disturbingly elated. A part of him had enjoyed doing that.

Ninon unclenched her hands and tried to roll over. Her muscles were uncoordinated and she needed help. Recalling his own experience with the venom and the paralysis it caused, Miguel reached for her, offering comfort with his body because he couldn't think what to say that would make this better. She curled close to him, accepting the shelter of his arms, though she didn't appear to be at all cold and had no trouble breathing now.

"How do you feel?" he asked, praying he hadn't hurt her too much.

"Different," she said. "Strong. My heart has never been so physically powerful and I can breathe again. Let's hope your gift to me allows me to remain this way—at least long enough to take out Saint Germain." She looked up and asked gently: "How about you? Are you cold?"

"No, not at all. Isn't that odd?"

"No, it's good. That's as it should be. I think."

After they had snuggled for a while, they dressed and began to talk of other things. Though they probably should have been planning their escape, instead they finally had the pillow talk they'd been denied before. It was rather more grim than for most couples.

"Your lips say *hello* but your eyes say *o Hell*." It was her small joke.

"Too many bad first dates," he answered. His brief smile didn't reach his eyes. It was weird to think that this day had actually been harder for him than it was for her. But it probably had been. To embrace his inner killer was to have his innocence die. That she had been a willing victim, and that he hadn't killed her was only small consolation. A line had been crossed for him and there was no going back—they both knew it.

"You look beautiful," she said. "More beautiful than before."

"So do you, though we're not very human-looking."

"No, not very. I like your black patent-leather eyes, though—all shiny and mysterious."

"Patent-leather eyes . . . That sounds too toylike, and I'm not a teddy bear stuffed full of love and kindness." Miguel's voice was neutral. "I am, in fact, probably full of something very, very bad. But you must know that by now."

She shrugged. "I'm not all sugar and spice either. Doesn't mean we need to slit our wrists or anything. Far from it." He looked skeptical so she added: "This is just a weird kind of postcoital-vampire depression you're feeling. Have a little faith. I think we'll make a good team. If you still want to go with me . . . ?"

He took her hand and laced their fingers. "I do. There's just one more thing I need to tell you about being a vampire and then I won't bring the subject up again."

"Only one? I feel lucky."

"Yes. But it's a big one. We are infertile, Smoking Mirror's get," he warned. "Our long life is purchased with the lives of our children and all the children thereafter. And only male vampires can make other vampires. I guess I should have mentioned this before."

"That's all right. I don't want to make more vampires. And I had a child. One was enough." More than enough. She had no desire to ever again experience the catastrophic intimacy of bearing someone inside her body, giving that child life, and then watching him grow old and die. Just as all her friends and lovers always grew old and perished.

You could have made him like you, given him the dark gift. The voice had returned. It sounded stronger too.

Damned him? My own son? No. I wouldn't do this to anyone.

Unless they were already damned like Miguel?

Ninon looked at Miguel but didn't answer. She didn't need to. The decision had been made and executed. She had turned Miguel only because he had already been contaminated by the darkness and in danger of being consumed by a greater evil that would cause him to harm others.

If she was his first, so too was he a first for her. They had traded hells and perhaps saved each other from cruel disease—at least for a time. But it wasn't something to put on a the calendar and celebrated every year.

"What about your . . . true father? The Scotsman? Is he your only other family?" she asked suddenly. "Is there anyone you will have to explain this to?"

"No. My biological father is long dead." He didn't mention his mother, and she didn't ask. "I have no siblings either."

"I'm sorry." Her brow wrinkled. "But if you've no family—no human family—to worry about, why come back *here* and face Smoking Mirror?"

"Not for consolation, that's for sure," he said. He gave a wry smile. "I think I came for the same reasons you did. I needed help. The urge to . . . to draw blood was getting overwhelming. I could tell that I had to do something about it. Or die. Don't think I didn't consider that option for a while too. I still keep it in reserve. Mostly, I was looking for a way out. I thought maybe the old tablets would tell me something."

Ninon nodded with sympathy. "I thought that too, and was upset when the largest stone in the museum went missing."

"I'm not sure I'll make a good vampire," Miguel said idly. He added, "I've always been a morning person. I know some of them can go out in the day, but they sure don't like it."

"You don't have to be good. Just good enough," she answered, telling a hard truth she hoped he was old enough to understand. There were some things you could never win at. Sometimes just surviving was a righteous fight. "Anyway, you may not have a problem with daylight. We'll have to see."

"I guess we will. Tell me something about *your* father," Miguel asked. "I'm trying to imagine him."

Ninon thought about his request. What could she say about a man as complex as her father had been? A shrink would likely say that her ambivalence toward love and relationships was all her father's fault. After all, he had been involved in—in fact, caused—a bad marriage. A very bad marriage. So bad that he'd had an affair with a married woman, committed murder to save her, and then had to flee the country for this crime when his daughter was only thirteen, leaving her to fend off the lechers and fortune hunters who saw her as easy prey with her father gone.

But for all that, she had loved him and was eternally grateful that he had taught her to be her own person. In life, one had to take the bitter with the sweet. She'd learned that lesson early.

Finally she said: "My father was a musician, though it was not fashionable in that era to be passionate about music or dance. Once he and his friend Gaultier had a duel of lutes and played for thirty-six hours straight. My father won when Gaultier collapsed from exhaustion. He taught me to play with equal passion even though the Jesuits and my mother thought it a sin. You play too?"

He blinked. "I did. Not anymore."

She touched the scars on Miguel's hands that had been obvious after the electrocution when all their scars glowed. He had similar ones on his feet.

"Miguel, did he . . . ?" she asked hesitatingly when he didn't say anything more. "I'm sorry. I shouldn't have—"

"No. It's all right. How weird that the scars show now. Usually they are invisible." He curled his fingers inward but only the index fingers could touch his palms without trembling. "Yes, it's Smoking Mirror's work. He felt that I was being stubborn about renouncing my Christianity."

"Bastard," she muttered.

"Yes, he is. And then some. What was it in Ecclesiastes—what has been made crooked cannot be made straight?" He flexed his hands again. This time it looked marginally easier. "The damage wasn't devastating, but enough to guarantee that I won't inflict my guitar playing on anyone—at least not any flamenco. And that was the only kind there was for me."

"Not into strumming those C, F, G folk songs? We'll see what happens now. Your muscles and nerves will heal faster than you can imagine. Your chest is already healing its burns." And inside she thought: *It's amazing your psyche isn't as scarred as your hands.*

"I'll hope, but I'm not expecting too much. It's better that way. Hope . . . hurts."

Ninon nodded, not making a single sympathetic noise since pity would just be a burden he didn't want. The proud did not want sympathy. She also had learned to travel light, to adapt to the new times, not die clinging to the old. Whenever possible she threw out unhappy memories, old grievances, dark emotions, but also hope and anticipation. People weren't designed to carry more than one lifetime's regret and bitterness. And one had to accept that sometimes you didn't get a happy ending. It was good that he knew this already.

But sad. Very sad to lose this too.

"I play," she told him. "I learned in Seville."

"I'd love to hear you," Miguel said and meant it. There was no envy in his dark eyes, and his generosity about this touched her gently on the heart. Few would be so charitable when their own loss was great. "Don't frown, Ninon. Really, it would be a consolation prize."

"You've paid top dollar for your father's sins," she heard herself saying, again angry at Smoking Mirror for doing this to his son. Though perhaps Miguel was truly lucky. He had lived this long. Some wizards killed their children—grandchildren too—in order to take back any power that had passed to them. That was what Saint Germain seemed to be doing as well, gathering up the power he thought his father had squandered on strangers—reclaiming his inheritance.

Miguel shook his head. "No, the price has been high, but not the highest. I've refused to give in to the toxin he put in my blood. I never killed. I still own my soul. I have free will."

Which he had compromised for her. And if the electrocution did not help, his hunger would be worse than ever, perhaps impossible to control. A simple thank-you didn't cover that sort of sacrifice, so she merely nodded.

"Are you ready to return to the land of conspicuous consumption?" she asked, changing the subject. "I think that is where we need to go—eventually."

"I'm certainly ready to leave here. But aren't we going after your magician? He's in Mexico, isn't he?"

"Yes, but in this we have an advantage—finally. He is actually following me now. Anywhere I lead, he will pursue. We have the luxury of choosing where this confrontation will take place. I think putting some distance between us and Smoking Mirror would be wise. One battle at a time and all that."

"Do we sneak across the border?" he asked. "I take it you don't want to leave too obvious a trail for anyone to follow."

"No, I don't. There may be some questions about the explosion that blew up my house and a neighbor's boat that went missing that night. And Saint Germain has probably got contacts in law enforcement. He was always good at befriending powerful politicians and he may have sicced them on me. Fortunately, getting across the border isn't hard. You should have no problems. Your identity is intact. You can just cross the normal way—if you go soon."

"Maybe, but your magician may figure out who I am and that we are together. He might try tracing you through me. Do you know a stretch of border where there aren't a lot of guards? In spite of what you've said about our bodies' ability to heal, I'd rather not be shot."

"Yes, I hear you. But even if we're caught, they'll let us go."

"They will? Why? Big bribes?"

"Not exactly." Ninon suddenly peeped at him through her eyelashes and gave him the dazzling I-think-you're-brilliant-and-I-want-to-give-you-a-handjob smile that worked on all heterosexual males age thirteen and up. St. Evremond had watched her use this on some of her enemies in the clergy and told her that he feared for the state of her soul.

Miguel whistled in admiration, though not in lust.

"You're good," he admitted.

Ninon laughed, tucking the seductress away.

"Practice, and you get better," she said. Then, with a frown: "Really, we need to get going."

"I know." Miguel reached for his belt and threaded it through his jeans. His movements were quick and sure. Usually there were hours of partial paralysis and uncoordinated movement after electrocution. This had to be the vampirism helping him recover. She also felt strong enough to bench-press a car. Two diseases taken together made quite a cocktail.

"Smoking Mirror has done one good thing," Miguel said. "There are no drug dealers round here, though they have tried to establish themselves more than once. Look around at a lot of these towns down here and you can see narco-dollars at work, buying guns and destroying lives with addiction. But not here. We won't have to keep watch for drug runners."

"I am the Lord thy dark god and thou shalt have no other god before me," she murmured. "Some people just don't like competition."

"And this town ain't big enough for two mass murderers," Miguel agreed. "And speaking of that . . . have you thought of a way to kill Smoking Mirror yet? He's going to be very unhappy about this turn of events."

"Not yet. I need to do some reading. I've killed zombies and ghouls, fought a demon . . . Actually, I mostly ran away from the demon, though I have learned how to banish them. But killing an Aztec god is a new one for me."

Miguel pulled open the small trapdoor in the roof. Rainwater edged over the lip and pattered on the dark floor below.

"Well, suffice it unto the day the trouble therein. We'll

take care of this Saint Germain first." He turned and pulled her closer. His body was hot, pouring off warmth into the cool air. Steam coiled around them.

Knowing that Miguel was also wondering if Smoking Mirror would send his minions after them, She asked, "How many vampires are here?"

"I'm not sure. Not many. S.M. keeps the population down. People would probably notice if they were invaded by masses of vampires, and feel moved to do something."

"They may know about them anyway. Have you noticed that many of the houses have their window sills and doors painted a peculiar shade of blue? Back in New Orleans, that was called *haint blue*. It's used to keep out wandering spirits. Maybe it works on vampires too."

"I wouldn't hold my breath. Most of the vamps down here are made near bodies of water. That's what seems to hold them, a tie to water. They feed on passersby careless enough to be hiking after dark. The only way most would get into town was if there were a flash flood."

"That's good—the water part. It should keep them from coming after us." Miguel hesitated a moment and she asked: "What?"

"The one exception seems to be my mother. She's been able to break free and travel to where I am, as long as it's over land. She's never crossed the ocean."

"Your mother?" Ninon shook her head. "You still . . . you still see her? Well, of course you do. Everyone has a mother, even vampires, and you would want to visit." She added to herself: "Vamps live long lives, too, so she won't be headed off to the old bloodsuckers home anytime soon. Damn. I think I'll have to wait to hear this story though. We need to get going. I'm packed, just need to fetch the cat. Where are you staying?"

"In my Aunt Elena's old house. It isn't far from here. I'd like to see her before I go—make sure Smoking Mirror hasn't hurt her."

"Let's split up then and meet outside the hotel. We should take both vehicles with us when we go."

"Okay."

Ninon reluctantly forced herself to the trapdoor and stared down at the ladder. It wasn't that she felt weak—not at all—but she was filled with a sort of strange, almost sexual lethargy that urged her to linger in this place. It wouldn't take much to convince her to drag Miguel back down to the floor and have sex with him again. Sighing, she knelt down and grabbed the ladder.

Miguel followed her down as slowly. His scars had mostly faded. The only thing that gave away his change was the blackness of his eyes—dark before, but now looking completely inhuman. They would have to get contacts for him right away. Until then, he would have to wear sunglasses.

The world had gone to war. Again. As much as Ninon hated the idea of facing battlefield bloodshed, she knew that she had to, or her conscience would never let her sleep again. The thought of almost-eternal life with no sleep was nothing to be scoffed at.

And this was different while still the same. Some wars were understandable. They were about food or land taken from those who had by those who did not. Others were fought for intangibles—religion or political ideology, some old and some new. It was a shame that real people got caught in real crossfires as these ambitious generals' theories were tested at the point of a gun. Montaigne had said that it was putting a high value upon one's opinion to burn men alive on account of them, but the world had never had a shortage of opinionated men.

However, Ninon had never intended, in answering the call to aid, that she would end up playing mother to a group of orphans with whom she shared no language. Childhood—hers or anyone else's—wasn't a place she ever wanted to revisit. But here they were—the tangible victims of someone's intangible ideology—looking at her with frightened, exhausted eyes. It has been almost three hundred years since she had helped an infant or cuddled a child, hungry, sick, and scared. And there were some things a woman never forgot, as much as she might try to, and being a mother was among them.

Ninon dropped to her knees and reached for the children.

Beauty without grace is a hook without bait.
—*Ninon de Lenclos*

After God made man he repented him. I feel this way about Redmond.
—*Ninon de Lenclos*

"The Queen's fate approaches," said St. Germain coldly. "Shall we see you again?" asked Countess d'Adhemar. "Five times more shall you see me. Do not wish for a sixth."
—*From the Diaries of the Countess d'Adhemar,* Souvenirs de Marie Antoinette

CHAPTER TEN

Ninon caught the barest glimpse of a hideous face hovering in the air above her and then something long and white struck at her head, knocking her flat in the hall outside her room. She felt a large mass falling towards her and lashed out with her foot, connecting with some *thing* that felt like a leather sack filled with rods of steel. She kicked again with her other foot, putting all her newfound strength behind the blow. The creature shrieked and backed away. She thought she heard it hiss: *Stay away from my son!*

When her vision cleared to the point that she was only seeing two of everything, she looked around and was delighted to find that she was alone except for the two Corazons who were growling in the depths of their twin cat carriers.

Ninon rested a moment longer and then tried to stand. And then tried again.

Because practice makes perfect. And if at first you don't succeed . . .

Six times proved to be the charm. She was up. Not jogging, but able to move if she hugged the wall of the passageway. She picked up the cat carrier, now only one in number but still a bit blurry, and tucked it under her left arm. The right she kept free so she could use her pistol. She wasn't anxious to start her career as monster-assassin of Mexico, but on the other hand, she'd suffered enough assaults for one day.

Eventually she staggered out onto the street. She had a hand at her temple where a goose egg was forming. No more being nice. The next thing that got in her way was getting shot.

"So, you've met Mamita. I thought I saw her fly by." Miguel handed over a flask and sunglasses. His expression was sympathetic. "It's scotch. Drink up. You've had a shock. Another shock."

"Did you say 'Mamita'?" Ninon took the flask even though you weren't supposed to drink with a concussion. If what Miguel had said was true, the alcohol would have almost no effect on her now.

"Old, ugly, bad breath, violent, levitates?" he paused then and reached for her face. His expression sobered. "Are you hurt?"

"Not really. I don't think we're going to get on, though. She said to stay away from her son." She took a small step away from Miguel and sipped cautiously. "Was it real? It looked real."

"The levitation? Yes and no. I think a lot of it is about the power of the mind. She believes that she levitates and her belief is so strong that she affects the minds of those around her." He paused. "Or maybe she levitates. I don't know. I can't do it."

Ninon drank again. Corazon growled some more.

"Your mother. . . . It isn't fair," she complained. "My parents are dead. I have nothing to inflict on you."

"Just your cat." Miguel peered into the carrier. "He looks angry."

"He doesn't like Mamita either."

"Then it's unanimous. Should we write bylaws and form a club?"

"Have you thought about killing her?" Ninon asked before thinking. "*Merde!* Sorry, Miguel—chock it up to blood loss. What a thing to say to you."

Miguel studied her for a moment and then reached for Corazon's carrier. "As a matter of fact," he answered, "I have."

Ninon looked at his back as he walked toward the Jeep. Miguel continued to surprise her.

She decided that maybe they should try the last few moments over again and said so.

"Okay. As long as you pretend my mother didn't attack you. I'm afraid that makes me angry."

"Done. I mean, there but for the grace of God . . . It could still be us one day."

"You're kind."

"Not really. I had a mother too. She was just more of an emotional vampire." Miguel turned around and she smiled at him. Unable to help himself, he smiled back.

"Hello, beautiful," she said.

Louis de Mornay looked up at her and then back down at the locket in his veined hands. The sun glinted in his thinning silvered hair. He had forgotten to put on a wig.

"You haven't changed at all," he whispered, his voice a mix of awe and fear. "You haven't aged a day."

"If you could see my heart you would know otherwise," she answered, understanding now that it had been a mistake to seek him out. Her presence would not comfort him for the loss of their son. She added aloud, "I'm just a dream, Louis. Only a dream. And I'll leave now that I've said my good-byes."

"Ninon!" he cried, but didn't reach for her, didn't look up from his locket. She saw each tear as it fell from his eyes and landed on the cold marble of their son's grave.

Men enjoy a thousand privileges that women do not enjoy.
Therefore I shall make myself into a man.
—*Ninon de Lenclos*

More genius is needed to make love than to command
armies.
—*From a letter by Ninon de Lenclos*

"N'avez pas peur, je m'en charge."
Have no fear, I am in charge.
—*Ninon de Lenclos*

Life is too short, according to my ideas, to read all kinds
of books and to load our memories with an endless number of things at the cost of our judgment. I do not attach
myself to the observations of scientific men to acquire science; but to the most rational, that I may strengthen my
reason. Sometimes, I seek for more delicate minds, that
my taste may imbibe their delicacy; sometimes, for the
gayer, that I may enrich my genius with their gaiety; and,
although I constantly read, I make it less my occupation
than my pleasure.
—*Self-portrait by philosopher, Saint Evremond, lifelong
friend of Ninon de Lenclos*

MIGUEL:

MY STORY

CHAPTER ELEVEN

Let's abandon all pretense, shall we? My real name is Miguel Stuart, though that isn't the name you know me by. I've been writing Ninon's story because she won't do it. She maintains that I'm the novelist, and since everyone is going to think this is complete fiction anyway, the telling of the story is my project. Fair enough, but I'm going to do it my way from here on in, because I don't really know what Ninon has been thinking since our mental connection was broken, and I have a feeling that any thoughts I attribute to her will be pale shadows of what is really on her mind. My own feelings I understand—at least in part—so I'll work with them.

You bought this thinking it was a romance, and it is. In a good story, especially a romance, you begin with a secret or mystery or an exciting revelation about the hero or heroine that will cause conflict and drive their actions for the remainder of the story. You've got one revelation now—this isn't a work of fiction at all. And the hero is actually a thwarted monster, and the heroine believes she's damned. Naturally they'll have issues. I can also promise that the hero and heroine will have some great adventures, brushes with the bad guy, mind-blowing sex, and then a thrilling final conflict. At some point, the villain, often like Scrooge, should have a change of heart and repent his evil ways and from there you move on to an exciting and morally improving finish where the boy gets the girl and they live happily ever after.

Sadly, I don't think you're getting all that in this tale—not if I tell the truth. Call me pessimistic, but I'm betting our villain just won't repent. We're going to have to kill the son-of-a-bitch. And I don't really know if happily-ever-after is an option for people with our kinds of problems. But I am getting ahead of myself.

So, where to begin this autobiography? Perhaps with the moment Ninon entered my life? Or should I begin at the beginning of my life, even if I don't know all the details from those long-ago days? Yes, maybe it's best to follow tradition and start here if I can sort it out in my own head. I mean, what am I?

What I know for sure is that I was born for the third time in the summer of 2006. Each time I've been born and died it's been in Mexico. (Which, since it is always painful, is a good argument for never going there again.)

Birth is always excruciating, and so is the life that follows—at least some of the time. I'm the only person I know who has two quasi-mothers and two fathers. Do I have to tell you that holidays are impossible? Filling out the family tree in the front of the Bible is out of the question, and my DNA would baffle the world's best genealogists. Not that I bother with these things, but sometimes it bugs me that I was stripped of options for a normal life before I was old enough to understand what I was losing.

Other things you should know but may not have gathered from the start of this story—women adore me but I don't have a girlfriend or even someone I see regularly. There's just too much guilt when affairs go wrong. Many people have relationships that end badly, but mine have the potential to be catastrophic. That's the trouble with having a mother who's a vampire with poor impulse control and a genetic stepfather—grandfather (I'll explain)—who's an Aztec death god. His name is Smoking Mirror but I call him S.M.—which is short for sadistic murderer, though he doesn't know that. Anyhow, with these unwanted connections, it isn't healthy for people to hang around me. One close call with a female grad student was enough to drive this lesson home. No male-pattern dimness here. She lived to see the dawn after our third date, but still has nightmares about the experience. Her therapy would advance, I'm sure, if I could tell her that she didn't really hallucinate the experience, but of course that isn't an option.

I used to only have one father: Cormac Stuart. He was a geologist. Back in those prenatal days I only had one mother too. Cormac met her in Mexico. It must have been nice—Mom, Dad, and soon-to-be baby makes three. . . . Too bad I can't remember it. It would have been nice to know my mother before she became a brain-sucking fiend. Fate—that bloody bitch—had other plans.

Mamita went into premature labor while on a hike to see her excited husband's discovery, an igneous intrusion near Cuatro Cienegas. At the first gush of blood, Mamita lay down by the side of small poza and waited while Dad—Cormac—ran to get the Jeep. He was fast but Mamita hemorrhaged massively and miscarried before he got back. The smell of blood in the water attracted the local death god, who specializes in women dying in childbirth, and while she was bleeding her life away, he dragged her into the water, gave her a vampire spinal tap and a lobotomy. Lucky thing for me, he didn't notice that I was still—barely—alive, or it would have been the end of yours truly. As it was, I was left on the bank for whatever predator would find me.

Poor Cormac came back with the Jeep and . . . well, I'm just imagining this part. He would never talk about it. He loaded up an unconscious and maybe drowned Mamita and his silent son—he did notice I was still breathing— and rushed us to the local doctor.

Cormac's grasp of Spanish was poor and his travel dictionary didn't cover the kind of phrases the panicked *medico* was laying on him. Look it up. You won't find "curse of the Aztec death god" in any conversational Spanish book. Still, Dad must have known the doc had something bad on his mind what with all the crucifixes being waved around and the doctor's refusal to do anything for his wife who wasn't dying in spite of massive blood loss and sucking water into her lungs. Dad decided to leave me with the doctor—I was having trouble breathing—while he took a dazed Mamita to her sister's home and tried to nurse her back to health and coherence.

My aunt was less than thrilled, but she did her best. So did Cormac.

Their marriage lasted only three days—well, three nights—longer. That's how long it takes for a full transformation from a loving wife into a brain-sucking fiend. Cormac woke up with Mamita's now very pointed, strawlike tongue probing his ear as she tried to get her first meal from his medulla oblongata. Fortunately she wasn't very skilled and didn't know her own strength, so Dad and Aunt Elena were able to get away without killing her. Dad always thought this was a good thing. Me? I'm not so sure. It isn't that I'm big on spousal murder, but it sure might have spared me some grief later.

Or not. It's hard to know how things might have gone. I mean, you can bob and weave, but can you really escape Fate when she's decided to punch out your lights?

What did happen is that we left Mexico that very night, but didn't get far over the U.S. border before Cormac came down with an ear infection that even the American doctors couldn't cure. It left him deaf on the left side, and the high fever caused a kind of amnesia about our days in Mexico. Or so he always claimed.

Cormac resigned from his job and we went back to Scotland to work the family croft with Uncle Seamus, who died soon after. Da refused to ever visit the Americas again. Cormac told everyone—including me—that my mother died in childbirth. Seeing how dreadful he looked and how eternally sad he was, no one ever doubted this, least of all me.

I survived a tedious childhood, bored because I was too bright for my own good and had too few intellectual distractions. I learned to play guitar, and did well in school—very well. They had me skipping grades, setting my O- and A-levels at an early age. I could have attended any university but chose Edinburgh so I could stay close to Cormac who, though he had no specific health problem, seemed to grow frailer with each passing year. There was also a girlfriend, Moira, my freshman year, but she died in a car accident before things got too serious.

I was young and my heart tender. I grieved for Moira for the better part of a year, but not as deeply as I should have—I see that now. Of course, there was no way to know that she would be the first and last girl I would have a long-term relationship with. Anyhow, I felt rootless afterward and wanted to get away.

Things were actually going great for me and passing fair for Cormac, who turned easily to the family trade of crofting and seemed happy to leave his twentieth century career to his overachieving son who visited often on holidays.

Like I said, I was growing ever more restless. My world felt too small. I was studying geology with an American called Dukie Deathergard whose father worked in some military-sponsored scientific think tank, and he was the one who lured me to North America. Deathergard—does Fate have a sense of humor, or what? Unlike his father, Dukie was a bit of a mystical poet and talked endlessly about the Four Corners area of the Southwestern U.S. where he had grown up. His love affair with the West was alluring for one whose horizons had been so limited. At his urging, I decided to spend my winter break looking at rock formations in the American West, maybe visiting a couple of grad schools, and paying my way—I naively assumed—by playing a bit of guitar on the streets as I sometimes did in Edinburgh. Cormac was nervous about these plans and sometimes muttered about having an ocean between us and disaster, but I put it down to the usual parental separation anxieties, nonspecific amorphous dread. Those of you with teens will know what I'm talking about. You'll also be able to predict that I didn't listen.

I loved the States, just as Dukie had said. The rocks really were stupendous, and the country vast beyond all imagination to someone raised on a small island. We also had some fun in Las Vegas. I won often because I am good with cards. But that soon palled. I was young and easily distracted, and when a couple of the other blokes we were traveling with suggested a road trip down into Mexico, I went along without much hesitation. I had some idea about maybe getting a few lessons from real flamenco guitarists and maybe picking up some of that Latin charm that the ladies liked.

That didn't happen. Fate—being a bloody-minded bitch, as I have mentioned before—arranged for me to miss the guitarist I wanted to see. What I thought was a freak storm stranded him in Nogales and, quickly disgusted by Tijuana sex shows that attracted my mates, I went south to Cuatro Cienegas looking for the famous igneous intrusions that Cormac had told me about. I also knew I might still have family there—I had seen a photo with Mamita and her sister—and though she had never contacted me, I decided to see if Tia Elena was still alive.

You can guess how it went. I didn't see my aunt, but met Mamita at the first full moon. I was camping at the poza where she died and got a little too interested in some old weathered sticks that looked a lot like bones—and of course they *were* bones, her refuse pile of old kills that she had laid out like a spider's web. Their crackling warned her I was near.

That meeting was a shock on many levels, for her as well as for me, though she had always been certain that I was alive. Vampirism has not been kind to Mamita. Mexican vampires live longer and stronger than their European kin, but not gracefully. She had aged far beyond what any human should, and had lost all desire to be tidy in person or place. She had developed a bad habit of just flinging her kills into any nearby water. She also was not big on brushing and flossing.

Her ugliness was shocking enough—she looks nothing like the photo I have of her—but while I was still sorting out the less-than-joyous news that this haglike monster pawing my arm was my supposedly dead mother, I met a hungry S.M. Less than delighted at Mamita's reunion with her long-lost boy, he immediately made sure I got my own involuntary spinal tap—but not a lobotomy.

That's where he went wrong or Fate got careless. S.M. was having too much fun torturing me and trying to make me renounce my religion. Not that he really cared about my religion. It was just a game for him, an excuse that he knew would bother Mamita. I didn't renounce my God that night. I might have, but it's hard to do when you're paralyzed and can't speak.

I thought for a while that my brain would implode and I would die from the horror of what was happening, but nothing that easy was in the cards. Maybe a brighter man would have known that this was the end of any chance at normal life, and killed himself when he had the opportunity, but I wasn't so bright. I was young, and hope and fear were about equal in me then—and both were cruel.

An agitated Mamita perched on a nearby rock and watched me being tortured. She said nothing, but apparently had one of her rare maternal impulses. While S.M. was grabbing a snack—another hiker who heard the muf-

fled screaming and blundered in on our exciting tableau—
she got me away from the poza. It was before the conversion was complete and my brains had been slurpeed. I
owe her for that, because I would have ended up a cruci-
fied, lobotomized brain-sucker if she hadn't been caring
and lucid enough to intervene at that moment. Anyhow,
this is what I refer to as my second birth and why S.M. is
sort of my father. Of course, since he also made Mamita
what she is, he's a sort of grandfather too. I have often
wondered what a geneticist would make of us, though I've
never been willing to actually find out. I work for the government now—what I told Ninon about NASA was sort
of true, though not what my job actually is. Was. So secret
that I still can't discuss it. Suffice it to say that I know
what happens when the Secrets Act gets invoked. At best,
governments are self-serving. At worst—and R&D pro-
grams are the worst—they are monsters without con-
sciences who wouldn't hesitate to make me into a lab rat
if they thought I had any useful potential for the weapons
program. I would kill or die to avoid that. Hell, I'd probably kill you if I had to. Sorry, but it's true.

If I ever get a tattoo—not likely, as I have enough
scars—I think I'll ask to have a 444 put on my chest: two-
thirds of 666. While I often feel far from a human, I'm really only about two-thirds corrupt. The remainder
is—was—still a human being. Or at least humane. The
rest of me isn't so nice, of course. I've been fairly kind in
the portrait I've painted of myself up 'til now because of
telling the story through Ninon's eyes. I know better
though, and so should you.

That trip I gained a compulsion to drink blood, an ability to hypnotize with my voice, and vampire-induced in-
fertility. In case I was ever insane enough to think of
passing this genetic curse on to my children, the option
was taken from me when S.M. injected his venom into my
spine. I did see a doctor about this at one point when I began having some very graphic dreams about dead babies

that was putting me off sex, and found out then that my semen is a dead zone. That was a lot to gain and lose before my twenty-first birthday. I sometimes meet up with the ghost of my former self in dreams, the *me* I might have been if I had never gone to Mexico. Though I tell myself that I am adjusted to my circumstance, I still wake up sometimes feeling wistful and lost, though I can no longer truly imagine what my life would have been like if I had stayed in Scotland with my father and raised sheep.

To this day my university friends have no idea how bloody lucky they were that they found their own way home from that trip. My control wasn't great around the third day after S.M.'s spinal surgery, and I'm not sure what I would have done if Mamita had not kept me confined and brought me animal blood to drink. As it was, all they got was Montezuma's revenge and a case of the clap that could be treated with antibiotics.

Eventually I sort of recovered my mind and strength. Dazed and feeling like a pariah, I went back to Edinburgh and, over Cormac's objections, I started the process of transferring to an American school. Dukie's father was a real help. I was offered a full scholarship to—should I name the school? Would they be proud of their alumnus? Probably not. I knew that I could not take my disease and soul-shame back to live at home where it would hurt my father every time he looked at me. Besides, the Americans really, really wanted me—and not just because I can count cards and do other numeric tricks.

I've done my best through the years to ignore the contagion inside me, but my body doesn't always see things my way. It goes without saying that I've had some holes in my life since then, and sadly none of the usual things can plug them. I can't get truly drunk or stoned, though I have really, really tried and consumed almost every outlawed substance, natural and man-made. The best I can achieve is a bit of buzz from jimsonweed, perhaps because it grows near Cuatro Cienegas.

As I mentioned, I won't do relationships, since I tend to have strong sanguinary impulses first thing in the morning. They come with the first erection of the day, and coffee doesn't help. Also, Mamita has managed to free herself from her poza and occasionally comes to visit, and she never phones ahead so that I can get girlfriends safely away. As with many mothers, she seems to feel that none of these girls are good enough for her son.

I spent some time in therapy, of course, but it didn't do much to help my violent impulses and dreams. Probably because I had to lie to my therapist—after all, I didn't want him to think I was insane. Sadly, it turns out that I have more snakes in my brain than Medusa, and some are hydras that multiply when you chop off their heads. You can't slay them all, not at one hundred and twenty-five bucks an hour, especially when you have a high-level security clearance that's under constant review. So instead I write novels under a couple of pen names. Paranormal fiction, they call them. Really, they're more autobiographical. That's where I exorcise my demons. I don't think my employers know anything about this. I've been at pains to keep the hobby from them. Still, even if they do find out, it won't be a breach of national security.

So without drugs and relationships—and no urge to play racket ball or golf—that pretty much left work to fill the void. And I was good at that, since I had so much time to devote to it. I did have a problem with blood sweats near the full of the moon. They were annoying and leaked reddish fluid all over my lab coats and scared my colleagues who thought—and they were right—that I have a blood disorder. They'd have preferred it if I left, but thanks to the higher-ups, and to the fact that my routine physicals—always scheduled for the evening—never turned up anything unusual, they couldn't make me.

But that seems to be over now. I saw this morning through without any urge to rip out someone's throat, and my white shirt is still white in spite of the moon being as round as a pie.

Which brings me to Ninon, the midwife—she would hate to be called mother—of my latest rebirth. And anyway, since I turned her, I guess in this analogy she might be considered my daughter. Whatever her relationship to me, she is a complete enigma. She's the most beautiful thing I've ever seen. She's also the scariest. You think I'm kidding? You don't know her then—though you should by now, if I've done my job as a writer.

So, to sum up, my rebirths have changed me. Now I can live for longer, for stronger—like Mamita—and because of Ninon, forever. Probably. Unless this wizard catches up with us.

I've heard about this Saint Germain guy from other sources, and I know there has to be more to him than long life and magic tricks. Whatever it is, it'll be bad. I don't think Ninon's trying to gaslight me. If anything, she's played her fear down. She barely broke a sweat when she was pinned under S.M. and he is the meanest thing I've ever encountered. And she's told me some stuff about this Dark Man—Saint Germain's father and her own childhood death god—and though my skin was creeping as she described him stripping her and then chaining her down for electrocution, she was utterly calm. So, if this Saint Germain can make her wary, I know we're in for one hell of ride.

But that's okay. Maybe it's leftover buzz from the lightning strike that ended my blood craving, but I feel ready to take on anything. However, if you have a weak stomach, my apologies. Best exit the story now.

For those who like thrill rides, fasten your seatbelts. Ladies and gentlemen, you're in for a rocky ride.

I have met people who worshipped their broken hearts as a sign that they are superior to others because they possess such great emotion. They feed these hearts with the incense of sorrowful or wrathful thoughts, until this smoke itself becomes an addiction and they have no more reason but only their fear and rage.
—*Ninon de Lenclos*

Every action we take, everything we do, is either a victory or defeat in the struggle to become what we want to be.
—*Ninon de Lenclos*

The ideal has many names, and beauty is but one of them.
—*Ninon de Lenclos*

The more sins you confess, the more books you will sell.
—*Ninon de Lenclos*

Chapter Twelve

Okay, we now return to our regularly scheduled program.

I felt calm as I waited for Ninon outside her hotel, my anxiety worn off the lining of my mental brake pads that had only barely stopped my earlier panic from roaring across the steep downward grade toward insanity. What can I say? S.M. affects me that way—especially when the bastard is crawling around in my skull, committing acts of vandalism. I knew that I'd have to have some brain repairs, and soon. But for the moment I was enjoying the absence of fear and the floating feeling that followed my death by electrocution. As I said, the only substance that can still get me high is jimsonweed, and for it to have any effect I have to smoke a joint about the size of a *grande* burrito, or eat an entire pan of brownies so fibrous they also serve as a colon cleanser. I don't do that often. This buzz was a rare treat.

The Hotel Ybarra had been invaded by tourists while we were out dying. People were in a party mood, but the Cheers bar it still was not, so I listened carefully to the gossip while I waited for Ninon to pack up her cat. It was easy; my hearing had always been good, but now it was exquisite.

There were a few tourists come to see the wonders of the pozas and a couple of boutique owners—women in their forties, I would estimate—looking for inexpensive imports that were colorful and yet still cheap. They had had a couple of margaritas to go with their new Vulcan-style face-lifts, and it was clear their credit cards were set to stun. They were going home with new stock, or they'd die trying. There was also another Anglo, a woman recently betrayed by her "rat bastard" husband. She had no credit limit and was in monetary kill mode. Her husband—rat bastard or otherwise—should be grateful that she discovered his infidelity while in Mexico. The local jewelry was fairly inexpensive, and even if she bought out the town, this would be marginally less expensive than paying for a divorce in California where they lived and had liberal community property laws.

The odd weather was mentioned in passing, but of vampires or death gods, there wasn't a single murmur. That was good. I hoped Mamita had the sense to get out of town for a while. I knew that we weren't being offered a clean escape route, a get-out-of-jail-free card from the mess we were in with either S.M. or this Saint Germain, but what we had been presented with was a quick getaway and a small detour from a really bad reality, a back road that might allow us to find a more advantageous position from which to fight the next battle. Clearly research and strategic planning were in order, and we'd do that better away from here.

I thought it a good thing that I'd brought my portable computer along. Aside from being able to write, I figured that the internet might actually be of some help. I hadn't had the thing open in days. Frankly, I'd been avoiding e-mail, though the town had an internet café I could have used. Partly, the avoidance was the fact that my mail is almost always disappointing. My colleagues aren't the kind to write casually—too many security hoops to jump through even on a home computer—and just how much does any man's penis need to lengthen, strengthen, be pumped up, or implanted? And, frankly, if you've seen one lesbian coed slumber party, you've seen them all. Of course, that wasn't the main reason I had been avoiding my in-box.

I was also dreading some bad news. I knew that my career at NASA was probably over. I'd been granted leave to visit Cormac and then, after the funeral, more time off to wrap up family affairs in Mexico. But vacation was long over and I hadn't reported in. So if not at that moment, then the next time they performed a routine security check on their AWOL employee, my termination would be carried through. I would possibly be declared persona non grata and probably have my U.S. visa revoked. They might do worse if they found out what I'd been doing while on vacation—like consorting with vampires and planning the killing of a vampire god. My explanation that these creatures were not really alive, or even persons, probably wouldn't help much either. And I am sure that an appeal for sympathy for my own vampirism would only get me labeled a security risk of the highest order. If they didn't believe me. If they did believe—I'd probably end up as an experiment in some bioweapons research unit. Of the two, being thought insane was better.

There was no way that I was going back to NASA. I couldn't simply disappear, though. They would investigate a suspicious disappearance very quickly and would soon discover that while my home computer system was hooked in to a Ma Bell approved outlet with all the security devices that allowed my employers to spy on me, I also had a second line that I used for my portable, and it was on this that I did some very interesting research as well as play a lot of Sudoku with a program I had written to generate puzzles. Acquiring the line had been fairly easy. I had borrowed it from my neighbors when they forgot to disconnect the landline when their daughter went off to college four years ago. It had taken some creative routing and a few lies to a pair of the most trusting people on the planet, but to this day my neighbors have been grateful for my "help" when they had a mysterious problem with their phones that the telephone company refused to fix free of charge because they said the fault was with the wiring in their home—which was utterly true. I had made sure that this was the case. I pay the monthly fees for this phone online from a blind account and since the neighbors never receive a bill for that number, no one is the wiser about my rerouting.

At least, not yet. That would change though, and then I'd have all kinds of three-letter agencies looking for me.

What I should do is resign—take early retirement. But not yet. Ninon and I might need access to some special databases and machines that could really crunch numbers, and they might not take official action to shut me out right away. That meant I had better check in—soon—and perhaps spin some yarn about a case of amoebic dysentery that had laid me up in village with downed phone lines.

Ninon stuck her head out of the bedroom window, waved at me once and then disappeared back inside. Then I caught a glimpse of what looked like Mamita. I didn't call out to her speeding shadow. If S.M. was after her, I didn't want to cause any delays.

Ninon emerged a few minutes later, her arms full of cat carrier, looking a bit unsteady and very angry. Her luggage was already in the Jeep. I'd checked. She had packed it before our meeting, knowing that whatever happened, she wouldn't be sticking around for a postmortem of the day.

But you've heard this part before. I don't want to bore you with too much redundant detail. I'll have to watch that, since I've slipped off the yoke of third-person POV discipline—which says as a popular novelist I have to keep internal monologue and descriptive narrative to a minimum, and not go on and on about things that are important only to me. The fact that it's a real story—and *my* story—is no excuse for being tedious. Still, I have to tell you that even annoyed, electrocuted, and concussed, Ninon looked like every man's ideal sex toy, the ultimate accessory for any heterosexual male's private fantasy—even for me. Especially me.

Ninon is one of the few women I've ever met who actually understands male lust and who would be completely aware that every man who looks at her would be thinking about doing some version of the dirty boogie with her. For some of those men in the bar, they would be imagining her looking up at them through her eyelashes and saying: *Spank me, Daddy.* Or maybe they'd like her in six-inch heels and nothing else, saying: *Suck on my toes—I know you want to.* Harmless stuff, these fantasies mostly, though most women would find it freaky to know men think of them this way all the time. Yes, we strip you and dialogue you with brainless ego-boosting patter, and have sex with you in all kinds of bad ways.

For me, it's darker stuff than bondage and unnatural sex acts. And she had looked up at me and into my soul, and then given me permission to do the really bad thing I'd been longing to do ever since S.M. had changed me. And just as I had feared, a part of me had enjoyed violating her, sucking her blood, pouring my poison into her body.

Does the fact that she knew my desire and gave me permission make it okay?

Ah! My head was indeed full of snakes that night—larvae implanted in my brain that were finally hatching out into wriggling nightmares of bloody violence. They still wiggle sometimes. I've got to wonder if writing all this down is exorcising my demon maggots, or keeping them alive so I can go on shadowboxing with that powerful thing inside me that I both despise and yet cherish because it is now part of me.

Perhaps that's why I always write at night. The shadows

are stronger then, words more potent and, being my ultimate opiate, they keep me from the temptation to examine my own life, from turning to see if that bitch, Fate, is
gaining ground on me, stripping me of my last shreds of
humanity. In the dark, I can't see I'm a monster.

Ugly, isn't it? But I don't lie to myself—and won't lie to
you. Much. Just enough to keep Ninon and I safe because,
gentle reader, you aren't the only one who follows my
work, and others are likely trying to piece together the
facts into a map that leads directly to their own gain, usually at our expense. So I shade the truth, practice a bit of
misdirection, lie about small things—but not the essen-
tials. Truth is a bitter drink, a vintage not much appreciated by the sinful, maybe because it doesn't go well with
fish or steak or brimstone. Still, I uncork the bottle from
time to time and take a sip for medicinal purposes. It
clears the mind. And on the day that it no longer tastes
bitter, I will know I'm not human anymore.

Reason says I should be bitter about this, but I'm not.
And that's partly Ninon's doing. I'd offered some of this
truth to Ninon, and she had accepted, hardly grimacing at
any of what had to be unwelcome revelations. She's kind
that way. I didn't like giving her poison, but she had to
know what I am and what she might become. Some things
you just don't keep secret.

But I'm digressing again.

"Hello, beautiful." Ninon managed a brittle but still
lovely smile. She reached over and twitched my shirt col-
lar into place. It was a casual act, a small maintenance
that women do for people they care about—children,
lovers, spouses—and I found myself smiling again because I doubted very much that she saw me as a child. Ninon thinks I'm beautiful, in a fallen-angel sort of way.
Most people—if they really believe in Hell—find Lucifer
scary, but as I've mentioned before, very little seems to
frighten this woman. Including occasional whiffs of brimstone, I guess.

"Are you ready to go?" I asked as she closed the passenger door on the Jeep. The upholstery was bald, like a dog with mange. It didn't suit her at all, but the cat seemed to like it well enough as a scratching post.

I looked into the back of her Jeep at the lumpy tarp. I had lifted a corner earlier and had to smile. Rope, flashlights, duct tape, an axe, a toolbox, work gloves, boxes of ammunition, cans of gasoline, and a camera bag. Great minds thought alike, though I had substituted a first aid kit for a camera, and I liked a shotgun with lots and lots of shells.

"Of course." This answer probably wouldn't pass a polygraph, but the answer was as nonnegotiable as junk bonds after the dot-com bust. What choice did we have? We had to be ready. "Do you want to lead, or shall I?" she asked.

"Whither thou goest," I answered. I wanted to touch her, but she looked pale and focused on what was to come. I wasn't sure what she was seeing, and didn't really want to know. I think we had both had enough togetherness for the time being. Neither of us was used to it, and we would need practice at sharing our thoughts and space.

"I goest north." She jerked her head. North was an interesting choice. Wouldn't be much there for long stretches at a time, but I didn't question her inner compass. She seemed to have a game plan, which was more than I had.

"North it is," I said, opening the door to the Jeep and helping her inside. As my father Cormac had been fond of saying, manners cost nothing, and Ninon, for all that she appeared very modern, would have come from a world where manners were valued. I wanted to please her. It was my way of apologizing for being a blood-sucking bastard who had enjoyed making her a vampire.

I think we are in rats' alley
Where the dead men lost their bones.
—*T. S. Eliot*

The aim of common sense is to learn to be happy, and to
do that it is only necessary to look at everything with an
unbiased mind. . . . A man's intelligence is measured by
his happiness.
—*From a letter by Ninon de Lenclos*

He is a worthy gentleman, but he never gave me the
chance to love him. . . . Women are never truly at ease except with those who take emotional chances with them.
—*Ninon de Lenclos about the Duc de Choiseul*

What does Ninon say about this?
—*Louis XIV*

CHAPTER THIRTEEN

At dawn, Ninon finally pulled her Jeep over at the edge of some no-name pueblo and I did the same with my SUV. We had been traveling without headlights. Neither of us needed them.

She got out slowly and stretched. The rising sun made the dark of her eyes glow like fire as she walked toward me. Her walk was graceful, but I could sense that her muscles were tight. Mine were too. We'd been off-roading in vehicles with poor shocks. Still, I sensed that something else was bothering her. I hoped it wasn't the first twinges of bloodlust.

We have free will to make the best of our situations as we travel through life, but the road we are given to travel is arranged by Fate. This one had been rough. I've said it before, but it bears repeating—what a bitch Fate can be. And it frustrated me that there was nothing I could do to ease the path for either of us.

"Welcome to historic Purgatory. Tourists, the line forms on the right," I muttered, getting out to do some stretching of my own as I glanced at the sun. It was coming up, but slowly, as if the hand of some dark god were trying to push it back below the horizon so that there would be more time for the wicked to be about their business. Disturbed at the idea of any other gods getting involved with us, I looked away.

The town wasn't an improvement of views. Purgatory was a good name. Except even Hell had rejected this place. It was dusty, forgotten, a no-man's-land. Not even the scorpions were stirring. I'd never been in a place so dead, and I couldn't see why Ninon had stopped here.

"All true, a horrible place—but it's Saint Germain's kind of place. I think it behooves us to stay here for a while and see what happens. Just leave the keys in the ignition."

I didn't argue. This seemed the kind of place one might want to leave quickly.

We walked. Slowly. It is hard to explain now why the abandoned pueblo was so sinister. Sure, the buildings hunched low to the ground, the edges worn away by the wind and the very adobe flaking away in leprous chunks, but so were many ghost towns and none had bothered me as this one did. Possibly it was the eerier silence there—not just the absence of people, but no cries from foraging birds, no yips from stray dogs. There was only this creepy breeze that brushed by like a stealthy cat and then moved on leaving dead calm behind.

Ninon picked a handful of debris at her feet and sniffed at the dried leaves and dirt.

"Hellebore, baneberry, belladonna . . . Yeah, he's been here—grave-dowsing. He's certainly improved on his father's technique. Dippel used to dig at random. Saint Germain has learned how to use magic to cause mass exhumations. Look around for the cemetery. I think we'll find it emptied." She turned slowly, stopping to look out over the ghostly asphodels that ringed the town. Their gray petals were shivering though there was no wind that I could feel. Perhaps they were mourning their comrades who had fallen under our tires.

"Emptied? You mean . . . all of them?"

"Yes. He's been raising the dead. Calling zombies. Unlike his father, he no longer has to dig them up to do the job. He's found the way to bring the mountain to Mohammad." She pointed. "Over there. See the toppled headstones? They are black because of lightning strikes. I guess we know what he was doing while we were playing with Smoking Mirror. Like this place wasn't horrible enough already. I just hope he hasn't been customizing."

A horrible place, Ninon called it. I thought she was being generous. There was more at work here than a lack of civic pride. Frankly, it looked like Hell had spilled its guts in the desert and then crawled away in shame. It smelled a bit that way too when the sneaky wind shifted to the west.

"Why?" I asked helplessly. "And if the dead aren't in their graves, where are they?"

"He does it because he can. Because it's quick and expedient, and sheer numbers can overwhelm even if individually they're fairly useless because their brains have rotted." She paused. "The dead could be anywhere. They prefer the dark but can move around in the sun—for a while. Keep an eye out."

"I think I'll keep two." We began to stroll down the street. Like gunfighters, we kept to the middle and watched each door and window, expecting an ambush in spite of the utter quiet.

I wondered, with a sort of low-grade dread, did Saint Germain want to kill us because he believed it was necessary, expedient? If killing was the correct word. Or was Ninon right? Did a part of him just plain old enjoy it? He might. And as I knew from my own experience, that urge wasn't necessarily his own fault. His humanity was withered. Parents can really warp their children, and a part of me felt pity for the child that had been raised by Ninon's Dark Man. I knew that my compassion didn't change what we had to do; I just felt like I should know this man before I helped kill him. Taking a life is personal. The why of it should be examined. I had never subscribed to the old saying, Kill 'em all, let God sort 'em out.

I glanced at Ninon. Her thoughts were closed to me now. I wondered if I was equally opaque, or if she could read me if she chose to. There was a lot I didn't know but felt I should. We were sort of kin now—though writing that makes me feel icky in an incestuous way.

I don't know if you can understand. Sharing blood with someone doesn't necessarily mean anything, and yet can mean everything. Ask anyone who has given birth, or, less happily, contracted AIDS. Blood counts. Certainly our little bonding ritual had made a tie more lasting than any social contract man ever drafted. Yet *bound* doesn't mean loved or understood. Look at S.M. and my mother. We all shared a bond, but I did not love them. My biological father was dead—no longer a part of my world—but I still cared for him.

And Ninon. Well, hell. I wasn't sure what I felt beyond intense attraction. One thing was certain—we had a relationship that was stronger, and that would in some form last longer, barring death by demon dismemberment, than any regular marriage.

Also, to use a clumsy metaphor, it was like I had walked through the first part of my life as a fixed telescope, seeing clearly enough but with only half the potential vision, and never able to turn away from my one view of the world. She had shown me how to be like binoculars that could turn in any direction. Linked to her, though briefly, I had witnessed vistas I had never suspected were there—some magnificent, some horrible—and I wanted that wider vision again so I could learn to fully see. Not exactly a Valentine motto. O, Love, wilt thou be my binoculars?

I cleared my throat.

"Yes?"

I'm a guy and therefore not big on talking about feelings. However, I am also a writer and understand the power of words. Words can take the strangest phenomenon and make it into something manageable, understandable. If something can be explained, it can, usually be contained.

Ninon began to smile at my silence. God! She was beautiful in the full blaze of the rising sun.

"Go on—ask. It isn't like you to be hesitant, Miguel."

"We're here to kill zombies?" I asked in lieu of what was really on my mind. It seemed best to sneak up slow on my other thoughts.

"Yes. We can't let Saint Germain set up strongholds. He'll be as bad as Smoking Mirror if we don't stay on top of him. I just hope that the zombies are still here and haven't been lured away."

I held the real binoculars to my eyes and scanned the horizon. I didn't need them but they gave me something to do besides ogle Ninon while we were waiting for whatever was going to happen. An inappropriate impulse, and I knew it. Just—she was so damned gorgeous.

Searching for distraction, I heard myself say: "You know, for years I thought that S.M. only went after me because I was Mamita's son. Also because I was unfinished business. As far as I know, I am the only male vampire he has ever made. I've been hunting up old stones that tell his story and so far haven't found a thing about him making male vampires."

Ninon nodded.

"I'm not sure why he favors women, except that his priestesses can't pass on the disease. I've thought sometimes that he had second thoughts about killing me because I have resisted making more vampires and therefore am no threat, but also because . . ." I tried to think how to put my thoughts into words. "I believe something has happened in the last few years, and he is holding me in reserve. Like banking your blood before an operation. Or finding an organ donor because you know down the road that you'll be needing one." I could feel Ninon staring at me. I didn't need to look over to know she was appalled but not disbelieving. This sounded a lot like what the Dark Man had done with her. Her understanding let me talk without guilt or shame.

"Are you an organ donor?" she asked, meaning a human organ donor. I knew what she was thinking because I'd already traveled this particular road of thought.

"No—and I've no intention of becoming one." Not for a human and not for S.M.

"That's good. Why take chances?"

I nodded. I didn't give blood either. Whatever had infected me, was staying with me. Except for Ninon. She was my one exception, and I didn't think there was any danger of her wanting to pass this disease on either. If anything, she was more repelled by it than I was, in spite of all evidence to the contrary. I had no illusions. She had asked for vampirism because it was expedient—she had changed me for that reason too—but she found what had been done to us morally reprehensible. She probably thought we were damned. I hadn't a clue how to address this notion, or if I even should. I couldn't really reassure her because she might be right.

"You don't know for sure why the Dark Man let you live?" *Or why Saint Germain wants you dead so badly?* But I didn't ask this last question out loud.

"He didn't 'let' me live. At first, I was proof that his experiments had finally worked. But later . . ." I half expected her to say that Dippel had grown fond of her, or perhaps he saw her as a sort of Bride of Frankenstein for his son. Her next words surprised me. "Later, after he began to get crazy, he tried to seduce me and failed. In a rage, Dippel made an attempt to kill me—some sort of ritual to take back his power, I think. When that failed, he sent his son after me. The son-of-a-bitch almost got me too. I didn't know who he was at the time, just an adviser at Court. And Saint Germain is so . . . beautiful. So charismatic." She shook her head. "But the longer I looked into his eyes, the colder and more frightening he seemed. He had me half-naked on a settee when I finally realized that he would prefer to fuck me, *then* kill me, but he would have been fine with doing it in reverse order so long as I eventually ended up dead." She smiled a little. I could hear it in her voice when she said, "I jammed a hat pin into his heart. He was more surprised than hurt, but it gave me a chance to get away."

The woman can chill my blood even when she excites me.

"You jammed a hat pin into his heart—and he wasn't hurt?"

"Nope. *You* don't have to worry about garden-variety stakes anymore either." This time I lowered my binoculars to look at her. She went on, "Unless your heart or brain is burned, vaporized, or ripped from your body, you will not die. You might hurt a lot, but you'll eventually recover."

"Sounds great. So what's the catch?"

"You sure you want all this now?"

"Yes." I wanted to know what made us different from the zombies we were hunting.

Her face was serious, even grim. But I still wanted to kiss her, to tangle my hands in her hair.

"We suffer. Terribly. Every few decades your body is going to need a little lightning. If you don't give it a shot of this 'divine fire,' old age will come on you with a vengeance. Any diseases you have will come back redoubled, and new ones can set in. We become the portrait of Dorian Grey. It happens fast, too—in me. Worse, it affects the brain as well as the body. However, I've known others who can wait months to get a tune-up once symptoms appear. Maybe you'll get lucky."

"But for you? How long do you have when this weakness sets in?" In other words, how long might I have before I had to find an electric chair of my own? She was probably right that this wasn't the best moment for such questions, since my mental upholstery, though overstuffed, wasn't exactly full of calm, rational thoughts and it would take little to tear open. Still, I felt compelled to ask. Given our present activities, it wasn't beyond the realm of the possible that we might not have another chance for a talk. I had to know what I was facing.

"How much time? Only weeks after the first symptom—and a shorter time each cycle. Or it was that way. I don't know what the vampirism will do. I'm hoping it buys me more time. It isn't always convenient to electrocute oneself." She laughed. "You'd be surprised at how many places never have lightning storms. Or only get them at certain times of the year. I can draw the St. Elmo's fire if there is a storm, but I can't alter weather patterns." She raised her binoculars. I didn't think that she needed them, either, at least not to see. "I almost died during World War One. I was in Belgium and the only storms we had for weeks on end were German artillery. I was badly wounded. I thought for a time I might die, but that mercy was not granted me."

"Can we die? I mean of disease or age?"

"I don't know. I don't want to find out." She stiffened suddenly.

"What?" I asked. "Do you see something?"

"I smell something. I believe that Hell is empty and all the Devils are here," she said, quoting *The Tempest*.

"Devils?" I never knew when she was kidding.

"Zombies at the least. How unpleasant to be right about this," she said, looking annoyed. She pulled her pistol from the small of her back and checked that it was loaded. Her hands didn't tremble. This was good. We were almost twelve hours into her conversion, but she seemed to be exhibiting none of the symptoms that had plagued me. She wasn't sweating blood and hadn't mentioned any urge to tear my throat out or suck my brains. There was no sign of any stinger growing on her tongue— I'd checked a couple of hours ago when we stopped to eat and answer the call of nature. I felt fine too. If this deal of ours had consequences, they were being delayed.

That suddenly made me nervous. As the saying went, if

it weren't for bad luck, I'd have no luck at all. This had to be Fate tempting us with false hope that all was well. The next full moon we'd probably pop out enormous fangs and suck the life out of everyone in Tijuana. Or Tacoma. I wasn't sure where we were going. "North" covered a lot of territory.

"At least we know we're in the right place for a fire-fight. I haven't seen anyone else around. We won't have to worry about human bystanders getting hurt," I said as I walked back to my SUV and reached into the backseat, doing my best Gary Cooper. I always liked him more than John Wayne.

I lifted out my shotgun and a box of ammo that I opened with one hand. I slipped shells into my shirt pocket. I carry a Mossberg pump-action, twelve-gauge, six-shot, if you care. It has a modified pistol-grip stock. Usually it feels more than adequate for any job. That day, I was wishing I had gone for a nine-shot model.

Passing the Jeep, I could see that Corazon didn't look happy with what he was smelling through the cracked window, but he wasn't frightened either, unless his contin-ued contribution of feline graffiti on the old seats was a sign of nervousness. I didn't think it was, since he stopped periodically to admire how sharp his claws were.

So, Ninon's cat wasn't afraid of zombies either. That sug-gested he had run into them before. If Corazon could talk, I'm betting he would have some strange stories to tell.

The cat looked up and met my gaze. His head cocked, and I swear I could hear a voice in my head say, *What makes you think I can't talk?*

I almost dropped the shotgun.

Understand, I am not completely anthropomorphic. I had a lovely terrier called Buster who was my closest childhood friend, and I was always fond of sheep and Mrs. MacTavish's old mouser, Gordon. I'm from Scot-land, land of second sight and wee people, but I've never shared a psychic connection with an animal. Being in the presence of this creature who appeared to be telepathic left me feeling wary and perhaps a bit jealous: This animal knew Ninon better than I did.

Ninon came closer. She wasn't wearing sunglasses. Before I could ask about the cat, who had gone back to polishing his nails, she said, "Yes, the town's empty except for zombies. We'll have to clean out this nest completely before we go on. We don't want enemies coming up behind us with sneak attacks." Moving beside me, she opened the Jeep's door and rolled the window all the way down. She and the cat stared into each others eyes for a long moment of communion. When she looked away I could see that her naked gaze was as cold as vodka in a freezer, and when she'd spoken her voice was calm and confident. You have to admire a woman who can look so good, so utterly female, and yet say something so ruthless. This was someone you wanted backing you up in a fight.

It also—strange as it sounds—gave me hope that maybe she and I could have something long-term and perhaps romantic. If zombies didn't do more than annoy her and she had a psychic cat, them a boyfriend who was the appropriated son of a death god and a vampire was probably just a bagatelle. And after that, the everyday trivia of survival would be nothing. Deciding who would take out the trash and who did the dishes, how you squeezed the toothpaste—that was a walk in the park.

In spite of everything that was happening, my spirits felt lighter. I was also made aware of just how tired I had become of constantly dreading the future, of the chronic worry about what I was becoming, which crept closer every night when I closed my eyes and the dreams started, and every morning when I woke up with a desire to kill my neighbors, the security guards at the plant, and every colleague unwise enough to address me before ten A.M. Whatever else happened, now I knew I wasn't alone.

I know Ninon had some moral reservations about turning me—she probably believed in a literal Heaven and

Hell and had a clear definition of sin that would include not offering innocent men the forbidden fruit of the tree of knowledge. But I wasn't innocent, and I was already standing with one foot in the worst of Hells. Sin or not, I'm grateful for what she did. I see our problems as ones of science and disease, not God and Devils. Though she might not think it mitigation, her version of mouth to mouth had pulled me back from torment—from maybe committing murder, which would be a far worse sin.

And what had she asked of me in return? Only to do the vile thing that I had secretly wanted—and she'd said that it was okay because it would help her as well. And it really seemed to have. I had found the one woman, perhaps the one *person*, that I could attack and not have die. I killed without killing. Almost, I could believe in a merciful God.

God—I hadn't thought of him in years, though I had been raised attending the local kirk. Yes, a Protestant church. My father had loved Mamita, but not her Catholicism. Still, I had not actually considered the subject of God and the resurrection of His son from the dead for a long, long time. Back then, I was into science. The Bible was metaphor and nothing more. But I was learning, and there were indeed more things in Heaven and earth than I had dreamed—a blasphemous thought, but I was in the select club of Resurrectionists now. Of course, frankly, other than Ninon, I didn't think I was going to like the membership. At least not in Mexico. The Risen God . . . The implications were terrifying. But just as there were no atheists in foxholes, I don't think too many people could stand where I was that morning and not wonder what else was out there and what it might mean.

I told Ninon about the idea of a Resurrection Club— minus any reference to Jesus. She didn't smile.

"You can still opt out," she said softly. Her dark eyes shone eerily, but she demonstrated all the worry of a napping cat on Prozac. The sun had finally forced its way into

the sky. I could feel its heat on my back and welcomed it.
I had always liked the sun, even when it burned. I always
felt like it was destroying the virus that lived in me.
"Miguel, nothing that has happened to you has been of
your doing. No blame attaches to you. You've killed no
one, and I can probably handle this alone. You can even
go back home now, take your life back."

"No way. It's not that simple and you know it."

Besides, I was too curious. And it seemed our chances
of survival went up if we each had someone else to watch
our backs while we slept. For we would need to watch our
backs. She was being optimistic if not naive. This wasn't
over. S.M. would hunt me to the ends of the earth, and so
would this Saint Germain when he found out about me. I
accepted this even if Ninon did not.

Besides, though Miss Manners had never covered the
delicate nuances of this situation—or if she had, I'd
missed that column—I felt sure that the etiquette of exchanging blood and spinal fluid, not to mention sharing a
bolt of heart-stopping lightning, said that you should stick
around for a while and see if the other person was really
okay and not going to turn into a bloodsucking berserker
at the end of the three-day incubation. It was the gentle-
manly and civic-minded thing to do.

Another whiff of bad air and the skin of my neck tightened. I was rethinking my idea that I could have kinship
with something smelling that rotten. This was way worse
than Mamita, and she fell squarely into the unpleasant
category of what Shakespeare had termed "a little more
than kin but less than kind."

"Okay, then. I want you to have this." Ninon handed me
a peculiar spike. It might have been some kind of garden-
ing tool, but I knew it wasn't.

"What's this?"

"A trench spike. I got several in Belgium. It's a weapon
of last resort, but the best for hand-to-hand combat. It
will stab through a metal helmet and skull without even

slowing." She paused. "The only drawback—aside from
the zombies being so close that they can bite—is that it
takes a certain amount of will to use the spike. This kind
of combat is very . . . personal."

I eyed the weapon with respect and then tucked it into
my belt. It had about a seven inch steel spike fitted into a
set of brass knuckles. The heavy weight was reassuring.

"Thank you," I said finally. "You have another?"

"Yes. And they work. I promise. Not that we'll need
them today. But just in case."

Suddenly, the dead were there, stumbling out of the
church.

"Holy hell."

"*Oui.*"

I looked at the zombies and felt like I had dislocated my
eyeballs. My brain insisted that I had to be looking at
something that was a trick, a distortion. It couldn't be
real. The things came shambling down the middle of the
town's only street, a lumbering funeral procession, or perhaps a small *dia de los muertos* parade. None were actually skeletons, but there wasn't a whole lot of flesh and
bone left to go with the sinew. Gender would have been
hard to determine without the tattered clothing that clung
to the corpses.

Ninon had warned me, but I hadn't really believed. My
brain dropped into a psychic blender and someone hit the
pulse button. My perception wasn't completely pureed,
but once again reality had spun around and I was facing
the wrong way. This couldn't be happening. I had accepted vampires and a death god, but this . . . Funny what
the brain sticks at, isn't it?

It was alarming to see that the dead had armed themselves with farm implements—pitchforks, hoes, shovels,
picks . . . a machete? They hadn't been buried with these
things, which answered the question of where they were
and what they'd been doing since we pulled into town.

"In spite of the hay forks and shovels, I don't think

they're going to a hoedown," I said, proud of my calm. I counted them. Only fourteen. There must have been more corpses in the graveyard, but perhaps the others had been too far gone for reanimation. I hoped so. There had to be some limit to what this Saint Germain could do. After all, there were a lot more dead people in the world than live ones. We'd be overrun if he summoned them all.

"No, they're headed toward us. They have our scent now and won't give up until they're fully dead. Good thing the sun is up. They'll be slower, easier to destroy." Ninon raised her handgun and sighted down the barrel. "It usually takes two shots to bring them down. One to the brain, one to the heart. Even then, you need to avoid them because if the brain isn't completely destroyed, the hands will grab at your ankles and they will bite if they have any jaw left. Don't worry, we'll burn them later. That will take care of the loose ends."

Don't worry, she'd said. *We'll burn them later.*

Reality clicked back into place. It was horrible, but I didn't doubt anymore. I also understood why Ninon did not consider these shambling creatures to be anything like us.

I pulled up my shotgun and pumped it. It would do more damage than one to the head and one to the heart. The things shuffled on, moving closer, uncaring of our weapons or perhaps not comprehending what they were. I chose a man, a peasant in black pants and what used to be a white shirt. As I watched, a rat scrambled out what used to be his stomach and dropped onto the ground, where it scurried away with a bit of dried intestine. It hit home then that these really were rotting corpses, and I had to swallow hard against my rising gorge. These were zombies, the walking dead. And they were looking at us like we were a free all-you-can-eat buffet.

I had some range with the shotgun, but I waited. When my target was close enough, I looked into the creature's blank, dusty eyes and felt relief. The soul had already departed from this thing. I was destroying flesh, but it wouldn't be murder. You can't murder what's already dead. At least, that's what I told myself that morning. I've since wondered if someone would ever look into my eyes and think the same thing.

Ninon pulled the trigger. The zombie in a wedding dress standing next to my entrails-challenged target snapped back, a small bloodless hole appearing in her head. She managed another step, but Ninon fired again, putting a second round in the heart. Quick, clean, and efficient. The creature crumpled to the street with a small puff of dust. I thought about complimenting Ninon on her shooting, but what she probably wanted to hear was my shotgun dealing with our problem.

I swallowed again and then let fly. As I had hoped, my gutless target and the creature behind him both fell over, blown back by what looked like a violent wind but was in fact lead shot. There was no blood from either, though an amazingly awful smell filled the air.

Aim, fire, reload. Repeat as necessary. It was actually over quickly—two minutes at most—and yet I spent an eternity there in Purgatory. I'd had bad nightmares before that day, but as Ninon had said, those dreams weren't my fault. I had no guilt for the things that had happened to me or my family. But any new nightmares that kept me from sleep—and they would come—would be what I'd bought and paid for with my own free will.

There's always a price, isn't there?

"Killing zombies. What a way to start the day." It seemed surreal that the morning should be so beautiful when we were wading through twitching corpses. They died hard, but guns had made the fight unequal—not that I was complaining. The scene was a whole lot creepier than the last act of *Hamlet,* or even a Jim Jones punch party. There, dead was dead. Here, we were standing in the Twilight Zone, where the unthinkable could happen.

"Burning them is even less pleasant," Ninon answered.

"But first we need to have a look around town and make sure we didn't miss any. Some might have been smart enough to hide."

"Okay," I said. "Do we split up?"

"Yeah—I want to be done before noon. We need to get on the road again. I want to find some shelter in a populated place and get some sleep while the sun is up. We both need it."

I nodded—reluctantly—and walked toward the nearest building with my shotgun ready.

My high was pretty much gone by that time, and I was thinking increasingly weird thoughts. Like, how zombies and vampires have one thing in common—neither are alive and they both need to have once been living. One cannot be born without a living mother, and one cannot be dead without first having been alive. But then there is Smoking Mirror. I don't know what he is. He exists, but he was not born and is not exactly alive.

Or maybe this was rationalization for the other thoughts that kept cropping up.

It came as a bit of a surprise, but once I looked, it became apparent that I had no firewall in my brain to prevent me from killing S.M. Today had proved that I could kill. Saint Germain probably wouldn't present a moral problem either. Our run-in with his zombies had convinced me he'd embraced his inhumanity—if he had ever been human. He might have been created by Dippel rather than born. This raising of the dead was an obscenity beyond obscenity. Like his crazy father, Saint Germain had maxed out his right to breathe. They say the acorn never falls far from the oak, and it's clearly true of other nuts as well.

To be honest, I felt a little bothered about killing these zombies. Or rekilling them. I still wasn't completely sure if that was okay. It was expedient and necessary, since we didn't know any rituals to put them back in the ground, but I still didn't like it. I still kind of identified with them. They were just unlucky—and admittedly smelly—dead folk being used by unscrupulous powers. Like Mamita was used by S.M. Left to my own devices, I might have left them alone. Who could they hurt in this abandoned ghost town?

But this was Ninon's party. She'd had a lot more experience with these things. Maybe the creatures really did want to go back to being dead and we were doing them a favor. If I had any brains left, I would be appalled at walking around in a rotting body and would want someone to put me out of my misery. And maybe they wouldn't stay in town. They had looked hungry. Starvation might prompt them to hunt.

She had also talked about not fighting a battle on two fronts—which was conveniently forgetting that we already had S.M. on our tails, but I didn't bring that up. She didn't mind that we were more than a little strange ourselves, so if these creatures set off her weirdo-meter more than S.M. then there was probably something very wrong and dangerous with them and we needed to make getting rid of them our top priority.

Also, every time she smiled at me, I felt it way down at the base of my spine. And maybe a bit lower. Yeah, I'd do just about anything for her. In fact, I already had. Maybe I should have been troubled about this, but I wasn't. Probably this was yet another sign of poor mental health, but I had long ago come to grips with the fact that I was going to go through life with a lot of unresolved issues and have to spend my days choosing the lesser of evils in life's nasty smorgasbord of unsavory alternatives.

"I'll look in the church," I called. I thought maybe that going into the building with the intent to kill anything in it would bother her. Even if she had renounced the Church, she had been raised Catholic and the symbols of the Church would have meaning.

"Okay. Just be careful."

I stopped in my dusty tracks outside the crumbling building and sniffed the air. I didn't smell any zombies but . . . This wasn't a soaring cathedral. It was a squalid building, painted tan—the color of apathy, fitting for a structure built by indifference and inhabited by sullen despair. It took an effort to push back the door the rest of the way, and not just because the hinges sagged.

The air hung thick and motionless inside the dark room. Though nothing moved, I could see dust suspended in the air, distorting and clouding the view of the fractured pews. I looked about quickly at the overturned altar and shuttered windows, but there was no place for anything zombie-sized to be hiding. Still, the room wasn't empty. Maybe the place was haunted by ghosts. Whatever inhabited that space, I'd sooner have sucked down cyanide than breathe that air into my lungs. It sounds melodramatic, but my very soul was offended. Ninon was right, this whole pueblo had to burn. Saint Germain had contaminated everything.

For a man I'd never met, I sure bore him a lot of enmity.

I did a quick check of the rest of the buildings. There were only four on my side of the street. I didn't look into any of the dark nooks and crannies. A professional burglar would have sneered at my efforts. Hell, Corazan would have sneered. But if there were any zombie rats, scorpions, or rattlesnakes about—a new and horrifying thought of the disease spreading into the animal kingdom had just occurred to me—I didn't want to see them.

When I got back to Ninon, she was pouring gas over the still twitching bodies. It didn't do much to improve the smell.

"I have another can in the back of the Jeep," she said. "Douse as many of the buildings as you can. It may not work, but I'd like to try to burn this place to the ground. We don't want to leave Saint Germain any refuge."

A woman after my own heart. If it was worth burning, it was worth burning to the ground.

I picked up the other red gas can in the rear of the Jeep and walked back the way I'd come. The exteriors might not burn enthusiastically, but the buildings had dry, rotting wood for guts.

Now, I don't mean to be gross, but just in case you ever find yourself in a similar situation, it turns out that zombies burn well. At least the old ones do. We used them as kindling in the buildings that didn't get gasoline aperitifs. I'm glad we weren't dealing with anything real fresh—those dried corpses were bad enough. The only really horrid part was the twitching, and after a while I learned to ignore it. Still, the job took longer than either of us had planned and I think we were both emotionally drained at the end.

For the record, I'm not a coward. Life on a farm can mean serious accidents without any real medical facilities nearby, animals have to be butchered, and so on. I was always proud that I had a cast-iron stomach and could handle whatever came my way. But neither am I a sadist. Nor have I ever been into exploding-head cinema, let alone attracted to splattered gore in real life—even when the brains being exploded had withered until they had the IQ of beef jerky. Or maybe it was the smell that got to me. Anyhow, it was time for another meal but I had no appetite. Ninon didn't seem inclined to eat either. Only the cat acted hungry, and he didn't do much more than chew on the broken neck of a small rodent he'd caught.

No appetite, but when Ninon offered me a flask and some oyster crackers, I took them. I unscrewed the cap, and my nose became more cheerful as it told my tongue to expect the smoky peat flavor of McCallum's whisky. I couldn't get drunk, but it was the flavor of home.

Ninon drank after me, one swallow like I had done, and then laid a cracker on her tongue. I wondered suddenly if she realized that this looked a sort of perverted communion. That used to be common on fields of battle—the priests giving communion or maybe absolution—and then sending the soldiers off to slaughter. What had the song from *The Survival of Saint Joan* said—something about cannon-fire being holy? That war was the Lord's machine?

Religion again. I shook the thought off, exhaled for a slow five-count, and then emptied myself of as much tension as I could.

I looked Ninon over carefully. It had been almost eighteen hours since I'd seen her naked. That was too long. Also, as weird as it sounds after what we'd just done, I really wanted sex with her again, but this time exchanging only the usual body fluids. Of course, not here. This was one bonfire that wasn't romantic.

My early optimism suffered a setback. I wondered if we would ever wander hand-in-hand through a park, feeding ducks from a shared bread crust saved from our picnic basket, or if we would ever tuck into a roast goose with chestnut stuffing on a snowy Christmas day while carolers sang on our porch. At the moment, both these things seemed unimaginable. Our lives could never be that normal. We would never have a cottage and kids and nine-to-five jobs.

My eyes grew hot and the lids stretched tight as the tissues swelled, but I didn't cry. It wasn't that I was trying to be macho—not entirely. It was more that the situation was way beyond tears, and I didn't feel like I could ask for sympathy from someone who needed comfort more than I did. I was mourning a new loss. She'd been living with this deprivation for four hundred years. No, I couldn't whine about this, couldn't ask for pity. Buy maybe sex . . .

Looking down, I patted my clothes and watched the dust puff off them as my eyes drained. I was filthy and knew that I smelled of smoke and gasoline and things far worse. No, it was hardly the most aphrodisiac of odor combinations—unless the woman you were with happened to get turned on by crematoriums. One didn't want to snuggle with anything that smelly either.

Nope, no sex for me. Not yet.

"Maybe we should have taken pictures," Ninon said.

"Pictures?" I blinked. Pictures are always the last thing on my mind. True, it would be nice to have a photo of us together, but I don't photograph well. I'm too ill at ease. No matter how many times I say "cheese" I always end up looking about as cheerful as the dusty taxidermied deer head on the wall of the steak house. For this reason—as well as other more practical ones—I have always refused to do an author photo. I just couldn't see how it would aid sales.

My father was never a fan of photographs, perhaps considering portraits to be a form of vanity. Or, maybe after Mamita, there didn't seem any point in family photos. There was only one picture of me from childhood, the only evidence that I was once young and happy. I don't look at it often anymore because it makes me sad. I keep it though, because it's proof that I was once normal.

It goes to show how tired I was that this was what occurred to me when she said "take pictures."

"For proof—documentation. Crime-scene photos. Though I don't suppose it would help any. Photos are so easy to fake these days."

For proof of the zombies, not the start of a family photo album. Duh! My brain really was fried.

Ninon turned away, looking about for something, maybe the cat. She sighed tiredly. We were both exhausted, mentally if not physically.

"What are you thinking?" I asked impulsively. Usually I'm good at the cold read—translating body language and facial expressions—plus I'm able to use the vampire stuff to hear heartbeats and to smell the mix of hormones and endorphins in people's sweat. However, Ninon gave me very little to work with. For the most part, I could see and hear only what she wanted seen and heard. She made a meditating yogi seem wild and out of control.

Normally, this lack of understanding wouldn't bother me. I like to be in control. To know things. I have enough weirdness in my own head; I don't need to be dealing with anyone else's bent psyches. But Ninon and I had—briefly—taken up residence in one another's brains. What I had seen intrigued me, and I wanted to know more—much more, and as soon as possible. I felt like I *belonged* in her head, and was even entitled to be there. Also, I wanted to be able to see beyond the horror show of our present circumstance, to know where we were going and why.

"Truthfully, I'm thanking my stars that there were no children in that graveyard."

"Children?" The words were like cold water poured down my neck. I shuddered. The thought was impossibly horrible. I didn't know—then—if I could have brought myself to shoot a child, even a zombie one.

"He wouldn't have spared them, you know," she said softly. "In fact, he'd probably have sent them first if he guessed it would be demoralizing."

I wanted to say something but for once words failed me. I still had a lot to learn about evil.

"Did I mention that I was at the Museo de Momias? I'm really praying Saint Germain didn't follow me there. I don't think he could resurrect any of those bodies but . . ." Clearly she had seen something that upset her. "No, it wouldn't work. They're too old."

Mummies. I blinked, my writer's brain kicking into high gear at the thought of a new story. "Do you suppose . . . ?"

"What?"

"Well, you recall all those curse-of-King-Tut's-tomb legends? You know, people being attacked by walking mummies who carry out the pharaohs' curse?"

She nodded, her face more serious than enthused. Ninon doesn't think like a novelist. "Yes. There was a case in Egypt in 1892 at a place called Hieraconpolis. They supposedly opened the door on a four-thousand-year-old tomb and found a 'live' mummy inside. I have always thought it was just Saint Germain playing a joke—he was in Egypt then. Still . . ." She frowned. "That's a horrible thought, isn't it? That someone else knew how to make zombies and actually left them in those dark tombs for thousands of years." She shuddered. "It can't be. They aren't like us. The risen dead—the revived corpses—they last only a couple of years. Five at the most, and that's in places like Finland where it's cold and there aren't so many exuberant flesh-eating microbes."

Exuberant flesh-eating microbes. Probably a story there, too, but I didn't feel like pursuing it.

Ninon glanced up at the sky. When she spoke again, her voice was distracted.

"It's always bothered me how most people eventually become mere fixtures in our lives, sometimes furniture that is no more than clutter, sometimes just wallpaper stuck in the mind. Even the brightest and best can sometimes be ignored, familiarity breeding indifference if not actual contempt. But, Miguel, I do not see you ever become just more wall covering. I wouldn't want you to."

"I should hope not," I said, surprised into awkwardness by the strange compliment.

Her next words were odd, as though she were following a meandering thought that I couldn't yet see.

"I'm a loner, Miguel. For many reasons. For a long time I saw the decline in manners as a decline in morality. It isn't that I miss the nit-picking of class etiquette of my era—well, only sometimes." Her smile was lopsided, but I was glad that it was back. "But I have for a long while been disturbed by the lack of empathy implied in acts of rudeness of modern postindustrial life. When we remove the social lubricant—the pleases and thank-yous—sooner or later the irritation of proximity with people we don't trust or like will lead to violence or other antisocial behavior. We will cease to be people to each other, cease to be humans. That is doubly dangerous if you are . . . different."

"Yes."

"And then I met my first zombie. My priorities have changed." She looked down. "You will find that it is not a simple platitude—one must adapt or die."

I tried hard to see what she was seeing, to grasp what she was trying to say. But I couldn't.

"Truthfully, I've felt trapped," I said, then added: "Not by you. Just by my life. By disease, I guess. I haven't wanted to adapt. I've wanted it to just go away."

She nodded. "But you know that everyone is trapped—it's the human condition. Most people just don't know it. Because they can download a selection of two hundred ring tones for their cell phones, eat at ten different fast-food joints, or get their iPods in five different colors, they think they have command of their lives. But choice among toys isn't freedom. It's nice, it's fun—but it doesn't make us free. Not in mind, not in soul. And we know that there are some obligations we cannot avoid if we are to retain any claim on our humanity."

"I know."

"Will you miss your work? Your colleagues?" She didn't ask about friends, probably because she knew full well that I couldn't afford to have any. I doubt she had any either. I'd had a decade of loneliness and it had eaten at me. How had she survived four centuries?

"Not much. I used to respect my boss, but I think he sold his soul for a time-share in Palm Springs. One of the guys at work said something about seeing it up for auction on eBay along with his mother's jewelry," I joked.

Ninon gave me a startled look and then said, "He wouldn't be the first. We settle so cheaply."

The first to sell his soul, I think she meant. Heaven knows they sell some weird things on eBay.

Ninon stepped closer and laid her head against my chest, and I could feel the tension in her body. So, she wasn't as unaffected as she seemed. In a way, this was re-assuring. Wonder Woman is great in a fight, but I've never been much tempted by her for a girlfriend. I raised a hand to Ninon's hair, but she was already backing away.

"Ready to go?" she asked. She was dirty, but the smile she turned on me was radiant, a blessing.

"More than," I answered.

"Thank you, Miguel. I can't tell you what it means to not be alone this time." She touched my arm. A small flow of warmth passed between us.

This time. I knew I wasn't going to like the rest of her zombie-killing stories when I heard them. Those ghosts of old loss and pain would probably cling to me. Still, I wanted to know. I'm haunted from the inside out. And Ninon was haunted, too—I could see it in her eyes. I just wasn't sure exactly how. Lost loved ones, lost ideals. In time—if we had that time—I would learn who her ghosts were and whether they needed exorcising.

Shall I tell you what renders love dangerous? It is the sublime idea which we often appear to have of it.
—*Letter from Ninon de Lenclos to the Marquis de Sévigné*

It is all very well to keep food for another day, but pleasure should be taken as it comes.
—*Ninon de Lenclos*

What is the worst of woes that wait on age?
What stamps the wrinkle deeper on the brow?
To view each loved one blotted from life's page,
And be alone on earth, as I am now.
—*Byron, from* Childe Harold's Pilgrimage

CHAPTER FOURTEEN

The sound of distant and disorganized thunder began stuttering toward us as soon as we killed the engines and stepped out of our vehicles in a new town. A hot and nervous breeze skittered by at knee level but did little to shift the honey-thick air that settled on our skin in a clammy blanket. If I were fanciful, I would say the wind had been frightened and doing its best to stay low to the ground as it fled the pueblo. I think Corazon felt it too, because the cat's fur raised momentarily and his eyes followed something I could not see passing through a hillock of low-growing wildflowers the color of prairie fire.

I sympathized with the cat's ruffled nerves. This time the sound of the approaching rainstorm didn't make me feel all perky and Gene Kelly-ish, having me wanting to be out singing and dancing in the rain. Usually a summer squall meant a break in the temperatures and would be welcome, but I'm afraid that all storms from here forward would feel sinister. Maybe they were natural, but I couldn't help suspecting that S.M. was systematically flooding the valley, attempting to find a waterway he could travel to lead him to us. And even if he failed, having storms everywhere we went was like sending up a flare for Saint Germain: *Yoo-hoo! Over here!* Nothing would make me as happy as looking up and seeing a boring old blue summer sky.

I had thought the only attraction of the town we'd come to was a gas station, but apparently I—and the Michelin Guide—had underestimated its charms. The door of the cantina Ninon had chosen for dinner had more than a few holes, some still occupied by bullets. I was hoping that it was some tasteless decorative desperado theme, or perhaps a drunken sharpshooting bet, but I knew this was too optimistic a hope to indulge. We weren't doing the four-star tourist circuit of Mexico, and we couldn't afford to let down our guard. Besides, a few of the buildings in the pueblo we'd burned had looked like this when Ninon and I were done with the zombie eradication. Until I heard otherwise, I'd have to assume the worst—i.e.: the town had been attacked by zombies and would be hostile to all newcomers.

"You know all the garden spots," I muttered to Ninon, then followed her into the cantina, holding the door open for her cat.

"Have faith."

It had nothing to do with faith, but I felt better almost immediately. The outside was scary but inside was gastronomic heaven. I sniffed appreciatively at the aroma of roasting pork and chiles that was dense in the air. It wasn't four-star—it might not even meet health codes—but it smelled heavenly.

The barman was so weathered he might have come from central casting, and he gestured us to a table that we took without any of the usual chitchat—not that I had been expecting sparkling dialogue from our grease-covered host. No menus were offered and none requested. My appetite was back and I wanted whatever was on the fire, healthy or not. After all, according to Ninon, nothing but decapitation could hurt me now. What was a case of trichinosis?

Not ready to abandon all caution, I glanced toward the kitchen as we walked past and saw a pair of women working there. Their days as beauty pageant contestants were long over, but they looked reassuringly human. Even if they hadn't, I might have still stayed to dine. The smell was that alluring.

"You're all but drooling," Ninon remarked with the small smile I found so intriguing. She petted Corazon, who had jumped into her lap. His sharp claws began kneading her jean-covered leg, and I could hear his rusty purr over the other diners' soft conversations.

"My appetite has returned and wants a fatted calf, pronto."

"I hope fatted pig will do." She smiled, but her eyes were busy scanning the room. She wasn't nervous precisely, but neither was she entirely at ease.

Both of us spoke softly in Spanish, doing our best to blend in. This wasn't a ghost town like the others we'd been through, but it looked like the kind of place visited only by the most die-hard of tourists. The ones who would shop for souvenirs in Hell. Or else crazy American quasi-conservationist backpackers who would go anywhere to see anything—even cactus, if it were rare enough. We were certainly dusty enough to make that last story believable. We might have hiked all the way from the border, sleeping rough along the way.

The last option for cover was drug-dealing, but I didn't think Ninon had the look about her. Besides, that was still considered a man's profession, at least down here. And besides, I didn't want anyone trying to buy product from us. It might piss off the local man of business, and we had enough headaches without angering the local drug traffickers.

The afternoon was waning and the room, with its small windows, was far from bright. Still, neither of us removed our sunglasses. Ninon's eyes had been too irritated by zombie smoke to tolerate contact lenses and I hadn't gotten any yet. Once it was full dark, no one would notice our unnerving eyes, but until then we needed to be careful. We couldn't possibly pass for locals. In this town, everyone would know everyone, so we were definitely outsiders. Our Spanish was very good, and we could probably convince most anyone that we were longtime residents somewhere south of the forty-eight contiguous states. But, then again, maybe not.

We had enough problems without having the villagers deciding we were foreign *brujos* come to hex the town. Does this sound like an odd thought? I suppose it was, but I had it all the same. Blame it on the last forty-eight hours filled with vampires and zombies.

The barman brought us plates of roasted pork and two bottles of Tecate. I guess we looked like beer drinkers—the kind that sip from bottles. Or maybe Monday nights were barman's choice and he got a kickback from Tecate. I didn't complain. Glass bottle, glass—what difference?

"He's like a well-mannered child," I said of the cat once the first pangs of hunger were assuaged. Corazon had taken the chair beside Ninon and was looking out the window while we dined. He didn't beg, didn't even give our plates a longing glance.

"Yes, and that's a bit odd. Usually he would ask for a bit of what we're having. I hope he's not getting sick." Her brows knit briefly.

"Well, he did have that tasty rat earlier," I said, tucking back into the pork with my bent fork.

"I suppose." Ninon ate more delicately but with equal relish.

"What? Your nose is wrinkling."

"It's just . . . children . . . I'm sorry, Miguel, if you wanted a family. I should have said that before. It's just . . . I don't think I have a proper biological clock," Ninon finally said, staring at the cat as she stretched the kinks out of her own back. I needed to move, too. We had put in some hard miles—if not as many as I would have liked—and the heavy food was making us sleepy. "Or maybe my batteries have shorted out in all the lightning. I have become a cat person. I find them good company— restful, fastidious, and not disturbed by my nocturnal ramblings. They are also great zombie detectors," she added with a laugh.

"Aren't they a bit self-centered?" I asked. Corazon walked over, leaned against my leg, and sneered up at me. He didn't waste any energy purring. He hadn't spoken to me again, and so I had to wonder if I hadn't imagined our communication earlier. I added pointedly, "Dogs are more loyal, and people are better conversationalists."

"Completely self-centered," she agreed. "But, unlike with a lover, I don't take the emotional neglect personally. Also, you don't need to raise them in a two-parent family. In fact, cats prefer having only one human in the home. Another would take time away from them—valuable time that could be spent dangling string or steaming fresh shrimp for their dinners."

Her tone was fond, and I swear the damn cat smiled. The animal was unnerving. I also didn't care for the trend of this conversation.

"I hope he won't mind me hanging around," I said, with what I think was admirable evenness.

"I shouldn't think that he would. Aleister—I mean, Corazon—is a very confident cat."

"Aleister? Your cat has an alias too?" I don't know why this startled me, but it did.

"Of course. Cats have nine lives and therefore need nine names. Also, while it seems unlikely that Saint Germain would know the name of my cat, there's no telling what he might know—and names have power. By the way, Aleister is not naturally dark-haired. We've both been resorting to artifice." She turned to me and smiled slowly. It was pretty close to the hand-job smile, but I sensed this one was sincere. "Do you think you'll like me as a blonde?"

"I think I'll like you fine when you've had a bath. Neither of us is exactly as fresh as spring rain." It was all I could do not to say something really stupid, like I'd love her as a Martian with six arms and green teeth. Even dusty and exhausted, I found her something more than merely beautiful. Of course, this attraction was as much emotional as aesthetic, which wasn't what she was talking about. I had a feeling we were a long way from any conversations of that nature. I don't know where her head was at, but seeing her reaction to the mention of kids and the snippets of thought about marriage when S.M. was in my head, I was betting that it wasn't in the rosy happily-ever-after. Not yet anyway. She wanted me physically and as an ally in this time of trouble. Beyond that, she would not look.

I reminded myself that passion—real passion—can be a ruthless taskmaster. If it needs to it can make you stupid, make you brave. But above all, it can make you blind. Ninon was right to stay focused. I'd have to watch myself too. It would be even dumber to confuse lust and need for love. After all, lovers come and lovers go, but evil goes on forever. It's about priorities.

Anyway, why chase love? It's an addiction. And Cupid's darts did a lot of damage. Not so much on entry—that hole was small. It was the exit wounds that did you in. Somehow, love has always been larger in its leaving than in coming. At least for me. Did I want to try that again? And with a woman who was commitment-phobic and had a bossy cat?

When we stepped outside an hour later, night had fallen and the air was full of invisible particles of pulverized rock. The gusting wind drove the microscopic knives into our exposed flesh. Corazon wisely went in through a window and didn't wait for us to open the Jeep.

"So, do we follow the lightning, or try to make the lightning follow us?" I asked, opening the door of the vehicle and sheltering behind it as Ninon climbed in. I didn't think there was much hope of the storm ignoring us. "Or can we avoid it all together?"

"Let's see if it will follow. I can't imagine that Saint Germain would want a showdown anywhere that there were witnesses. But on the other hand . . ."

"On the other hand, he's a psychopath," I finished. I debated trotting out my theory about S.M. trying to follow us by creating seasonal rivers and decided against it. It sounded a mite paranoid.

"Exactly. We'll head for the next village. There is a small hotel there—or was. I haven't been there in a long while. If it looks safe, we'll stay the night."

"Okay." I might have discussed this longer, but that wind was vicious and I wanted out of it.

Ninon had been generous with her use of the word *hotel*. It was a place that rented beds with slightly more legroom than the Jeep, and had indoor plumbing, but that was about all you could say for it. It didn't take a genius to spot the fact that there was a definite theme to the towns we visited. If they were not dead and abandoned, they were in extremis, were villages whose aging hearts had almost given out. This Saint Germain had an affinity for all things dead. Of course, so did Smoking Mirror. These poor bastards didn't have much chance.

That was our last normal—well, normal by our standards—night in Mexico. The last moments of quasi-innocence—at least for me—before Saint Germain chose to attack. I think back on this time like a fever dream—vivid but surreal, ugly but beautiful. Perhaps it was my heightened senses, but those days were Technicolor, with a heat that burned the brain like Hell everlasting, and every blessed sunset took me by surprise when the Hell did actually end. Then, only moments later it seemed, came the freezing night, where the world drained of color.

If anything, my senses during the night became more acute. Hearing, smell, taste, sight, touch—and something else—were acute enough to be called painful, so sharp they cut the nerves like glass. Ninon had promised that I would adapt, but I knew she was worried because she also was suffering from heightened stimulation.

Burning day and night both seemed unending as we lived through them, and we wore them like a hair shirt. I could almost imagine that we had been transported to some parallel universe, a place where the twentieth and twenty-first centuries had never happened and magic ruled the planet. I knew that there were towns and cities fairly close by where the modern world went on at its normal frantic pace, but we never went near them. Saint Germain's evil was old and thus flourished in old places. Until he was dead, this would be our domain.

We registered as man and wife—the Garcias, I think— and went to our room. We didn't touch, though we were finally alone. This not because of coyness, or a pretense of modesty on her part, nor the need of a shower. Ninon doesn't do contrived modesty. Nor would she feign a headache if she wasn't in the mood.

"It's matter of energy," she said. "I think I've hit a wall. It isn't so much my body as . . . well, my senses."

"I know," I said. The constant stimulation was exhausting.

Whether we eventually made love or not, we would share the sagging double mattress and the twin misshapen pillows in yellowed linens that looked uncomfortably like the shrouded corpses of two dead sheep. Unless . . .

I looked at Ninon.

"Yeah. I'll get the sleeping bags," I volunteered. And the guns. I had a definite itch that would be calmed only by the presence of firearms.

Ninon nodded, her nose wrinkling. I sympathized. I didn't want to sleep on anything that reminded me of corpses. As it was, we were probably in for some weird dreams.

Still, this felt safer than sleeping in the Jeep or my SUV. I could all too easily imagine water from the storm creeping around us while we slept, and waking up to an enraged S.M. ripping off the door and then our heads.

"Do you really think he's trying to find us?" Ninon asked suddenly. She and the cat both turned to look at me.

"Saint Germain?" I asked.

"No, Smoking Mirror."

So, she could read my mind. Or maybe she just understood how I thought.

"I don't know. And I'd rather not find out tonight. We really need some sleep. And to shower. I'd like to do that without worrying about what's coming up the drain."

She said, in a far-away voice as she lifted the yellowing curtain and looked into the night through the room's one lone window, "Life has to be kind of dull for S.M. these days—no new pyramids going up, no sacrifices of blood or gold being made to his glory. Just a few sorry vampire priestesses that are too brain damaged to be much company."

"Are you saying you feel sorry for him?" I asked, certain that she did not but trying to understand.

Her eyes refocused and she shook her head.

"Hell, no. I'm saying he's probably bored *as well* as nuts. That's doubly dangerous. Too much free time to think about us and brood. Best bring the guns and all the ammunition we have. Which reminds me, we are going to need to find a gun shop and get more ammo."

"Already on the list for morning," I assured her.

Ninon nodded. "Of course," she added softly. "You know . . . he may not be trying to find us. He might be looking for Saint Germain."

And I had thought my nightmares couldn't worsen.

"I really hope you're wrong about that," I said.

"Me, too. That meeting must never take place."

Women have always refused to recognize what most marriages are. Wives are slaves to their husbands. Even the convent seemed better to me. I am not saying that we should not love—to fight against nature's passions is to invite a life-long torture. Yet, a woman must consider carefully before she sets a legal seal on her deeper emotions. Passion is fleeting; marriage is not.
—*Ninon de Lenclos*

That which is striking and beautiful is not always good, but that which is good is always beautiful.
—*From a letter by Ninon de Lenclos*

I tell you on behalf of women: There is not one of us who does not prefer a little rough handling to too much consideration.
—*Letter from Ninon de Lenclos to the Marquis de Sévigné*

We would willingly say to men: Ah! In Pity's name, do not suppose us to be so very virtuous; you are forcing us to have too much of it!
—*Letter from Ninon de Lenclos to the Marquis de Sévigné*

CHAPTER FIFTEEN

"There's a storm coming at us—fast. We've been followed." Ninon turned from the window. Her eyes shone like patent leather.

"S.M.? Or Saint Germain?"

"Could be either. I suspect the dear Comte may be beating the bushes, trying to flush me into the open. He might be hoping the lightning will get me high and I'll be stupid enough to drop my guard."

"Could that happen?"

"Only if I got careless." She turned my way.

I had already half-decided that sex was a dumb idea and I wouldn't bring the matter up, even though I felt better after a shower. Then she touched me. It seemed that all the latent heat in my body roared to life and then stabbed through my skin where it actually left marks. At least this time the stimulation was enjoyable. Ninon moaned softly and leaned into me. She felt it too—the spreading fire. It didn't burn the flesh exactly; rather it melted the will. All other senses folded in on themselves. There was heat and want—that was all. We were playing with fire, literally, but I didn't even bother with a token protest about needing our strength for tomorrow. Corazon would have to stand guard for a while. I hoped Ninon was right about him being a good sentry.

We fell back onto the bed, Ninon beneath me. I caught my weight on my forearms and hovered there, taking in the view. Inches away, and she was still flawless.

Her hair lay over the edge of the bed in a dark fall of curls. Beautiful. I touched the strands, marveling at the silken texture that remained in spite of the dye. It was soft, like her mouth, and again I felt flooded with a surge of desire that was close to religious ecstasy—the kind that transforms saints and mystics and makes sane men do mad things.

This was what I had been wanting. It was the balm of Gilead. It was forgetting, a divine madness that made the pain of senses into a tool we could direct rather than a scourge that hurt us at will.

I am not one who worships from a distance. One didn't need to touch Ninon to be grateful for the beauty she graced me with, and to be aware of the exquisiteness of the occasion, but my appreciation has always been more earthy, more hands-on, and it certainly added to the pleasure of the moment.

I undressed her first, enjoying the resistance of the buttons of jeans that only reluctantly revealed the velvety skin of her belly by tantalizing inches, until they could be pulled down her hips and stripped away altogether. Her shirt went next. She wore a bra—a confection of shell pink and darker rose lace that was more alluring than functional, though it extended down her torso and had a series of small ties that had to be undone. I didn't mind at all as I kissed around the edges and then pulled the laces free one by one, pushing the silk away from the perfection of her breasts and body.

Her flesh smelled slightly of wet cornflakes, and I was puzzled until I realized that she was burning off the chemicals that gave her a fake tan. As I watched, she went from gold to cream.

Her breasts were gorgeous, her belly an expanse of perfect skin overlaid with a golden mesh of scars. I didn't stop there. There was too much to explore, to reacquaint myself with. Our first time had been too fast and too long ago.

She was stronger than her fragile appearance suggested. I loved the delicate articulation of the muscles beneath the velvety skin. Ah, the beauty of the female body! There is nothing like it. Nothing at all. And Ninon . . . No knots of bulging muscle to betray her strength, or coarse hair to mar her skin, just the smooth, almost liquid flow of movement when she moved to wrap herself around me.

Done with the first round of tactile appreciation, I took her left breast in my mouth and nibbled with the edge of my teeth. Her skin was both sweet and salty.

Ninon obligingly tightened like a bowstring beneath me, arching that graceful back and moaning as if the breath were being pulled out of her against her will. She turned her head and bit my shoulder. Her teeth were sharp and the bite almost painful. Such animal response was both thrilling and also a warning. I paused for a moment. We both had beasts inside us that could be moved to bloodlust. Because we had not shown any of the usual symptoms of vampiric bloodlust, it didn't mean it wasn't there. The hunger rising between us was not of the usual sort that happened between man and woman. The aroused appetite was enormous, an implacable lust that needed to feast.

At my hesitation, Ninon made a noise that was part moan and part growl. It had no words, but I knew exactly what it meant: *Here dwell monsters. Continue at your peril.*

I understood the danger, but didn't care. My own monster was unafraid and it wanted her very badly.

"Go on then," she whispered.

She undressed me without haste. As the clothes were

stripped away, her eyes filled with ever-growing heat. She looked raptly at the soft net of golden blemishes that now covered my chest and back. They matched the gold netting of lightning strikes that covered her body. They weren't scars exactly, but some kind of erectile tissue called to life either by the storm or by our arousal. She looked too at the marks of the stigmata clear on my skin now and didn't turn away. I was bothered, though, and I moved toward the bedside lamp. She reached out quickly and caught my hand.

"No. We'll have no darkness here. No shame, no hiding." Her voice was rough. "I'm not afraid to see you or for you to see me. We are what we are. You should know that the only way I ever do things is with my eyes wide open."

I thought of who she was and what she was and nodded. My jubilant beast tried again to break free. It wanted a chance to again take her blood.

"So be it," I managed to say.

She reached for me then, but it was my turn to stay her hands. I kissed them as I tried to calm myself.

"Slowly." My voice was rough, filled with the energy of the storm outside and my rising passions. As had happened before, I was beginning to feel a bit high.

"And yet the matter seems urgent." She had that smile again, the small one full of secret amusement.

I followed her line of sight and looked down at my penis poised between us. I laughed once. No, it didn't want to go slowly. It all but wore a neon sign that said URGENT. That creature of greed! Self-interested, careless, greedy, always wanting to have its way—and right now. It never suffered from ambivalence or caution. Still, better this beast than the other.

"Miguel?"

I realized I was still grinning as I imprisoned her hands, and Ninon was now looking more than a little amused. Laughter was an inappropriate response to the moment, but I was feeling more than a little buzzed and very wild. I think she was too.

Fate—or S.M.—tried a last time to interrupt us, but it was a miscalculation. Fists of wind struck the shutters and made them rattle like old bones. The storm was strengthening outside but that only made me higher and my desire stronger. I knew that we should leave this until the squall passed. It's what sensible people would do. But I knew we wouldn't play it safe.

"I don't want to be cautious or sensible," she murmured. Her hair began to stir as static electricity crept through it. I could smell ozone. She laid a hand on my cheek.

I realized that I was humming like a plucked guitar string. My muscles had taken in an electrical charge, drawing from the atmosphere inside the room and the rising storm beyond. My body was begging for a chance to expend the energy in Ninon. My beast was shaking, too, demanding to be fed.

"I wish I could think of something romantic to say. Because you deserve it." My voice was low and uneven as I looked into her black eyes and tried to explain. "But I am almost all animal now—and perhaps a bit crazy."

"Words are sweet, but desire is enough." She again managed to sound reasonable in spite of the pulse hammering in her throat. I loved that about her—her calm and focus. She did not fear her beast because she believed utterly in her control over it. "And sometimes a little madness is a good thing. It lets us know we're alive."

Desire. That was all she would speak of. I understood. No mention of other emotion would be allowed to intrude too far into the proceedings.

Ninon tugged her hands free and this time I didn't stop her when she reached for me. Maybe it wrong to let the beasts have any rope, to relax our vigilance, but we were going to take the chance.

I crouched above her, ignoring the creaks of the rope

bed as I lowered my mouth to hers. It was like kissing lightning. Power poured from my mouth to hers, mixed with her own storm and then rebounded, stabbing through my nerves where the charge redoubled. I pulled back with a small gasp, breaking the circuit. I stared at the pulse of veins in her throat. It hammered hard, like a prisoner demanding escape from her cell. My own heart answered. Or perhaps it was the beast, the bloodlust, demanding to be let free.

The air was cool on my skin, but not enough to stop the heat that was burning through it. Her hands slipped around my butt and traced the cleft. One hand slid over the other and then slipped over my cheeks and then between, the other roamed around to the front of my body. Her touch was not entirely gentle, and I felt every stroke in every nerve. In that moment I was all sensitized flesh and hunger for things I was afraid to put a name to.

"Your aura is so bright," she whispered.

So was hers. I could feel the light and heat beginning to dance over my skin. The reaction was too intense. I knew that we should stop.

"So beautiful," she whispered, and then turned back to my lips. She cradled me in the relative coolness of her body, accepting my heat—even demanding it. She still did not fear the beasts inside or the storm around us.

Amazed, I moved down to her breasts, crisscrossed in a relief of gold now, and suckled, being very careful to keep the stinger curled under my tongue. She twisted fingers into my hair and pulled my head back toward her lips. Though I should have been a gentleman, I didn't cooperate. Instead I slid lower, biting the underside of her breast with enough force to mark but not break the skin. The beast was excited by this, and I could feel my tongue trying to uncurl itself. I turned my head and distracted myself with the sensation of her smooth, heated skin under my cheek.

Though she resisted slightly with her handholds, I slid

lower. Her scent aroused me, a patchouli that was generally feminine and yet specific to her. I knew that I would always be able to recognize her, even without sight or touch.

My hands flexed into the muscles of her thighs, urging them to open. She resisted briefly and then gave in, crying out when my thumb flicked over her clitoris and then slipped inside. Her legs moved restlessly, shifting over the nylon of the sleeping bag and making it sigh.

I set my mouth to her, enjoying how this flesh also changed. I wanted to devour her, to draw blood, to stab into this softest flesh with my tongue. I also thought that I would ignite—perhaps electrocute us both. The electricity dancing over our skin was visible now and surrounded us in a halo of gold.

We had to end it at once; it was too dangerous to wait. Sex games could come later when the storm passed. We had dared Fate and our beasts enough for one night.

I slid back up her body and her legs whipped around me, as though securing her against another escape. She was strong, stronger than any woman I had ever been with. She was also ready. I slid into her and the tempest was on us immediately. There was a flash of radiance, a sheet of white that ran down our bodies in both directions from where we were joined. I covered her mouth as she screamed. The shock threw her into erotic convulsions, and I followed immediately, burying my face in the nylon to muffle my own beastly roars.

And just like that, the storm—inside and out—was gone.

"That was reckless," she said softly. "But I think we're okay."

"Your hair," I said, reaching for it. The color had changed to dark gold.

"Dye doesn't last. I have to recolor it every few days. Plastic surgery doesn't work for long either. I've tried. Tissues simply rearrange themselves back into their intended order." Ninon snuggled against me, fitting into my arms as if she had always been there. She looked relaxed, without pain, and I realized that I felt better too. The sex had burned out my nerve endings and I could no longer feel.

I knew I should think about this new information, but instead I slept.

I dreamed of Cormac that night. It felt real, but I knew I was dreaming when I saw the croft as it had been in my childhood, and therefore wasn't terribly surprised when he showed up. He came in through the only door, covered in raindrops and smelling of wind.

"Hullo, Da."

It hurt to see him. It might be different for you, but for me, most memory is about pain; good moments are about loss, and the bad . . . well, they are terrible. Instead of relaxing in his presence, I felt my body brace itself.

"Hullo, son. Have ye some room by the fire?"

Son? He hadn't called me that in years. We both preferred Miguel.

Uneasy, I shifted over reluctantly so that he could pull up a chair. The peat was burning low but gave out a welcome heat. Steam rose gently from the kettle and I knew in a while he would ask me to make some tea. All was normal, except that it was somehow subtly wrong.

"I didn't think I'd see you again," I told him. "You always said that dead was dead and you had no plans on becoming a ghost."

"True, true. But it's only right that I meet your lass. She's a bonnie wee thing, I hear." I couldn't quite make out his eyes in the dark, but something about them was different. Also, his accent wasn't quite right. He sounded more like me when I lapse into Scots.

"Aye, that she is," I agreed, trying not to stare.

"Shouldn't you introduce us?" he asked, smiling gently and waving a hand at a cot on the side of the room. I turned my head and wasn't surprised to see Ninon there.

I resisted this idea though, had I been awake and Cormac real, I would have done precisely that.

"How? This is just a dream," I hedged.

"Aye, but it would take only a small effort for you to contact her." His accent had disappeared. "Just reach out for her with your mind and tell her that you want her to meet your father. She'll let us in."

Father. Cormac hardly ever referred to himself as my father. He was Da or Dad to me, and Cormac to his friends.

At that moment a strange and unpleasant odor reached up and clawed at my nose, insisting on my attention. I sniffed discretely. The smell was coming from Cormac, a smell I was coming to know and dread.

No, I thought. No! Don't let this be.

"I . . . I don't know how." But a part of me did.

"Sure you do, son."

There was something very, very wrong with his eyes now. And he kept calling me son. This wasn't my Da. It was some evil phantom wearing his memory. The disappointment was crushing.

Just then I heard a cat howl and felt a sharp pain in my leg. The thing that looked like Cormac gave a growl of his own and leaned toward me.

I jerked awake and found Ninon hovering over me. Her fair fell over her now pale skin, a thick veil that parted at her breasts, letting her nipples show through. For once, this sight didn't move me to lust. Perhaps it was the low, menacing growling that filled the air.

I looked in the growler's direction. Corazon was at the end of the bed, his fur sticking out until he looked like puff adder. I felt blood on my leg from where he clawed me. Sweat was pouring off of my body. The room was stifling, but that wasn't why I was perspiring.

"It was Saint Germain, wasn't it?" Ninon said. "He was trying to get into your head."

Saint Germain? That sounded right.

"He was in my head." My voice was raspy. I watched the cat, waiting for his fur to flatten. "He was trying to get into yours."

She reached for my face, forcing my head her way. Her eyes had widened.

"Through you? He knew you?" she asked. "He was trying to work through you? To get at me?"

"Yes. I pretended not to know how." I swallowed. My eyes flicked downward. Corazon was beginning to calm, but I feared our already tenuous relationship had suffered a setback. A pity, because I was truly grateful that he had brought me back to the here and now. "I didn't know it was him. Not at first. I thought it was my father."

Ninon laid a comforting hand on my chest as though to soothe my troubled heart. And in a way, she did.

"I'm so sorry, Miguel. I shouldn't have seduced you. That's his favorite trick—the sneaky, conniving bastard. And I'm afraid that it's bad news that he's found us this way. We just have to be glad he didn't send a demon."

"It won't happen again." I'm not sure why I said that. There was no way I could know it was true, except that I was really determined to not let that foul thing back in my brain. The lesson was learned. I didn't want to see any more impersonations of people I knew and cared for.

It's odd how emotional pain works. Those nails hammered into the heart can kill you if they go too deep, but they can also pound important lessons home. For me, all my heart lessons centered around loss—loss of family, loss of options, loss of trust. I understood; bad things did indeed happen to good people. Justice was a concept rarely seen in real life. And hope was foolish, because it left you vulnerable. Translated, that meant: Cormac was dead, no one would punish S.M. or Saint Germain unless we did, and I couldn't trust anyone except Ninon. Maybe not even her.

"No, it won't happen again. I'll watch for him now as

well." She was definite. "And he's played his high card, using your father that way. An Achilles' heel is only vulnerable if you don't know about it. He's done his worst. You'll be wary now."

I was really glad to hear her say this, because dread lingered in me. But I realized she was right. He had played his high card. There wasn't much left. Moira, my childhood sweetheart, was long dead and mostly forgotten. She would lack power as a weapon even if I fell for the same trick twice. Cormac was the only person from my old life that I had ever loved completely, the only one I had trusted enough to let into my heart and dreams—and I'd damn sure bar the door against him if he ever appeared again.

Which left only Ninon. I had a bad feeling that she was my second point of vulnerability. Saint Germain would never get to my dreams through her, but there were so many other ways that she could be taken hostage.

I didn't say any of that. Instead, I rolled from the bed and began gathering my clothes. It was almost dawn and time we were moving on. We had a wizard to kill and I was coming to understand, more each day, that this wouldn't be easy.

My indisposition continues, my friend, and I never go out in the day.
—*From a letter by Ninon de Lenclos to St. Evremond.*

Vulnerant omnia, ultima necat. (All hours wound you, the last one kills.)
—*Latin proverb*

A woman is much better persuaded that she is loved by what she guesses than by what she is told.
—*Letter from Ninon de Lenclos to the Marquis de Sévigné*

A true friend is the greatest of all blessings, and that which we take the least care of all to acquire.
—*François de la Rochefoucauld*

CHAPTER SIXTEEN

As I mentioned before, time had become meaningless; it belonged to another world. I did send off my deathly-sick-in-a-one-phone-village message to my boss before we left the next morning, asking for an extension of my leave, for all the good it would do. It might buy a little time, but I had every expectation of someday reaching my house—assuming I even got back, which was a large assumption—and discovering that it had been cleaned out, basement to attic, by one of the many three-letter agencies who were concerned with the comings and goings of certain kinds of scientists. This violation of my privacy probably should have bothered me, but it all seemed to belong to a life that was over. Anyway, Saint Germain had taught me what real violation of privacy was. The rest was nothing when compared to that.

If my old life was gone, then departed too was the terminal loneliness that went with it, the awful backdrop for my life that had become a depressing wallpaper of the mind resisting all my previous efforts to strip or paint over it. Ninon had burned it away.

True, I was leaving the comfort of the known, and a lucrative and prestigious career, to chase a homicidal maniac who wanted his ghouls to eat me, but the trade was worthwhile. I still find it somewhat amazing how I walked away—first physically and then mentally—and left it all behind without even a twinge of regret. That's what rage and determination—and lust—will do for you. Like a snake, I just shed that constricting skin and moved on.

I also started keeping a journal, the notes that have turned into this story. Perhaps it is different for you, but I find that writing puts me in control, that it allows me to blunt the edges of cold hard truth, dressing them in optimistic padding that sometimes—*sometimes*—helps me look at hard things without getting cut and bruised. This works for me because the mind is strong, and belief can indeed move mountains. It often lets me believe that all will be well even when statistics say otherwise.

As we drove out along the road—a horrible stretch of cracked paving and then dirt that I suppose could have been worse, but only with a direct act of divine intervention—I found myself thinking about a conversation I'd had with Ninon some time before. A day ago? Two days perhaps? I had lost track. We had been speaking about Saint Germain. I had expressed curiosity about him and wondered if he had been the victim of the standard abuses we hear so many sociopaths were subject to.

Her reply had been adamant. "You must not think of him this way—as a person, a victim. He has renounced all claims to humanity. Do you think that in the past I've never had moments of compassion for him?" she asked. "Times when I pitied the creature for the horrible childhood he must have had? Of course I have. But, Miguel, the thing with someone who has formally embraced evil is that no amount of kindness can wipe out what was done to him. It's too late for love or therapy. The bridges are burned. This is a case where no sufficient reparation to him or from him can be made. The broken cannot be mended, not by us. Maybe by God. Maybe." She paused. "Understand this: He doesn't want to change. He's not looking for a way out of this situation, a chance to redeem himself. He likes the power and wants more. Maybe it's because Daddy didn't love him, perhaps it's his growing insanity, I don't know. All I can say is that he will kill us—and many others—if he is not stopped."

I had changed—aged, grown harder. Seeing those zombies—and, yes, his using my father's image as a way to trick me into letting him get near Ninon—had colored in the remaining gray areas for me. Ninon was right. Saint Germain, for whatever cause, was evil. And evil, true evil, cannot be seen as anything but black in a white world. You have to be absolute in your thinking because evil is absolute; it will show no compassion or mercy. It is not human and that is not its nature. To think of evil in any other way is to invite its invasion through chinks in your armor.

I was also wondering a lot about Fate these days, what Ninon might see as God's will. Perhaps I just suffered from really bad luck. Actually, I knew I suffered from bad luck. The only question was whether it was random, a statistical fluke. Why had I come back to Mexico? Was it really for help? Trying to find some long-lost cure for my disease carved into ancient stones? Or was it that I could feel myself giving in to S.M.'s power and wanted to be near someone—anyone, even my brain-impaired mother—who understood what was happening? Or was it—maybe—a higher purpose that brought me? Had I been selected as a tool? A comforting thought, but was I rationalizing because I was squeamish about what needed to be done?

Have you ever noticed that self-appraisal can turn into paralyzing second-guessing? I decided to quit before I got to the part where I was asking God about the meaning of my life. Some questions and doubts were just too big when you were on a zombie hunt. You can't afford those kinds of distractions when you are facing the worst moments of your existence.

I wished, not for the first time, that I had a dog. I'd wanted a pet for a long time but had known it was impossible. I'd gone to an animal shelter once and caused a panic. The dogs had been terrified of me. Maybe now that the change of electrocution had blunted the worst of the blood-hunger, I could get a pet and have it not be afraid of me.

Ninon's Jeep picked up a rock and flung it at my windshield, breaking my reverie. I peered out the side window. The sky said it was noon and so did my bladder.

I pulled up alongside Ninon as soon the goat path we were on widened enough to do so without losing paint to the nasty flora and knifelike stones that lined the path, and I shouted, "Ready to eat?" It was hard to see her. We were kicking up a dust trail worthy of a cattle stampede. She nodded reluctantly. Now that she had decided on a path, she resented the time we had to give to food or even rest, but she also knew we needed both since neither long life nor vampirism conferred cast-iron kidneys.

"I know a place. Turn up here," she shouted back. She jerked her head to indicate that we should take the left fork that we were rolling up on at about thirty-five miles per hour. The slow paced bothered her too, but any faster and we'd have needed to find a dentist to fix our loosened teeth. Thank heaven for seatbelts. We would have been concussed without them. The road wasn't so much potholed as chasmed.

I was about to fall back behind Ninon—the dirt road wasn't really wide enough to accommodate both vehicles—when I saw Ninon's eyes widen as she leaned forward over her steering wheel. My own gaze jerked forward and there it caught on something unexplainable. In front of us stood, or rather crouched, a satyr. I say satyr because he—it—had the face and torso of a man, but its legs were all goat—backward joints and all. Except it was a hairless goat and seemed to lack genitals, almost as though someone had sewn a badly cured hide over a goat's legs. Nudity in this situation was shocking enough, but there was another anomaly. This . . . this *thing* had what looked a great deal like a bloodied human arm dangling from its mouth.

It was the worst thing I'd ever seen.

You know, I may have to stop using the word "worst." Every time I think I've seen the worst, something else happens to prove me wrong. I used to think that the creepiest thing you could do to a corpse was embalm it. Then I ran into Mamita. Then I saw zombies. I'd thought they could never be topped. But I was wrong; this thing increased that magnitude of wrongness tenfold.

Looking at this nightmare creature, I had one of those moments of shock that can't last more than a second but that feels like an eternity. As my foot moved toward my brake, Ninon punched her accelerator and aimed her Jeep right at the creature, planning on mowing it down. I admit—this shocked me. It was so repellent that I didn't even want to touch it with my SUV.

I quickly lost sight of it in the churned-up dust that boiled under my skidding tires and Ninon's acceleration, but not before I saw it grin a challenge and toss the remains of its dinner at Ninon's windshield.

Ninon applied the brakes. Fortunately I saw the red lights and was able to swerve past as her Jeep did a one-eighty. She was barely stopped before she erupted from her vehicle with gun drawn, saying something in French that I have never found in a phrase book. I couldn't help but notice that, surrounded as we were by the triangular stones, she looked like she was standing in a giant shark's mouth, shouting imprecations at the sky as the huge fish swallowed her in one dusty gulp.

She let off a shot, but only one because it was immediately apparent that ricochets off the surrounding rocks could be dangerous to us and the vehicles. Anyway, the creature was gone, vanished into a stand of cactus and then down one of the many tunnels created by the piles of cracked boulders dumped there by some glacier many eons ago.

I had a bad moment when I thought Ninon might be crazy enough to accept the challenge and chase it into the labyrinth, but even enraged, she was too canny to get lured into what was probably a trap.

Corazon apparently had some doubts too, because he flew out of the window and planted himself in front of her, his back arched and his hair standing out all over his body in a way that was almost comical. Almost. I knew now that this stance meant Saint Germain—in some form—was somewhere nearby.

I ran up to Ninon, telling myself to keep breathing, that this atavistic fear could be ignored. This new creature was nothing worse. Okay, the last zombies hadn't been eating anything when we saw them, but dead was dead, and zombies weren't so bad as foes went. Sure, this thing had suffered from a hideous birth defect, but however warped, it was still just a body without a soul or much in the way of brains—a ghost. Zombies had physical presence but were haunts just the same; human once but no more. And statistically, it was a lot more likely that I would be hit by a bus or struck by lightning—well, that last was a given—than end up eaten by anything, let alone a zombie. They weren't fast enough to catch us, and they weren't that bright. The ones we had seen back in that ghost town were obviously more than a few French fries short of a Happy Meal. Maybe this creature had appeared to be deliberately flinging down a bloodied gauntlet, but that was just a trick of the light aided by paranoia. There was no need for me to feel so cold and revolted. I was a big bad vampire, damn it! I didn't have to be afraid of anything on two legs, no matter how weird those legs were.

"Not a zombie. A zombie wouldn't be out feeding at noon," Ninon corrected, as though hearing my thoughts.

She walked over to where the arm had fallen and picked it up. She sniffed delicately. My eyes locked on the thick gold wedding band still encircling the ring finger of the bloodied hand that hung limply. It didn't take Sherlock Holmes to deduce that this was a man's arm torn off at the shoulder. It also hadn't been torn off for long, because there was little smell of decay and no rigor mortis.

"Not a zombie?" I repeated. I had heard her the first time; I just didn't like the news and was appealing the verdict.

She dropped the arm at the base of some spiny plant and rubbed her fingers on her jeans. I saw her point— who'd want to go on touching the thing if they didn't have to? And we really couldn't keep it. We didn't even have an ice chest to store it in. Besides, I couldn't see us strolling into some police station and trying to report this to the local authorities. She had her priorities straight. Still, the coldness, the ruthless dismal of the act made me shiver. As I have mentioned before, Ninon can be scary.

"No. It's a ghoul, a genuine Frankensteinian monster. Those are worse. Real bad. A zombie will try to kill you if it's ordered to, but ghouls kill just because they like to eat people. They're also fast and very strong and can endure daylight if they must. Some of them are fairly bright. They can think for themselves. They have initiative."

"And you are saying that was a ghoul." I know, I know! I sounded like an idiot, but I just couldn't take it all in. At least I didn't ask her to explain the thing I was really wondering about—like, how the hell something like that was created. A Frankenstein monster? Was that possible, sewing together human and nonhuman parts? But such questions had to wait. She had covered the points that were relevant. They were fast, strong, smart, and liked to eat people. The remedial course in Monsters 101 could wait.

"At least one. Usually they travel in pairs or even packs. Damn it! Saint Germain's working too quickly, or else he's been down here for longer than I suspected. How the hell will we ever get a jump on him?" For the first time I heard frustration in her voice. She turned back to the Jeep.

I had no answer for her, just growing determination to rid the world of this sick bastard. Any trace of compassion for him was long gone. His blackness got blacker and blacker.

"We need more guns and more ammunition." She opened the door for Corazon. Crimson flags of rage were flying in her pale cheeks. She hadn't had time to reapply the self-tanner or dye her hair.

"Do you think that man was alive? When it took his arm? Should we look for him?" I asked, unable to help myself. It was a stupid question. The dead don't bleed—not that much—and the arm was covered in clotted blood. That guy was a goner.

"No, he was dead." Ninon looked me in the eyes as she said this, but I knew she was lying to spare me.

"It's going to be a real pleasure to kill this son-of-a-bitch," I said, and I meant it. And I wasn't speaking of the ghoul, though I wanted that abomination dead too. The very thought of it sharing the earth and air with humankind offended me.

Again, Ninon understood. In a way, it was reassuring that we both still identified ourselves with the human race.

"Yes. Sadly, yes." Ninon walked back to her Jeep. "I keep telling myself that we have no choice. I hope that will make it better when the time comes. He's the last, you know. The only one who knows how to raise the dead, to make these ghouls and zombies. If we kill him before he finds an apprentice, it's over—for good or bad."

"Thank you, God, for each small blessing," I muttered. As a scientist, I should have wanted to preserve this information. As a human—even only a nominal one—I could only wish it gone.

"Truthfully, I never thought the day would pass when I

would rejoice so completely in another's death. That I can kill now without regret brings me no happiness."

She meant that she feared we were turning into monsters ourselves. I felt bad that I could offer no comfort, but what could I say? I already knew that I was half fiend. My brain—my emotions—were simply slow to catch up with the reality of my changed body and circumstances.

"Well, looking on the bright side . . . ," I began.

"Yes?" She slammed her door and examined a dent her ricocheting bullet had put in it.

"This makes me feel better about the vampirism. It seems positively natural by comparison."

Ninon nodded, clearly distracted by other thoughts.

"Never mind food. Miguel, we need guns. I know this other place. It's kind of drug-dealer hangout, a clearing house for marijuana and cocaine. I would have avoided it if I could, but they have the kind of things we need there. They might even have grenades."

Grenades. Of course.

"Also—and I am sorry for this—I think we may have to steal some things," she went on.

"Sure," I said. Then: "Why steal?"

"It wouldn't be wise to let these people know we have money. We already have enough things trying to kill us. No need to add drug dealers to the lists."

"Excellent point." And why balk at a little thing like robbery after all the rest?

We climbed back into our vehicles and headed for Ninon's den of thieves, where I would begin my career as a bandit. It was nothing compared to what I'd already done, and I wasn't feeling particularly enthused.

I do not agree with what you have to say, but I'll defend to the death your right to say it.
—*Voltaire*

The human heart, which will be the subject of these letters, presents so many contrasts that whosoever lays it bare must fall into a flood of contradictions. You think something stable in your grasp and then find that you have seized a shadow. . . . I confess that I am not free from grave scruples since I can scarcely be sincere without slandering my own sex a little. . . . We will undertake a journey of morals together.
—*Letter from Ninon de Lenclos to the Marquis de Sévigné*

He was a man beyond definition; with a soul of pulp, a body of wet paper, and a heart of pumpkin fricasseed in snow.
—*Letter from Ninon de Lenclos about the Marquis de Sévigné*

It is easier to know men in general, than men in particular.
—*François de la Rochefoucauld*

CHAPTER SEVENTEEN

We stopped just outside *La Boca del Conchinillo*. The Mouth of the Suckling Pig—how appropriate. We could see the town rising before us, the buildings seeming to do a slow shimmy, caught in the waves of heat emanating off the desert floor. Once again this was another slice of Hell, only this one came with barred windows and barbed wire on the tops of the buildings. It looked a lot like a prison.

Ninon emerged from her Jeep wearing the dress she'd had on the first night I tried to seduce her. The dress was vintage—a work by Alfred Shaheen, she told me later—with a winged bust that would have looked a bit like the back end of a '56 Chevy Bel Aire had Chevrolet made any cars in two-tone neon.

Her hair was loose and she wore red lipstick. She looked like a '50s Hollywood vamp, the kind who always hung out with gangsters. She batted her eyes at me and had me convinced that she was a brainless bimbo, that if she'd ever managed to have a thought it had gone and died of loneliness waiting for company to show up. The outlines of her plan began to suggest itself. In a movie it would be amusing—but, here? I wasn't entirely enthused. If fact, I didn't like it at all.

"Does it hurt when your IQ falls so hard?" I asked.

She wrinkled her brow and pouted, as though trying to understand were a labor just this side of childbirth.

I laughed reluctantly.

"Really, is this wise?" I persisted. "Couldn't we just sneak in and take what we want?"

"There will be alarms and watchmen. Someone will have to distract them. And I think they are less likely to put a bullet in me than in you. I bet they'll even be happy to give me some gas."

I had a crude thought that they would definitely want to give her something, and it wouldn't be fuel. I didn't say anything, though. All those mandatory on-the-job sensitivity seminars had trained me well. Anyway, she was probably right about us needing a diversion while I stole things, and the less alarming the diversion the better.

We traveled the rest of the way to town in her Jeep, kicking up a plume of dust that would be visible to any lookout. Corazon didn't like it, but Ninon made him wait in my SUV while we went into the village. I didn't argue the call, but had a strong suspicion that I would return to find that the annoyed animal had carved his initials in my upholstery. If not worse. I really hoped he contained himself. Nothing smelled quite as bad as cat urine in a hot car.

The Jeep didn't smell at all. I was grateful. So many rentals and secondhand vehicles smelled like a gym locker. Ninon and Corazon were obviously fastidious.

Ninon pushed in a tape and the sounds of Sourdough Slim's yodels filled the air. This made me flinch, but I reminded myself that she wasn't trying to be stealthy. An upfront approach would help ease any suspicions about her.

We stopped just at the edge of the still village, leaving the Jeep in the open but screened by a large stand of prickly pear. Sourdough's lament about a strawberry roan was cut off midsong.

We waited. And waited. No one approached, nothing moved. We looked at one another, feeling vague unease. Drug dealers weren't this careless. We decided to be a shade less open in our advance. No act would fool a ghoul or zombie.

As we crept closer, we finally heard the distant strains of music. Guitar—good guitar—can usually make my hands ache with old longing, but I felt nothing that day. Partly that was because this was a recording, but also the air of desolation was thickening. I was tempted to suggest turning back, but knew Ninon would refuse. We needed weapons and our options were limited.

We made our way through the available shadows as we approached the only building in town that showed signs of life.

The windows of the squat house where a boom box played were shuttered but in bad repair, so it was easy enough to lay an eye against the crack and have a look-see at what was beyond. We had apparently arrived on poker day. Four of humankind's more primitive specimens were bellied up to a round kitchen table covered in American currency and surrounded by a minefield of beer bottles. None of the poker players would be trying out for Mr. Universe anytime soon, but they didn't have to worry about anyone kicking sand in their faces either.

If this weren't off-putting enough, the air was thick with smoke and the sound of the Gypsy Kings, who they were torturing by playing it on a CD player that had seen better days. Dust is hard on electronics and cars. Ninon and I both carried spare air filters for this reason.

We backed away quickly. Neither of us was smiling.

"I don't like this," I whispered, looking up and down the street. "It's too dead. If we hadn't seen those guys, I would think this was another of Saint Germain's zombie towns."

"It does seem abandoned. But maybe the drug dealers prefer it this way," Ninon suggested softly. "I haven't smelled any zombies or ghouls yet."

I sniffed. I didn't smell any either. Still, there was something nasty riding the air, causing a feeling of impending violence that tickled the hairs of my nape.

"We need guns and ammo and anything else we can find. If Saint Germain has made a ghoul pack . . ." Ninon spread her hands wide. Sometimes she is very French. I knew what she meant though. We had to deal with this. It wasn't like we could call a support group.

"Okay," I said. "You're sure they keep the guns around back?"

"Yes, I can smell them."

Once she mentioned it, I also smelled the faint odor of gun oil. Maybe that was what was bugging me—guns, violence. It was a good match. I told the small hairs on my nape to lie back down. They didn't listen.

"I'll be quick," I promised. "You be careful. Scream if anything goes wrong. Anything."

"I'm always careful." Ninon got up and adjusted her dress—and not to make it more modest. She swayed toward the door, balancing on those ridiculously high heels that they call stilettos.

In spite of my promise to hurry, I hung around long enough to make sure that she wasn't gunned down immediately upon walking through the door.

I shouldn't worry about her, I scolded myself. These were, after all, mere males. But I remained, pressed against the shutter.

I could see straightaway that Ninon's main target was a middle-aged man, a Latino Jackie Gleason. He looked marginally friendlier that the others. She made her voice high and giggled nonstop as she swayed in on ridiculously high heels telling a tale in fractured Spanish about getting lost and running out of gas. The sound was grating but she was doing a stupendous impersonation of a woman so stupid that she almost needed her own branch on the great ape family tree: one above gorillas but below chimps and humans. Had I been part of the crowd, the only thing that would have saved her from strangling was the fact that she was so damned beautiful. But then, I have perfect pitch. Maybe these guys were tone-deaf. Maybe they were really just gorillas who had managed to shave and liked feeling intellectually superior to someone for a change. Mr. Muscle on the far side of the table certainly looked closer to a gorilla than a Homo sapien.

Certain that she had successfully distracted everyone in the room and that they were not offering her anything more deadly than leers, I slipped around back to see what I could discover.

It was easy to find the place where the weapons were stored; I just followed my nose and those upright hairs that twitched. Warmer, warmer, hot!

The room seemed as empty as the rest of the town, but I remained cautious. First stop for the new cat burglar was a small barred window where I again did a bit of reconnoitering. A quick peek told me the room inside was empty. There also was a locked door with a barred window, but the catch was flimsy and I am very strong. I also wasn't worried about being heard above Ninon's shrill laughter, shouts of *Tequila!* and the Gypsy Kings that could be heard even through two sets of walls. It seemed certain that nothing short of a raid would get their attention now.

The air inside was stale and the light almost nonexistent. I saw no obvious gun lockers, no weapons of any kind. In fact, under normal circumstances, there was nothing there that would have encouraged me to linger. But these were hardly normal days, so linger I did, looking for the useful weapons my nose could smell.

Excepting an exquisite woman—to which I am as vulnerable as the next man—I am a less-than-usually visual person. I live more in my mind than most men, but because of my heightened sense of hearing and smell, I tend to use these senses as much as I do sight. Perhaps that is why I was less than moved by the portrait in front of me.

I don't mean to be critical—after all, art is a personal choice. But I saw that this artist wasn't especially gifted. In fact, I am sure it was an amateur piece. It was a woman—actually just a very graphic diagram of the least interesting parts of the female body. So bad was it, I felt safe in assuming that it had never graced the covers of any of the finer men's magazines. Still, it drew me more than the more tasteful watercolors on the other wall. I laid my hand on the frame and began to feel around it. I had a strange woman's breast nearly pressed against my eye.

They say that a picture is worth a thousand words—but not in fiction. Not unless it's exceptionally good art and the author exceptionally awful. All a picture can do is show. Give me a thousand words and I will make you smell and taste and feel. This portrait was maybe a small but tasteless step down from the velvet dogs playing poker, however it still interested me because of the gun safe I smelled behind it. Breaking in might have been a challenge, but fortunately it had been left open.

I wasn't interested in the money or the documents inside, though a more larcenous man would have pocketed them. But I was very happy to see the 9-millimeter handgun ammunition and the semiautomatic rifle. It was a classic, the M1 carbine. If you're not up on your guns, let me explain my enthusiasm for this find. This model has been made since the Second World War and is still in production today. It's perfect because it's lightweight, has a short muzzle that is good in tight places, rarely jams, and ammunition is readily available. Especially in this drug dealer's back room. He had stacks of it. I found a paper sack and began loading it. With this treasure, we could take on a small ghoul nation.

I still preferred my shotgun in a tight spot, but this would be excellent for Ninon. It would be great long range, much better than her pistol. She'd be pleased.

I didn't waste time searching the office for the missing handgun that went with the ammo; it was a sure thing that one of the poker players had it at the table. More would have been better, but this was a good score and things were going smoothly. Ninon was going to be sorry about the lack of grenades and rocket launchers, though. Still, I was thinking we were golden. Mission accomplished.

On the way back to her, I suffered my first distraction. I was passing a second small door, something that might open into a utility closet, when I heard a familiar but not immediately placeable sound. *Thump-bump, thump-bump,* like a really slow heartbeat. I also smelled something. Something at once appealing and unpleasant.

Hesitating, I slung the shotgun over my shoulder with the carbine and laid an ear against the door. The sound got louder but no clearer. *Thump-bump, thump-bump.* It was too rhythmic to be someone knocking, but something about it . . .

Knowing it was unlikely that I would find more weapons, I still put my hand on the doorknob and gave it a slow twist. It wasn't locked. I looked about quickly before I entered. I was still alone. Nothing moved in the sun-baked street. Nothing.

The door opened without protest and I found myself, not in a utility closet, but in the kitchen part of a small, low-ceilinged house. The thumping noise was coming from through an open door to the left. I approached slowly, skirting a small table with a coffee cup and a vase of dying flowers. I put my bag of ammo and the rifle down. I was alone, but I walked quietly and warily, my breath held.

The owners must have been fairly wealthy people by local standards—perhaps Americans who had retired down there, drug dealers who decided to splurge on a few comforts for the housekeeper. The place had a paved floor, a gas range, a small refrigerator, and a washer and dryer. It was the last two appliances that were tucked in the small laundry room and laboring diligently. New, compact, and sparkling white, they were also smeared with ugly stains that could only be blood. Now that I was inside, the odor was drifting my way.

Someone was hurt, I thought. Then: Someone is dead.

I thought about the ghoul's arm.

I looked left. *Thump-bump, thump-bump.* There should have been flies gathered in the blood, but none had ventured near because of the pounding that shook the machine. I had seen this before when loads of heavy sheets or comforters were severely unbalanced. The washing machine had begun walking across the floor, its metal feet scraping deep grooves in the adobe tiles as it teetered.

I crossed the room slowly, hating the smell of rotting lilies, burnt coffee, and semi-fresh blood. The three smells, each bad enough alone, were unutterably horrible together in that hot, airless room.

Thump-bump. Thump-bump.

It wasn't just the washer. Something heavy and solid was rolling around inside the dryer, making a slamming sound that was audible even over the clanking of the swaying washer on spin cycle. Reluctantly, I leaned down and peered in the dryer's dark window—and was immediately sorry I did. What I assume were the house's late owners peered back at me as their heads tumbled by, frozen expressions shocked and outraged.

I gagged and reeled back against the rough wall, feeling dizzy. The washer moved closer, pleading to be spared another spin cycle, but no power on earth would have been able to get me to open and see what was going through the rinse.

It took a moment for my disorientation to wear off, but as soon as my brain unlocked I began thinking hard. I know that such an act of barbarism should suggest insanity or some brutal drug-dealer's revenge, but it somehow didn't. This was beyond bizarre, beyond revenge, beyond insanity. It was like the severed arm that the ghoul had thrown at Ninon. It was a challenge, a taunt, aimed at us. Something done to provoke us into action. I realized that we were *supposed* to find this—and this terrible idea, once born, raised those small hairs on the back of my neck until they stood on end.

We were *supposed* to find this, and be outraged. Therefore, someone knew that we were here. Someone cruel and insane.

We had two candidates. But since there was no lake or stream nearby, I was betting on it being Saint Germain.

I glanced at the corner of the dining room I could see from where I stood pressed against the wall, making sure I was still alone. I was. And this time I noticed that there was a wooden ladder leaned against the wall, leading up to a trapdoor in the ceiling. The square was not sealed tightly and stray shafts of sunlight leaked into the room.

Ignore it, I told myself. *Whatever's up there, you don't want to see. It might even be a trap. Just signal Ninon that the job is done and get out of here.*

Yet, a moment later I was climbing the stepladder up to the roof, arguing that I needed to know if the Jeep had been found and perhaps tampered with, or if there was anyone—or anything—between us and a safe getaway.

I ventured out slowly, looking for booby traps or sentries, or, I admit, ax-wielding maniacs. But nothing sinister was up there except a selection of dead cockroaches and a few cracks in the slanted adobe that needed immediate repair. The clay was burned in several places and I suspected that it had been hit with lightning.

The thought was further cause for anxiety, but I didn't hurry away. The roof offered an excellent view of the town, and more than ever I wanted to be sure that Ninon and I wouldn't be running into a trap when we tried to leave.

I could hear the faint strains of music coming from the left. Just music. No screams or gunshots, not even any more shouts for tequila. That was good. That probably meant the homicidal housekeeper was having a coffee break somewhere else before starting the ironing on the entrails, or whipping up cannibal smoothies.

I squatted down and crab-walked to the low wall that encircled the roof, being careful to avoid the cockroach carapaces. There were clay drainpipes around the edge at four foot intervals, large enough to stuff my hands in, but I would have to lie flat to see out of them, something I was reluctant to do. I listened some more, my breath held. Nothing moved, nothing disturbed the eerie silence. Not so much a bird called or a dog barked.

Zombie town, I thought again. I couldn't smell them, but that didn't mean they weren't there, hiding in the houses, waiting for dark.

Inch by inch, I raised my head until I could peer over the wall. What I saw was not reassuring. No one was near Ninon's Jeep, but something very bad had happened here recently—and I didn't think it was drug dealers looking for a little privacy and sending the townfolks for vacation in Puerto Vallarta. For one thing, people didn't go off and leave their house and car doors standing open.

And there was that open gun locker, full of cash but only one weapon.

I looked south. Some the buildings near the town square had been decked with bunting for a fiesta or perhaps a parade, and it hadn't yet begun to fade in the summer sun. That would happen very quickly, in only a day or so. Obviously, they couldn't have been up that long. There was also a table of food—almost black with flies—and half-empty punch bowls laid out in the village square. Worse still, a few torches were still flickering. Whatever had happened, it had been recent. I didn't see any bodies or blood, but the place was as dead as a graveyard. Whether the people had enjoyed their party or not, they had been driven away or killed before they had a chance to take the decorations down and finish their sangria.

If it were the latter and they were dead, I thought, *God grant that our enemies' destruction will give them consolation for their lost lives.*

I rubbed a hand over my face. It was Hell at high noon,

a landscape worthy of Dante. I hadn't prayed since childhood, but my subconscious recalled its teachings and began reciting the prayer for the dead.

I had another moment of dizziness. The heat was worse
now than it had been all day, especially up there in the
open with the baking cockroach carcasses. Summer was
here and the lightning-damaged adobe was baking itself
into powdered clay that fell from the walls softly like a
swarm of dead moths. I watched the plaster fall off the
building across the street, mesmerized, as it seemed to
float on the air to the soft strains of wheezing flamenco
guitars.

I think maybe the sun was baking my brain too. Something must account for my sudden stupor.

As I stared at the flaking plaster and thought about
dead moths, Saint Germain walked into the square. A
breeze, perhaps stirred up by his passing, made the
bunting flutter. He paused at the feast table where he
helped himself to whatever was in the punch bowls. I
turned my head slowly and blinked twice and then twice
again, unable to believe my eyes. I'd never seen him before, and yet I knew beyond any doubt that this was our
enemy. I also finally caught of whiff of spoiled food and
what could only be human blood.

He sat casually on the edge of the table. I watched his
throat work as he swallowed the red sludge and had a sick
feeling—part disgust but part envy, I have to admit—that
he was drinking blood.

Saint Germain was drinking blood. From a punch bowl.
All alone. Something wasn't right. I mean, less right that
even we expected. Ninon hadn't said anything about him
drinking blood. Could he be some kind of vampire after
all? I shook my head again. This was Alice-through-the-
Looking-Glass time.

I should have left then, don't you think? Found Ninon
and gotten the hell out of Dodge, even if I had to shoot
the poker players to do it. But I didn't. I just squatted

there, stunned as any deer in headlights and watched the man—if a man he was—drinking blood and swinging one foot gently as he killed some time before doing God only knew what.

I have no explanation for this paralysis. None. All I can say is that I simply hadn't reckoned on being so damned fascinated and stunned by our enemy. Ninon had warned me, told me of his beauty and his ability to hypnotize and seduce—Hell, I knew he was dangerous because of my dream. Had he tried a front-on assault, or again tried to invade my thoughts, I would have been ready for him. I think. But nothing of what he did, how he looked or stood or moved, had anything to do with deliberate seduction. It wasn't aimed at me; it just *was*. He wore his authority like he did his skin. The power of his stance, the arrogant tilt of the head, his radiance—these were with him all the time. And they were as beautiful as they were horrible.

I'm going to confess something difficult now, because it may be the only thing that will make you understand what he is. I have no homosexual leanings, no bisexual fantasies. But in that moment, a part of me longed for him. If not as my lover, then as my brother, my father, my teacher. I looked down from my perch on the roof and for a moment the desire to see his eyes overcame my intention—my need—to kill him. I forgot I had a shotgun. I forgot the heads in the dryer. I forgot Ninon was with a gang of potential rapists. I wanted so badly for him to look at me and smile that I nearly called out, nearly flung myself off that roof and ran toward him.

I thought: The wonder wasn't that Ninon had been seduced into trusting him, but in that she had seen his evil before it was too late.

It was that thought of Ninon and her hat pin that saved me from revealing myself. That, and the attack by the ghoul—our old pal, the satyr.

For those who have never had experience with hand-to-hand combat or any kind of life-and-death confrontation in a war zone, let me explain what happens. Reactions in battle can be divided into three phases. The first is recognition of danger. The second is formulation of a response. The third is to carry it through. All of this must happen faster than in daily life.

Many things can affect response time to danger; age, health, general alertness, training—vampirism. I was lucky that day to have had at least three of those things in my favor.

Had there been an eastern breeze, the smell would have warned me sooner. As it was, the only hint of peril I had was the fall of a speeding shadow over my right shoulder. My subconscious mind—which processes things faster than my conscious—knew that shadows moving so fast were unusual, probably unnatural, and likely dangerous. I recognized this straightaway. Moving out of the way seemed the correct response, and I did so with all the speed my vampirism-enhanced muscles could give me. I moved very quickly indeed—know this—but it still wasn't fast enough. It was on me before I could raise my shotgun or even stand up to my full height. In less than a second, I was involved in a life-and-death struggle.

Most of you won't know this, and thank whatever god you worship that this is so, but such fighting is very personal. You look into your enemy's eyes, smell the breath—and in this case the rotting body. This isn't pleasant, but it does make you focus. I had no trouble forgetting about Saint Germain's beauty and giving my full attention to dealing with the satyr.

Many people would react with fear. I didn't. Rage at the creature for having the affront to try to end my life made me ruthless and inventive. I found myself willing to commit acts of violence I had never before imagined, and made every attempt to carry the ideas through. Nothing worked. In fact, its first blow spun me about like a top.

I know why I wanted to be quiet during our duel— Saint Germain and the potential for the rest of some ghoul pack joining us was a great incentive to silence—but I'm not sure why the satyr didn't cry out. Maybe it was pride. Maybe it couldn't. Perhaps when it was being stitched together, vocal chords hadn't been deemed necessary. In any event, I was very lucky.

It was on me. I felt the wiry hair of its forearms as it wrapped them about my face. It had been going for the neck, hoping for a quick snap, or perhaps to tear my throat out, but I'd dropped my head in time. Long, filthy nails punctured my cheek though, and blood flowed into my mouth and down my face. It tried to turn my head, succeeding inch by inch.

I thought about the heads in the dryer and resisted.

My arms were pinned by something that felt like a steel bar, and they went numb almost at once. The shotgun slid from my fingers and my ribs began to scream that they were being crushed. I tried kicking back but it did no good; the satyr's knees jointed the wrong way to cause a break. Knowing it was a risk to expose my throat, I threw my head back as hard as I could and felt the satisfying snap of the creature's nose and cheekbones breaking. I did it again and think I smashed its teeth. Something punctured my scalp with what felt like roofing nails. A normal man would have screamed and curled up in a fetal ball. This creature's arm didn't loosen much, though, and it still held me too close for me to use my arms to defend myself.

But it did pause before going for my neck again. I think that I'd surprised it. Its previous prey hadn't been as quick or as strong.

It hissed through broken teeth but still didn't call out. It belatedly occurred to me that maybe like a zombie he didn't actually feel pain. I could smack it with my head until my skull shattered and only I would feel it.

This was bad news.

I pushed backwards and tried again to move my arms—no go. I was pinned and my chest was being crushed. My vision began to darken. Synapses began firing off warnings, telling me that I wasn't getting enough oxygen. I leaned my head back a fraction of an inch, opening my airway.

It worked. The monster tried again to pull my face around, but my neck was strong enough to resist. We breathed heavily as we struggled in place, our heads touching but sharing no thought or words, though I wanted—insanely—to ask it who it was and how it had been made, and why it wanted to live in that rotting body. Mostly I wanted to know if it believed it was Fate that had brought us here, to this place at this time, so that we would try to kill each other.

Weird, I know. But my brain was starving for oxygen. I was thinking lots of strange, alarming stuff. Like, across the street the failing adobe continued to fall in soft shushing flakes. They were no longer gentle moths, but rather a flock of ghostly ravens come to pick my bones. At the same time, I realized that I was thirsty and wanted to taste raspberry iced tea again almost as much as I wanted another breath of air. Mostly, I longed to wash the taste of those rotting fingers out of my mouth before I vomited.

I was also feeling fatigue. We had only been locked together for seconds—a minute at most—and yet so great was the effort I was exerting against the creature's enormous strength that my arms, legs, and neck were nearly exhausted. This was no wrestling match. No referee would rescue me. There would be no respite until one of us was dead; and that would be me if I didn't do something to break the stalemate.

As I said, it's very personal.

We listened to the music for another moment. Or, I did. Who knows what the satyr thought as it stood there crushing the life out of me. I swayed in place, thinking that music wasn't the soundtrack I would have chosen for a climactic fight scene and wondering what the hell I could do to get out of this mess. Then I felt the monster's muscles gather for another attack. It tried to kick my knees, to knock me to the floor where its greater weight would be an advantage, but the knees that had saved it before were a hindrance now. Its foot—hoof—struck my calf and I felt the skin split. That hurt, but the muscle was intact and I didn't fall. I couldn't. I knew that if I was pinned, I was dead.

Again we paused, our breath heaving. We were at an impasse, but that wasn't good enough. I didn't know how strong the thing was. It seemed likely that I would tire before it did. Then it would eat me alive.

Two other thoughts occurred to me:

The bad guys might actually win this one.

Ninon might die.

That was unacceptable, absolutely intolerable. My brain released another surge of chemical rage. I had to kill this thing, quickly and quietly. And, it finally occurred to me, before Saint Germain or his ghouls found me or Ninon and we were overwhelmed.

I twisted hard to the right, away from the hand buried in my cheek, feeling skin tear and more blood fall. I kicked out again, not trying for knees this time but rather the feet. Ever had your toes crushed? It's painful. Splintered hooves would have to hurt too. It was fast, though, and he swung its right hoof out of harm's way, so I continued to bring my knee up, going for the groin.

I hit, I know I did, but there was no reaction except to continue the momentum of the turn I had started, spinning us both toward the trapdoor in the roof. We twirled twice like drunken dancers doing the Viennese waltz, slipping in my blood that gushed freely, and then we finally fell apart.

I caught a break. The creature's left hoof got caught in one of those cracks that fissured the roof, and it very nearly overbalanced and toppled through the open trapdoor. I didn't give it time to recover its equilibrium. I leapt at it and slammed my fist into its body, accidentally punching through the desiccated flesh and into withered organs. I gave a half twist of the wrist and then grabbed. I'm not sure what I had—liver, gallbladder, appendix, something. I hadn't paid much attention to my anatomy lessons, and anyway everything inside was sort of leathery and fused. I gave a backward yank, pulling out organs and, as a bonus, a loop of intestine. That was still soft and squishy and very full of red pulp.

Its arms swiped at me and it tried to bite, but my second hard jab to its torso tipped it through the trap door opening. Intestines un-spooled and then ripped free with a splash of blood as it fell, but that didn't stop it. I stood there gaping at the bloated, oozing rope in my hand as the damn thing came popping right back out. Its broken teeth were bared and it reached for me confidently, sure of my death.

Pride goeth before a fall, that's what Cormac always said.

I had forgotten in those first moments of shock that I wasn't dealing with a living person. My brain, now with oxygen restored, was finally functioning again. The only thing that would kill this creature was to rip out its heart or brain. My shotgun was out of the question—and not just because of the noise, but because I would never reach the gun in time. I did a quick calculation as the creature launched itself toward me. Ribs would be easier to break, but it might take me a moment to find the heart. There wasn't any confusion about where the brain was. Pulling back my arm, I slammed into its head with all the remaining strength I could summon.

All I did was dent its skull and make it fall back into the darkness. I also broke my right hand.

Two falls from the roof. Its neck should be broken, but the nightmare refused to end. There was another hiss and then it came back up. This time I was ready. My brain had recalled Ninon's deadly gift, tucked into my boot, a personal weapon for a personal battle. I got out the trench spike with my left hand, and brought it down with all my might as the damned thing popped out of the trapdoor.

It must have felt the spike go in, but the beast's upward progress stopped only when my knuckles hit its skull. The blow was numbing from fingers to elbow. My aim wasn't great either. The front of the spike was protruding out of the thing's upper side jaw. Still, my hit had to have wiped out massive amounts of brain.

There was a long enough space of time for me to worry that this method would not kill a ghoul, to see the enormous teeth that were not flossed or brushed. Then the creature stiffened, thrashed once more and fell a third time through the trapdoor, slowly pulling free of the spike with a disgusting, sucking sound.

I waited, breathing hard, listening for cries of alarm and nursing my broken hand and bruised calf. It didn't do its Jack-in-the-box trick but I could hear it whipping about below, louder than the washing machine it had filled with victims. It still wasn't screaming, but it was hissing and making too much noise as it lashed about in what I hoped were its death throes.

I did some mental cursing and then dropped through the door, not bothering with the ladder. I landed beside the thing and used my downward momentum to bury the trench spike in its chest. I must have found the heart, because it hissed once more and then finally stilled.

I got up slowly and wiped the spike on its chest, doing my best to clear the dark red slime it used for blood. I reached up and pulled a selection of its teeth out of my scalp and then pushed the torn flesh of my cheek back into place. That hurt like a son-of-a-bitch and I would probably need stitches.

"Mary, mother of God," I murmured, regressing to boyhood and calling on Mamita's Virgin for help. I whistled when I spoke, the air passing through the tears in my face. No one answered, and so I passed another rite of passage alone, took another step away from my humanity and into the realm of monsters without any witnesses except heads in a dryer.

I hurt everywhere. It took a bit longer this time for me to climb out onto the roof that second time. The smell of baking intestine left me sick. I no longer hungered for blood. When I did finally get around to looking over the wall, Saint Germain was gone. So was the music. I was truly alone.

That felt ominous, trying to throw off my lingering shock. I cursed again and then picked up my dusty shotgun.

Time to find Ninon. We were going to do what I should have done when I stumbled into the grisly scene in the laundry room—namely, get out of town as fast as we possibly could. I didn't care what Saint Germain and the ghouls were up to anymore. We had grossly underestimated our enemy. Or I had. Ninon was right—we needed weapons. At the moment I was telling myself that until we had attack helicopters and a small army—and maybe a priest and a shaman—I wasn't taking him or any ghouls on again. I'd won this battle, but no way would I win the war. Not without help.

My honored father:

I am eleven years old. I am big and strong, but shall certainly fall ill if I continue to assist at three masses every day, especially on account of one performed by a great, gouty, fat canon who takes at least twelve minutes to get through the Epistle and the Gospel, and who the choirboys are obliged to put back on his feet after each genuflexion. This is all depressing, I can assure you. Well, I am done twiddling with the rosary beads while mumbling Aves, Paters, and Credos. The present moment is the one for me to inform you that I have decided to no longer be a girl, but to become a boy. As I am now a son, it is your duty to take over my education immediately and I shall tell you how it is to be done . . .

—*Letter from Ninon de L'enclos*

It is with true love as it is with ghosts; everyone talks about it, but few have seen it.

—*François de la Rochefoucauld*

CHAPTER EIGHTEEN

While I was having my face ripped off, Ninon was having some adventures of her own.

The Gypsy Kings played on in an asthmatic fashion. Maybe they needed some of the tequila the men had been drinking. Maybe they were just stoned from the marijuana smoke.

Two of the men held Ninon. A third—the fat one—held a gun on her while the fourth came up behind. He seemed to have guessed that it was safest to aim for her head. Or someone had told him that he should handle her that way.

These four weren't ghouls—not yet—but their breath stank of blood and rotting flesh. There was also a lack of intelligence in their eyes that suggested some sort of brain damage. She didn't think they were victims of a vampire attack, but something was wrong with them. They were a long way from being human, and even their mothers would say so.

She wasn't screaming, though that was what they wanted—and she wouldn't, no matter what they did. Not unless she had to shout to warn Miguel away. Ninon had seen Saint Germain walk past the shutters outside less than a minute before. She'd had no more than a glimpse of him, a few slices of his body that moved by in a blur, but it was enough to shake her. Her enemy was here and she didn't have a single bloody weapon to defend herself with.

Saint Germain was here. How? How had he known she would be here?

The man behind her tore her dress. The vandalism made her angry. He reached around her, squeezing her left breast roughly and shoving his hand into her panties. He pushed a dirty finger inside of her and bit down on her shoulder, drawing blood. She knew that she was supposed to be afraid, to whimper and plead, but she found the idea of rape so much less horrifying than being ripped apart by ghouls that she couldn't work up much fear. And she felt no shame, though humiliation was their aim. She wouldn't give them that either.

Anyway, these were dead men. Dead, dead, dead. All she needed was a moment when the gun wavered from her head and she would take them. Wisely, she kept her eyes lowered; the fat one with the gun might be bright enough to read her intent if she looked him in the eye, and he was nervous enough to shoot.

The man behind her got bored with her unresponsiveness. He came around her left side and then stepped in front of her. She looked up but kept her face blank, not telegraphing her intent until he stepped between her and the gun. The moment she was shielded, Ninon jerked her right arm forward, throwing her unprepared captor toward the gunman. His headlong stumble wasn't anything to put in a Hollywood movie, but it served her purpose well enough. Jackie Gleason was pinned between a body and a heavy table.

She spun then toward the stunned creep holding her left arm and used her right hand to double him over with a shot to the diaphragm that broke the tip of his sternum.

His eyes before she hit him were terrified, and she wondered what she looked like, or if he simply read his destruction in her face. As he doubled over she saw that he had a gun tucked in the small of his back. She had to reach over him to snatch it, letting his contorted face press against her bare torso.

Jackie Gleason was shouting at the gaping dress-ripper to move out of the way. It didn't occur to him to move himself around the table. She had no such problem with mobility. The gun wrenched clear of the goon's waistband and she stepped around her shield to put a bullet into Jackie Gleason's head. The strangeness of the weapon did not strike her at the time; she was conversant with firearms of all eras. The noise of the shot was uncomfortably loud but still satisfying, because it was one of the many sounds that meant death for her enemies.

A part of her was horrified at what she was doing, but it was a small part that didn't protest.

It was a tough decision, but she chose to shoot the man who had had her right arm first. The dress-ripper was closer, but the other guy had a gun and he was finally groping for it.

Time slowed down. Intellectually, she knew why. The pituitary gland was being stimulated by the hypothalamus. Adrenaline—actually adrenocorticotropin—was washing through her body, helping her muscles prepare to do what they needed to survive. Inside, the vampire virus that Miguel had infected her with had woken up and leapt joyfully into action. The organism's bloodlust took over immediately, aiding her already prepared muscles into new autonomic reflexive actions. It said prompt, aggressive deeds were called for. It tightened her finger on the trigger before her conscious mind had a chance to weigh options and make any pacifist decisions about running away.

Ninon might have been able to override the monster in her blood, but she chose instead to let its instincts guide her. She had sought precisely this kind of help, and this was no time to be slowed by doubts about what she had done. She sensed its utter ferocity and will to live. It would do whatever was needed to keep her alive. It was a natural killer. She was not.

Thanks to her supernaturally fast reflexes, the second goon was down before the dress-ripper reached her. The noise from her gun was very loud, dangerously so given that Saint Germain was somewhere nearby, but she couldn't take all four of them in a fistfight. Not yet. Her vampirism was still gathering strength.

A quick glance assured her that the man whose diaphragm she'd torn was still lying on the floor and no threat. That just left the one who had wrecked her lovely dress and bitten her shoulder. She was especially angry with him.

The CD player stopped playing with a loud pop and then a sizzle that suggested some power surge. Ninon looked at her arms and realized that she was glowing, all but setting the room on fire.

Damn. There would be nothing now to mask the sound of guns. That might be all right though, if Saint Germain had continued walking. The walls were thick and would dampen sound. Still, she wouldn't risk it if there were any other way. There was just the one man left to deal with, and she could break his neck if she could get around behind him.

Her muscles were gathering themselves, preparing for a leap, when on her left a door opened and yet another man, one with a gun, rushed into the room. Blood smeared his lips and chin. More danger. The organism in control of her brain didn't care. It had calculated and decided that she could take him as well.

The fourth man had her now. Her left hand, the one without the gun, whipped up and shoved hard against the dress-ripper's nose, pushing it upward into his brain. She pushed off against him, using him as a brace, and launched herself into the air before he even fell over, putting to use an all-but-forgotten karate kick a retired CIA spook had taught her one night when he was very drunk and hoping to get laid. The fifth man, the one with the gun, had no chance to bring it around before she hit him, her right heel serving as a pick that broke through his sternum and drove itself into his heart. He was dead before he hit the floor.

Unfortunately, it took a moment to free her foot and, already off balance, she was dragged down with him. Inside she screamed in frustration at being snared by this corpse. She wrenched violently until the heel snapped off.

Damn it! Damn it! Now she'd wrecked a pair of shoes.

She heard the door to the street open and threw herself around with desperate speed, aiming in that general direction with the pistol she still held in her hand, but she had no chance to do more than catch her breath before someone who looked a lot like Saint Germain pointed a shotgun at her.

"*Bonjour,* Ninon. Now say good-bye." It was Saint Germain's voice, Saint Germain's eyes.

Her finger tightened on the trigger, but her gun was empty. She opened her mouth to scream at Saint Germain and tried to leap at his weapon to push it away, but the room filled with explosion and a fine mist of shredded blood and tissue catching her midflight knocked her backward.

I think it took Ninon a moment to realize that she hadn't been shot, that it was Saint Germain's exploded chest covering her almost naked body in blood, and not her own.

"Miguel?" Her voice was hardly recognizable. I didn't blame her for asking. Last she had seen me, my face was whole and I wasn't limping.

"We've gotta go. There are ghoulth all over the plathe." I had developed a lisp. The left side of my face wasn't working right. Muscles had been severed.

I jumped over Saint Germain—amazingly, he wasn't

dead—and reached out for her. Ninon didn't recoil, but the look in her eyes gave me pause. Her gaze was fixed on Saint Germain and she was shaking. It wasn't with fear either. Lightning also danced over skin. That wasn't sexual arousal, though I think it was lust of another sort. I was facing a wild animal who was nearly beyond control. The vampire had finally woken up in her. I think I understood what she was feeling. I wanted Saint Germain ripped open and to wallow in his blood. I wanted to tear him limb from limb, as the saying went. As his bitterest enemy, her desire had to be even stronger.

However, even if I were inclined to give in, we simply didn't have the time to indulge the monsters within. There were other ghouls still about.

My eyes finally adapted to the dark and I took in the rest of the slaughter. I was impressed. Five bodies, not counting the twitching Saint Germain who was actually attempting to get to his feet. Ninon had been busy. No wonder her bloodlust was roused. I couldn't imagine how she had managed not to fall on these creatures and lap at their blood. I shuddered.

Saint Germain reached for me, grabbing at my sore leg. Since the time for silence was long past, I took the handgun from Ninon, an old revolver, and loaded it with the ammo in my pocket. I turned and emptied all the bullets into Saint Germain's head. I shoved the empty gun into my pocket when I was done. Then I got Jackie Gleason's gun and emptied it too. Small-caliber weapons, museum pieces really—they didn't even have magazines but required the loading of individual bullets—and they didn't do as much damage as I would have liked.

To the best of my recollection, I didn't think once about the fact that I had just performed an execution-style shooting. All I can recall thinking was that we were out of ammo now. I had taken the carbine and the rest of the ammunition out to the Jeep before doubling back for Ninon. It wasn't until I was back in town that I had seen the other men—ghouls—and Saint Germain. I'd considered going back for the carbine but then the shooting had started.

It took several long seconds for the bullets to do their work, but Saint Germain finally fell back to the floor. His head was pretty much gone and he looked real dead, but I didn't for one second believe it. I was filled with supernatural dread and no longer expected natural law to prevail. He would rise again. Whatever was animating him, it wasn't just in his brain. Call it irrational fear, but I didn't think we were getting rid of him so easily. This was no zombie to be put down with a bullet. And evil—real evil—doesn't retreat that effortlessly. It was the second thing in this world that was eternal.

A second look at Ninon showed me that she actually was wounded. My shot had gone through Saint Germain and into her. But just as she had assured me, the wounds weren't lethal. I watched as she dug out the spent shot with her fingers. Her skin returned to normal and she began to shiver. More than anything else, I was unhappy with the look in her eyes. Terminal horror can leave the eyes looking permanently harrowed. I didn't think she was there yet, but we needed to get away from this horror show as soon as possible. Too much more and she'd never be able to pass for human again. It might already be too late for me.

I knew I'd probably feel really bad about this later, but at that moment, I didn't let myself care. We were both breathing and able to run—that was good enough.

"That's not Saint Germain," she whispered finally, pressing a hand to the small wounds in her chest. She was beginning to look sick, her skin turning a faint shade of green that made her lipstick look like an old wound. I felt for her; the downside of an adrenaline high was awful. She would be recognizing just what she had let the blood-lust do. Even if you don't feel guilt, ever after you have a fear of the monster within because you know what it can do. Also, she probably hurt. I knew we would mend quickly, but for a while, my face had been very painful. I guess our gifts didn't include an escape from pain.

"Miguel—*cher!* This is not Saint Germain."

Her words registered, both the endearment and the bad news.

"What? But it hath to be." I looked at the body. His face was pretty smashed, but he looked like the man I had seen from the roof. I thought the clothes were the same. Of course, a white shirt and jeans was pretty standard.

"No."

I began to doubt. Perhaps it was that he was almost disintegrated, but I didn't feel the same psychic pull toward him.

Ninon insisted: "That's not him. It looks like him but . . . maybe it's a clone or a doppelganger or something."

A clone—his evil doubled. Before I could digest this horrible idea, we heard an ominous combination of hissing and growling fill the air. It was coming from the south, the square where the aborted fiesta had taken place.

"Come on! Thith way." I grabbed her arm and pulled toward the back of the building. She stumbled over one of the bodies but I held her up. "The ghoulth have found uth. We need to run. Fatht."

Ninon didn't need to be told twice.

We raced through the gunroom and out into the back street. We were both hobbled. My calf was damaged and she had broken a heel; still, I think we would have qualified at any Olympic track speed trial. Funny. Having a pack of ghouls racing after you and no more ammunition for your empty guns can put wings on you feet.

I am in terror. I have seen my man in black! The man with the red tablets bearing my name and the dozen bottles of elixir—the one who appeared before me seventy years ago. And I heard him say he has a son who will be called St. Germain.
—*From the letters of Ninon de Lenclos*

If we are to judge of love by its consequences, it more nearly resembles hatred than friendship.
—*François de la Rochefoucauld*

A woman who is through with a man will give him up for anything—except another woman.
—*"Lesson in Love" by Ninon de Lenclos*

Your heart needs occupation
—*Letter from Ninon de Lenclos to the Marquis de Sévigné*

CHAPTER NINETEEN

I'd been fixating on the weird mix of weaponry that we'd found in that town, probably because it was better than thinking about other things. Maybe I was being influenced by American cinema, but I had always thought of modern drug dealers as being more high-tech. Had many fled at the first sign of trouble, taking their newer guns with them? And if some had departed on an urgent mission, why leave those other unpleasant specimens behind?

These trivial thoughts were soon displaced. Thirty yards away, it became apparent that in our absence my SUV had suffered an engine extraction and extensive re-modeling of its exterior by King Kong or a tribe of cudgel-wielding freaks. A closer inspection showed that Corazon also appeared to be missing.

Ninon was understandably upset. But not for long. That cat has more than nine lives, I swear, and as soon as Ninon called he reappeared, wet from doing God knew what and dragging another limp-necked rodent that looked severely withered. He seemed unharmed but a little dazed. I didn't blame him. My run-in with a ghoul had produced a similar effect.

Unfortunately, Ninon couldn't call my engine back as easily as the cat. It continued to lie in the flattened cactus by the road, its torn engine mounts facing skyward as it played at the automotive version of roadkill. I didn't want to think about what could be strong enough to rip an engine out of an SUV, but I had to admit a graphic image or two crossed my mind before I shut down my imagination and remembered to breathe.

"I'm glad this car wasn't a phallic symbol for me or anything," I muttered.

That got a small smile.

"Actually, I see this as a good news–bad news sort of thing," I went on. I had stopped lisping. Amazingly, my cheek was already beginning to heal, the skin and muscle knitting back together. I had known that, as a vampire, I was supposed to have good recuperative abilities, and Ninon assured me that our little divine fire trick would make them even better, but I had never been tempted to test the theory before. Not that I was feeling smug and immortal, but it was a very small silver lining in an otherwise stressful day.

"I can see the bad," she said, picking up a punctured gas can. Only a small amount of fuel sloshed around the bottom. Shrugging, she went to the back of the Jeep and pulled out fresh clothing and some wet-wipes. The hole in her chest had scabbed over and she looked fairly healthy when she wiped the blood away. "But the good?"

"Well, eventually the SUV will be found and traced back to me. If I want to disappear, to fake my death, this should do it. Especially if I leave some blood behind for dramatic color." I picked up some of my clothes that had been flung about in the cactus. Not all of it was shredded. That was good, because my current selection was looking less than haute couture.

I was also relieved to find my portable computer, safe inside its very expensive case. I made a note to never complain about the cost of computer bags again.

"No blood," Ninon said immediately, and I felt like smacking my head. Of course no blood. I didn't want them trying to match my DNA and getting too interested in the anomalies. "The rest is good though—especially if we burn it. The last time I had to disappear I went missing in the Bermuda Triangle. That always felt a bit cliché. A car accident in the wilds of Mexico is much better."

That was my Ninon, ever calm, always thinking. We both began to clean up and then dress. Though we didn't say anything, we were sniffing the air at regular intervals, checking that we were alone.

"If you have any money stashed away under your real name, you'd best arrange to collect it. Once you 'die,' you need to stay dead," she said suddenly.

I nodded.

"If we do a transfer and large withdrawal at a nearby town, they will probably assume that you were followed by thieves and killed in a roadside robbery. I guess that's more good news. And you won't have to pay any more taxes this year."

I shivered a bit. Too many geese walking on my grave all at once. One thing though, the ghouls scared me more than the IRS.

"Is there a nearby town? I mean, one large enough to have a bank?" I asked.

"Yes. At least, there was. I don't think we can take anything for granted from here on out. Saint Germain has gotten unbelievably bold."

"How long can a ghoul live?" I asked. "What about zombies?" In other words, how long could these things chase us? Or force us to chase them?

"In this heat a zombie, assuming it was in prime condition when it was raised, would last no more than five years—three is more likely. A ghoul? I don't know. Not much longer. Even if they avoid the sun, the heat and other organisms will continue to eat away at their flesh. Of course, if Saint Germain keeps replacing failing body parts . . . I don't know. The zombies I'm less worried about. If we can kill Saint Germain, they'll wander about their own locales until they rot. The ghouls, though— they'll follow us. And failing that, they'll move into populated areas looking for prey. We're going to have to kill them." She finished dressing and then tucked her pistol into her belt. I noticed that she had also retrieved her trench spike.

"With a shotgun, a carbine rifle, a nine-millimeter handgun, and an antique revolver for which we have little ammunition? I forgot the trench spike—those work really well," I added.

She nodded. "Yes. Until we can find something better. Maybe . . ." She broke off, spinning about with reflexes that would make Corazon proud. She snatched up her trench spike and continued her pivot so that she was facing the body when it hurtled out of the sky.

Her spike landed dead center in its chest. Ninon grabbed the thing's right arm and flipped the creature onto the ground. She cracked it like a whip, dislocating the thing's shoulder. The noise it made when it hit the ground was shrill enough to pierce the eardrums. Without thought, without any conscious instruction, I grabbed up my own spike and drove it into the creature's head. It bucked twice, then stilled.

It was only then that I realized that we hadn't been attacked by a ghoul.

Ninon realized this at the same moment, and backed away hastily. As I watched, every last bit of color drained from her face.

"Miguel." Her voice was barely recognizable. I wondered for a moment if she was going to faint. "Please tell me that isn't your mother."

My mother? I looked back down at the withered thing

with leprous skin and talons. Its mouth was open and I could see the pick on the end of its tongue. It was definitely a vampire. Could that be Mamita? My eyes ran over it repeatedly, unable to take in what lay before us. Finally, I focused on its abdomen.

"No," I said at last, finding myself oddly relieved. "There's no appendectomy scar. Anyway, this poor thing has eczema or something."

"Not eczema—sunburn, I think," Ninon said, slumping against the Jeep. She drew a couple of slow breaths and color began to return to her face. "She's been out in the sun for a while. Maybe *she* wrecked the SUV and not the ghouls."

It was possible, but I didn't think so. Vampires tended to get mad at people, not things that couldn't bleed.

"How did she get here? I don't smell any water." I inhaled deeply and regretted it. The creature was definitely starting to rot. The deterioration was rapid; we could almost see the body caving in. The movies had got that part right.

"With all the recent rain, there could be underground aquifers." Ninon shrugged. Vampires obviously weren't her area of expertise.

Then we looked at one another, our eyes widening. If a vampire could travel to us via underground rivers, so could S.M.

I reached down and pulled out our trench spikes. This time the sucking sound bothered me. I went to the back of the Jeep and used a few more of Ninon's wet-wipes to clean them off. I worked quickly. The thought of S.M. lent me speed.

"Put all the clothing and rags in the SUV," Ninon said, picking up the damaged gas can again. "We're going to burn it all."

"Don't," I said, as she reached down for the body. Ninon hesitated.

"We should burn it too."

"I know. But I'll do it."

"You don't have to. I can—"

"I'll do it," I repeated. "There's no need for you to get messy again. Just get anything useful out of the SUV packed into the Jeep."

She nodded, but we both knew that wasn't the reason I didn't want her touching the body. That creature wasn't Mamita, but it could have been. This was my job.

"Miguel!" she said again. I looked back at her. She was pointing to the side of the SUV. Someone had written in the dust: *Lara Vieja*. There was something about the handwriting that was familiar, but then I had only seen one letter from Mamita. And most graffiti looks alike so I wasn't inclined to jump to conclusions.

"What does that mean?" I asked. "Old Lara? Is that who this creature is?"

"No. Lara Vieja is a ghost town. It was wiped out some years ago in a flash flood."

"So this would be a clue then?"

"A dare, I think. Or a warning. Maybe both."

I thought so too. Everything the ghouls had done had been a taunt.

Still, that writing bugged me. Ghouls were brighter than zombies, but could they write? Or did we have a friend? Maybe it was someone who was an enemy of our enemy and willing to help us find him.

"Do we take the dare?" I asked.

"The world is a big place. Saint Germain could be hiding anywhere. I don't see that we have a choice."

I saw many choices, but I didn't think Ninon would go for running away and not stopping until we reached the Arctic Circle.

We stayed only long enough to see things catch fire. By then there wasn't much of the vampire's body left to burn. I still felt sick seeing it consumed by flames.

Ninon turned away first. She opened the driver's-side door of her Jeep and then said to me, "Do you want to drive?"

"Like I've never wanted anything in my life," I muttered.

I took the keys she held out to me. Under any other circumstance I think we would have held each other, offered comfort and consolation. But we couldn't afford the time or the weakness that sympathy brought about. If we had ever had any doubts about the situation, now we knew: We were at war. The place had been named and the battlefield was to be Lara Vieja.

"Miguel?" Ninon asked after I had driven for a few minutes in silent driving. I glanced at her, but she didn't turn my way. The scenery seemed to enrapture her. Or maybe she was watching for ghouls. "That creature was attacking us, wasn't it? I didn't overreact?"

I had never heard Ninon sound uncertain. The question surprised me a little.

"Yes, it was attacking," I said, and made my voice definite because the vampire had been after her. Her, Ninon. The next part came out more easily than I thought it would. "And if you see another vampire coming at you, you must not hesitate because you think it's my mother. Believe me, she wouldn't hesitate to attack you if she thought you were threatening me."

"Miguel . . ." She swallowed. "You know that S.M. controls these vampires. He's been in your head and you still have some powers of resistance. You can't hesitate either if one comes at you. Even if it's your mother."

"I know." I reached over to squeeze her leg. She turned to look at me with somber eyes, and I forced myself to nod affirmation. I still felt ill. "And I won't hesitate if she attacks me. Or you."

It wasn't a hollow promise. Anything that came at me or Ninon—ghoul, zombie, vampire, Mamita, S.M.—was going to end up shot or spiked.

"I'm so glad my own mother's dead," Ninon whispered. "Seeing me now . . . it would kill her. Or Saint Germain would."

It wasn't a joke. I wished my mother were dead, too—though not quite enough to want to be the one who killed her. And not enough to want her die by any method S.M. devised.

Men are more often defeated in love by their own clumsiness than by a woman's virtue.
—*"Lesson in Love" from* Carte du Tendre *by Ninon de Lenclos*

To achieve greatness one should live as if they will never die.
—*François de la Rochefoucauld*

It is not only for what we do that we are held responsible, but also for what we do not do.
—*Molière*

CHAPTER TWENTY

Our run-in with the vampire had me thinking about Mamita. I had thought that maternal-connector nerve severed, my mind made up about her and therefore no reason to feel pain at the thought of her escaping from a life of slavery. After all, I barely knew her and had no real bond, no reason to care beyond basic human decency, and I had less and less of that all the time. But somehow I did care. I also had questions bubbling back to the surface of my consciousness. Stupid, bitter questions about why and how she had ended up as a vampire. I've read up on the Aztec birth rituals once, the ones that invoked the gods. It made me wonder: Did Mamita, in her delirium, accidentally conjure S.M. to save herself? Or maybe by attempting a Christian baptism of her infant so I would not die in sin and end up in Limbo, and that was how her blood got in the water? The later seemed more likely. I couldn't picture her accidentally murmuring the conjuring ritual— *Come, O god, to see my child, come into the world of too much heat and cold and wind. I give his blood for the sun to drink and may this water carry away all stain and make this child worthy.*

No, it was more likely her blood that drew him. He loved women who were dying in childbirth. The smell would have been like chum in the water, drawing the nearby shark. It was probably just bad luck.

The thing was that Mamita either didn't know what had happened or wouldn't tell me, and since I wasn't going to ask S.M., I would probably never have answers. I just had to accept that maybe there hadn't been any reason for this tragedy, no one to blame.

We found a town with a bank and no noticeable zombies, and arranged for a transfer of funds and a large cash withdrawal from my bank accounts. I didn't empty them completely or close them down; that would look too much like a deliberate attempt to disappear and I didn't need my former bosses mounting a paranoid search for me. Not immediately. We needed to get a few miles under our belts before anyone else started hunting us.

I sat in the small office with my smoky clothes—I had changed, but all our clothes were burdened with a smoke pall—and did my best to look unimpressive, trying to imagine that I had less personality than a vegetable. Somehow I don't think I succeeded, probably because Ninon and I didn't dare take our sunglasses off. I think the manager of the bank thought I was a stupid gringo trying to set up a drug deal, and Ninon the evil girlfriend who was leading me astray. He wouldn't be surprised when the SUV was found torn apart and my body missing. Theoretically, this was a good thing. In actual practice, I didn't enjoy being looked at like I was stupid scum, another ugly American.

Ninon was an old hand with these sorts of transactions and was very charming, but in spite of what they show you in the movies and the manager's earnest desire to please her, this moving money across borders is not exactly instantaneous. Perhaps if we had been in the Caymans or Switzerland where they did these things daily. Still, though I would have to come back the next day to pick up the cash—greenbacks, not pesos—I felt somewhat better about actually taking a concrete step, committing to a course of action. I've never been good at fence-sitting. A balancing act takes more energy than engaging in an actual fight.

I haven't talked about my job in any specifics—and won't—but I should explain that what the government values me for isn't something they can easily find and replace. I am unique and they won't be happy with my loss. I have what you might call hyperfocus, a sort of pattern recognition ability that borders on being psychic. Put simply, I just know things—even about subjects I have no training in. They show me data, often raw numbers or strange collections of facts from newspapers or the internet, and I can somehow glean massive amounts of information from very little data. The fact that I often don't know what I'm working on is meaningless; I have seen top-secret information that I might pass on to someone else. Really, the only way out for me—at least as far as the more paranoid government types are concerned—is feet first. This disappearance was a drastic step, but a necessary one. I knew it, but it was still a bit eerie killing off Miguel Stuart.

We blew a little of our traveling money and had a car alarm installed in the Jeep. Again, we got some weird looks for wanting to alarm the old thing, but I thought Ninon's idea perfect. It was belling the cat. We couldn't stop ghouls—or vampires—from trashing the Jeep, but at least we'd know they were doing it. If the town had run to high-tech, I'd have picked up motion sensors for our hotel room door and to set up everywhere we went, an early warning system that bad guys were creeping up on us. We needed all the edge we could get.

I was still thinking fondly of attack helicopters, but resisted the urge to ask anyone about purchasing dynamite or military-grade weapons. The place was too small even for a gun store, and we didn't want to be remembered too colorfully when my bosses finally arrived in town looking for answers about my disappearance. A drug deal gone bad they might buy. It wouldn't be the first time an American had gone on vacation and done something stupid. Trafficking in arms was another matter.

A gun store wasn't all that was missing in this minimetropolis. The town's temples of commerce were limited in their choice of couture as well. They had shorts and T-shirts that advertised beer and cigarettes, and one pair of jeans in my size that cost three times what they would in the States. There were no dress shirts to be had at any price. I found myself looking at stacks of Joe Camel T-shirts and hats that stank of burned rubber, and longing for my closet of clean button-down cotton shirts and suits; and I knew it was probably worse for Ninon who selected a few things with an air of despair. It was bold to tempt Fate by making plans, but I promised myself a trip to expensive stores in a major city soon. I feel so much more competent and desirous of living when I wear clean clothes that fit.

The evening was better. We had a peaceful night in a hotel that offered room service, undisturbed by any branch of the living dead family, though I had at first rather thought the place too much like a rest home where people might be waiting for the bitter—or maybe welcome—end. I actually hesitated before entering the lobby. One didn't usually see so many elderly people in boater hats and matching shirts gathered in one place, except at campaign rallies in Iowa in an election year. Or with tour groups of retirees, usually going to Reno or Atlantic City to blow their kids' inheritance.

As I'd stood outside the hotel, reluctant to step inside, Ninon began staring at me with a brow raised, asking silently what was wrong. A quick look around showed me that there was a tour bus outside. I was still feeling a bit creeped out by the general air of decrepitude, but we decided to register.

The condemned man and woman, we enjoyed our last meal, a sensual feast by anyone's standards, and then we slept. It was sleep with one mental eye open, on the lookout for intruders, but for the first time ever I enjoyed the simple act of sleeping with a woman in my arms.

The next morning, we started out early heading north. Ninon was driving, so I had the sunrise full on my right cheek. It was beautiful, full of pinks and reds, but I was coming to hate the sun. Being out in it day after day was making me feel like cured leather. However, it was better than rain and the attendant problems that could bring.

Ninon told me that we were near Chihuanuan, almost to the U.S. border. I couldn't smell the Rio Grande, but took her word for our location, especially when she again left the paved road in favor of what looked like an old wagon-train path.

"This is it."

The remains of Lara Vieja were beautiful and sad painted in late-morning light. Most of the smaller buildings had collapsed in the flood that had temporarily drowned the town, and were returning their clay to the earth from which it came. Their sandstone foundations were all that survived the torrent, leaving only faint signs of what would have been a bank or café, a market, a school, and homes.

The flood had been bad. Bad enough and fast enough to be supernatural in origin, though it had happened before Ninon and I were in Mexico, so maybe it had nothing to do with us. I hoped the people had escaped the deluge but suspected they hadn't. There weren't any bones or bodies about, but experience told us that didn't mean anything one way or another. Scavengers of any ilk could have carried off the corpses.

The town was a ruin, but the church and hotel remained more or less unscathed, tattered but still proud to be doing their civic duty for whatever ghosts lingered. Their furniture had been swept into the streets and the walls water-stained to a height of seven feet, but I could see though the open doors and missing windows that the frescos and chandeliers in the ceiling remained intact.

The church vault and hotel wine cellars were probably intact too—the perfect place for a zombie to enjoy a little siesta.

It would be a damned shame, I thought, if we had to burn this place. We were certainly prepared for this eventuality. We had a lot of gasoline in the back of the Jeep. I didn't plan on getting caught short again.

We slowed to a full stop in the middle of the village square. Only faint traces of the plaza's giant pavers remained, cracked, crumbling, also anxious to be done with this man-made incarnation and to return to the earth from which they been plucked. We got out of the Jeep, listening and watching and reaching out with other senses.

Beautiful it was, but there were many things not to like when you were thinking defensively. The town was rimmed with cracked boulders and a thick stand of cactus, and burnt-out sagebrush and greasewood littered with church pews, smashed sofas, torn beds, a sign for a *farmacia* now long gone, and even an old claw-footed bathtub—all providing excellent cover for anyone who wished to remain unobserved as they crept up on us. Also, shooting into that mess would mean risking wounds from ricochets.

Guns were a last resort anyway. Reconnaissance was called for.

"They're here?" I asked, not referring to the townspeople.

"Yes. Listen." I did, and still heard nothing that suggested life or movement. I suppose the absence of sound was the biggest giveaway that the bad boys were around.

Again, just as was the case in all the other ghost towns we had visited, there were no signs of coyotes or any animal habitants. Birds, snakes, burrowing animals—none of these were shy and should have moved into these ready-made homes as soon as the waters receded, but there was nothing, not so much even as a scorpion clinging to the decaying walls. There was also no graffiti, no broken bottles, no bullet holes, no sign that any human predator had come to gnaw on Lara Vieja's carcass. Something was keeping them away. The only question I had was whether it was Saint Germain or S.M. who'd been at work.

I turned and looked out over the desert. No animals breathed or chirped or barked. The wind was back, though, its idiot gibbering slipping through the opened doors and missing windows, and it told sad insane tales. It was bringing storm clouds with it as well. Ozone was building in the air.

I turned slowly, looking first at the red-stained church with its bell still hanging from a giant blackened beam and then at the hotel of two-toned pink plaster, a deeper hue where the water had raged. Its wrought-iron balconies were still there, its blue-paned French doors, their glass broken but closed however futilely against the sun. Its carved sign was still legible over the arch of the main entrance: Hotel Loyola, 1864.

Ninon grimaced as the hot wind came, blowing its fetid breath over our tired bodies.

"Is this Smoking Mirror's work? But why would he do it?" Ninon asked. "There must be a reason. This large a flood would take effort."

"He doesn't need a reason. Being pissed off is enough Maybe someone slighted him."

Ninon looked a question at me.

"Seriously. You may think you know how to hold a grudge, but I promise you that good old S.M. can hold a grudge longer and stronger than anyone. After all, he's immortal. He has had time to work vengeance into an art."

"Do we know that?" she asked, looking up into the sky.

"That he's immortal?" That stopped me. I thought about it, trying for a paradigm shift and finally having a slight one. "No, actually we don't. Those stone tablets are hundreds of years old, so we know he's long-lived. But they don't actually say he's immortal."

"So it might be good news for us. He could be killable by standard means."

"Or not." I shook my head. S.M. was too large a problem. Suffice it unto the day the troubles therein and all that. "So, any thoughts about our current dilemma? Do we start with the abode of God? Or do you prefer the abode of men?" I asked. "I suppose we could rummage in the dump for a while. It looks like a great place for ghouls to hide."

"The church will be more open with fewer places for anyone to hide," Ninon said. She went to the back of the Jeep, fetched the carbine, and filled her purse with ammunition. She slung the strap across her chest, leaving her arms free. She had her spike and pistol tucked into her waistband already. Her shirt was loose, the bottom buttons undone so that she could draw her gun easily. I approved. It would probably be a long time before either of us went weaponless again.

"Works for me. Let's go pray and see if we can get the angels on our side." I already had my shotgun and the second of Ninon's straw purses filled with ammunition. The trench spike was in my boot, but I added a crowbar to my burden. I had a feeling we might want to open things that were shut.

"*Bon.* Yes, let's go kill for Christ, since this seems to be what God wants," Ninon said, closing the back of the Jeep.

The slight blasphemy surprised me. It said so much about the depths of anger and loathing she had been hiding from me and perhaps from herself.

Her words were defiant, but I wasn't surprised when Ninon paused outside the church, showing a rare moment of hesitation. I didn't blame her. Even I, as irreligious as I am, felt reluctant to go on. This had been holy ground, a place of worship, a house of God. Its wall were imbued with faith. You didn't have to be a devout Catholic to think twice about committing the worst of all sins right there in God's living room.

"This is stupid. I'm a living fossil," she said quietly. "I'm a creature of another era. I wear twenty-first century rationalist trappings of science and logic, but in my heart I still believe in God and the Devil and see this as an omen."

The adobe crackled, and a small chunk of plaster fell at our feet. Perhaps it was protesting the relentless violation of the sun that attacked it day after day. Or maybe it really was warning us away.

"Miguel, I am older than this church, more than four centuries old, and today I feel the weight of every one of those four hundred years. I would give anything to be able to walk away from this confrontation. But I can't. I keep thinking maybe this is how I am supposed to atone for what I did all those years ago in taking the Dark Man's gift. Or maybe it is just like that old proverb—*Who must do the difficult thing? He who can.*

I nodded. "And we can."

"Yes."

"Saint Germain may be banking on this."

"I know."

"I never used to believe in God," I confessed. "And I didn't believe in Evil—not the kind with a capital E. I'd always kind of thought that a certain amount of general badness was spread like cosmic dust at the time of the Big Bang. It was random and rare."

"And now what do you believe?"

"I don't know if I believe in the Devil per se. But I do think that there is evil—intelligent evil. It might have been the case once that wickedness was rare, but it's plain that distribution of evil is no longer random and widespread. I'm seeing patterns down here—and, not to brag, I am never wrong about patterns." I tried to explain. "It looks to me like there are some people and places that are vacuums with special filters, and they eventually manage to accumulate enough small evil that they evolve into something else. Call it karma or the wrath of God. Maybe it's just bad luck or an anomaly or too many of the wrong subatomic particles. Whatever. These last couple of days I've been asking myself, in this brave new world, where we really fit on the food chain."

"Have you decided?" she asked. She seemed less curious than simply waiting for judgment to be passed. She didn't question my beliefs or what I thought I was seeing, didn't insist that this was God and Satan fighting it out on earth with their chosen warriors.

"They used to tell us in school that when all other life was gone from the planet, there would still be cockroaches. I'm thinking now that the roaches have been replaced by something more persistent. The last things that will be moving on this earth are zombies and S.M.'s vampires."

"And us. Maybe."

"Maybe."

"Well, whatever the case—God's chosen or the victims of bad ions—we have to go on."

I didn't want to agree—if this were bad ions and not God's plan, then we had no moral obligation to make a suicidal stand—but Ninon straightened her spine and started for the church. I wasn't about to let her go in there alone. I don't know precisely what she was thinking as she marched to the door, but I could hear my grammar school teacher quoting one of her favorite sayings: *The coward dies a thousand deaths, a brave man only one.*

"Let's do this," she said under her breath. "I'm sick to death of Mexico. Miguel, if we don't die today, I want to go someplace that doesn't reek of zombies and where the sun is more kind."

"Amen, amen, amen," I murmured. I could have said something else—"Hell, yes," came to mind—but I figured it didn't hurt to be a bit pious—just in case Ninon was right about us being God's lieutenants.

The interior of the *iglesia* smelled damp and ancient and more than a bit bitter. I wasn't enthused about sucking down into my lungs the many kinds of mold and mildew brewing in the rotten plaster, though let's face it, airborne contaminants were the least of our problems. Neither was the cat enthused about the smell. He took a short sniff and then elected to remain outside. Smart beast. He would probably outlive Ninon and I. He would have been a good early-warning device, a canary down the coal mine, but Ninon petted him once at the door and then walked away without a word of reproach.

I thought that if I ever reincarnated, I'd like to come back as Ninon's cat.

We scanned the church quickly. It had been swept clean of altars, religious art, and pews. The only sign that we were not the first visitors was the small army of footprints in the thin coat of reddish silt that covered the floor. The tracks went back and forth from the front of the church to an iron gate that guarded a set of damp stone stairs heading down toward what I assumed were the burial vaults. Some prints were barefooted, and some wearing only one shoe—not a standard way for tourists to dress but quite common for zombies. The church was older than the rest of the town, and the monks who had founded it had practiced crypt burials. Zombies would feel right at home, and the good brothers' remains would make for a nice snack if zombies or any ghouls started feeling peckish.

We listened to the sound of dripping water echoing up from the dark. It wasn't relaxing. Water meant the possibility of vampires or even S.M. himself. I envied the people who had to choose only between the Devil and the deep blue sea. Our menu of the awful was so much more extensive.

There was also a kind of mist in the air, full of particles too fine for the nose to filter, so fine that it could slip beneath your eyelids even if they were closed, and it got inside the body and irritated the mind. I think it may have been a physical manifestation of some of that less-than-random evil I'd been telling Ninon about.

"I'd feel better if we checked out the hotel before going down there," I said softly. "There's just the one way in and out, and I'd like to know that we didn't have anyone creeping up on us from the rear."

Ninon nodded and began backing toward the door.

It was a relief to be back outside. It was a bit like whistling past a graveyard, but I began humming "Hotel California" as we crossed the plaza. It just seemed appropriate in a place where you might check out but you'd probably never leave.

Ninon shook her head at me and refused to smile at my morbid humor.

"You really need to learn how to have more fun," I told her.

"Don't tempt Fate," Ninon warned. "I've known her a long time and she's horrible."

Like I needed reminding.

The hotel was equally unappealing once we were inside. As expected, the lower floors were bare except for the registration desk, which had been nailed down. It was a massive affair of wood and stone that could have doubled as an Aztec sacrificial altar. In fact, I suspected it might have been just that, and thought maybe that was what had drawn S.M.

Because you stepped down into the lobby, a small body of water was trapped there in an eight-inch-deep pool. Filled with silt, mosquito larvae, and growing slime, it made slurping noises as we waded across. I tried not to think about leeches, but failed. We should have been happy at any sign of life, but I couldn't work up enthusiasm for things that wiggled in water.

That floor was taken up with the lobby, a room probably used for dining, and lastly a small kitchen, long and narrow with a giant cast-iron stove and a hand pump in a stone sink. There were also microwave ovens. It was raging paranoia that made me open the old oven and look inside. No severed heads. No ghouls or zombies. Nobody had been cute with the microwaves either.

We found three staircases on the ground floor. Two went up and one went down. The main stairs for the guests were wide, hung with decorative wrought-iron lanterns and had shallow-front steps in hand-painted tiles that could be easily negotiated by an elderly person or a lady in high heels. The others were for the staff, who apparently didn't need space for their elbows or lanterns to light their way. Perhaps I misjudged the builders, but I sensed an attitude that said if the dark stairs broke the peons' necks, so what. Labor was ubiquitous and cheap.

It wasn't pretentiousness that made us take the guest stairs up to the second floor; we just liked having room to stand two abreast and shoot things without there being any danger of us catching one another in a cross fire. The puddles of sunlight that came at regular intervals were also welcome.

The windows of the upstairs hall were small transoms over the bedroom doors. They let in small amounts of light but no air. The heat was beginning to build, turning the hotel into an oasthouse. A wise zombie would opt for a shady and cool basement, but since wisdom wasn't their main trait, I remained alert as we investigated.

We forced open the first door we came to—numbered 301 for some odd reason, though it was on the second floor. The weight of the water-swollen wood had made it sag on its hinges, and the bottom of the door scraped over the floor, making more noise than I liked. The room beyond must have once been beautiful. It had a now badly faded tapestry spread on the bed, and a steamer trunk made of mahogany. I opened that with gun poised, not caring if Ninon thought me nervous. But nothing was there except a pair of kid gloves that had shriveled into mummy hands. The chewed interior had once been a haven for spiders and rodents. Nothing but dust lived there now.

We tried a couple of other doors but found the rooms to be all the same. After a while we gave up searching. If anyone were hiding up there, we'd hear the opening of a swollen door.

"Ready to go up?"

I nodded. There was a third floor, attic rooms for the same peasants who didn't need lights on the stairs. The heat would be brutal and the air a miasma of bad smells, but this wasn't an occasion for careless speed. We went quickly but cautiously, and again found nothing but filthy cobwebs and rodent droppings—and one old rocking chair beside a small table with a glass jar filled with dried, faded flowers. We were back in the lobby in less than ten minutes. I know because I have one of those watches that can take a licking and keep on ticking.

That left the basement, which we never did explore. Like the lobby, it had been made of stone and lined in adobe. We could see that the whole downstairs was the world's filthiest swimming pool where bottles of wine and rafts of rotting wood floated. There might be zombies down there in the water. They didn't need air, or so Ninon said—a thought I found horrible and which would supply me with new food for nightmares—and the odds of our being hurt by them were too high to risk exploration. Our eyes were good in the dark, but not in sludge. Anyway, any zombie dumb enough to stay down there wouldn't be a problem in a fight. They would have spent the last several months turning into stew.

That left us with the church crypt, the place where we had always known we would have to explore. The walk across the plaza was too short, and the church as dark and unpleasant as ever.

We stood outside the iron gate that guarded the crypts. I had my crowbar, but I made no effort to force the ancient lock.

"Okay, I have a new plan," I said to Ninon.

"I'm all ears."

"We go down slowly. Very, very slowly. We look for Saint Germain's laboratory and the man himself, but at the first sign of trouble, we hightail it back up here, slam the gate, pour gasoline down the stairs, and make like it's an arsonist Fourth of July." I know torching historic landmarks was a real no-no, but that day I simply didn't care. If it meant avoiding a pack of ghouls and seeing the real Saint Germain, I'd have arranged a weenie roast as I burned down the Louvre.

"I like it. Except for one thing. We have to be sure that Saint Germain is actually down there. The real one, not just a clone. We have to kill him, Miguel. We have to. Otherwise he'll just go on chasing us, making more ghouls, and generally doing evil. Until he's dead, this isn't over."

I nodded. There wouldn't be any peace accord with this guy, and he didn't believe in live and let live.

"I hear you. But in spite of that supposed clue, there is no guarantee that he is down there, you know. If I were him, I'd make like a general and lead my troops from far, far away."

Ninon frowned. "He's very arrogant. I'd think he'd want to be here to see me die."

"Maybe, but only if he's more stupid than conceited."

She sighed. "He isn't stupid. Just . . . crazy."

"Okay then."

"All right, let's go get the gasoline and lighters. If we have ghouls chewing on us when we come up those stairs, I don't want to be fumbling with the car keys."

"Damn straight."

Fetching gas and two flashlights took another five minutes, but then the delays were exhausted and it was time to face the horrible task.

The subterranean crypt was about what we'd expected, cold, dark, still, and damp. The stair was narrow and the wall and treads covered in black gunk that we did our best to avoid. The monks must have been pressed for burial space, because we encountered our first slime-covered skeleton standing at attention halfway down the stairs. I didn't examine how this feat of erection had been managed. The wool of its cassock had all but rotted away, leaving the browned rotted bones to protrude at will. Somehow, the wooden cross around its neck had ended up jammed in its teeth. I didn't care for its amused grin as it bit into the black wood, or the way the hollow sockets seemed to follow us as we passed.

Recuiscat In Pace, Hermano. And please stay dead.

I was bothered that there was no sign of a generator or power lines. It seemed unlikely that Saint Germain would want to work in the dark. If this were his base, there should be some sign of human—or whatever—occupation.

Things looked more hopeful at the base of the stairs. We shone our lights around slowly, taking it in. There were at least two rooms down there. In the first one, the stacks of skeletons had been pushed aside to make space for three folding tables, the type used by traveling massage therapists. And mad necromancers. There were also power cables leading away from some sort of an electrical device. Ninon inhaled slowly and began to follow them. I went the other way.

One table had a nice collection of glass beakers containing assorted fluids that had disgusting clots floating in them. Behind it there was a tank full of reddish liquid plenty large enough to float a body. I went forward cautiously, sniffing the air. The chemicals burned my nostrils like a snort of ammonia, though it wasn't anything I had ever smelled before. I wasn't up on cloning, but this looked a lot like the Frankenstein labs where Boris Karloff used to hang out.

"Could this be one of the Dark Man's labs?" I asked.

"Miguel." Ninon's voice was urgent but not panicked. I followed her light around a wall of stacked skulls and saw her looking down at a body—a skeleton, really, though it looked fragile, almost powdery. A skeleton wasn't so unusual, but this one wasn't covered in slime, so it had been brought down there recently. It also had a couple of other odd things wrong with it. The head had been severed with a clean cut and there was a wooden stake driven through the thing's chest.

"Can you tell if it was a vampire?" Ninon asked, bending down and inhaling slowly. She coughed and recoiled. I hate that our sense of smell is so keen. It's a useful tool but everything about our travels seemed to smell terrible.

"No, but I'd say it has all the general outlines of a vampire slaying." It looked too tall to be Mamita, or that's what I told myself.

"Then S.M. has probably been here to see Saint Germain."

"And gotten a really negative answer to his plan for taking on a new apprentice." I thought about it. "Maybe that's when S.M. sent a vampire to find us and tell us about Lara Vieja."

"To tell *you*. That thing wanted to kill me." Ninon added, "And I doubt it was S.M. I think it more likely that it was your mother."

Mamita. That made some sense. S.M. probably wanted me dead more than he wanted anything. I looked back at the skeleton. Odds really were against it being her. I refused to let myself think about her being dead. There was bound to be some emotion, and I had to stay focused.

"So, that leaves us just ghouls and zombies to worry about," I said, trying to sound cheerful. It was impossible in that space. Words simply fell dead in the moldering air.

"And maybe Saint Germain."

We both looked over at a heavy door set into a wall—a real one made of stone. It was clad in copper and carved with all sorts of saints being tormented. It didn't say Abandon All Hope Ye Who Enter Here, but then, it didn't need to.

"Do you hear anything?" I asked, straining my ears.

"No."

"Smell anything?"

"No." She waited a beat and then added what I least wanted to hear. "But they're here. I can feel it. And we have to open that door. The fire won't get through otherwise."

"Let's go get one of the gas cans now," I suggested.

"You go. I think it would be unwise to leave this door unguarded. If I can feel them, it may be that they can feel me." Ninon eased the carbine off her shoulder and tucked it under her arm. "At least now they're contained. We can get them all."

"You know, they always split up in horror movies and someone always gets killed. I really think that you should come with me."

"This isn't a movie," she said impatiently. "Go. And be quick. I hate this place."

I did too, so I stopped arguing and headed for the stairs.

We die only once—and for such a long time.
—*Molière*

Neither the sun nor death can be looked at with a steady eye.
—*François de la Rochefoucauld*

Talk to your lover about herself, and seldom of your own self. Take for granted that she is a hundred times more interested in the charms of her own person than in the whole gamut of your emotions.
—*"Lesson in Love" from* Carte du Tendre *by Ninon de Lenclos*

Absence diminishes mediocre passions and increases great ones, as the wind extinguishes candles and fans fires.
—*François de la Rochefoucauld*

CHAPTER TWENTY-ONE

I encountered a ghoul in the stairwell.

Fortunately, this time I smelled the creature before I saw it—or it saw me—and I turned off my flashlight so my eyes could adjust to the dark. I stood in silence, looking up until it appeared, peering down toward me from the top of the stairs and snuffling after our trail.

Now that danger had actually arrived, I was calm and able to think clearly. Given that Ninon sensed a crypt full of bad guys on the other side of the copper door, and that I wanted them to stay there, there was no choice but to take this one on with a trench spike and pray for a quick, quiet kill. Besides, a single blast from my shotgun might not put it down, and I probably wouldn't get a second shot before it was on me. Anyway, that would also alert all the other ghouls to our whereabouts. Assuming they didn't already know. They might not.

This ghoul had to be a rogue who had been out hunting for lunch in the cactus while we explored the hotel. We'd been wading through water for a lot of our search, and since they seemed to rely on scent and sound rather than sight, it might not be sure of our lingering presence. If I could take this one before it raised the alarm, we stood a good chance of starting our barbecue and getting away before the rest of them knew we were in town.

Okay, I had to kill it. Alone. And quietly.

Confronting it headlong while climbing up slimy stairs wasn't my first choice of attack strategies; I'd be at a terrible disadvantage. Sneaking up behind from another route wasn't a viable choice, either. I was at the bottom of the only flight of stairs. I considered my options, looking for ways out as I waited unmoving for the giant, snuffling head to withdraw.

As I mentioned before, I'm not good at waiting, but I had no idea what to do as long as that damn thing sat there like the stopper in the end of a bottle. Ninon had pointed out that we weren't in a movie, but I was willing to turn to Hollywood for inspiration. I decided to try the old lob-a-stone trick that they used in spy movies where smart American prisoners wanted to distract the evil Nazi guards. Fortunately, the stones in the wall were loose from their extended stay in the water, and I was able to pry one free with only minimal difficulty.

The throw was an awkward one, so I took my time. I was careful to pitch over its head. Smacking it in the face would be really dumb since it would tell the thing I was there and also piss it off.

Fetch, Rover! Chase that rock, I thought as I chucked the stone high.

Wonder of wonders, it worked. I saw the ghoul's silhouette whip around, and then it disappeared just like it had read the script and knew its part. I climbed quickly and silently, controlling my breathing, being careful not to let my shoes make any sucking sounds as I scrambled through the slime, using the crypt's wall of dead brothers' bodies to keep my balance. Oddly, the last bit of the stairway was the worst. I ran out of skeletons and there was nothing to hang on to but slime-covered stones.

Though I made no noise, the creature sensed me before I made it out the door. The ghoul turned quickly as I jumped—or, more accurately, skidded—into the room. It was fast, but I had momentum and a trench spike on my side.

Haste makes waste—I've found the saying is actually true in combat, at least for me. My first blow missed its heart. I'd have to work on my technique if I lived long enough. I might have screwed up with the spike, but I lashed out with my foot, spinning the thing about and making a fine effort to shove the thing backward down the stairs. I'd do anything to keep it from getting its gorilla arms around me.

It grunted at the impact of the heel of my boot, but its left hand shot out and grasped my ankle with what felt like an iron claw. The right hand flailed but held fast to another object, even though it might have been able to save itself by grabbing at the iron gate.

My eyes finally adapted to the brighter light and I understood why it hung on so tight. It had a hand grenade! A bloody great hand grenade, just like in the movies—which I would be sure to tell Ms. This-is-real-life-and-not-a-movie. No more sneering. Hollywood had been right about everything—about splitting up being stupid, about the rock trick, and now about the bad guy turning up with bigger guns.

Our gazes met as the ghoul pinwheeled at the top of the stairs. The thing had evil eyes, yellow eyes that must have come from a goat. I saw also an intelligence there that hadn't existed in the zombies we'd seen—as Ninon had claimed. If there had ever been any doubt about what I was fighting, it was ended. This was a ghoul, a thinking being.

However, that consciousness was where any connection between our species ended. This thing wasn't even remotely human. It had no hair and the skin looked burnt, almost waxen. As with the other ghoul, the underlying bone structure was subtly wrong. For one thing, the legs and arms were too long for the torso.

Alarmed and repulsed by the feel of the talons crushing my ankle, I dropped to the ground, changing the thing's center of gravity and pushing it off balance. As the creature fell backward, I kicked out with my other foot, twisting in the air and connecting hard with the thing's face. The monster fell into the darkness.

Thank God that ghouls don't scream. The sound of it landing should alert Ninon to be on guard, but I hoped it wouldn't be loud enough to alarm anyone else.

I scrambled quickly to the edge of the stairs and watched its tumbling fall while I nursed my throbbing ankle. Thank goodness I'd been wearing boots or I'd also have to deal with missing tissue. If I kept this up I'd end a walking topographical map in scars of our visit to Mexico. As it was, the leather of my boot was torn clean through.

The thing grunted as it hit the wall, ricocheting like a pinball back and forth between the stony surfaces. An audible punctuation of each blow forced a small bit of air from its lungs. It reached bottom finally and then let out an enraged hiss that vibrated the air of the stairwell. I loathed that sound. Why the Hell didn't they scream like normal animals? It *had* to be lacking vocal chords. Maybe Saint Germain believed that ghouls should be seen and not heard. Probably not a bad policy. Their conversation would likely be limited to demands for food.

But both silence and resilience are ghoulish features. Like the other ghoul, this one was unhurt by its fall. All I had accomplished by shoving it down the stairs was to piss it off and keep it away from the fuel. If Ninon weren't down there, I'd dump the gasoline on it and set it on fire.

But Ninon was down there, and the beast hadn't rushed back up to get me.

Ninon—that was a psychological kick to the head. For the first time, fear touched me and I felt my hastily erected scaffolding of courage shimmy beneath me.

"Bloody Hell." I trusted my ankle to hold out a while longer and jumped down the stairs after the ghoul, trench spike ready.

It scrambled away from me as I landed, trying to hide in the dark. That didn't work. My eyesight is very good in low-light situations. The beast was still clinging to its grenade but hadn't pulled the pin. Maybe it knew it wouldn't survive if an explosion went off down there. Maybe there was enough awareness that it didn't want to die if it could avoid it.

Or maybe its creator was down there and it didn't dare risk hurting him unless left with no other choice.

We had a temporary standoff. The ghoul snarled silently at me with its long inhuman teeth. Apparently it wasn't good with waiting either. With unbelievable speed, the creature bounded halfway across the floor. It was on me a half-second later, nails of its right hand clawing at my face—what is it about my face that attracts them?—and jaws snapping as it tried for a lock on my throat with its filthy teeth.

I couldn't land an effective blow with the spike. The ghoul was too close and my swing hampered. Instead I rolled backward, using the thing's momentum to force it over my head. I pulled my knees into my chest and then let fly with a kick that would do a mule proud. Again I threw the ghoul off, shoving as hard as I could into the soft part of its body as I flung it away.

There was a horrible cracking noise as my boot punched a hole in the creature's gut, knocking some organs loose and tearing gristle. A gush of dark sludge cascaded down my leg. It burned like acid and smelled like the sewers of Hell, but I didn't pause. I already knew this loss of organs wouldn't stop the thing. I rolled over and kicked out again, aiming for the head.

I connected, but did no damage. The thing hissed and headed back for the stairs—and up toward the gasoline. It looked enraged now, and I knew if it got to the top that it would probably drop the grenade down on Ninon and me and then throw the gas cans in after.

I jumped in pursuit, landing on the creature's back and striking downward with the spike. Something clattered to the floor and rolled away. I'm sure I hit the heart, but it slowed the creature very little. My weight knocked the air out of its lungs, but the monster apparently didn't need air to live.

Very aware that the grenade might have had its pin pulled and I had only seconds left, I jerked the spike out of its chest and aimed for its head. The blow was an awkward one and went in sideways, skipping along the skull without penetrating more than the skin. I was getting ready to try again when Ninon arrived. She came up on the left, quickly and silently. Her spike went in smoothly and was pulled out the same way.

More sludge gushed out of the ghoul's body, and I shoved it away from me. It took a moment for the thing to die. We scrambled back as it lashed at us, avoiding its awful jaws and tearing hands while it thrashed on the slimy floor.

Finally it quieted. Nothing exploded.

"Is that the only one?" Ninon whispered.

"I think so. Turn on your flashlight. There's a grenade down here someplace."

"A grenade?" Ninon is the only woman I know who could sound happy at this news.

I shared her joy when we found it with its pin in place. It would make opening that damn door so much easier. All we had to do was take a quick peek, and if there were too many undead, we'd toss in our little explosive, slam the door, and get the Hell up those stairs.

"Are you okay?" she asked me, laying her hand on my arm.

"Better all the time," I said. I ignored my throbbing ankle and retorn cheek.

The natives tell of sickness that darkens the soul, causing a thirst for blood of their brothers ... Once darkened, there is no method of healing save death itself.
—*From Father Esteban Negron of Bartolome de las Casas*

One certainly has a soul; but how it came to allow itself to be enclosed in a body is more than I can imagine. I only know if once mine gets out, I'll have a bit of a tussle before I let it get in again to that of any other.
—*Byron*

As long as men believe in absurdities, they will continue to commit atrocities.
—*Voltaire*

Perhaps being old is having lighted rooms inside your head, and people in them, acting. People you know, yet can't quite name.
—*François de la Rochefoucauld*

To live without loving is not really to live.
—*Molière*

CHAPTER TWENTY-TWO

Things went as planned. We opened the copper door, took a look at the piles of napping ghouls, and made use of the grenade. It was a first for me, killing the undead so easily, and I have to admit I enjoyed it.

We felt the concussion on the stairs, to which we'd run. It was painful enough on the eardrums that we both gasped. We fetched a can of gasoline and went back down to the basement. I didn't care for the way the plaster was falling and how the ceiling beams groaned. We opened the copper door, now rather bent, and looked inside. It was full of bodies, but bodies that were still moving.

I'm going to blame our hesitation to enter on architectural instability. We should have gone in to see if we could find Saint Germain, but neither of us could make ourselves wade into the filth of exploded ghouls. Instead we opened a can of gas and tossed it at one of the small fires smoldering on the timbered walls. We waited for the whoosh of ignition and then slammed the door shut again.

The second bang was smaller, or maybe our ears were too damaged to hear.

We staggered out and back up into the church, covered in slime and smudged with smoke, heading for the other gas cans on shaky legs. Probably we could leave the church to burn on its own, but we were taking no chances. There was that lab downstairs and it might be put to use again.

I knelt down, reaching for one of the red cans, when a trio of creatures flew at us out of the dark beams overhead, two of them grey fleshy nightmares that were all teeth and tearing claws, the third something more recognizably human. There was no time for the mind to translate the eyes' revolted warnings into words of alarm, and no time for me to aim my shotgun before they were on top of us. Fortunately, the lead monster blew past and headed for another danger we hadn't sensed.

My stomach muscles contracted as I braced myself for a blow. I knew with certain dread that I was being slow—too slow—and I was lucky when the second creature passed me by. Ninon wasn't as stunned as I. Her body moved seemingly without effort, dropping her flashlight and bringing her gun to bear first on the blond man who had entered the church, and then on the second vampire who deviated from its course and came at her with claws extended. Too close to me to risk the shot, she dropped her rifle and seized its arm. Using the thing's own momentum, she flung it into the remains of the vestry with skull-crushing force that broke both its withered body and chipped the adobe of the wall. A shower of falling plaster burst like a popping vacuum cleaner bag, but before it settled on the floor Ninon had spun about, picked up her rifle and re-aimed it at the man. Saint Germain.

The third vampire turned from its attack on Saint Germain and reached out for Ninon. As I had promised, I did not hesitate. I grabbed the creature by its bald head, and also using the hurtling body's own momentum, I let it reach the end of its tether and then efficiently snapped its neck the way you would crack a whip. I swung about in a small circle and then threw the dead creature into Saint Germain's path.

My timing could have been better. The final vampire, a mass of hissing fangs and ripping claws, was dropping down on Saint Germain, and the live and dead vampires collided. The sound of crunching bones was loud as the monsters smashed together, but it was soon replaced with an even more disturbing high-pitched hissing as the live vampire did its best to both rid itself of its dead companion and tear off Saint Germain's head.

Ninon stood with the rifle ready, but she did not shoot. It took a long minute but the vampire succeeded in decapitating its victim. Yet not without cost. Saint Germain managed to punch through its body and rip out its heart. Apparently a stake wasn't needed to kill a vampire, just the removal of its heart. The pair collapsed seconds later, both falling to the floor, one missing its head, the other the seat of its spirit that Saint Germain clutched in his dead hand.

Ninon and I stood in silence, our attention fixed on Saint Germain's corpse. Both of us expected it to rise, but it didn't move.

I eventually became aware that the leprous skin of the second vampire's face was clinging to my hand, where it had peeled off the creature's skull like a surgeon's latex glove. I made a sound of disgust, shaking my fingers to be rid of it.

"Are they vampires?" Ninon asked, glancing nervously at the three bodies and then up at the darkness overhead. Nothing moved, but she wasn't reassured. She kept the rifle ready.

"Yes." I already knew what I would find, but I knelt by Saint Germain and turned the final vampire over. It had an abdominal scar right where its appendix used to be. Ninon came over and knelt beside me.

"Is it your mother?" Her voice was a whisper.

"Yes. That's Mamita."

"I'm sorry," she said.

And I knew that she was. Mamita had been a vampire, had attached her, but the monster was still my mother, and Ninon—compassionate creature that she is—was sorry for my loss. I think I was too. "She died saving you."

"Again."

Yes, she'd died saving me, while her friends had tried to kill Ninon. How was I supposed to feel about that?

"Miguel?" Ninon cleared her throat. She got to her feet, gun again ready. "We might have a problem."

"You don't think this one is Saint Germain either?" I asked, coming to my feet as well. My confused feelings would have to wait.

"I can't be sure but . . . No. I don't believe it's him. He doesn't feel old enough, evil enough. I think he's another clone."

Clones. Great. The evil asshole had a Xerox machine.

"We burn the town anyway," I guessed.

Ninon nodded. "Oh yes. To the ground."

Writing is like prostitution. First you do it for love, then for a few close friends, and then for money.
—*Molière*

In the arithmetic of love, one plus one equals everything. Two minus one equals nothing.
—*Ninon de Lenclos*

Grammar knows how to control even kings.
—*Molière*

Today a new sun rises for me; everything lives, everything is animated, everything seems to speak to me of my passion, everything invites me to cherish it.
—*Ninon de Lenclos*

CHAPTER TWENTY-THREE

Smoke billowed into the sky in ugly black cyclones, marking the end of Lara Vieja. Ninon turned her back on the smoldering church and smiled at me. Her face was filthy but radiant. Had mere mortals been hanging about they would have fallen to their knees and shielded their eyes. As it was, I hoped the old gods weren't watching, because from all I'd read they were a jealous lot who didn't want humans to be too beautiful.

"The ghouls are all gone. We didn't get Saint Germain but we can leave this place."

I wanted to share her happiness, to believe her, but hope was a temporarily forgotten emotion.

"Are you sure?" I asked.

"Yes. I don't think even Saint Germain would have more than one ghoul pack. And I'm thinking that he has probably retreated across the border, out of reach of S.M."

"I hope you're right. I'm tired of being the public defender against the undead in Mexico."

Corazon appeared suddenly on the hood of the Jeep, carrying another withered mouse.

"The prodigal returns," I said. "Did you have a nice lunch, cat, while we were killing monsters?"

The cat tossed his lunch away and licked his lips slowly. A tiny bit of what looked like bone flickered in the sun.

Ninon gasped just a bit ahead of me and had Corazon up in arms before I could say a word. She held him in front of her at face level. The eye contact between them was intense and unblinking.

"His tongue . . . ! S.M. must have gotten to him somehow," I said. A vampire cat? As ever, just when I thought I'd seen it all, something else came along to demonstrate my ignorance.

"Or one of those vampires."

"No. Only S.M. can make vampires. It had to be him."

"*Merde!* So he *was* here."

"Yes, and content to wait and see if we managed to kill Saint Germain."

Ninon nodded but was clearly distracted.

"*Mon chat,*" Ninon said, shaking the beast gently. "I am not angry that you are a vampire, but we must have some rules, *non?* You cannot go about simply sucking everything. Next we will have an army of undead mice."

Corazon did his best to look limp and helpless, but it was hard when he clearly thought she was being hysterical. Of course he had rules! What did she think he was—some brainless canine who would forget himself the first time he became excited?

"I don't think this happened today," I said slowly. "He's been sucking rats and mice for a few days now. He's been careful too."

I didn't say this just to reassure Ninon. The cat did seem to have rules, or at least a routine. I had twice seen him with dead rodents. Thinking back, I realized that he had obviously drained their blood and then broken their necks. Even supposing that he was contagious—did his being male make him a carrier even if he were a cat?—his prey would not be resurrecting. A whole spine was needed to make a new vampire. Even if he somehow figured out how to inject venom into the tiny spines, with a broken neck they would not revive.

Ninon relaxed and pulled the cat close. Corazon closed his eyes and began to purr. He did his best to look cuddly and adorable, no monsters hiding in there. You'd never know that his new favorite hobby was drinking blood and sucking mouse brains.

"I'm sorry, *mon cher*. I should have protected you."

I didn't say anything then, but I strongly suspect that Corazon isn't unhappy with events. He has no moral dilemmas to plague him, and now he's very, very strong and will live an even longer life.

We burned all of the pueblo. It was probably overkill, but why take any chances? Lara Vieja is really and truly gone. Nothing remains, not even the ghosts.

When we were done with that last bit of arson, we went back to town and collected my money from the bank and its sorrowful manager. The hotel there was tempting, offering food and showers, but I still didn't like it. So we traveled a few more miles west before renting a room at a cheap motel. We didn't stay the night, just paused long enough to change and bathe. We drove on to Tijuana. Ninon arranged a new passport for me there. As the joke goes, she has low friends in high places who are happy to do things for money.

We found a quiet place on the outskirts of town to grab a bite to eat where there were only a few tourists and the beer wasn't too flat. It wasn't yet cocktail hour and we were able to perch almost alone on the tall swivel chairs that faced a long, fly-spattered mirror that showed us the only entrance into the building. The single sound to mar the quiet conversation was the occasional laughter from a pair of college kids who were high on pot and the exhilaration of being someplace where they felt free to be as naughty as they liked. They reminded me a bit of myself, all those years ago, and I sent up a small prayer that they have a safe journey home.

We did a little shopping after dinner, splitting up for a half hour or so while we hunted up clothing—neither of us could stand the smell of the rubber decals on the last T-shirts we'd bought. The area didn't run to department stores and American brands, so that rather left us with local goods. For me that meant mostly linen smocks that had too much embroidery for the tastes of the average American male. They were loud, but I forced myself to buy one anyway.

Ninon brought me another present that night, a guitar. It's a thing of beauty. The wood gleams like a golden sunrise and it's inlaid with mother-of-pearl.

"For when you're ready," she said.

I held it for a while, admiring the craftsmanship. I don't know if I'll ever play it. My hands are healing more every day. I think that eventually I will be physically capable of the motor control needed to play flamenco guitar. It's my will that's lacking. I am not sure I have music in me anymore.

"Where would you like to go now that this is all over?" I asked her that night in our room, propped up against the headboard and watching the local news. It wasn't all over, but we were pretending it was because our souls needed a vacation. That meant crossing the border back into the States and trying to recapture something that looked like a normal life while we decided what to do about Saint Germain.

"First to a waffle house where I can get lingonberry syrup. Then—briefly—to New Orleans. I have a home in the French Quarter and haven't been back since the hurricane. The caretakers say all is well there, but . . ."

"New Orleans? Is that wise? I mean, haven't you had enough of haunted places? Turning out haunts is practically a cottage industry there." There was also the matter of Saint Germain's spies.

"Yes, I know. But I am more than half-ghost myself any-more. Anyway, we won't stay long. I just want to see it again. It is more my spiritual home these days than Paris and I miss it. I'd like to show the city to you someday, when the rebuilding is done." She looked at me and I felt relief. I hadn't really thought that she would want to split up once we were in the States, but she hadn't said anything one way or the other. "Do you want to go to Califor-nia?" she asked.

I did, but I shook my head. It was too soon to risk it. Miguel Stuart needed a while to drop off the govern-ment's radar.

"Later. Maybe. Have you ever seen the wine country? There's nothing like it in the fall. It's the only time of year when death is beautiful. I went to a grape-stomp there three years ago. It was wonderful. Messy but lots of fun."

It was her turn to shake her head. "I would love that. I haven't seen a grape harvest since I left France."

"We'll do it then. Maybe next year."

She shifted over and leaned back into my arms. It had been only a few days between us, but already she seemed to belong there.

Ninon turned her face up and our eyes met. I wondered what she saw there. I wasn't entirely sure of what was there for her to see.

She touched my cheek.

Do I love you? her eyes asked, more of herself than of me.

Couldn't you love me as a possibility? As a hope for the future? my eyes asked back.

I . . . I don't know. You? Can you love?

I don't know either. Sometime I think that neither of us would recognize love if it walked up and kissed us on the lips.

"Perhaps. If I loved you . . ." She stopped.

"If." I waited. My heart made its presence known with a small thud that knocked against my breastbone.

"If I loved you, I would say stay with you. . . . If you loved me too," she added.

I smiled a little and my heart settled. "If I loved you, I would go. . . . If you didn't love me too."

"If."

I nodded. "If."

"I am not good at relationships. At least, not ones with lovers. And I have always been opposed to marriage. You know that."

"I do. And I have always left a Do Not Resuscitate order on my relationships too," I said. "When they were over, they were over. But this could never be anything so simple."

"*Oui.* I think we're both past that now. We are, after all, resuscitated for good and all." She looked away, her tone becoming brisk when she spoke of our plans. The conversation about emotions was over, but I still felt happy with the start. "You know what we must do now? We need to find Byron—Lord Byron, the poet—and warn him about Saint Germain. He is the one who killed Dippel, and he and his wife are probably in as much danger as we are."

"How do we find Lord Byron?" I asked, only mildly surprised by her announcement that the famous man still lived. Perhaps she had mentioned it before, somewhere in my dreams. Every day we did more and more talking with our minds.

She smiled at me, knowing that the idea that we were not alone, that there were others like us was very reassuring.

"We'll take out ads in all the major U.S. newspapers, especially *The Times Picayune,* since he will be searching for us there."

"Why?"

"Because he knows I lived there once. He has also lived there before."

"Okay. What exactly would this ad say?"

"Oh, perhaps something like *Lord Byron, phone home.*

Except, we will use an e-mail address. That will be harder to trace." She smiled a little, that small Mona Lisa smile that said she knew something that I didn't. "And we will use his most recent name, Damien Ruthven, of course."

"Damian Ruthven—the book critic?" I recalled when he had disappeared. It had caused quite a stir until Hurricane Katrina came along and distracted everyone from the mystery. "Well, well. Then there's something else we can do to get his attention. I just need a little time for cleanup first." I pointed at my portable computer. I'd been lucky that it was spared when the SUV was wrecked.

"Your story?" she asked. "*Bon!* That is a brilliant idea."

"I rather think so. He'd be sure to pick up any book about Ninon de Lenclos and Saint Germain."

"*Oui.* And read it cover to cover."

"I'll start work as soon as we're back in the States. It won't take long. It's all there and just needs some polishing."

"*Bon.*" She reached for the phone. "I think I would like some champagne."

And so this part of our story closes. I'll send this manuscript off to my editor when we settle in . . . well, someplace. It's the final book in my contract. There probably won't be another for a while. I can't risk contact with anyone from my old life. Chris will probably manhandle the book quite a bit—he may even edit me out of it in an effort to protect my pen name—but enough of it will remain to get our story into the hands of anyone who knows what's going on with Dippel's dark children, and that's all that matters.

Yes, much has happened and much is still happening. We haven't heard from S.M. again, which was truly worrisome. However, Ninon and I have begun to accept what feelings we have for each other—and what else can you ask for in a romance? I warned you in the middle. I can think no more perfect ending for this book than Ninon and I to walk off into a spectacular sunrise and whatever will be the rest of our—we hope—long lives. But this isn't an ending. Far from it.

Still, every sunrise is spectacular now, and east seems as good a direction to travel as any.

Editorial Note: This is a last message supposedly in the hand of Ninon de Lenclos, left in the book after much debate.

Byron, mon cher, I have let Miguel tell this story for me. His words are so colorful and he paints a flattering portrait, oui? But I must add this postscript in my own hand so you know that it is true. We have seen nothing of Saint Germain since returning to the States, but I do not believe that our troubles are over. Whoever it was who died that day in Lara Vieja, it was not our nemesis. I know the Dark Man's son, and this doppelgänger was not he. So write soon and we will make a plan. Miguel has an e-mail address under his nom de plume: <u>melaniejaxn@hotmail.com</u>. We will check it often.

Adieu, Ninon

Yes, Marquis, I will keep my word with you, and upon all occasions shall speak the truth, though I sometimes tell it at my own expense. I have more firmness of mind than perhaps you may imagine, and 'tis very probable that in the course of this correspondence, you will think I push this quality too far, even to severity. But then, please to remember that I have only the outside of a woman, and that my heart and mind are wholly masculine. . . .

Shall I tell you what makes love so dangerous? 'Tis the too high idea we are apt to form of it. But to speak the truth, love, considered as passion, is merely a blind instinct, that we should rate accordingly. It is an appetite, which inclines us to one object, rather than another, without our being able to account for our taste. Considered as a bond of friendship, where reason presides, it is no longer a passion and loses the very name of love. It becomes esteem which is indeed a very pleasing appetite, but too tranquil and therefore incapable of rousing you from your present lethargy.

If you madly trace the footsteps of our ancient heroes of romance, adopting their extravagant sentiments, you will soon experience, that such false chivalry metamorphoses this charming passion into a melancholy folly nay, often a tragical one: a perfect frenzy! But divest it of all the borrowed pomp and opinion, and you will then perceive how much it will contribute both to your happiness and pleasure. Be assured that if either reason or knight errantry should be permitted to form the union of our hearts, love would become a state of apathy and madness.

The only way to avoid these extremes, is to pursue the course I pointed out to you. At present you have no occasion for anything more than mere amusement, and believe me, you will not meet it except among women of the character I speak of. Your heart wants occupation; and they are framed to supply the void. At least give my prescription a fair trial, and I will be answerable for the success.

I promised to reason with you, and I think I have kept my word. Farewell.

Tomorrow the Abbé Châteauneuf and perhaps Molière are to be with me. We are to read over the Tartuffe together, in order to make some necessary alterations. Depend upon it, Marquis, that whoever denies the maxims I have here laid down, partakes a little of that character in his play.

—*A letter from Ninon de Lenclos to the Marquis de Sévigné*

AUTHOR'S NOTE

Welcome to the second book of what I call my Not-so-dead Poet Society stories. Let's talk a bit, if you have time. Come closer, so my computer-weary eyes can see you. My battered fingers are reaching the end of their endurance, but I want to share a few more things with you before you go.

First of all, let me thank you again for climbing aboard my runaway literary train and taking a wild journey with me. I hope you enjoyed this visit to the modern Ninon's world—this *Dangerous Liaisons* of the Underworld where she lives, at least in my imagination. I pray her shade is comfortable with what I have done in her name. If you meet her in dreams some night, please say a kind word for me.

The historic Ninon de Lenclos has always fascinated me, not simply because she was one of the great minds of the seventeenth century, but because of her lifelong moral convictions about the rights of women in an era when they were still burning uppity females at the stake for disagreeing with the clergy or king.

Some may find the notion of Ninon as being moral an odd one. After all, she rejected the standards of her time that equated all female virtue with chastity, which was to be traded in for a husband. But one must recall that she had been raised as a man, trained to think and reason as men did in that era—and believe me, the nobles of seventeenth-century France weren't saving themselves for marriage. They were not looking at any mathematical or philosophical equation that said nobility or virtue in a male equaled virginity. Ninon likewise scorned the idea that penetration by a man was the same as moral ruin. The generic penis simply did not have that much power over her.

She also saw that once a woman was sold into marriage, her property, her fortune, her body—and those of all children she bore—were owned by the man who purchased her with an "I do." Men of the upper classes—probably the lower ones too—were faithless and often cruel, and women had almost no legal recourse for any abuse perpetrated on them. Ninon refused this church-sanctioned slavery, though her mother's simple and sincere faith moved her. Faith was not what she quarreled with; It was the liars and scoundrels (like Cardinal Richelieu) who used the Church to pursue political and personal power agendas.

But though rejecting the institution of marriage, and clear in her own mind that the first rush of romantic love could not last, she nevertheless knew that one could die of loneliness if one never loved. So she chose lovers and friends. And not indiscriminately. Indeed, not even rank, fortune, fame, or beauty were passports to her bed or drawing room. She gave her favors only where she found pleasure and joy, and for only so long as pleasure and joy lasted. This is all very clear in her letters, which are a genuine version of the novel, *Dangerous Liaisons* (a side fact, the seducer Valmont in *Dangerous Liaisons* is based on a real person, the Duc de Richelieu).

And, oh yes, in additional to all this, Ninon also managed to write a treatise on male-female relationships that is as relevant today as it was in hers. She edited the plays of Molière; was influential in the evolution of St. Evremond's philosophies and remained his lifelong friend even when he was exiled; defended Descartes when the Faculty of Theology brought him up on charges of blasphemy; paid for Voltaire's education (that ungrateful bastard); moderated the harsh policies of the infamous and manipulative Cardinal Richelieu, as well as indirectly advising a very silly king; was admired and consulted by the Queen of Sweden; ran a nightly salon where all the finest minds in Europe gathered in spite of Church disapproval. She was a gifted musician, spoke several languages . . . and she ran an informal school of lovemaking where she taught Frenchmen that foreplay begins with the mind and not the breasts. In fact, the reputation the French have of being great lovers can be traced straight back to Ninon's education. She was loved by men and women alike, and when the French queen tried to have her locked up in a convent, Paris rioted.

Of course, many of the stories about her are apocryphal. I doubt very much that she ever sold her soul to the Devil for eternal beauty. Just as with Byron, when she died friends rushed in to canonize her. Then enemies tried to vilify her. And, to a certain extent, they both succeeded. It remains for history to pass verdict on who and what she really was. Sadly, I have never found a journal or diary. The ones quoted in this book are made up.

The villain of this story is cut from equally grand cloth, and a part of me hated to cast him as a bad guy. But if you accept that he was his father's son (that is, the son of the Dark Man from *Divine Fire*), then madness and corruption would eventually come upon him and therein lay the seeds of ruin.

The historic Saint Germain remains a mystery. This prophet and alchemist—and artist and musician and metallurgist—seems to have been born in 1712 and many think he died in 1784. But there were reports of him turning up, meddling in the politics of Europe as late as 1822. (One would think this an easy matter to verify—after all, all one need do is check his tombstone. However, there seem to have been at least three graves scattered about Europe, and none have the same date of departure.) In all this time, he was never seen to age, nor did he ever eat in public, so his youth-preserving diet remains a mystery. He admitted to traveling into other lands with his mind and talking to the dead. Many think he is a vampire, and who am I to say no? Especially when it makes for such a good story.

If you have curiosity about these two amazing figures, I have listed some reference books that are a good starting place for getting to know these charismatic seducers. And that is what they were: master seducers and puppeteers both personally and at a societal level. We don't think of them as we do Don Juan or Casanova or other great lovers, though they were every bit as charming and siren-like. But their larger accomplishments overshadow their personal love lives. They could seduce without sex and they belong on the list of great charismatics like Joan of Arc, Rasputin, Lenin, Kennedy, Malcolm X . . . even Elvis Presley. People who could topple governments, begin and end wars, move people to faith and riot. Had they been English instead of French (or Hungarian—the jury is still out about Saint Germain's real nationality) we would have read about them in high school history classes.

As for Miguel—well, I let you make up your own mind about him. I like heroes with some edge to them, men who come with a bit of a twist.

If in your reading you happened to feel like you were actually experiencing high noon at the OK Corral—with ghouls—you were. I tried to banish it, but the soundtrack to every spaghetti western I ever saw kept playing in my head. Except at Lara Vieja. That was really the sunken city of Guerrero Viejo. I wanted it in the story but liked it too well to burn it down in the end, so I changed it for the book. It's so great to have that power.

If you enjoyed this story and haven't read *Divine Fire*, try to find it. That book is about another of the world's great lovers and original thinkers, Lord Byron.

There! The exorcism is complete. This story is done and Ninon no longer haunts me. I can rest.

Thank you again and—as ever—your company has been lovely. Please write—to Melanie or Miguel—at:

Melanie Jackson
www.melaniejackson.com
PO Box 574
Sonora, CA, 95370-0574

RESOURCE LIST

Life, Letters and Epicurean Philosophy of Ninon de L'Enclos, The Celebrated Beauty of the Seventeenth Century by Charles Henry Robinson

Nymphos and Other Maniacs by Irving Wallace

The Technique of the Love Affair by Doris Langley Moore

The Immortal Ninon by Phyllis Tholin

Ninon de L'Enclos and Her Century by Mary C. Rowsell

Ninon de Lanclos by Emile Magne

The Comte de St. Germain: The Secret of Kings by Cooper-Oakley

The Art of Seduction by Robert Greene, Joost Elffers

A Field Guide to Demons, Fairies, Fallen Angels, and Other Subversive Spirits by Carol K. Mack, Dinah Mack

Dictionary of Angels: Including the Fallen Angels by Gustav Davidson

Two Pleasant Hours in the National Museum, The Most Important Monuments and Relics by Jose Jimmenez Gomez

Daily Life of the Aztecs by Jacques Soustelle

The Zombie Survival Guide by Max Brooks

DIVINE FIRE
MELANIE JACKSON

In 1816, Lord Byron stayed at the castle of Dr. Johann Dippel, the inspiration for Mary Shelley's Baron von Frankenstein. The doctor promised a cure for his epilepsy. That "cure" changed him forever.

In the 21st century, Brice Ashton wrote a book. Like all biographies of famous persons, hers on Lord Byron was sent to critics in advance. One Damien Ruthven responded. He suggested her work contained two errors—and that only he could give her the truth. His words held hints of long-lost knowledge; were fraught with danger, deception…and desire. And his eyes showed the experience of centuries. Damien promised to share his secrets. But first, Brice knew, she would have to share herself with him.

THE SAINT

MELANIE JACKSON

One hundred and sixty years ago Kris Kringle walked the earth spreading the message of love and peace. Then he was kidnapped and given a drug that wiped out his memory, while the goblins hijacked Christmas.

Kris has been found. But he's not what you think. He dislikes the fat caricature the goblins stuck him with. He's the most powerful death fey living, who gave up mortal women because none could complete him. That's why he needs Adora Navarra. Only she can help take back his image and punish the wicked. And only she can complete him....

MARJORIE M. LIU

THE RED HEART OF JADE

The grisly murders are just the beginning. Dean Campbell, ex-cop and clairvoyant, is sent to investigate. He is with the Dirk & Steele Detective Agency, that global association of shapeshifters, psychics and other paranormals devoted to protecting life. But there are those who live to destroy.

In Taipei, he finds the remains of burned-alive men and women that reveal a pattern far more deadly than any he has foreseen. Someone knows of a power that can change the world, and of a woman who can complete him: Mirabelle Lee, the childhood sweetheart he'd once thought dead. Now, all that remains is blinding light and searing pain. And beneath it all is...
The Red Heart of Jade
